In his most powerful novel, *The Right Choice*—the third book of his dynamic trilogy—Jim Carson continues with the final story of Mack Shannon in his epic rags-to-riches series.

Set in the river town of Memphis along the banks of the Mississippi River and the "way-down-South" Conch City of Key West, the story begins with newly appointed Federal Judge McKenzie O'Connor. Always late, she races to her first self-defense gun lesson at the home of Captain Kevin O'Shea of the Memphis Police after receiving threatening anonymous letters. This one lesson saves her life when she is confronted with a drugged-out, lifelong criminal.

From one disaster to another, Mack is continuously fighting off attacks by his nemeses, Crazy Ray and Dago—most egregious, the kidnapping of Mack's daughter, Irish.

With skill and passion, the author moves quickly through a rich range of characters:

Dr. Jin Girod, M.D. and veterinarian, a true Cajun and soon to be a part of Mack's family.

Amala Kahn, beautiful Moslem, deceptive, con artist. Captain Kevin O'Shea was thinking marriage—Amala was thinking money.

Dr. Devi Shah, eminent neurosurgeon who comes to Mack's rescue.

Nico, you will have to wait and see for yourself.

There's Elizabeth and Darcy, Romeo and Juliet, Scarlett and Rhett, and now you have Mack and McKenzie.

THE RIGHT CHOICE

"THE RIGHT CHOICE." A great read! It made me miss three of my favorite TV shows. I couldn't stop reading and as soon as I finished, I ordered book one, "A CHASING AFTER THE WIND" and book two, "A MAN'S HUNGRY HEART." Forget TV, I'm going back to reading again. Thank you, Jim Carson.

— *Deborah Diane Miller, 2025*

Jim Carson is a gifted writer. If you read, "The Right Choice," the third book of his trilogy just published this year (2025), you will know why. His characters jump off the pages as real people, especially the protagonists Mack Shannon and McKenzie O'Connor. It is a fast read, a page turner, a rags to riches story that you will go back and read over again.

— *Robert Pinner, 2025*

Finally, Mr. Carson has come out with the last book of his trilogy. I have been eagerly awaiting (checking Amazon and his website) for his third book in this series. Wow, the wait was well worth it. First, I went back and read the last two chapters of the sequel so I could follow the end of the story and pick up where the new story, *The Right Choice*, begins. Guess what? Those two chapters hooked me again. I binged, and read all three books over a weekend. It was great, it was like watching a great TV series. Chapter after chapter, thoroughly researched and skillfully crafted, the storyline flowed with such powerful narrative and artful dialogue, three books became one.

— *Steven R. Pepper, 2025*

What I like best about Jim Carson's riveting writing style is his books read like a combination of fiction and nonfiction, especially his latest book, "The Right Choice." I learn something new every time I read one of his books. I'll read something incredible about his main character, Mack Shannon, like losing an engine flying his airplane, Hookah diving while lobstering in Key West, or snow skiing deep powder on Black Diamond slopes in Aspen. I'll say to myself, that can't be right. Then, I google it and he's right. He must do a tremendous amount of research, or could Jim Carson be Mack Shannon? :)

Uh-oh, what about romance? No problem, there's lots of strong and passionate women, especially the fiery redhead protagonist, McKenzie O'Connor.

— J. Anthony, 2025

THE RIGHT CHOICE

A NOVEL BY

JIM CARSON

Also by Jim Carson

A Chasing After The Wind

A Man's Hungry Heart

THE RIGHT CHOICE

For my son, Jim Carson.
"You did good, Jimbo."

CONTENTS

"The ultimate dream is finding out what we were made for. It is said that the two best days of our lives are the day we were born and the day we discovered why. This is a life-long journey of discovery all the way up to our final breath."

— C. S. Lewis

CHAPTER 1

The sun was directly overhead while she waited for the red light to change. It was a beautiful cloudless day, perfect for having the top down. She was about eight miles north of downtown Memphis at the intersection of Highway 51 and Watkins Street. Her mind drifted, reminiscing the many twists and turns her life had taken. Like the concrete statue of Lady Justice outside the courthouse, Judge McKenzie O'Connor weighed the scales of her successes and failures, both professional and personal. One scale was a lot heavier than the other—her personal life sucked.

A loud horn behind her blew twice jolting her back to reality and fired her Irish temper. She fought her normal reactions: give them the bird, blow *her* horn, or do a burnout and let them eat some rubber smoke. She unclenched her jaws, took a deep breath, and repeated her New Year's resolution, *Avoid trouble! No confrontations! You are a federal judge now, appointed by the President of the United States. Curb that Irish temper!*

With a bit of cheekiness, she took her time turning left onto Watkins and headed towards Shelby Forest State Park. Siri told her to turn left at the next intersection on Fite Road and go five miles and she would be at her destination. She had been to Captain Kevin O'Shea's house before, a long time ago in the wee hours of the morning and a little tipsy. Okay, probably drunk, if she had been stopped and tested. He had a lot of bad boy in him, a little too dangerous for her legal reputation. But it was a trait she had always been attracted to and found rarely available being surrounded by lawyers most of her working life.

McKenzie didn't remember his place being this far back in the sticks. It was in the middle of nowhere for God's sake. She turned left on Fite Road, shoved the floor shift into second gear, and raced around the first curve. The two-lane blacktop country road was narrow, but her beloved vintage Porsche 356 Cabriolet, a high school graduation present from her father, hugged each curve as she braked and shifted around one bend after the other. She slowed to a stop when she saw the green mailbox nailed to a tree, a marker O'Shea told her to look for. She turned into the driveway, stopped and studied what looked like a washed out incline.

She had been receiving these weird anonymous letters, somewhere between insulting and threatening, and decided to get some professional self-defense training. At least something more than the minimum training she had received years ago to get her conceal carry license. It had been over a year since she had fired her revolver. She liked the idea of the protection it gave her but hated wearing a gun. It felt all right in the pocket of her judicial robe while on the bench but it was hard to conceal in street clothes and uncomfortable to carry.

She shifted into first gear and when rocks started flying into her fender wells, she slowed down and crawled up the dirt and gravel drive. She gritted her teeth when she heard her oil pan drag over a large rock. Her car was much too low for this. She thought about parking and walking until she saw a pack of mix-breed dogs running down the drive toward her, jumping and barking. She rolled up her window and kept driving. At the top of the hill she saw O'Shea standing in the middle of the road—tall, challenging, with both hands on his hips. He was dressed in jeans and a white tee shirt. His arms were covered with multicolored tattoos, one arm a complete sleeve. A holstered automatic was belted on his right hip. The bright sun glistened off his curly red hair and his welcoming smile stretched from ear to ear. *What a stud muffin.*

"I was coming to see if you would make it up the driveway."

"Driveway? That's not a driveway, it's an *obstacle course!*"

"When are you going to get a *real* car?" O'Shea said as he opened her door and help her out.

"The same time you get rid of that *bubba* truck you drive." She nodded toward his beat up, camouflaged, 4x4 pickup parked in front of her.

He gave her a hug, paused a second to see if she was receptive to a kiss, but felt the slight barrier that signaled a hug was enough. They had been together before, a chance encounter at a political party that ended at his place with a naked chase through the woods. A wild night he relived often. He never was quite sure if it was just a horny itch she had and he was there at the right time to scratch it, or . . . It didn't matter; he had enough fields to plough.

"*Touché.*" He threw up both hands. "Hold on, don't move," he said and jogged over to a metal building and entered a walk-through door on the side.

McKenzie could hear the roar of a powerful engine as the overhead door began to open. From the dark inside rolled out a matte black, stealth-style, *Hellcat.* Red and blue lights flashed from the grille as if announcing the premiere of a James Bond movie.

O'Shea jumped from the car and bowed, "Voila, my new 'Bubba ride.'"

"Boys and their toys." She said, shaking her head.

"This is no toy . . . 204 miles per hour! The torque on that supercharger will pin you to the seat."

"Great, where are you going to drive a car 204 miles an hour? Is that a police car?"

"Yes and no. It's on loan to me from the Dodge dealership on a trial basis. If the department doesn't want it, I'm gonna buy her."

"You've named it a *her* already?"

"No, Dodge named her. It's a Dodge 'Hellcat' with 707 horsepower, just like you, wild and untamable," he said flashing his big boyish smile again.

"Are we going to shoot bullshit or shoot guns?"

"Okay, okay. Come on, the dogs won't bother you; they're my alarm system." O'Shea removed a black baseball-style cap from his back pocket and put it on his head blocking the sun from his eyes.

McKenzie saw the gold oak leaf sewn on the cap above the brim. "Congratulations on your promotions, *Major* O'Shea."

"Thanks. What time do you have to be back in court?"

"I have a jury trial starting at two o'clock."

"Good timing, I have to be at the Police Academy at two. We'll get a good hour of work. Did you bring your weapons?"

"I only have one, my Chief Special."

"Where is it?"

"On my ankle, but it hurts when I wear it."

"At least you have it on you. Most people leave their weapon in the car or at home. We'll get into that later. Let's go down to the shooting range."

McKenzie followed O'Shea down a footpath through the woods, each dog brushing against her leg as they raced ahead.

She had first met O'Shea some years ago—how long *had* it been? It was at the Beethoven Club 100th birthday party, whatever that date was. He was a captain at that time on the Memphis Police Department, moonlighting as security for the birthday party. Back then she thought he was the most egotistical bully she had ever met, a typical cop. Now, he was the commander of the Swat Team or TACK Unit as Memphis Police called their high-risk operation team and the newly formed and much publicized Gang and Drug Unit. She had used him as an expert witness in her courtroom many times and recommended him to others. They had agreed to no exchange of money for trading favors. She called it *quid pro quo*. He called it a *freebie*. She had met a lot of different people at that birthday party, influential people, especially the host, Mack Shannon.

Mack Shannon. Just saying his name made her smile, yet sad. She had asked herself a thousand times, *why?* Why did she send him that letter severing their relationship? He had sent her a couple of Christmas cards after her letter, but how many years ago had that been? She couldn't remember the last time she had even heard his name. No one ever "rattled her cage" like he did. She could hear his voice now; remember his touch, dream of his kisses that left her breathless.

"Let me have your Chief Special," O'Shea said while looking at his watch. They were standing in front of a plywood countertop nailed between two trees with a variety of guns and ammo, spread out on top.

McKenzie bent over and pulled up her pants leg, which caught on her holster. She fumbled around and finally removed her revolver and handed it to him.

"Okay, we might as well address this now. A couple of things first, you never hand a loaded gun to another person, bad habit. Second, if you ever have to draw from an ankle holster . . . snatch your pants leg up and drop to a knee position and with both hands . . . well . . . it doesn't matter now, you're dead. An ankle holster is for a backup, not for a quick draw. Most gunfights are over in 3 seconds.

"But I wasn't drawing to shoot . . ."

"I know, but you weren't under the pressure of someone shooting at you either. Nowadays every street thug is carrying a weapon, most likely an automatic with a large mag. It used to be accuracy first, speed second. Now gangs spray everything with rapid-fire first. Tests have shown that an *untrained* shooter with a Glock 19 can empty his 15-round mag in 6 seconds, including drawing their weapon. No one can draw from an ankle holster and get a shot off under that kind of fire power."

"What then?"

"If that's all you've got, in your case, *run*, as fast as you can. Put something between you and the bad guy; a car, a utility pole, anything to get enough time to draw your weapon. But most important is avoidance. *Don't get into a gunfight* or any kind of confrontation. Back off, walk away; you're not the police. It's not your job to send him to hell. Your job is to stay alive. You live in one of the top five most dangerous cities of violent crimes in this country: murder, rape, armed robbery, and aggravated assault. There are thousands of drugged crazies out there. I don't need to tell you about Tennessee's 'stand your ground' laws. If you feel your life is in danger and you can't leave safely—forget laws and everything else—draw your weapon *first*. Stay calm, try to diffuse the situation, but if he pulls a gun on you, shoot him; if he walks toward you with a knife or baseball bat—shoot him—*Bang! Bang! Bang!* Three shots at a time, then move, and find cover if you can. If he's still coming keep firing, and *please*, don't try to wound him or any headshots, that's only in the movies. We'll get into this more in future lessons."

"I feel like I've been in a gunfight already."

"Just relax, the more you shoot and practice it becomes natural. Today I want to get you matched with the right weapon, a practical and comfortable holster, and get you familiar with firing it."

O'Shea was holding her S&W .38, "This model 442 is a great backup weapon for an ankle holster: black finish, aluminum frame, hammerless," he balanced it up and down in the palm of his hand. "Airweight they call it, a bit of exaggeration, still very light at 18 ounces. Lighter than the 26 ounce Baby Glock, but you've got 11 shots in the Glock compared to 5 shots in the S&W. I'd like for you to keep wearing this gun as a backup, we just need to get you a more comfortable ankle holster." He opened up a box of 38 specials, and handed her the revolver. "Let's shoot. Remember, with a revolver double tap, and move, you only have 3 more shots, so while looking for cover, top off . . . reload."

After shooting the box of 38's, O'Shea handed her the weapon he thought she should carry: a subcompact, 9mm semiautomatic Glock 26 Gen 4, the "Baby Glock," with 11 rounds, 10 in the mag and 1 in the chamber. "Everybody has their favorites. I'm a Glock man, but I've got a lot of guns on loan here and you can fire all of them and see what *you* like best."

"What are you carrying?"

"A Glock 21, Gen 4, 14 rounds." He removed the mag and ejected the round in the chamber, and handed it to her. "It's a .45 caliber hollow point with a 13 round mag, it weighs a little over two pounds. It's more for open carry, although some carry it concealed. You can fire it later if you like."

McKenzie fired 200 rounds with the Baby Glock: right and left-handed, sitting, kneeling, tucked, prone, speed loading while walking and running and firing at different targets, then she fired 2 magazines, of 14 rounds each with his G-21.

They were drinking bottled water as they walked back up to her car and she hurried to get inside because of the dogs. O'Shea stopped and removed a brown sack from his truck and handed it to McKenzie.

"What's this?"

"Open it."

She looked inside and removed a soft black leather shoulder purse, and looked up at O'Shea.

"Look inside," he said.

There was a flap over a couple of zippers and when she lifted the flap she saw a Velcro holster sewn to the inside of the purse with a Glock 26 in the holster.

"It's a gun purse," he said, taking it from her. He put the strap over his shoulder and lifted the flap. "The flap hides the gun and you keep your phone, keys, billfold, and other stuff in the zipper parts. Anytime you're walking to your car, from one building to another, or anyplace you feel uncomfortable, you can keep your hand on your gun at all times while it's hidden by the flap. Get in the habit of scoping all areas before walking into one." He dropped the flap back over the gun. "It's opened at both ends so you can fire from any position or jerk the purse off with your left hand while holding your gun. It's an easy carry: summer or winter, inconspicuous, comfortable, and concealed. There are two extra mags held by Velcro strips inside. The gun is loaded. Unload it when you get home or in your office and practice, practice, practice. Draw and dry fire different ways: while walking in the yard, sitting at your desk, watching TV, whenever. Next week we will see what you think. Bring those letters from the crazy; I want to read them. I'm not so sure I shouldn't call the Director of the FBI."

"Not yet. I used to get all kinds of threats when I was over in Chancery and nothing ever came of it."

"Bring me those letters."

"How did you know I would like the Glock 26 best?" She asked, looking at her watch; it was 1:40.

O'Shea just smiled and leaned over the convertible and kissed her on the lips.

"Thank you, and for the Glock too, but I'm warning you," she said, smiling, "you go to all this trouble and when it comes down to it . . . I don't think I could shoot a human being. I've shot birds and rabbits hunting with my father and deer hunting with my uncles, but . . . to kill a person . . . I don't want to do that." McKenzie said.

"Most people don't, but there's always druggies and degenerates preying on the weak, they care less about killing you as you did about killing birds and rabbits. You'll get over that feeling, it's all in the training."

"I'm going to be late," she said, making a U-turn in his drive, waving. "Let me know what I owe you."

CHAPTER 2

She steered down the left side of his steep driveway in low gear without dragging the bottom of her car. Once on Fite Road she shoved the gas pedal to the floor and the Porsche leaped forward. Hurrying, she eased through the red light on Highway 51 North. The speed limit was 55 but quickly changed to 40 mph. McKenzie checked her speedometer and the needle was a little past 70 mph. She was lane changing and passing on both sides of traffic when she glanced in her rearview mirror and saw the blue lights of a police car closing in behind her. *"Damn!"* she shouted, and moved to the right lane as she slowed to 40 mph thinking he might be chasing someone else. No such luck. He was right on her tail now and turned his siren on for her to stop. She pulled off the right side of the road and watched as the cop walked up to her. He was a Deputy Sheriff, not Memphis Police.

"Cut your engine off, Ma'am."

"Officer, I have an emergency . . ."

"Ma'am! Cut your engine!"

McKenzie turned the key off and reached over to get billfold from her purse on the passenger seat and saw that she had left the flap partially opened and the butt of her new gun was sticking out.

The Deputy saw the gun at the same time and shouted, "Don't move!" His right hand was on his gun as he snatched her door open with his left hand and ordered, "Out of the car!"

McKenzie, furious, swung her legs around to get out of the car and unconsciously reached back for her phone.

"Stop!" The Deputy shouted again, stepping back and drawing his gun. "Do not touch that gun!"

"I was reaching for my phone, are you craz . . ."

"Out! NOW!"

"All right, all right!" she said, getting out with both hands in the air. "I'm a federal judge, you idiot. I'll have your job for this." *Damn O'Shea. This is all your fault.*

They both turned when they heard another Deputy Sheriff's car pull up with his lights flashing. A Captain walked up, "What's the problem, Deputy?"

"Speeding, sir, and she has a gun in the front seat."

"Did she pull it on you?"

"No sir."

"Holster your weapon, Deputy. Ma'am you can put your hands down."

"Are you sure he's not going to shoot me?"

The Captain walked over and looked in the front seat. "I assume you have a permit for that, Chancellor?"

"Yes I do. You know me?"

"Yes Ma'am. I used to be a Court Bailiff in Circuit Court for Judge Bailey."

"I'm a Federal Judge now."

"Congratulations, Judge. Will you excuse me a moment?" He motioned for his Deputy to follow him to his car. Standing at the Deputy's car he said, "What do you want to do?"

"She ran a red light and was doing 80 mph, Captain."

"Have you ever worked in the downtown jail, Junior?"

Junior shook his head.

"You think you would like that kind of work?"

"No sir."

"You're going to owe me a big time Christmas present, Junior."

Junior nodded.

"Why don't you get back in service and let me see if I can cool this redhead down." The Captain stepped aside and watched Junior get in his car and leave. He walked over to McKenzie.

"Judge, let me apologize for my deputy's overreaction. He's a rookie and all our men are a little spooked since one of our Deputies was shot last week."

"I read about that, how's he doing?"

"He died yesterday, left two young kids. He never had a chance . . . walked up behind him at a red light and shot him in the head. It was best he didn't live."

"I'm so sorry, Captain," she said, walking to the driver's side of her car. "If I can do anything . . ."

He shut her door after she got in and leaned over the top, "Your Honor, I was thinking a one day suspension for my Deputy would teach him a good lesson. Would that heal the embarrassment we caused you?"

"Whatever you feel is appropriate, Captain." She started the Porsche.

"Am I free to go? I'm really late."

The Captain stepped back, "Of course."

She revved the engine a couple of times.

"Oh, one last thing, Your Honor." He leaned over the top again, "I know these cars are called 'Speedster,' but remember, speed kills. Be careful . . . slow it down."

"Thank you, Captain. Have a nice day." The engine was revved when she released the clutch and the car fishtailed out into the traffic, her back wheels slinging loose gravel at his feet as passing cars swerved and blew their horns at the red Porsche.

The Captain stood watching, *Go ahead, missy; keep it up . . . one night I'll be cutting you out of that tin can.*

McKenzie's cell phone was ringing; she knew it was her office calling. *Damn! Can you believe this . . . now I'm really late.* At 70 mph her tachometer pegged past redline, and she shifted into a higher gear while searching to find her cell phone.

CHAPTER 3

In downtown Memphis, on the river bluff overlooking the Mississippi River, a Cadillac Escalade cruised north on Front Street at a slow rate of speed. The driver's dark tinted window was cracked only about three inches, but you could still hear the blaring music a block away. The driver, Pookie Moss, pounded on the steering wheel to the beat of the rap music, and shouted in sync with his favorite hip-hopper, Drake:

Own it, own it, own it, own it, own it, own it, own it, own it,
Go own that shit, own that shit, own that shit, you own that shit . . .

In the back seat was Pookie's brother, Tayshaun, the Grand Master of the Vampires, the largest drug gang in the tri-state area. Both wore black hoodies with their gang sign, a small red V with drops of blood printed over the left chest.

"Cut that shit down," Tayshaun shouted, "you can't hear a word I'm saying to you."

"What's up, Tay?" Pookie asked. He was so small he could barely see the top of Tay's head through the rear view mirror.

Tay opened the backseat console, removed a hand full of "Rosebuds," picked one out and dropped the others back in. He removed the cork from each end of the 4-inch long glass tube and blew the tiny, 2-inch silk red rose out the other end onto the floorboard. "You know that liquor store over on Auction; stop there, I'll need a bottle of Remy after the dentist."

"Two o'clock, right? At crosstown?" Pookie twisted his head from side to side, constantly checking the side view mirrors. His paranoia was full blown after bingeing on crack cocaine for the last 48 hours. He scratched his head frantically; his long nails digging into his scalp for "coke bugs."

Tay removed a Chore Boy copper-scouring pad from the console and broke off a small piece and stuffed it into the end of the glass tube. He then opened an Altoids tin and inside was a solid white ingot, like a bar of motel soap, with some small loose "rocks" scattered around it. He picked up one of the rocks, pushed it into the end of the copper filter, and lit it with a long Bic wand lighter. The hot vapors immediately absorbed into his blood stream and within 8 seconds reached his brain. He fell back against the seat, his head resting on the headrest, his eyes closed, his "crack-lips" (blistered from the glass pipe) moving but no sound. Wrapped in euphoric vapors, he rocketed into a cosmic world of excessive and uncontrolled happiness, excitement, and joy . . . but only for a few minutes.

The vapor of the burning crack worked its way slowly to the front seat. Pookie squealed, like a little girl, "Crack Time!"

Tay leaned forward with his head bent and his eyes open, fully dilated, showing just two black olives. He stared at the dozen or so tiny red roses scattered deep into the black mouton floor mat. He watched as the roses started to grow their long stems out of the black "soil" gathering into a tall lush bouquet between his knees. Smiling, he reached out to pick one . . .

"Hey my brother from the same mother, ain't you going to share?" Pookie said as he pulled up in front of the liquor store.

Tay's few minutes of bliss were over. He got out of the car, wobbled a little until his vertigo subsided, then scanned the surrounding neighborhood. There had been a lot of chatter about a rival gang looking to make a hit on the Vampires. He leaned in and said, "I don't want anyone seeing us, park in the back," and walked into the liquor store.

"Damn, Tay, you leave me nothing, not even a little toke. No love, man." he shouted. *I just needed a little bump to kill these bugs crawling over me."* He eased the big SUV over the driveway entrance to the rear parking lot.

A couple of stores down, sitting in an unmarked car, eating a late lunch at McDonald's was Hector Gomez, a rookie undercover cop. He watched the black SUV stop behind the liquor store and park. *Wow, cool ride: 24-inch rims and low-profile tires, looks new.* He saw the driver's door open and picked up his binoculars to see who was driving. *He looked like a kid, but he was dressed like a gangbanger: black hoodie, hip-hop jeans and COOGI sneakers. Did he steal the car? He's jumpy—looking around in every direction.* Hector kept watching through his binoculars. Now the boy was in the back seat, then out and in the driver's seat again. Smoke was coming out of the tailpipe, so the car was still running. *Was he waiting on someone in the liquor store? Was it an on-going robbery? Let's see what the little man is up to.* He placed his binoculars on his passenger seat, finished the last bite of his burger, and backed out of his parking space.

Pookie opened the ashtray in the backseat and found the glass tube Tay had used. He blew the small amount of burned residue into the ashtray and picked out the tiniest rock from the Altoids tin, one he figured Tay would never notice. Sitting in the front seat he fired up the pipe.

Hector, with long hair, a thin mustache and goatee, dressed like a gangbanger, pulled onto the parking lot of the liquor store and parked behind the SUV. He paused, thinking of the best way to approach the vehicle. Fresh out of the police academy he thought about calling for backup, but if it turned out to be some kids trying to buy alcohol he would be the laughing stock of his department. Still . . . he picked up the radio mic and asked the dispatcher to run a license number check on the black SUV Escalade Cadillac, and that he was leaving his car to check on a suspicious person parked in the SUV behind the liquor store on Auction between Second and Third Street.

Sergeant Bobby Davis, in an unmarked car, had just left police headquarters at 201 Poplar and turned north on 3rd Street when he heard officer Gomez's radio message. He was just five blocks away and decided to drive by and check on his newest rookie.

Hector eased up along the rear side of the SUV, loud music was playing and he could see smoke coming out of the top of the driver's side window. It was a funky smell, but not marijuana. He stopped just behind the driver's door, his cap on backward, wearing wrap-around sunglasses and tapped on the side of the door, "Hey, wassup, man?"

No response. He waited. "Hey!" he shouted, and banged on the side of the door. Hector jumped backward immediately and drew his weapon. The sound of the doors automatically locking was ringing in his ears. Then the window on the driver's side started closing. He held his breath, both hands on his gun. He couldn't see inside the dark window as it closed all the way. *Oh hell! What now?*

Pookie had both hands on the steering wheel, his head drooping against his forearms. He was zonked, trying to ride out his celestial joyride as long as he could. Ohhhhh man . . . *Baby mama! Blast off! Was that shit cut with rocket fuel or what?* He leaned back, slumped down in his seat. A loud shout and banging on the door jolted his nerves as he jumped upright. He checked all the windows and the rear view mirror and didn't see anything until he looked through his side view mirror. *What the hell? A wetback gangbanger.* He pushed the button to lock the doors and another to close the top of his window. At the same time he patted the shoulder holster under his left arm to make sure his gun was there. He checked the windows again and didn't see anyone else; was there more than one? Where's Tay? He checked the side view mirror again . . . *the spic has a gun!* It's a hit. I knew it. Have they shot Tay?

Hector's hands were shaking as he pointed the gun at the window. He had an expert firing record at the police shooting range, but had never shot anyone, never been hunting even. *What are you doing?* He asked himself. *You can't shoot this kid, what's he done? Back off.* Hector holstered his gun and started backing away, but not fast enough. It all happened so quickly. Before he could draw his weapon again, the driver's door swung open and he saw a huge gold Desert Eagle pointing at him. The .50 caliber bullet, smashed into his chest like a 12-pound sledgehammer.

Where's Tay? Where's Tay? The words were screaming inside Pookie's head. *They've killed him!* He unzipped his hoodie and removed the five-pound gold Desert Eagle with the moniker, "Napoleon," due to Pookie's Napoleon complex. He fired two shots, first was a bull's-eye, center of the chest, and the second shot went high and right due to the powerful recoil. These deafening shots set off a chain of events—actions that were continuous, like the aftershocks of an earthquake. Tay came running out of the back of the liquor store, one hand in the air waving and screaming "No! No!" the other hand carrying a paper sack. Pookie was standing over a body spread out over the pavement next to the car, his Napoleon hanging from his hand almost touching the ground.

"Tay!" Pookie shouted, smiled and started running toward his brother, "Man, I thought you were dead. Where you been?"

Tay grabbed him, dropping the two bottles of cognac onto the payment, and shoved him into the driver's seat. "Go! Let's get out of here, you've killed a cop."

"What? He ain't no cop, look at him," he pointed his Napoleon at the body on the ground, "he's a Mexican gangbanger."

Tay had jumped in the front passenger seat, "Don't you hear his radio, see the spotlights and the antennas on that car, he's undercover . . . put that damn gun away and *drive!*"

Pookie made a U-turn screeching out of the parking lot onto Auction Street and turned east running the red light at 3rd Street.

Sergeant Davis, driving north on 3rd Street, two blocks from Auction heard the gunshots. He switched on the emergency lights and siren and stomped the accelerator to the floor. "310 responding to shots fired, 3rd Street and Auction." Davis knew the liquor store was between 3rd and 2nd Street and he would have to turn left on Auction. He saw the light was green, no traffic coming in the opposite direction, and started his left turn when he saw the black SUV barreling down on him. He stood on his brakes as his car skidded sideways crashing into the oncoming Cadillac, tearing metal from front to back. His car stopped when it slammed into the curb, teetered on two wheels for a few seconds, then rolled over onto the sidewalk, with the wheels still spinning.

Davis heard the sirens of other officers responding as he unbuckled his seatbelt, grabbed his handheld radio, and climbed out his opened window unhurt. A sick feeling came over him as he ran across the parking lot and saw Hector spread-eagle behind his car. He kneeled down to check his pulse, he was still breathing but a large hole was blown in the middle of his body armor. Davis jumped up and pulled his gun when he saw a young black man running toward him. He aimed and shouted, "Stop!"

The man stopped with both hands in the air, "Don't shoot! I'm a paramedic with the Memphis Fire Department. I saw the whole thing. Can I help?"

"Thank God." He holstered his gun. "Please . . . his name is Hector."

Two police cruisers pulled onto the lot as Davis pushed the key on his radio, "310, officer down, officer down, rear parking lot of liquor store on Auction between 2nd and 3rd. Send EMS, STAT!"

The radio was immediately jammed with calls until the dispatcher took control, "Listen up. Everybody listen up. Please stand by . . . stay off the radio, one at a time with your call number. I'll keep you informed. We have an officer down in the rear of a liquor store on the north side of Auction Street between 2nd and 3rd Street, be aware of EMS and fire units responding. 310, are you shot?"

"310. No, I'm not shot. Officer 325 shot in chest, unconscious, but breathing. Two black male suspects, driving a black Escalade are traveling east on Auction at a high rate of speed."

CHAPTER 4

Racing south on Thomas Street, 30 mph over the speed limit, McKenzie O'Connor saw that the light ahead at Auction was green and speeded up. If she made the light, she might not be late for her 2 o'clock jury trial. She took a quick look at her watch while crossing the intersection, but when she looked back, all she saw was a black wall. The explosion shattered her senses.

Major Kevin O'Shea had decided to go to Police Headquarters downtown first and then to the Police Academy on his way back home. He had just crossed Wolf River on Highway 51 N when he heard the radio call, "officer down." He pressed a button on his steering wheel that was wired directly to his police radio speaker, "500 . . . " he said.

"Go ahead 500," the dispatcher said.

O'Shea flipped a switch that turned the red and blue flashing lights on in his grille, "Say again location of suspects in black Escalade."

"500, two black males traveling east on Auction at a high rate of speed."

"500 responding. I'm headed south on Thomas Street crossing Wolf River." He placed a magnetic blue strobe light on his roof, tightened his seat belt, hit the switch for his siren, and stomped the gas pedal. The 707 horsepower engine came alive. From a block away you could hear the whine of the Hellcat Hemi supercharger as he raced to intercept the Escalade at Auction. He started naming the streets that had stoplights he would slow down for: *Firestone, Chelsea, and Jackson.*

O'Shea could hear sirens approaching as his car skidded over gasoline and oil spillage and came to a stop on the far side of the intersection. It looked like a war zone. The tangled wreckage of a three-car collision; smoke, steam, broken glass, and twisted metal was strewn all over the place. One side and half of the top of the black Escalade was wedged underneath a city garbage truck. The driver's door was blown off its hinges into the middle of the street and a small body was lying next to it. The complete frame of a small sports car was imbedded deep into the backseat of the SUV, like a harpoon shot from a cannon. Two garbage men were trying to free the driver from the exploded airbags on the sports car.

"500 on the scene, intersection of Auction, Danny Thomas, and Thomas Street. Send fire department, EMS, and backup. Suspect's car, black Cadillac SUV, disabled in a three-car collision."

"That big black car busted through the red-light . . . must have been doing a hundred." An old man standing on the curb with a walking cane said to O'Shea as he got out of his car.

"Is that the driver?" O'Shea said, pointing to the body in the street.

"That little red car was flying too, almost went right through that black car. Wildest thing I ever saw, so loud it shook the ground I was standing on. That boy there and the door came flying through the air as if dropped from an airplane. Yes sir, he was the one driving."

"Where's the other man that was in the black car?" O'Shea was scanning the surrounding area the whole time. He heard someone scream from across the street and saw the men pulling a body out of the mangled red car.

"Oh, the garbage men dragged him out from the other side of the garbage truck, I think he's dead. They told me to get away from there."

O'Shea started walking toward the body in the street while the old man was still talking. He had his Glock 21 in his hand by his side. He stood over Pookie who was face down, one of his legs was twisted backwards, the bone sticking out, and blood was pooling around his head; he appeared to be breathing. *Damn, he's just a kid.*

Yeah, and the venom from a newborn Cobra is enough to kill 50 men. He gave him a short kick to the broken leg—no movement, no sound, and with the toe of his shoe he pushed him over on his back. He pulled the hoodie down and saw the tattoo on his neck, a red V with two drops of blood. The rumor was that the drops of bloods represented how many people you had killed. He shook his head and with the barrel of his gun, flipped the hoodie open and saw the shoulder holster and the gold gun. *Damn, a Desert Eagle; .50 caliber.* He reached down to remove the gun and something hit him hard in his left arm just below his shoulder, twisting him and knocking him to the ground. He heard two more shots and saw they were coming from under the garbage truck. He rose up on one knee and fired three shots from his .45.

Tayshaun Moss was not dead. After the garbage men pulled his unconscious body from the SUV, covered in blood from multiple head cuts, they left him for dead. Then they went to extricate the woman in the sports car. As Tay regained consciousness he heard sirens approaching, wiped the blood from his eyes, and crawled underneath the garbage truck, hiding and looking for Pookie. He saw the SWAT cop with his flashing lights park and walk across the intersection to Pookie, who was lying motionless. Tay wiped the blood from his eyes again and saw the cop kick his dead brother's body. He fired three shots at the cop with his 9mm. When returned fire tore up the ground around him, he fired two more shots, then rolled out from under the garbage truck and started hobbling off across a vacant field toward a boarded up convenience store.

O'Shea took off running toward his car, firing four evenly spaced shots under the garbage truck. He sat inside his car, gasping for breath, his heart racing as he looked for his first aid kit. He watched the fire department EMS truck stop near the body in the middle of the intersection; one fireman pushed a gurney over to the body in the street and the other ran with an emergency backboard to the two garbage men working on the sports car. O'Shea shouted at them to back away but with sirens screaming in all directions, they didn't hear him.

Sticky blood was running down his sleeve covering his hand while he tried to open the first aid kit. He took a couple of deep breaths trying to control his heartbeat, placed his gun on the car seat, wiped both hand on his pants and wrapped an ace bandage from the kit around his arm to stop the bleeding.

The old man still standing on the curb didn't say anything, he just pointed at the shooter running across the field.

Slow down. Take your time. No stupid mistakes. O'Shea nodded his head at the old man and keyed his mic, "500, shots fired, shots fired! Need backup. I've been hit in the arm. In pursuit of a black male on foot, east side of Danny Thomas at Auction."

He picked up his Glock, ejected the magazine, and reloaded with another mag of 13 rounds of hollow point. He watched as one of the garbage men and the fireman rushed to the EMS truck carrying a bloody body half-covered in a blanket. His car was still running. He jerked it into gear and floored the gas pedal. He swerved around the rear of the garbage truck, crossed the intersection, and jumped the curb. He saw the shooter stumble and fall in knee-high weeds, and then struggling, he stood and fired three shots.

O'Shea skidded to a stop about 30 feet away and dove out the door as two shots tore through his windshield. He crawled off to the left through the weeds, and waited, counting the shots the shooter had fired, *8 shots. He's got 1 shot left . . . maybe.* He peeked over the top of the weeds and saw the shooter limping away, dragging one leg. He stood, took aim, fired three times and watched the shooter go down. He moved forward with small steps and both hands wrapped around his Glock. Six feet away he saw the shooter propped up on one elbow, an arm waving above the grass with a gun in its hand, "I'm hit, I'm hit . . ."

O'Shea quickly scanned the surrounding area . . . *Too late asshole.* O'Shea fired two times, point-blank. *I'm the last cop you'll ever shoot.*

CHAPTER 5

Inside the EMS truck, McKenzie O'Conner, semi-conscious, was placed on the bench seat leaving enough room on the left side of the truck for the gurney. The fireman, this one a paramedic, had removed the straps from the backboard, inserted an IV, and injected 2 ml of Fentanyl. He removed the blanket, checked the two tourniquets on both her legs and heard a loud shout from his partner. He stepped to the back door and saw his partner leaning over the body in the street, frantically waving at him. He adjusted the leaking oxygen mask on her face, covered her back up with the lightweight fire department blanket, grabbed his medical bag and took off running.

"What'cha got?" the paramedic asked, standing behind his partner.

The EMT moved away from the body.

The paramedic looked down at the Fire Department blanket covering the body and sticking out the side, pointed up at him, was the biggest automatic handgun he had ever seen.

"Whoa!" he jumped back, dropped his bag and raised both hands in the air.

"Put your hands down stupid," Pookie said. "Which one of you has the morphine?"

"We don't carry morphine." The paramedic said.

"AHHHHHH!" Pookie screamed in pain, "Don't give me that shit man, I'll *kill* you!"

"We carry Fentanyl, it's in the truck." The EMT said.

Pookie shoved the gun up close to the paramedic. "You want to play games with me, be a big hero, *huh*? Load me on that stretcher and get me on that truck *now!*" He was struggling to breathe, "And stay in front of me. Don't be thinking about running or dropping me 'cause my finger is on this trigger and I'll blow a hole right through your head." He grimaced in pain. "One more won't make no never mind."

"We need to set that leg first before moving you; the bone has broken through and . . ."

"I'm not blind, dumb ass. Do it in the truck . . ." he groaned, "Set me up where I can watch you . . . Go!"

The two firemen loaded Pookie onto the stretcher and rushed him to the truck. The rear door of the truck was open and McKenzie could hear someone shouting as the gurney was rolled through the door. Her pain had subsided, but she felt nauseated and closed her eyes when she saw the bloody thighbone sticking up through the man's pants leg. *Was that a large gun he was waving at the two firemen?* A dark cloud closed in over her.

"You," Pookie pointed the gun at the paramedic, "get me that shot *now* and then fix this leg. You," he shouted at the EMT, "get up front and drive, get us out of here."

"Where to?" the EMT said.

"I need him here to help set your leg." The paramedic said.

"AHHHHHH!" Pookie screamed again. Holding the gun with both hands he fired two shots through the roof. The explosion rocked the truck. "NOW! Get me that shot!" He pointed the gun in the paramedic's face, his eyes bulging.

The EMT pointed to the front cab, motioning he was moving up front through the walkthrough to the driver seat.

The paramedic started laying out an IV set, a start kit, and a saline bag.

"What's all that shit?" Pookie reached over and smacked him on the side of his head with the gun barrel, "Put a needle in my arm *now*!"

The paramedic hurriedly tore the paper away from the syringe with his teeth as blood ran down his neck, stuck it in an ampule of Fentanyl and withdrew the fluid.

"If you OD me I'm going to blow a hole through your chest before I pass out." Pookie said while watching the paramedic's shaking hand insert the needle in his vein. He took a deep breath and leaned back on the tilted stretcher waiting for the drug to take effect. He knew that Fentanyl was a 100 times more potent than morphine and had a heroin like effect; he felt the pain fading, like letters erased from a chalkboard, one line at a time.

"Who's that?" Pookie said, pointing the gun at the blood-soaked sheet wrapped around McKenzie's knees. "Is she dead?"

"No, sedated. She was in the sports car . . ."

Hearing the two shots fired, O'Shea jumped in his car as his radio squawked the arrival of another car, "211 on the scene at Auction and Danny Thomas, shots fired from inside the EMS truck . . ."

"211. Anyone shot?" said the dispatcher.

"211, standby."

O'Shea wheeled around the garbage truck and saw two policemen, their guns drawn, standing behind their parked cruiser blocking the rear of the EMS truck. With the blue light on his roof still flashing, he skidded to a stop in front, blocking in the truck. Shielding himself behind his car, he waved his gun at the driver, motioning for him to get out of the truck.

The EMT shook his head and pointed to the back part of the truck. O'Shea eased around the back of his car and duck-walked over to the truck. The EMT watched O'Shea and slowly unhooked his seatbelt. He jumped when the door was jerked open and he was yanked to the ground and half-dragged behind the police car.

"WHAT?" Startled from his Fentanyl trance, Pookie quick-fired wildly toward the sound of the front door, the recoil so strong the gun almost jumped from his hand as the windshield exploded splaying glass over O'Shea and the EMT.

McKenzie's eyes popped open as she screamed in shock and pain. Her ears were ringing so loud she couldn't think. *Who was shot?* She knew she couldn't just lie there and do nothing and die. This kid was whacked out; she could be next and then the paramedic. Under the cover of the blanket, she pulled the taped IV from her right arm, rolled onto her side, and tried to pull her legs up but couldn't move them. Finally, she got her hand under her right thigh and pulled her leg up high enough to remove the .38 special from her ankle holster.

"Where's the driver?" Pookie shouted, smacking the arm of the paramedic who was holding both hands over his ringing ears. "Look up front and see."

The paramedic saw the blue flashing light in front of the truck and cautiously leaned around the walkthrough, "He's gone."

"That chickenshit! I guess he didn't believe me when I said I'd kill you if he ran."

"He couldn't go anywhere, there's a police car blocking the truck."

"Then you drive. Back it up now and if you run, I'll kill her." He pointed the pistol at McKenzie.

The paramedic looked through the window of the back door and saw multiple police cars with their lights flashing, "They've got the rear blocked off too, police are all over the place."

"This is the Memphis Police Department, the truck is completely surrounded and you have no chance of escape." O'Shea was behind his car talking over a hand held loudspeaker. "You have two hostages inside, I need to know that they are okay. I'm going to call the paramedic on his cell phone so we can . . ."

Pookie leaned over into the walkthrough holding the gun with both hands and pulled the trigger on the .50-caliber. The other windshield exploded, shattering glass in all directions as he screamed, "You come in here and I'll kill you and everybody else." Pookie was sitting upright on the stretcher, both hands on the gun, waiting to see what they were going to do. A terrified look came over his face, *how many bullets do I have left?* He couldn't think. He searched the pockets of his hoodie but the extra magazine was not there. He knew he had at least one bullet in the chamber, but how many in the mag? Still groggy, he made a fatal move, he automatically slid his thumb up and ejected the mag.

Even with the reverberation of the explosion, the paramedic recognized the familiar sound of a magazine being ejected from an automatic. He couldn't believe his eyes when he saw the gun in one hand and the magazine in the other, knowing an automatic would not fire without the mag in the gun. He leaped with both hands together high above his head, and came smashing down with all his might on the broken bone protruding from Pookie's leg.

Never had Pookie thought that anyone could still be alive and experience such pain. His air passage closed off as if his chest was crushed and the blow to the femur drove the bone into his hip almost jarring him from the stretcher. His heart stopped beating; there was only pain. His scream mixed with vomit horrified McKenzie as the magazine flew from his hand, but not the gun. Instinctively he knew the gun was his lifeline. It became part of his hand and he used it like a 5-pound hammer in a murderous frenzy as he pummeled the head of the paramedic.

"STOP!" McKenzie shouted, her .38 special pointed at him.

Pookie jerked around, his bloody gun barrel pointed at her.

She could hear Kevin O'Shea's strong voice inside her head: *If he pulls a gun on you, shoot him—Bang! Bang! Bang!*

She didn't know how many times it went *Bang*. She was still pulling the trigger on an empty chamber when she saw O'Shea standing in the walkthrough with a bewildered look on his face. "Well, I'll be damned!" He said and holstered his gun. "What the *hell* are you doing here?"

CHAPTER 6

ajor Kevin O'Shea took the steps two at a time as he hurried through the doors of the Winchester Medical Center. He had heard of Boutique hospitals before, but this was a first.

The place was more like the Peabody Hotel. He should have come here to be sewed up. Naw, his insurance would have frowned on that.

After signing in, he was escorted to Judge O'Connor's suite by a retired policeman working as security. O'Shea recognized the man but didn't remember his name. He said that he was assigned to the judge and that she had been in surgery for over four hours and was now resting in her suite. He could see her but shouldn't stay too long.

As O'Shea walked down the halls, he noticed how overly complaisant everyone was. They had big smiles, and were dressed in upscale street clothes as if they worked in the executive office of a Fortune 500 company. No lab coats, scrubs, even security wore coats and ties. The only uniform in the place was his all-back SWAT attire, including the black sling holding up his left arm.

There was a 'Do Not Disturb' sign on the door; he tapped lightly and went in. McKenzie was propped up in the bed with a pillow under one-bandaged knee, the other in a soft cast. Her nose was taped up and a bandage one wrapped around her hand. Her face was red and swollen, and starting to show bruising. Numerous IV lines were hanging from a pole, including a morphine drip with a computerized pump (PCA) and one for antibiotics. She still looked somewhat groggy, but when she saw O'Shea her eyes gleamed and she tried to smile while waving him in. Surprised, he turned instantly when the bathroom door opened and he stared at a tall older man dressed in a polo shirt and khakis.

"Kevin, you remember Bishop O'Brien?" McKenzie said.

"How are you, Kevin? Congratulations on your promotion." O'Brien said, extending his hand.

O'Shea had a puzzled look on his face until he realized it was McKenzie's priest. Without his clerical clothes, he had failed to recognize him. He doffed his cap and shook O'Brien's hand, "Of course, how are you sir? Sorry about that . . ."

"It happens all the time. Oh, I didn't know you were injured."

"Nothing permanent, a couple of stitches and some antibiotics."

"Well I'm glad you're safe. I was just leaving. I'm playing in a foursome out at Spring Creek and I don't want to be late." He leaned over the bed and kissed McKenzie on the cheek and as he passed Kevin he patted him on the back and whispered, "Thank you. I understand you saved her life," and hurried out the door.

"If you hadn't said his name I would never have recognized him." O'Shea said standing at the foot of her bed.

"I know."

"I tried to get here sooner, I thought they took you to The Med, but . . ."

She motioned for him to come closer. "I need a hug," she whispered.

He leaned over the bed and wrapped one arm around her.

"Ohhhh." She held on to him as if she were drowning. Tears gushed from her eyes and her body shook with heavy sobs.

He waited, trying to think of something to say that was appropriate.

She pushed back from him and reached for a tissue. With her head down, she dabbed her eyes and wiped her nose. "I'm sorry. I hope I didn't freak you out."

"What, me? Do I look freaked out?"

"No, I'm the one that's freaked out. I killed . . ." she dropped her head in her hands, "a young kid."

"McKenzie, look at me. You shot him in self-defense. He would have killed that fireman and you, and maybe me. It was a clean shoot; I'm proud of you.

"Did you call for Father O'Brien?" he asked, changing the subject.

"No, he was visiting a member of his church down the hall and saw them wheeling me in. Why?"

"Just making sure it wasn't for your last rites," he smiled.

"He was hearing my confession."

"Your confession? What did you have to confess?"

"Kevin! I committed a mortal sin; I killed a human being."

"Listen *Judge*, you killed a crack head who shot two cops. His days were numbered. I'm sorry you had to go through this, but it's not mathematical logic; you die or he dies . . . 100 percent self-defense. What did O'Brien tell you?"

"I can't tell you that, it's a confessional privilege, you should know that."

"Just trying to get you to talk to me."

"What do you know about "mathematical logic" anyway?"

"It sounds good . . . I read somewhere it was higher math."

"I told him everything that happened. I asked him *why* God put me in that situation? He said, pretty much the same that you just said, maybe to save that paramedic's life, like you saved mine."

"He said that?"

"Yes, and you did save my life. I'll forever be thankful." She reached out and grabbed his hand. "Without that backup gun and the words you repeatedly forced into my memory . . . I *would* be dead."

"It was a miracle that crash didn't kill you. Your car looked like something from the junkyard."

"Thank God, my father insisted on having those airbags installed. I'll trade a broken nose anytime for a face though the windshield."

"What about your legs?"

"My left one will heal, its' not too bad. My right knee, they're not sure. The surgeons inserted some screws and plates, but if that doesn't work, I'll need a complete knee replacement. No more tennis for a while anyway."

"I'm sorry, are you in any pain?"

"No, this pump takes care of that. I'm just thankful to be alive."

"This is some hospital. Is this the one your husband built?"

"Yes, Randolph built it with a couple of other doctors and when he died they changed the name to Winchester Medical Center in his honor."

"I was thinking that if you wanted to talk to someone about the shooting, we have a psych doc on call that specializes in shooting cases."

"Can he do anything for me that talking to you wouldn't do?" She saw a puzzled look on his face. "You know, like you said, the two of us talking it out now?"

"What do I know about a woman's mind? I could give you the wrong advice."

"What has *women* got to do with it? You didn't give me the wrong advice when you told me . . . *Bang! Bang! Bang!*"

There was a light tap on the door and McKenzie's legal secretary, Abby Jones, walked in and hurried across the room. "Oh my God, I was scared to death when the police called me, they said you were dead . . . I was almost crazy. I got Director Maddox's cell phone number from your computer and called him and he tracked you down." Abby tried to hug her but backed away afraid she might hurt her. She held her good hand and kissed her on the cheek. "Are you in much pain?"

"You called James Maddox, the Director of Police?" O'Shea asked.

"Damn right I did. Why?"

"Abby, you remember Major O'Shea?"

"I do, he's the one giving you the shooting lessons. The Director told me you saved her life with that leg gun; you did good Major. Can you teach me next?"

Abby turned back to McKenzie and stared at her bandaged legs, swollen face, broken nose, and the growing purple discoloration under her eyes.

"What's wrong?" McKenzie asked.

"You look like one of our domestic violence cases." Abby said.

"I feel like one too. There's a mirror in the bathroom, let me see."

"I'd better go," O'Shea said. "I've got to run by Baptist Hospital and check on officer Gomez; he's lucky to be alive. If you need anything, just call me." He opened the door and an older woman stumbled into the room as if she had been eavesdropping. O'Shea's habit of thinking that everybody is a suspect, something he'd learned in Leadership Training School at the FBI Academy. It warned him to take a mental snapshot of this person. Did he know this . . . woman, or was it a man? Dyed blond hair hung out the bottom of her baseball cap.

"Sorry, I saw the sign on the door and wasn't sure I had the right room. Is this Judge O'Conner's room, I have flowers to deliver." A heavy coat of pancake makeup covered her rough complexion and her arched eyebrows looked penciled in above her tinted glasses. She wore a long pleated skirt and an open blouse.

O'Shea stared at her Adam's apple, then shifted to the long black delivery box with a red ribbon and bow. *Nice, I should have remembered to get McKenzie flowers . . . I'll send some later.* He stepped back, "Come on in, you got the right room." He said goodbye again and closed the door behind him.

Abby said, "Nice" and reached for the box of flowers.

"No!" the woman said pulling the box back, "I was told to give them to her personally."

Abby snatched the box from her, "Back off *girlie*, you've done your job."

Abby removed a card stuck under the ribbon and handed it to McKenzie, "I wonder who sent these?"

The woman said, "I don't know! I just do the deliveries." She moved to the side of the bed and took McKenzie's hand, "I'm very, *very*, sorry you were hurt, Judge." She backed up all the way to the door, fumbled in her purse, removed her cell phone and snapped off two quick photos and rushed from the room.

"What the hell was that? I almost wet my panties, I thought she was digging in her purse for a gun," Abby said.

"Why did she take our pictures?"

" Beats me. Probably to prove she delivered the flowers. Is there a vase around here?"

"I think there's one in the bathroom closet," McKenzie said, her curiosity increasing as she opened the envelope and saw the writing in red ink on black paper. She read each word as an eerie feeling crept over her:

Though I turn, I fly not—
I cannot depart;
I would try, but try not
To release my heart.
And my hopes are dying
While, on dreams relying.

Thus, the bright snake coiling
Wins the bird, beguiling,
To come down and see:
Like that bird the lover
Round his fate will hover
Till the blow is over
And he sinks — like me.

Strange poem, she thought. She started to read it again when her fragile nerves were shattered by a horrific scream from the bathroom. Then a loud crash of what she imagined was the glass flower vase. She sat trembling, staring at the bathroom door as Abby staggered out holding her bleeding hand.

"It bit me . . . it bit me." She looked up at McKenzie whispering the last words. Her eyes were terrifying, searching for help, as she crumpled to the floor.

CHAPTER 7

O'Shea got to the end of the curved driveway of the medical center and stopped. Something was bothering him. He put the Hellcat in park, the engine still running. It was that delivery woman. He had learned not to brush these forewarnings to the side. Something just wasn't right. Out of the corner of his eye he saw an old Volkswagen Beetle racing out of the parking lot and knew it was her. But the baseball cap was gone and a shiny baldhead replaced the blond wig. He grabbed his binoculars and focused on the license number calling it out to himself as the Beetle passed the front of the medical center. He shoved the gearshift into reverse, stomped the accelerator and sped back up the driveway to the entrance.

The door was open when O'Shea got to McKenzie's room. Abby was spread out on the floor with a pillow under her head and a nurse hovering over her.

"What happened?" O'Shea said.

"Kevin! A snake bit Abby! Look, her hand bleeding!"

"A snake . . . where the hell did a snake come from?"

Abby was moaning and looked as if she was in shock. He took her hand, wiped the blood away, and examined her finger.

McKenzie nodded toward the nurse, "She called the emergency room . . . a doctor is on his way."

"Well, nothing to worry about, it's non-poisonous. A little peroxide and a shot of penicillin and you'll be like new again."

"Whhhat?" Abby's head popped up from the pillow. All three stared at him as if he was some kind of witch doctor. The nurse finally spoke, "How do you know?"

"You see those little pinpricks making a half circle, a poisonous snake bite would have two puncture marks from its fangs. Where's the snake?"

"What are those little white things in the blood? McKenzie asked.

"Baby teeth that broke off when the snake bit her." O'Shea said.

Abby jumped to her feet immediately as if nothing had ever happened, "I'm going to knock more than it's baby teeth out, that damn snake scared the you-know-what out of me."

"Whoa, hold on," O'Shea grabbed Abby's arm. "Is the snake in the bathroom?"

"Yes, it was in the box of flowers and when I reached in to put them in the vase I felt this sting and dropped the box. The snake was just dangling there, hanging on my finger until I slung it off. I almost had a heart attack."

O'Shea stepped into the bathroom and shut the door. The place looked like a fight scene: a broken vase, scattered roses, black flower box upside-down and the top, was halfway in the shower . . . but no snake. He swept the broken vase into a corner with his boot, scooted the roses away from the box into a pile and placed them in the sink. The black box was upside down and when he lifted the corner he heard the snake hissing. "Wow little fellow, I'm not going to hurt you," he whispered. The small, black, yellow and red-banded snake slithered to the corner, coiled, raised his head and hissed.

O'Shea sat on the toilet seat thinking about the difference between the deadly poisonous Coral snake, and the nonpoisonous Scarlet King Snake; both were black, yellow and red banded. He kept saying the different axioms over and over to himself:

Red Touch Yellow - Kills a Fellow
Red Touch Black – Safe for Jack

And then he remembered another one: *The Coral Snake has a black nose.* He double-checked; the snake's nose was red. He slide his boot over to the snake, *"I know, I'd be pissed too if someone yanked my teeth out."* The snake uncoiled and O'Shea gently picked it up, watched as it coiled around his arm. He picked up the box and the top and walked out of the bathroom.

"Oh my God!" Abby shouted as she backed away, stumbling over a chair and falling into the nurse. "Get that thing out of here!"

"It's a harmless King snake," O'Shea said, holding it up and letting it uncoil from his arm and fall into the flower box.

"What pretty colors." McKenzie said.

"The Kings are very unique; they're immune to poisonous snakebites. A free exterminator you might say that loves to feast on rattlesnakes, copperheads, and cottonmouths."

"What made you come back?" McKenzie asked, propped up in the bed now.

"I had a weird feeling about that delivery woman; I think it was a man. I noticed his Adams apple was too large for a woman, and under all that makeup was a shadow of a beard, but I let it pass."

"Look at this," McKenzie said handing him the note."

O'Shea read the note, looked up, then read it again. "I knew something was wrong, I felt it. Is this the same freak that's been sending you those letters?"

"I don't know," McKenzie said, shrugging her shoulders. "What does it mean?"

O'Shea read Poe's poem again, "*Though I turn, I fly not—I cannot depart;* It looks as if he's saying he can't leave you alone. This last part is what I'm concerned about, *Till the blow is over, And he sinks — like me.*"

"You think he's going to kill her, don't you?" Abby said.

O'Shea folded the note and stuck it in his shirt pocket thinking . . . *black paper and red ink, that's got to have some spooky significance.* He pointed at McKenzie, *"You,* get me those other notes and letters from this nut case . . . *today.* I'll be in touch." He turned and was out the open door before anyone could say a word.

CHAPTER 8

"Dear friends in Christ, we have gathered together today to witness Raymond Flynn and Charles Parker publicly committing themselves to one another. In the name of the Church, we bless their union: a relationship of mutual fidelity and steadfast love, forsaking all others, holding one another in tenderness and respect, in strength and bravery, as long as they live. If any of you can show just cause why they may not lawfully be married speak now; or else for ever hold your peace."

Ohh shit, what have I done? Crazy Ray said under his breath while holding both of Dago's hands.

"I require and charge you both, here in the presence of God, that if either of you know any reason why you may not be united in marriage lawfully, and in accordance with God's Word, you do now confess it . . . Therefore, let us pray in the name of Christ that they may be strengthened by the promises they make this day, and that we will have the generosity to support them in whatever they undertake and the wisdom to see God at work in their life together. God be with you. Amen."

There were no lights on in the house, the blinds and shades were closed and Crazy Ray sat in complete darkness except for the gas burning logs in the small fireplace. He hadn't slept in the last three days, except for nodding off in the recliner, and not since his delivery of flowers to the judge in the hospital. *Bam*, what an adrenaline rush—he opened the door and almost fell into the cop's lap for God's sake. And he knew the cop, a real badass; dressed in all black SWAT gear. Did the cop recognize him? He *was* staring hard at him. No way, it had been years since the kidnapping plus his disguise made it impossible.

Crazy Ray fell back in his recliner, his pupils constricted down to pinpoints, his heavy eyelids fighting to stay open. The three oxycontin's he crushed and snorted were kicking in, playing havoc with his central nervous system. He stopped breathing, his chin dropped to his chest, his mouth opened, with saliva drooling from his mouth. He gasped, as if a defibrillator had shocked him. His head fell back and he started breathing again with gulps of air, his eyes wide open. He watched as his body levitated, hovering above the living room. A wide crack appeared in the floor, expanding as it zigzagged across the room. The coffee table tilted over breaking the glass top and the end of the couch slid into what was now a large sinkhole. The recliner teetered on the edge until the floor gave way and swallowed the recliner with Crazy Ray in it. The last thing he remembered was watching the fading light of the living room as he dropped through the mineshaft like hole.

His fried brain jumped from hallucinations to delusional perceptions as he watched an image of himself open a cigar box and remove a S&W .357 Magnum. He had forgotten how heavy it was. He pushed the cylinder release button, ejected 5 of the 6 bullets, spun and closed the cylinder, cocked the hammer and placed the barrel against his throbbing temple. He hesitated, took a deep breath and pulled the trigger. The sound of the firing pin in the empty chamber caused him to flinch. Would he have heard that sound if a bullet had been in the chamber? The cold stainless barrel felt good pressed to his head. A single bullet and there would be no more pain. No problems, no regrets . . . no nothing. He opened the cylinder and reached for another bullet.

"Hey Raaaaymond, I'm home." Dago shouted, as his tank-like 240-pound frame tromped across the living room dragging his roller suitcase with a backpack on top. He flipped on the light switch. "What's with the fire logs burning its 65-degrees outside?"

The noise and light roused Crazy Ray from his stupor. He leaned forward dropping his face in his hands, "Cut those damn lights out, my head is killing me, and don't call me by that name."

"My, my, aren't we touchy. I thought you would be glad to see me. What's wrong? Are you sick? Have you been taken your medicine?"

"I've taken so many pills I've forgotten what I've taken."

"I thought you were following the drug schedule on your computer?"

"I can't remember . . ."

"Did you take the pills the new doc gave you?"

"I think so," He slurred his words into a table fan blowing on him. "They're the ones making me so sick, I think."

"Are you stoned?"

"I took a couple of oxys for this damn headache . . . and smoked a joint to settle my stomach."

"You are going to die if you don't get off that shit and stay on schedule with your ARV pills."

"I wish."

"No, you don't. You watched that doctor boyfriend of yours die from AIDS, going from 200 pounds to an 80 pound skeleton is not a pretty sight."

"Don't talk about him, and I don't have AIDS."

"Okay, HIV." Dago stepped on something soft and picked it up; it was a blond wig. He reached over and pulled the chain on a table lamp. "I need to take a look at you.

"My God, Ray, tell me you didn't go to the hospital to see that woman? She's a *federal* judge, man; she'll lock your ass up in a federal prison for life. It won't be like that 'Club Fed' you were in down in Pensacola."

Crazy Ray struggled to stand, swayed a bit, then got his balance. All he had on was black pantyhose, and a lace camisole with a padded bra. His lipstick was smeared and the pancake makeup no longer covered the red cutaneous lesions on his face.

"I've got to go to the bathroom. I have diarrhea."

Dago followed him to the bathroom, "What happened at the hospital? I know something happened, I can tell. Did she recognize you?"

Crazy Ray opened the bathroom door and turned back to look at Dago, "Are you joining me?" and slammed the door."

"Crazy bitch," Dago said, banging his fist on the door. "We need to talk." He started to walk away but turned back and kicked the bottom of the door, "You need to take a shower while you're in there; you stink."

It all started in parochial school. Dago was walking down the outside stairs at Holy Names, saw a large crowd in the rear of the schoolyard and walked over to see what was happening. The younger one of the two brothers was holding a redheaded kid while his older brother punched the kid in the face over and over. Dago remember the kid because of his red hair and the freckles on his face, but you couldn't see any now for all the blood. Dago slammed his large fist on the back of the older brother's head, knocking him sideways to the ground, and was ready to kick him when someone shouted. "Here comes Sister Agnes George." The crowd scattered, Dago grabbed the redhead by the collar and they ran down an alley adjacent to the schoolyard. "You the one they call Crazy Ray?"

"Yeah, what about it?"

From that day forward they were inseparable.

It all seemed to evolve from the day Dago brought Crazy Ray home with him after the fight in the schoolyard. He had no place to go. There was no father in the picture and after his mother ran off with a drug dealer, the landlord padlocked the doors of their house for nonpayment and put all their belongings on the street. Dago's mother's house was only a two-bedroom but she offered their couch for him to sleep on and soon after, he was sleeping in the same bed with Dago.

There was nothing sexual involved. Dago was asexual. He never had sex with a woman or a man. Well, when he was a kid, he let a lecherous old fag give him a hand job, but it was more out of curiosity than anything else. He didn't know Crazy Ray's sexual preference; it was something they never talked about. He knew Crazy Ray was a tomcat—with men and women—and had a torrid love affair with his married doctor, Randolph (Randy) Winchester, an eminent anesthesiologist who died of AIDS.

Dago never understood why they got married; loneliness on his part for sure. He was never able to sleep by himself without having horrible nightmares and had slept in the same bed with his mother until Crazy Ray moved in. Two men married to each other sounds ridiculous. They never marched in a LGBT parade, flew a rainbow flag, or held hands in public. Mainly it was something Crazy Ray wanted to do, to be different, to shock people. They had never discussed any role-playing between them, or designated any feminine or masculine chores. It was Dago's house; he had always done the repairs and cleaning. That's how he learned some of his maintenance skills.

Dago removed the dirty dishes from the sink, threw the mildewed coffee grounds into the foul-smelling garbage can, and put on a fresh pot of coffee. While it was percolating, he filled the sink with hot soapy water and started washing what appeared to be every plate, glass, and silverware in the house.

Dago sat at the kitchen table with pen and paper making a list of demands for Crazy Ray if he wanted to continue to live in Dago's house. A steaming cup of coffee waited for Crazy Ray when he came out of the bathroom, a towel wrapped around him, and his long red hair dripping water.

"We need to talk," Dago said.

"About what?"

"Just sit down and listen." Dago pushed a chair out with his foot.

"Not another sermon?"

"Call it what you want, but I'm not going to live like this. I like order, you like chaos. I work out of town all week and come home to a pigsty. You don't work, you don't clean, the yard is overgrown, and you don't contribute one dollar to this household. You disappear for no reason, stay gone weeks at a time, then show up unexpectedly like a stray dog; starved, beat-up, and not a dime in your pockets. I don't know if you're dead or alive."

Crazy Ray jumped up from the chair, "You want me to move out, to leave? Just say the word and I'm outta here!"

This time, Dago was waiting for this familiar threat. He stood up, towering over Crazy Ray, poking him in the chest with each word, "Yes, I want your ass outta here, *now*. It shouldn't take you over 10 minutes to get your shit and go. You're a real wacko, Ray. Why do you think they call you Crazy Ray? Anyone who would dress up like a woman, stalk and threaten to kill a federal judge *is* crazy. And you're jeopardizing *my* life. You're a psycho, man; the cops will put you down like a mad dog for what you've done, and without any warning . . .

"There are garbage bags under the kitchen sink to carry your shit in." Dago moved to the living room and picked up his suitcase.

There was a shocked look on Crazy Ray's face as he watched Dago unloaded his suitcase into the washing machine. He turned abruptly and stalked off to his bedroom. He had moved out before but not when he was this sick. "Okay, if that's what you want," he shouted and started emptying the drawers in his dresser, throwing everything onto the bed. His weak body and mind opened the door to fear, and tremors set in. His body started shaking and sweating profusely as Meniere's vertigo reared its ugly head. He grabbed for the dresser as the room started tilting, then spinning, faster and faster, until his legs collapsed. He fell face first, vomiting into the opened drawers. The mirrored dresser tumbled over on top of him.

Hearing the crash, Dago rushed to the bedroom. He muscled the dresser off Crazy Ray with ease, and clothes flew across the room as he jerked the bedspread from the bed. He lifted Crazy Ray, the towel falling from his naked body, and placed him on the bed. He took the towel and wiped the sweat from his body and the vomit from his face. He hurried to the kitchen, broke open an ice tray into a pot on the stove, threw a kitchen towel in with some cold water, and dashed back to bedroom with the iced towel. He patted the towel across Crazy Ray's forehead and eyes. "I'm so sorry my darling, I didn't mean to call you those names. You'll get over this; it's just another attack of vertigo. I'll get your motion sickness pills."

Dago didn't know why, but he had this deep feeling of responsibility for Crazy Ray. The only other person he felt that way about was his mother, and now that she was gone the only person he had was Crazy Ray. Maybe it was because he felt guilty about running off to Mexico and leaving Crazy Ray alone after he kidnapped Mack Shannon's daughter. He did try to call him before he crossed the border, but Crazy Ray didn't answer and he was afraid to leave a message.

After a year of living in Mexico, Dago moved back to Memphis but failed to locate Crazy Ray. He assumed he was in prison or dead, until late one night he showed up at his door with a wild story about a towboat crew rescuing him from a tree floating down the Mississippi River. Unfortunately, there was a warrant still out for Crazy Ray's arrest. Tito saw him going into the neighborhood grocery and turned him in for the $10,000 reward. At three o'clock in the morning the SWAT team surrounded Dago's house, kicked the door in and took them both to jail.

Dago's lawyer won his release after 60 days in jail. He argued there was no proof or witnesses that Dago was involved in the kidnapping. Mack refused to let Irish come back to Memphis to testify. Besides, she would swear to tell the truth about Crazy Ray, that he did her no harm. Regardless, Crazy Ray was sentenced to 5 years in prison by Chancellor McKenzie O'Connor. He served 3 years and was released on good behavior.

Whack. Whacko. Psycho . . . Dago's poisonous words bounced around in Crazy Ray's head to the beat of the whirling blades of the lawnmower. Later, when he thought the pounding had stopped, but the beat continued to the incessant dripping faucet as he cleaned the kitchen. He was trying to hold off mixing the painkillers with his other drugs, but it was all too much.

The dripping faucet was Dago's fault; he said he was going to fix it, but left it dripping to punish me. He was no different than all the others. The conspiracy was from all directions. Just wait. Judgment will be forthcoming and payback will be hell. Dago, you'll be first on my list. *Oh, no worry Judge O'Connor; I'm not through with you yet, the letters and the snake were just the opening scene—you and Mack Shannon. All of you are on my list.*

He sat at the kitchen table in front of his computer drinking coffee and typed in the word, *psycho.* He knew what the word meant, but wanted a more detailed explanation—*a crazy or mentally unstable person.* He then type in the word crazy—*mentally deranged; demented; insane.*

Insane? How would an insane person know if he didn't do the chores Dago had written down: cut the grass, scrub the floors, clean the house, that he wouldn't have a place to live? How would he know that? Why would he care? Dago, my oldest friend says I'm deranged, a psycho. How could he say that? I'll make him wish he never called me that. He looked at the gas logs in the fireplace and thought about burning the house down to prove his point. Now that would be crazy, and stupid—*Where would I live?*

He started banging both temples with the heel of his hands, jumped up and knocked over the chair, howling. He grabbed his coffee cup and threw it across the kitchen, shattering it against the drip, drip, dripping faucet, *Oh, Holy Mother of God, where is my sweet Randy when I need him the most. He always knew what to do when I was like this.*

CHAPTER 9

Mack Shannon stood up from his redwood chaise lounge, removed his sunglasses and pressed his fingers on his flat stomach. He squinted from the bright sun as he checked his skin to make sure he was not getting too much sun. Even with his black hair, now streaked with gray, and a medium dark-complexion, he still had to be careful; he was Irish, albeit Black Irish, but the Key West sun had no mercy on any skin. Besides, he had gotten an hour of sun early this morning on a long run with his daughter and had planned to go diving for lobster later this morning.

He lowered the top half of the lounge chair and sighed as he eased himself facedown sinking into the soft cushion; *I wonder what the rich are doing now?*

Years ago he was that ultra-rich dynamo that worked 24/7 and never took a day off to relax in the sun. He lived a worldly life of luxury without limits. When that world crashed around him, he remembered what Akhenaton said 3,000 years ago, "To be satisfied with a little, is the greatest wisdom; and he that increaseth his riches, increaseth his cares; but a contented mind is a hidden treasure, and trouble findeth not."

No more. Those days were over. He was in paradise now and if he had known retirement was going to be this good, he would have quit the rat race years earlier. He had enough assets put away to live comfortably the rest of his life. He sold the big house on the peninsula jutting out over the Gulf of Mexico and paid cash for the house and the remodeling he was in now.

Nevertheless—from time to time—his ego demanded to be heard. He *did* miss the challenges, the attention, and even the obsequiousness from others. And his Marine Corps training would always be a major part of his thinking and action. None of that training advocated sitting on the sidelines. Right or wrong, for him it had always been: Press on, Ooh-Rah! Charge! *Act and you shall have dinner; Wait and you shall be dinner.* Wasn't there a middle ground, somewhere between "wasting away in Margaritaville" and "master of the universe?"

He heard a bicycle bell ring as the pool gate opened. "Conch express," Irish shouted, pushing her Conch Cruiser through the gate. She removed a paper tray from the bike basket and walked over and placed it on a low redwood table between the two chaise lounges. "Your Majesty, your breakfast is served."

"Thank you little darling, you saved my life, I was dying for a coffee fix."

She removed the top from a Styrofoam cup of café-con-leche and handed it to him. "Uno grande," she said as sweet steamy milk-vapors escaped. "I only got one sandwich but I had it cut in half." She unwrapped the pressed Cuban bread sandwich.

Mack sipped the hot coffee and bit into the bacon and egg sandwich with melted cheese pressed out the sides, "What am I going to do when you're gone?"

"That cute little Cuban girl that made the sandwich asked about you and keeps hinting about coming over for a swim. She has an unusual and pretty name, Savanna. I'm sure she would bring you coffee every morning."

"I'm old enough to be her father . . ."

"Didn't seem to bother her."

"Yeah, sure . . . Are we still going diving?"

"Vamos, Papa. I've got my bathing suit on under my shorts."

Mack motioned to Irish with his hand to slow the 18-foot Dolphin as it silently glided across the glass top surface. From the front of the boat, he studied the sandy bottom 30 feet below as it crawled forward. Spotting the first coral head, he sliced his finger across his throat signaling to his daughter to cut the motor. Mack eased the anchor over the side feeding the line hand over hand to the bottom. The stern of the boat settled east as the anchor seated in the sand. Mack watched his daughter climb the poling platform, her diving mask on her head, her snorkel dangling to the side. *My God*, he thought. She stood fearlessly, hands on her hips, smiling like a bronze sun goddess. The sun had climbed almost overhead with golden sunrays bursting through drifting cloud shadows surrounding her. *So beautiful . . . thank you God, you did good.* They had come a long way, just the two of them, and soon it would be time to let her go. "What?" she said.

He just shook his head. "Time for a little hookah diving," and cranked the air compressor and started feeding the two 100-foot yellow air hoses with regulators into the water. With his facemask and snorkel on his head, he eased himself over the side into the warm, turquoise blue gulf stream.

"Daddy! Daddy look, there's a big Stingray on the bottom." She pointed just behind the back of the boat.

Mack found the end of one of the floating air hoses, purged the regulator, stuck it in his mouth, and waved at his daughter to follow him.

Irish pulled her mask down, stuck the snorkel in her mouth, and leaped into the water from the poling platform. Floating on the surface face down she saw nothing on the bottom except the roiling sediment where the Stingray was. But as the stirring sand settled back to the bottom, she saw a huge black mass headed straight toward her. She quickly realized it was way too bulky to be a Stingray and had no tail . . . more like the size of a Manatee.

Mack, treading water, had stopped halfway down and watched as this large prehistoric creature ascended into the clear water and started circling him.

It's a giant sea turtle, Irish thought, *but what's that dragging behind it.* She watched as her father hitched a ride on its back, its powerful flippers like long rowing oars, pulling them to the surface with ease.

Mack reached high up on the long teardrop-shaped back of the turtle, grabbed the collar of the soft shell, pulled himself forward and swung each leg around its long accordion like neck, as if riding a bronco. He removed his diving knife from his leg sheath, and with both hands pulled the turtles head back as far as he could and started cutting away the large, plastic garbage bag lodged deep into the creases around its neck and stretched tight under its left flipper. This was not the first time Mack had seen these industrial strength, 60-gallon size black bags. He had used them on his construction sites as liners for 55-gallon drums to collect trash and construction debris. But this was not from a construction site; it was from a floating kitchen, a cruise ship kitchen that fed thousands of people around the clock, from a week to months. Rotting vegetables, fruits, meats, and whole skeletons of fish poured from the plastic liner as Mack sliced and tore at the black bag.

Irish grabbed the trailing end of the bag as the turtle surfaced and started circling the boat. Mack was now under the turtle trying to pull and cut the bag from the armpit of one of its slow moving, 6-foot long flippers. They both were holding tight to the long bag, and the turtle, undaunted by all that was going on, started to dive, pulling both of them down with him.

Mack pointed his finger to the surface, motioning for Irish to let go and get to the top for some air. Holding on to the bag now instead of the turtle, he hand crawled up the bag and with one quick slash, the bag was cut from the flipper. Irish, floating on top and breathing through her snorkel, watched her father kick to the surface, dragging the bag behind him as garbage spilled from the hole in the bottom. "Sharks! Daddy, look." Mack looked behind him and saw two shark fins cutting through the water, "Time to get in the boat, baby girl." He removed his fins, tossed them into the boat and boosted Irish onto the deck and climbed in behind her dragging the bag. "Daddy, there's another one."

"Yeah, at least they'll clean up most of the garbage." He reached over the side into the water and snatched up a floating magazine. He waved it at Irish, "World Cruises, this is where the garbage came from. Those bastards!"

"Daddy, watch your language."

"Sorry . . . it just pisses me off."

"Can't the government stop them?"

"No. They ban plastics, but they are allowed to dump tons of garbage as long as they are 3 miles out. I mean everything: solid waste, raw sewage, pure *shit* and urine, even tampons and toilet paper right out of the toilet, every day . . . *3 miles!*"

"For real, Daddy? How can they do that?"

"Over 30 million passengers a year pooping in our oceans."

"*Ugh!* Like, why can't they stop them?"

"Money honey—*tourism*—over 35 *billion* dollars a year. The cruise ships have been fined millions, but there is no ocean police." Mack started pulling in the air hoses, a curious shark followed one of them to the boat. "Nobody cares anymore; it's like spitting in the wind." He started the trolling motor and set the remote autopilot.

"Like, we're not going to dive anymore?" Irish asked."

"Irish! Stop that. When did you pick that up? Every other word you say is *like*."

"Sorry."

"Terrible habit."

"Yes sir. Can we dive some more?"

"You want to dive where the sharks are feeding? Let's move to another spot."

Irish was standing on the forward deck with her arms stretched out, her head back, and her long blond hair flowing in the sea breeze.

"Look, there's our Leatherback again," Mack, pointed about 30 yards in front of the boat.

"Pull up beside her, let's see if she's okay."

The turtle stopped swimming when Mack pulled up beside it and shut the trolling motor off. Irish was looking down at the turtle when it turned its head and looked up at her.

"Ahhh, look Daddy, she's thanking us." She leaned over and rubbed its back.

"How do you know it's a *she*?" Mack asked.

"Is it a male turtle?"

"I don't know."

"The correct gender pronoun is *he and she* or *his and her*."

Mack shook his head and thought, *liberal academia. You're the one that sent her to private schools.*

Mack said, "I'm a man, right? So when *I'm* talking, I use the pronouns *he, him* or *his.*"

Irish, still rubbing the turtles back, "Okay, I'm a woman. When I'm talking about an unknown species I'll say *she, or her*, right? How do you know she's a Leatherback turtle? It looks like a lot of other turtles to me, except a lot bigger?"

Mack laughed, knowing it was futile to continue, and regardless, he would never want to diminish her free spirit. "Okay, hardhead. The first thing is the size. *He's* the largest turtle in the ocean, some as big as 2,000 pounds. Tap on its back, see, not a hard shell, it's more like leather, hence the name Leatherback. Another distinguishing characteristic is the shape of his shell, hydrodynamic, like a speedboat, so it can move through the water without a lot of drag. See those 7 bony ridges running down his back. Only the Leatherback has those. And do you know why *he's* a diver and swimmers best friend?"

"Why?"

"He exclusively feeds on jellyfish, over 400 pounds a day."

"That's a lot of jellyfish."

"Depends on the type of jellyfish. Some weigh as little as an ounce and some weigh over 500 pounds.

"500 hundred pounds? No way . . . you're joking right? You sure this is not some Irish malarkey?"

"Google it."

CHAPTER 10

Crazy Ray sat in his lawn chair in the backyard drinking a cold beer while admiring his yard work. He took the bottom of his shirt and wiped the sweat from his forehead. The yard was cut, hedges trimmed, and leaves raked and bagged. A cool breeze blew down from the north sending a chill over his body and plucked the last clinging leaves of the season. This would be the last time to cut the yard; he felt good. His doctor had changed the dosage of his medicines and he was back on a regular schedule. Dago had hugged him and said he was sorry. What he needed now was money.

Crazy Ray's monthly disability check of $1,420.00 plus Medicare (full disability due to his HIV disease) was not enough for him to live on. The day they released him from prison he received $500.00 "gate money" for food, clothes, and transportation, but that was gone the first week. He then applied for Social Security Insurance Emergency Supplement Benefits of $1,500.00 and $310.00 a month for Mandatory Disability Benefit for every month he was incarcerated. From the Welfare Office he received $520.00 of food stamps every month for himself and his wife, Dago. These benefits were to help him reestablish himself as a productive member of his community.

Crazy Ray's phone started ringing; he looked down and saw it was Dago and hit the speaker key. "What's up?"

"Guess who I just saw."

"Where are you?"

"West Memphis."

"What are you doing in Arkansas?"

"I'm working, I told you we were remodeling a truck stop over here. You want to know who I just saw or not?"

"Sure, give me a hint."

"Ten thousand dollars."

"Give me another hint."

"Damn, that was a great hint. Are you stoned?" The phone went silent. "Okay, I'm sorry. How about the name, Tito. Does that ring a bell?"

"Tito! That ratfink son of a bitchin stool pigeon! Where is he now?"

"He just drove off. I stopped at a food truck over here for lunch and . . ."

"You didn't lose him . . ."

"Hold your horses, just listen. I'm sitting in my truck eating my tacos when this new Range Rover pulls up and out rolls fatso Tito. I wanted to run him down there in the parking lot but there were too many people around. Anyway, he walks to the backdoor of the food truck and opens it with a key and walks right in."

"He's working in a food truck?"

"You gonna let me finish or not?"

"Okay, okay, go ahead."

"No, he's not working in a food truck, he's owns the food truck, a fleet of them called 'Road Runner Chow'".

"You're shitting me?"

"No, I went back for a couple of more tacos, chatted up the guy in the truck, and he told me about the other food trucks, and guess what?"

"I'm all ears."

"When he walked in the back door of the food truck, he had an empty backpack and when he left it was stuffed . . . and I bet it ain't stuffed with tacos."

"Did you follow him?'

"No, but I got his license number. You remember Billy, down at the tire store, his brother's a cop and for twenty-five bucks he'll get me the address."

"Bingo! Payback time." Crazy Ray said.

"Not only that, we're going to take *all* his backpacks."

It was late at night and Dago was driving, squinching his eyes as he looked for the address. "What's that number again?"

"I told you three times, it's 2 8 5. It's on a corner. Where are your glasses?"

"Is this the corner, up here on the left?" Dago said.

"Slow down, let me look. Yeah, this is it, Sunset Road. Turn here and stop . . . cut your lights. Damn, you sure this is the right address, this place is top shelf. Where did Tito get this kind of money?" Crazy Ray said.

"Duh, he is a drug dealer."

"This copy from the assessor's office says it's appraised at two million four hundred. It's listed in the name of Maria del Carmen Acosta."

"Yeah, Billy said the Range Rover was in her name too. You think that's his mother? Is he married?" Dago said.

"How would I know? Is Tito's last name Acosta?"

"Tito is all I've ever heard."

"Pull around to the back and let's have a look."

"You can't see much with this brick wall around the place."

"Hold it! Turn your lights off, the gates are opening."

Crazy Ray removed a pair of binoculars from the center console, adjusted the focus on the driver of the black Range Rover as it turned into the driveway; it was Tito. Halfway through the double gate, Tito stopped when he saw the lights of a Chevy Suburban parked inside the gates. Mid-South Security Alarms and Patrol, was painted on the door of the Suburban and a German Shepard, his large head hanging out the window, watched everything that moved. The patrolman got out of the Suburban, walked over to Tito, had a short exchange of words, and Tito drove up to the house as the gates closed.

"Breaking in here is not going to work. Head back to the house, I need to rethink this."

Dago sat in his pickup truck in the parking lot outside the "Road Runner Chow" food truck, eating a taco. "You were right, same day, same time; here he comes." Dago said to Crazy Ray. They watched as Tito in his black Range Rover pulled around to the back and parked facing the door of the food truck. He hurried inside carrying his folded backpack under his arm.

"Back up so your rear fender is blocking him in," Crazy Ray said, as he put his sunglasses and baseball cap on, and nodded to Dago to do the same. He opened his door and stepped out, "Leave the truck running, I'll be behind the Range Rover."

Dago reached down into the side pocket of his door and removed a black sock. He lifted the sock by the toe and caught the black silencer as it fell into his hand, removed the Glock 17 from his holster and screwed the silencer onto the end of the threaded barrel. He pushed the mag release and counted the cartridges in the magazine and then, with his left hand, he pushed the

Dragonfly-slide back and made sure there was a cartridge in the chamber. Satisfied, he unbuckled his seat belt, laid the pistol across his lap, and waited.

Crazy Ray watched Tito stop as he exited the food truck, and stare at the pickup blocking his SUV.

"Hey, move your truck, you're blocking me," Tito shouted.

Dago heard Tito shouting, but continued looking straight ahead as he held up his middle finger against his glass window while finishing off his second taco.

"I'll take that finger and shove it up his ass," Tito mumbled, and marched over to Dago's truck and banged on his window, "Hey dumbass, move your truck." Tito pulled his shirt up to show his holstered pistol.

Dago lowered the window and pointed his Glock out the window, the silencer almost touching Tito's chest. "Who you calling dumbass, fatso?"

"Dago! I didn't know that was you."

"Yeah, I bet you didn't." Dago said, getting out of the truck. "Don't even think about reaching for that gun; I've been ichin' to shoot your ass anyway."

"No, no," Tito said, putting both hands in the air. "Why would I shoot *you?*"

"Someone's been looking for you. Put your hands down, stupid."

"Who's looking for me?" He heard footsteps behind him and half turned to a loud burst of electricity, like a blown transformer. His backpack flew from his shoulder as a million volts exploded into the side of his neck. He hit the ground hard.

Crazy Ray put the stun gun back in his pocket, tossed Dago a zip tie and rolled Tito over face down. "Tie his hands behind him." He then removed a roll of duct tape and wrapped two quick turns around Tito's head to cover his mouth and eyes. He tossed Dago the roll of tape, "Wrap his feet together." Crazy Ray removed Tito's keyless remote fob, then his gun, and opened the back door of the Range Rover. He tossed the backpack on top of Tito and said, "I got his feet, let's load him up."

Dago, in his pickup, followed Crazy Ray driving the Range Rover, but instead of going back across the river to Memphis, Crazy Ray turned on a side road that crossed under the Memphis and Arkansas Bridge and stopped. Dago pulled up beside him and lowered his window, "What's up, I thought we were taking him to the house?"

"Change of plans; follow me." Crazy Ray turned down a narrow dirt road toward the river, but after a quarter of a mile, he stopped when the ruts in the road became deeper and full of rainwater. The last thing he wanted was to get stuck in Arkansas gumbo. Even with 4-wheel drive it was like quicksand; once stuck, it was impossible to get out without a tow.

Crazy Ray walked around the SUV and opened the backdoor, removed his box cutter knife, and cut the tape from Tito's ankles. He pulled him out from the back seat, stood him up, and cut the tape from his eyes. "I'll remove the tape from your mouth, but I don't want a word out of you, understand?"

Tito nodded his head.

"What's going on?" Dago said, walking up from his truck.

"It's too muddy, I don't want to get stuck. Get that old ski rope I threw in the back of the truck and follow us down to the river." Crazy Ray said as he removed the tape from Tito's mouth.

Tito struggled, tried to get a deep breath as the tape was pulled off, his eyes bulging with fear. "What are you doing?" he shouted. "Why are you doing this, Ray? I'm sorry about what happened. I got money now, we can make a deal, right? I'll give you the Range Rover too, that's a hundred grand."

Crazy Ray hit him hard in the nose with his fist knocking him back onto the seat and stuck the tape back across his mouth. "I told you no talking."

"What are we going to do with this rope, hang him or see if he can ski?" Dago said as he walked back from his truck twirling one end of the rope.

"Help me stand him up. Now tie that rope around you and the other end around his chest. We don't want our bait to fall into the river . . . not yet."

As they got closer to the water, the overgrown hanging trees and shrubs narrowed the muddy road down to no more than a deer trail. They walked in single file, Dago bringing up the rear, swinging his end of the rope that he had tied around his waist at Tito's head, "Did you think there wasn't going to be any payback for ratting us out, Fatso?"

Tito moaned, shaking his head.

"Yeah, Tito, you *should* moan. I moaned for 1,095 days locked in prison waiting for this day." Crazy Ray shouted back.

"Me too, 60 days I spent in that filthy, stinking jail downtown. I'm taking the Range Rover." Dago said.

The trail ended at a wing dike that ran 100 feet out into the rapid current of the river. Most of the dike was underwater, with knee-high weeds and a few young cypress trees pushing their way up between the riprap.

"Look Tito, the river's up. It's flooding, now you'll float better." Dago said.

"Almost over the top of the dike." Crazy Ray said.

"How'd you find this place?"

Crazy Ray started walking out to the end of the dike, careful of the wet stones and broken concrete. "I used to skip school and come down here fishing. I caught a monster catfish out of here one day."

"You, fishing? I'd like to see a picture of that."

Crazy Ray faced Tito and put his finger to his lips, then snatched the tape from his mouth.

"*Please*, please Ray, untie my hands; it's cutting into my wrist."

"Shut your mouth," Dago said, hitting him again with the rope. "Where is that reward money, the ten grand?"

"I swear I didn't get any reward money. They refused to give it to me, said I was a criminal and had no rights. But I can pay you, just tell me what you want?" Tito said, stumbling across the riprap.

"We want that house of yours on the corner, your food trucks, and your car." Dago said.

"That's my wife's house, and the food trucks belong to her father, Juan Carlos, I'm not lying. But I've got money put away."

"Yeah, I bet. Stuffed in those backpacks, right?" Dago said.

"No, I work for Juan Carlos Acosta. He'll kill me if that backpack is not delivered today. I'm just a peon; all I do is the pickup and delivery."

"Sure, Tito, we believe you. Where is this money you have put away?" Crazy Ray said. They had walked to the end of the dike, the rushing current in front, and the calm inlet behind them.

"It's in a safe place."

"Is it all cash? How much do you have?" Dago said.

"You'll let me go if I pay you?"

"Of course." Crazy Ray said.

"It's all cash, about a hundred grand. I'll give you half."

"You're not in a good position to negotiate."

"You're not either. I know you Ray, you wouldn't risk losing fifty grand."

Tito said.

"I think it's time for you to take a little swim," Crazy Ray said, moving toward Tito.

Tito stepped backwards in defense, stumbled, tried to right himself, stumbled again and fell headfirst into the river.

The mighty Mississippi River, the third longest river system in the world, with all its whirlpools and deadly undertow, grabbed him like a hungry alligator. The slack in the rope tore across the dike, tightening to a loud snap as Tito shot downriver and jerked Dago forward, pulling him over the rocky edge into the river. He fought to hold on to a large stone with both hands, the rope taut, dragging the bottom half of his submerged body out into the current.

"Help! Help me, Ray! I can't swim."

Crazy Ray worked himself over the riprap to the edge and stopped in front of Dago.

Dago lunged with one hand and grabbed Crazy Ray's ankle in a death grip.

Crazy Ray fell backwards, pulling and kicking with his other foot trying to break free and suddenly he stopped. He leaned forward and in a broken whisper said, "I - can't - help - you - Dago," then exploded, "*REMEMBER, I'm a wacko!*"

Dago screamed, begging Crazy Ray to help, as his hand slipped from Crazy Ray's ankle to his pants leg.

Crazy Ray reached in his pocket, removed his box cutter, and sliced his pants leg free. He waited; the water was up to Dago's chest now. He watched to see how long Dago could hold on to the rock with one hand. He stared out onto the river, at the end of the rope, watching Tito bob up and down.

"You said I was insane, Dago." He reached down to the rock and sliced each finger to the bone, "you said I was *DEMENTED.*"

CHAPTER 11

"Are you sure you don't want me to put a line out for you, two's better than one for catching supper."

"Noooo sir." Irish said, while spread out on a beach towel on the deck, "I'm going to soak up some rays."

"You got on sunscreen?"

"Yep."

Mack reached into the livewell and removed a cigar minnow to bait his hook.

"Hey, Daddy, what's wrong with your little finger?"

Mack looked down and watched the cigar minnow slide from his right hand. He tried to catch it but had no control, his little finger was flapping up and down like a live fish in the bottom of the boat. He grabbed and squeezed it tight with his left hand.

"This has happened a couple of times before. I think I've pinched a nerve somehow or fell asleep on it. It goes away eventually."

"You need to get that checked, Daddy. It could be something serious."

Mack removed his left hand and the tremor in his little finger had stopped. He picked up the minnow, baited his hook and cast out the live bait. "Have you decided on what school yet?"

Irish sat up as the trolling motor pushed the boat across the smooth surface without a wake. "You ready for me to leave, getting tired of me, huh?"

"No darling, I love you living with me. You can stay as long as you like."

"To tell you the truth, Daddy, I'm a little bored. I mean, all this sunshine, beautiful water, wearing flip-flops and cutoffs every day, playing tennis and riding my bike everywhere . . . like, we're in paradise, right?"

"It is paradise."

"I know, but I'm not . . . what's the word, *challenged.* Like . . . oops, sorry, didn't mean to say that word again. I've got to stop that. But you know what I mean. I feel like that Jimmy Buffett's song . . . *wasting away in Margaretville.*"

"Well, at least you got to practice your tennis and Spanish a lot."

Irish smiled, "I'll miss all my Cuban friends at the tennis center and El Siboneys. You'll have to send me their fried plantains; I love those things. I'm sorry, Daddy. I really do love Key West, but . . ."

"No, no, I understand, Key West is not for everyone. I get a little bored myself, but a couple of days in Miami traffic and I'm ready to get back to Key West on my conch cruiser."

"What do you think about this? I narrowed the schools down to my top five. I know Harvard is a great school, but it's too elitist for me and I don't want to spend 6 to 8 months of every year in cold weather. I'm a southern girl, I love the sun."

"I bet I can pick your top five. Are they all south of the Mason-Dixon line?"

"Yes sir. Well, I don't know how far west the line runs."

"You're still talking about *law* schools, right?" Mack jerked his line out of the water and the bait was gone. He baited his hook again.

Irish nodded her head. "I'll confess up, I've already applied and been accepted."

"Really? Then why ask my opinion if you've already picked the school?"

"You always taught me to be assertive, weigh all the options and take a shot. Besides, I had to apply early if I wanted in. Can I tell you the schools I picked from and you guess which one?"

"Well, I know it's not an Ivy League school . . ."

"Duke, Vandy, Stanford, UVA, and Emory."

"Hmm, Emory I know very little about, other than it's in Atlanta, but the other four are top shelf schools. My first choice would be UVA then Vanderbilt."

Irish shook her head. "Nope, it's Stanford."

"Stanford Cardinal. That's as far away from Key West as you can get, why Stanford?"

"A bunch of reasons."

"Hold it!" Mack's fishing line started zinging back and forth across the water as he reeled in his line. "Hand me the net." He lifted the fish out of the water and into the boat before she could get the net.

"Nice Grouper, Dad."

"Ahh, too small." Mack removed the hook from its mouth and eased it back into the water.

"There goes our dinner. It looked plenty big to me."

Mack patted the top of his knee, "From here to the bottom of the boat; if it's longer than that, we can eat it. Tell me why Stanford." Mack removed another cigar minnow and baited his hook.

Irish fell back, spread-eagle on the deck, looking up at the sun, "I picked Stanford 'cause I wanted sunshine, and a beach close by. Plus, Stanford offers a joint degree in Law and an MBA in the same time frame, 3 years. Their Business School is ranked #1 in the nation and their Law School is rank #2."

"I should have known, the highest rated and most expensive, I imagine."

"I got it from you."

"Got what?"

"You're always saying, '*I'm easy to please, I like the very best.*'"

"I thought Churchill said that."

"No, he said, '*I cannot live without champagne. In victory, I deserve it, and in defeat, I need it.*'" She laughed.

"I agree with him on that too."

"I know we don't have a lot of money now, but you did say you still had those bonds put away if I decided to go to graduate school."

"I did and I do. I put those bonds in your education fund when you were a wee thing. I should have started a 'Daddy Fund' at the same time for when I get old."

"You're never going to get old."

"We all have an expiration date stamped on us somewhere."

"Now that I confessed about Stanford, I need to confess one more thing you may not approve of."

"What's that?"

"Stanford has everything I was looking for. But sometimes money and top grades are not enough to get in the best schools. I needed a letter of reference to go with my application, ideally from someone associated with Stanford."

"I don't know anyone at Stanford." He stood up in the boat to cast his line farther out.

"Sorry Dad, but you do."

"Oh really . . . who?"

"After filling out my application online, I started surfing their website and absentmindedly clicked on the Board of Trustees. I couldn't believe it when I saw the name of a trustee I had met before. It's someone that you know a lot better than me."

He turned and looked back, "Again missy, *who?*"

"McKenzie O'Connor . . . she's an alumna and a federal judge now."

Mack felt weak-kneed, as if someone punched him in the stomach. He moved to the bow and sat on the deck and thought to himself—*what a wuss.* How can just hearing her name short-circuit your nervous system? Was it his age? Had he been sitting on the sidelines too long?

"Daddy, you okay?"

Mack reached over the side and splashed some water on his face. "Yeah, I'm okay. Maybe too much sun."

Irish pulled his hat from the center console and tossed it to him, "Here, you need to wear this."

"Did she ask about me?" *Damn! I shouldn't have said that.*

"She did. She was very curious and asked if you were married? What happened between you two?"

"She's a married woman."

"Not anymore. I asked her if she was married and she told me her husband was a doctor and had passed away from a long illness. She wrote me a great letter of recommendation."

"Does she still live in Memphis?"

"Yes sir, she was just appointed to the U. S. Courts of Appeals."

"That sounds impressive."

"It is one step away from the Supreme Court. She's a very smart woman . . . beautiful and rich."

"How do you know that?"

"I googled her. Her husband left her a fortune, plus she has family money of her own."

"Money is not everything."

"Easy to say when you have it."

"Nobody gave it to me, I worked my ass off 24/7 . . . easy for you to say."

"I'm sorry, Dad, I didn't mean it that way. I couldn't live without you. You made it so easy for me and I thank God ever night for you. Why don't you move out to California with me, we could get a place together, maybe close to the beach."

"I've got a place right here, a block from the beach and it's paid for."

"But you'll be all by yourself when I leave."

"I like being by myself."

"Not all the time. You need to find yourself a woman, Daddy."

"No I don't. I don't need *more* problems. I've got all the women I need."

"I'm not talking about that kind."

"What kind?"

"You know what I mean, the Green Parrot, the Sloppy Joe's type. The kind of women I'm talking about, you're not going to find in Key West."

"How come?"

"Key West is too small, the good ones are married, and you're too picky."

"You are too."

"I got it from you. Besides, I'm moving to California."

"Yeah, good luck with that. With all the kooks out there; you'll need it." He reeled in his line to check his bait.

"Daddy, that's not fair."

"You're right, I'm sorry."

"How about this? You could fly me out to Stanford when school starts next month. Judge O'Connor is giving a 'Welcome to SLS speech' to the first year law students. That way you could kill three birds with one stone."

Mack had a puzzled look on his face. "Okay, okay, what three birds?"

"Well, number one, I wouldn't have to fly commercial. I could help you fly and we would have more time together. Two, we could take Judge O'Connor to dinner and you two could reunite. And three, you could look the area over and maybe change your mind about moving out there."

Mack just shook his head, *"Women."*

His cell phone started ringing. Irish found it in the console and handed it to him. He stared at the 504-area code and started not to answer. Then he changed his mind.

"Hello."

"Is this Mack Shannon?"

"Who's calling?"

"Jin Girod. Is this Mr. Shannon?"

"What's this regarding?"

Mack could hear exasperated mumbling, "Can I ask you a couple of questions?"

"You already have."

"Damn man, lighten up."

"Wait a minute *Ms.* Girod, you're the one who called me."

"What a hard ass," she mumbled again. "It's *Doctor* Girod, Mr. Shannon, Doctor Jin Girod. I'm in New Orleans."

"Is that Jen for Jenny?" Mack said, yanking her chain a little more.

"NO! It's J-I-N for Jin. It's Chinese."

"And what would a Chinese doctor in New Orleans be calling Mack Shannon for?"

"All I want to know is do you have a lost dog?"

"*What!*" Mack sucked in a deep breath and waited.

"Oh, now I have your attention, huh? Just tell me what kind of dog you had and what is her name?"

"It's been a long time since I've had a dog, and it was a male dog, not a female."

"Was there a microchip implanted?"

"Yes! His name was Bear, a black Bouvier.

"Mr. Shannon, what city do you live in?"

"At the time, I lived in Memphis."

"Now that wasn't so hard, was it Mr. Shannon? I think I have your dog."

"But you asked me what *her* name was?"

"Mister Shannon, I think you can figure that out. Do you want to say hello to him? He's right here beside me?" Jin put the phone to Bear's ear."

"Bear . . . Bear, can you hear me, big boy?"

Bear started barking.

"Well, Mr. Shannon, you passed our DNA test. I guess you're the Daddy."

"My daughter is with me, can she say hello to him?" Mack handed the phone to Irish, "This lady found Bear."

Irish could hear Bear barking. "Bear, where are you? I've missed you so much. I love you, Bear." Irish cried out.

Bear threw back his head and let out a long mournful wolf call.

"Hello?" Jin said.

"You have my dog!" Irish said, crying.

"I'm sure I do, honey. You want to come get him?"

"Can I?"

"You sure can. Let me talk to your father."

CHAPTER 12

A snapshot of tragedy raced through Crazy Ray's head: two men screamed to live, then were swept away by the milk-chocolate river current and sucked under like quicksand to their death. Crazy Ray stood out on the point of the wing-dike watching the Mississippi River and listened to the distant caw of a crow, the low rippling sound of the current, and felt no guilt about Dago or Tito. The camera lens clicked shut, permanently erasing all memory of his actions. It was just payback—business was business. There's great splendor in payback, it keeps everything in balance, and it's more powerful than success.

He thought about the big catfish he had caught years ago and wished he had a cane pole to rig up and some big fat Catawba worms for bait.

He scanned the Memphis skyline across the river . . . *time to leave, better get back home.* He took a deep breath, stretched out his arms wide, leaned back and shouted to the sky, "Thank you, Lord!" He made the sign of the cross, turned, and started back across the dike.

For some reason, as he hiked back up the trail, he started thinking about Judge McKenzie O'Connor. Why? Maybe it was unfinished business, time to balance the books, or more payback. Although he felt no animosity toward her, she did send him to prison. But on the flip side, she was married to the only man he ever loved, and took loving care of him to the day he died. She didn't desert him or dump him in some hospice. Randy died peacefully in their home with around-the-clock nurses. Her payback would require a little more thought.

It didn't take him long to figure out which vehicle to take. He doubted the Range Rover was worth a hundred grand but he would find out soon enough. He had a list of prison contacts for every crime that was ever committed, two or three for boosting cars. He took an oil rag from under Dago's seat and wiped his fingerprints off everything in the truck, not that it really mattered, he was just being extra cautious. When he finished he took Dago's Glock and wrapped it in the rag and shoved it under the seat. Most likely someone would steal the truck or the cops would tow it and come knocking on his door. 'He's out of town working on a job,' is all he would say. He figured when Dago and

Tito floated up, the cops would check their criminal records and assume that it was just another drug deal gone wrong.

The Range Rover was a sweet driving machine with less than 1,000 miles. He turned off the cruise control as he dropped off the bridge in downtown Memphis and checked his speed. The last thing he needed was to be pulled over by the cops. That thought reminded him about Tito's backpack full of money. He turned onto a side street and stopped. He knew he was in a rough neighborhood and snatched a quick look at the rear seat floorboard and saw the bag. The black Range Rover had money written all over it and he fought with himself to open it now or wait. He turned back onto Summer Ave and headed east. He figured he had three days at the most to get rid of the Range Rover—get it home, park it in the back and search it completely. Mexico would be the number one place to sell it.

Dago had no written will or relatives of any kind. As far as Crazy Ray was concerned, the house was his now. Who would question that? He pulled in the drive, got out and opened the chain-link gate and parked the SUV up close behind the house. He reached behind the front passenger seat, removed Tito's backpack, and hurried into the house. He dropped the backpack onto the kitchen table, unzipped it, turned it upside down and shook the contents onto the table. There was no money.

Spread out over the table was ten bricklike packages tightly wrapped with duct tape. He knew it was drugs, either cocaine or heroin. He picked up one of the packages and weighed it up and down in his hand, knowing a 'brick' was a kilo, and a kilo weighed a little over two pounds. He removed his box cutter knife, sliced a cut in the brick, and with the tip of the razor dug out a small amount of white powder and dumped it in the palm of his hand. He had snorted plenty of coke in his time and licked his finger, dabbed it on the powder and rubbed it on his gums. There was no numbing sensation, just a slight bitter taste, and no smell. China White? Maybe. Twenty-two pounds of China White heroin, what's that worth? Depends on how pure it is. In a lot of places China White heroin was cut with Fentanyl. He needed someone to test it and see if it had been stepped on. He didn't have time for that, he would sell it as pure China White, let the buyer test it. He needed a quick sell; sell it wholesale. Ten kilos to one person for a nice round figure of five hundred thousand, a dealer pushing it on the street would get twice that much, minimum, or even double that, especially if the purity tested as high as a four.

He opened an overhead kitchen cabinet and removed a brown paper sack and dumped four burner phones on the table. Each phone was marked with a number and the date of purchase. He turned on his laptop, found the number of Tony, a cellmate of his in prison that had served time for grand theft auto and now lived in Jackson, Mississippi. He punched in his number.

Crazy Ray told him he had a 2017 high-end luxury SUV with less than 1,000 miles that needed to be moved immediately. Tony told him he didn't have that kind of money but for $200 bucks he would put him in touch with a Mexican in Houston, a big-time dealer that loved to wash money on deals like this. Crazy Ray agreed, told him the number he was calling from was only good for twenty-four hours. Tony said someone would call him within the hour.

True to his word, one hour later his phone rang,

"Hello."

"Is this Senor Ray Flynn?"

"Yes, who's this?"

"I understand you have an item for sale?"

"Yes."

"I need photos of the exterior, interior, and odometer showing the mileage. Is that a problem?"

"No problema."

"Ah, tu hablas Espanol?"

"No, just a few words. Should I text the photos to this 832 area code number?"

"Si. We will be in touch today if interested."

In less than an hour Crazy Ray received a text telling him a representative, Vicente, would meet him at 12 noon tomorrow at the rear of the closed weigh station at the Mississippi/Tennessee state line on the east side of I-55 to inspect the item and close the deal.

Crazy Ray texted back that he would be there. He opened an empty prescription vial and dropped two tablespoons of heroin in it and stuck it in his pocket. Back on the computer he scrolled down his contact list to the name Boone, a mute that owned a small junkyard. He lost his vocal cords when a roadside bomb in Afghanistan sent a baseball size piece of shrapnel into his Adams apple. Crazy Ray texted the following message: *need your services tomorrow at 11 am at my house. Bring up-to-date license plate and Shorty.'* Boone was hired muscle—big, black, and intimidating, and a great supplier of anything military, including weapons. Crazy Ray had never seen him in anything but his unlimited supply of camo fatigues stolen from the U. S. Army Depot.

Crazy Ray checked his rearview mirror looking for his old Volkswagen Beetle as he turned off I-240 onto I-55 south to make sure Boone was still following him. He slowed the Range Rover till the Beetle caught up and both exited on Stateline Road into Mississippi. Crazy Ray turned onto a side road leading to the closed weigh station and maneuvered around a half-standing wooden barricade with a *Posted No Trespassing* sign attached. He saw the lone pickup parked about a hundred yards behind the small weigh station building. He stopped for a moment and noticed that one door and a large window in front of the building were boarded up with plywood, then drove around to the back dodging potholes, and parked twenty feet behind the pickup. Boone stayed parked in front of the building where he could watch the pickup and the closed road. His favorite companion, *Shorty*, a sawed-off automatic shotgun, rested in the front passenger seat of the Beetle.

It was a waiting game. Just when Crazy Ray was about to give in, the door of the pickup opened and a small, white haired Mexican stepped out. There was no one else in the truck. Crazy Ray somewhat relieved, yet cautious, that this old man was the representative. He adjusted Tito's gun inside his waistband, exited the SUV, and walked over to the 'representative.'

"Buenos Dias, Senior Ray?"

"Yes. And you are . . .?"

"Vicente." He nodded his head toward the Beetle. "I see you came with an associate?"

"Just my ride home. Assuming we reach an agreement."

"Bueno. Muy bien. Do you mind if I inspect?" Vicente asked while walking over to the Range Rover.

"That's why we're here."

Vicente opened each door including the trunk, and examined the interior and exterior and then walked around the SUV stopping at intervals to inspect the undercarriage. He asked Crazy Ray to start the engine and pull the release to raise the hood. Satisfied, he shut the hood.

"Okay if I test-drive it?"

"As long as I'm with you."

They both climbed into the Range Rover and Vicente drove around the building where Boone was waiting in the Beetle.

"How about testing it on the interstate?"

"No. Can't do that."

Vicente looked suspicious.

"No paper work. No title. No insurance, etc." Crazy Ray said.

"Oh, okay . . . comprendo." Vicente drove back to where his truck was and parked the SUV. He stared at the odometer, "Very nice, low mileage, like new. I need to make a call Senor Ray." He exited the SUV, walked over to his truck and called a number on his cell phone.

Crazy Ray lowered his window and could hear Vicente talking in Spanish. He knew that if anything was going to go bad, this was the time. He lifted his shirt and removed Tito's pistol and watched Vicente walk over to his side of the Range Rover with his cell phone in his hand.

"My boss will pay $25,000 dollars for the car."

"I was thinking more like $35,000."

Vicente relayed the offer over his phone.

"He said 'if you have someone else that wants to buy the SUV, then you should sell it to them.'"

"Okay, okay. Do you have the $25,000 cash with you?"

"No, senor, but it is close by. I can have it here within minutes."

"Let's do the deal. Can I talk to your boss about another deal?"

Vicente turned his back to Crazy Ray and spoke into the phone in rapid Spanish, longer than necessary to ask one question. Crazy Ray was suspicious, *is Vicente talking to himself? Is he the "boss?" Why the deception?*

"The money is on the way. My boss said it is best to complete one deal before moving to another. He will call you tomorrow after checking out the Range Rover."

Crazy Ray removed the prescription vial and handed it to Vicente, "A sample for your boss to test if he decides he's interested in a second deal."

Crazy Ray turned quickly at a roaring sound behind him as a large Peterbilt semi-trailer truck, pulling an enclosed car-hauler trailer, stopped in front of them. They watched as the rear ramp door lowered to the ground a few feet from the Range Rover. The driver hurried over to Vicente and handed him a padded manila envelope.

Vicente held the envelope out in front of him, "Your money has arrived, Senor Ray. My keys to the SUV, por favor."

CHAPTER 13

"*A*re we close, Daddy?"

"About ten miles out."

"Can I land it?"

"Sure, pull your seat up. Let's check the conditions." Mack switched the radio frequency. A continuous recording started: *Lakefront Airport information Bravo one three five five Zulu weather. Wind three zero zero at one seven, visibility five. Five hundred few, one thousand two hundred scattered, ceiling three thousand overcast, temperature two seven five seven, dewpoint eight. Altimeter two niner eight seven. VFR aircraft say direction of flight. All aircraft read back all hold short instructions. Advise controller on initial contact that you have Bravo.*

Mack changed the radio frequency again. "Ok, call approach."

"No Daddy, you do the talking. They talk too fast for me, I'll mess up."

"You're the pilot-in-command. Put your headset on, I'll back you up." He opened her student pilot logbook and removed a laminated card titled 'Landings Instructions' on one side and 'Take-Off Instructions' on the back. "Just remember to take your time, you control the microphone, don't let them rush you. Let's review," he stuck the instruction card on a clip attached to the instrument panel. After she read the landing instructions out loud, Mack said, "You're good to go, baby girl. Speak in segments, New Orleans will pass us on to Lakefront."

Irish took a deep breath and whispered to herself, rehearsing what she wanted to say. She pressed the mic button and with her deepest voice said, *"Lakefront Approach . . . Bonanza One Zero Seven Echo Sierra . . . ten miles southwest . . . at three thousand . . . inbound for landing at Lakefront with,"* she looked over at Mack and he mouthed the call sign for the weather, 'Bravo.'

"With Bravo," she said.

"Bonanza One Zero Seven Echo Sierra, Lakefront Approach, radar contact, altitude indicates three thousand one hundred, traffic, eleven o'clock, opposite direction, altitude three thousand six hundred."

Mack pointed out his window at the airplane 500 feet above them.

Irish nodded, *"Seven Echo Sierra have traffic in sight."*

"Seven Echo Sierra, maintain visual separation with that traffic and contact

Lakefront Tower, One One Niner Point Niner. ”

“*Seven Echo Sierra, One One Niner Point Niner. Thank you.*” Irish said.

Mack switched frequencies.

Irish pushed the mic button, “*Bonanza One Zero Seven Echo Sierra . . . Lakefront Tower . . . eight miles southeast . . . inbound for landing with information Bravo.*”

“*Lakefront Tower to Bonanza One Zero Seven Echo Sierra, enter right downwind, runway Three Six Right, report entering right downwind.*”

“*Seven Echo Sierra will report right downwind.*”

“That a girl. Watch your air speed. Trim the nose up a wee bit.”

“*Lakefront Tower . . . Seven Echo Sierra . . . right downwind for Three Six Right.*”

“*Seven Echo Sierra, cleared to land.*”

Irish turned on final approach for Runway 36R and said to her father, “Wheels down” as she flipped the landing gear switch.

“It’s windy, you’re crabbing a little, give it some right rudder.” Mack said. “Now adjust your trim again, nose up.” He tapped on the attitude indicator, “Watch your gyro. That’s it. You got it now. It’ll land itself.”

The plane touched down on the runway. *“Wow.”* Irish said.

“Good landing, baby.”

“It was! Was it really, Daddy?”

“Perfect, *Miss Earhart.*” Mack switched radio frequency to ground control and took over the radio communications. He pointed to the FBO building and said to Irish, “We’ll park there.”

“You have the controls?” She said, remembering the change of command he had taught her.

“I have the controls.”

She released the yoke with a big sigh, shaking both hands in the air nervously, “I need more practice landing.”

“We’ll practice some touch and go’s when we leave if they’re not too busy and some when we get back to Key West.”

Mack stared at Irish. He thought about how her mother used to shake her hands in the air like that when she got nervous, and how much Kate and Irish looked alike—that same Nordic look—blond hair, almost gold color and those arctic blue eyes. When he first found out Kate was pregnant, like most men, he wanted a boy. But it was not to be. He got a double whammy; Kate died giving birth and left him alone with a girl. After a long period of withdrawal and self-doubt, he resolved to play the hand he was dealt. He told God, out of spite for not giving him the boy he wanted, he was not going to give any special allowances for her being a girl; she would have to tough it out like everyone else. But now, after all these years, he figured Irish and he were about even-steven; she was as tough on him as he was on her and had taught him as much as he had taught her.

A lot of changes had taken place since her birth. Financially, he had gone from rags to riches and back to rags. Well, not back to rags literally, but certainly metaphorically. His "crash" was a great lesson. Very few men in their lifetime were successful enough to bankrupt a billion dollar project. The catastrophe of the Trinity Town Towers was reported worldwide, but not a fault of his; only God controls earthquakes. Still, lesser men had jumped from buildings or blown their brains out over such loss. That never crossed his mind; he came from nothing, so it wasn't strange territory when it happened. Like a broken heart, it just took time to heal. Daily, he practiced the old habits of psycho-cybernetics—the mind-body connection—while running LSD's (long slow distances) along the beach at sunrise and around the island. His subconscious mind sucked the powerful affirmations he studied years ago of Napoleon Hill's three P's: Positive thinking, Perseverance, and Patience. Music was a big part of rebuilding his self-image. Nina Simone's soulful rendition of "Feeling Good" played over and over throughout the house and Mack hummed the words unconsciously—*A new dawn, a new day, a new life for me . . . and I'm feeling good.*

"Look Daddy!" Irish pointed.

Mack looked out Irish's window as he taxied the plane and saw a tall woman standing on the tarmac outside the door of the service center. She was dressed in tight shorts, a cutoff tee shirt showing her tanned midsection, and running shoes. Mack thought of Cher and her much-publicized belly button. The wind was blowing her long black hair horizontally like the weathered windsock mounted on the rooftop above her. Standing beside her like a foreign dignitary, was his beloved Bear. *Hmm . . .* could that be *Doctor* Girod?

As soon as the engine was shut down, Irish was out the door, jumped from the wing and started running toward Bear.

Jin Girod unclipped the leash from Bear's collar and whispered, "Go."

Irish stopped and braced herself for Bear's jump when she saw him running to her. She wrapped both arms around his huge chest as he stood on his back legs, his paws over her shoulders, licking the tears running down her face. She staggered from his weight; they danced back and forth until he stopped abruptly. His attention alerted elsewhere. He raised his head, twitched his nose and sniffed the scent of his master. He raced to the side of the airplane and watched as Mack stepped down from the wing carrying two backpacks. Bear squatted on his haunches, frozen in place like a concrete statue, waiting, his tongue hanging out.

"Well, look who's here," Mack said walking over to Bear. "Where have you been all this time, big boy?" He sat the two backpacks on the tarmac and stuck out an open hand.

Bear lifted his paw and placed it in Mack's hand with a low whine.

Mack looked into Bear's black eyes, half-hidden behind all the hair, and felt them boring through him. He wondered what was going on in that large head. With both his hands he patted his chest rapidly.

As quick as a triggered rattrap, Bear's hindquarters fired, catapulting his 110 pounds onto Mack. Mack grabbed two fistfuls of thick hair and stumbled, falling backward, dragging Bear on top of him. They rolled over and over, wrestling like old times. Bear broke loose; jumped, barked, and growled as Mack grabbed and pushed, sparring with him. He noticed how big and healthy he looked and how soft his fur was; he even smelled good.

Mack wasn't sure—never researched or discussed it with anyone—but had always thought that there was a special bond between male animals and male humans, especially Bear, and Satan, his 20 pound ebony Persian cat. The more he thought about it the more he was convinced. In years past it was the same with his champion stallion, Midnight Explosion. And now, even his Key West parrot, Sunny, a gregarious Sun Conure, would bite any woman that came close. But, maybe it wasn't male or female; maybe the bond was because they were all A-type personalities? Irish for sure an A-type, and he definitely had a special bond with her. Another A-type, recently resurrected by his daughter, was McKenzie O'Connor.

Jin walked over to Irish and handed her the leash, "Hello, I'm Jin, and you must be Irish." They both watched the rough-play of Mack and Bear. "Well, there's no doubt Bear has found his family."

"Ohhh, thank you so much," Irish said, wiping the tears on her face and hugging Jin.

Mack walked over and stuck out his hand, "I'm Mack Shannon, and you must be Doctor Girod?" A loud rumble of thunder exploded as they shook hands, followed by a flash of lighting across the darkening skies.

"Wow," Jin said, looking up at the sky, "does that always happen when you first meet someone?"

Mack smiled, "Only with special people." *She has a wee bit of age on her, but a great body.*

A light drizzle blew across Lake Pontchartrain as a cold chill of déjà vu came over Mack. The same thing with thunder had happened when he first met Kate, Irish's mother.

"Call me Jin, everyone does." *Nice teeth. He's a little older than I thought, but the gray streaks in his hair gave him a . . . an adventurous look.*

Mack, lost momentarily in the memory of his wife, exhaled, "Jin, is that short for Jennifer?"

"No. Its J I N, a Chinese name."

"Are you Chinese?" She didn't have the eyes of an Asian.

"My mother's mother was from China and my father was born here, with French heritage."

Bear was leaning hard against Mack's leg; he grabbed him by the nape of his neck and shook him. "Bear is a big part of our family, you have no idea what it means for us to have him back. Please, what do I owe you?"

"You owe me nothing."

Mack noticed she wore no makeup and her face was unblemished, with not one wrinkle, although he had a strange feeling they were close to the same age. He looked down at her worn running shoes. "Are you a runner?"

"Yes." She looked at her shoes and smiled with both arms out wide. "My running gear. A group of us are training together for the Rock 'n' Roll Marathon. Are you a runner?"

"Yes."

Bear pushed against Mack's leg. "He's in tremendous shape. Has he been running with you?"

"He won't let me run without him."

"You have taken great care of him. Surely, I can repay you in some way?"

"No. We are great buds. Doctoring him was a labor of love; he will break a lot of hearts around here when he's gone."

"I don't know what to say; I feel . . . indebted?"

"Okay, how about taking us all to dinner tonight at my family restaurant;

they allow dogs."

"Daddy, it's starting to rain." Irish said.

Jin pointed to an old white 4-door Chevy Suburban with an unpainted front fender parked beside the service center, "Let's get in out of the rain while you think about it."

Mack handed Irish one of the backpacks, "You all go ahead while I check the weather and talk to the base operator about topping off the gas tanks."

Bear followed Mack inside the service center. Irish and Jin hurried to the truck.

CHAPTER 14

Mack had been to New Orleans a couple of times for Mardi Gras, but that had been years ago. The city had changed . . . a lot. He was in the front seat of the Suburban, while Bear and Irish rode in the back leaning forward between the bucket seats. Jin, like a tour guide, gave a running commentary as she exited I-10.

"There's the Superdome and up ahead is the medical center," she turned right and stopped in front of Tulane University Medical Center. "Irish, this is where I went to school . . . thousands of hours."

"Is this the Vet school?" Mack asked.

"No, this is Tulane's medical school. I went to Vet school first, at LSU in Baton Rouge, but when I found out my father had Alzheimer, I decided to go to med school."

"Ohhh," Irish said. "Is he better now?"

"Yes. He's in a better place."

"I'm so sorry," Irish leaned forward and put an arm around Jin's shoulder.

"Thank you, sweetie.

"Straight ahead is the Mississippi River, so let's turn here on St. Charles. It follows the river from the French Quarter along the Garden District to West Riverside, and then over to Audubon Park."

"Where we headed?" Mack asked.

"Why? You in a rush?"

"No, just wondering."

"What did your weatherman say?"

"Overcast with possible thunderstorms."

"No flying then?"

"No flying. I try to avoid flying in bad weather. Is there a hotel close by?"

"I have a place you and Irish can stay." She turned toward Irish, "Up here on your right is the main campus of Tulane where I went to undergraduate school, and across the street is Audubon Park."

Jin made a U-turn, crossed the trolley tracks and skirted down the side of Audubon Park toward the river. She pointed out the Audubon Zoo and the Children's Hospital. At the end of Terminal Drive, she stopped in front of an ancient stone wall with a large, recessed archway. English ivy covered the wall and archway. Jin pushed a small remote clipped to her sun visor and the two heavy cypress gates opened to the inside of the archway. On the left side of the column where the ivy had been cut back, were colorful ceramic lettered tiles, *EMPYREAN GARDENS*. Underneath the name was the address—*200 East Drive—Est. 1854.*

"Wow!" Irish said, "Open-o-sesame."

"Welcome to my humble abode and your hotel for the night." Jin said as she pulled through the archway into an idyllic garden of white blooming magnolia trees and purple wisteria.

Mack perused the garden, admiring the Spanish moss draping from the live oak and the bald cypress trees, a light fog hugged the ground. "You live here?" he asked.

"Yes. Live *and* work." Bear started barking and she stopped the truck. "Irish, would you let Bear out, he loves to run through the garden asserting his dominance over the other animals."

"Can I go with him?"

"Sure, if it's okay with your dad."

"Be careful," Mack said, watching them scramble from the back seat.

"Wait!" Mack shouted. An old man, tall and bent, had burst from the wooded shrubs. He stood completely naked in the middle of the drive, white as a ghost, almost translucent through the misting rain and ground fog. He took a deep bow smiling, his long white beard and white hair down his back dripping rain, and then rushed back into the bushes on the other side of the drive.

"What was *that* . . . Rip Van Winkle?" Mack said, and turned quickly to the back seat, "Irish, back in the truck."

Mack heard Jin shout, in what he guessed was Chinese, and saw a large Asian man dressed in white pants and shirt, hurry past the front of the Suburban, chasing the old man into the woods. Bear, howling like a coon dog, was right on his heels.

Jin started laughing, her hand over her mouth, she said, "Welcome to your first Chinese fire drill."

"What's a *Chinese* fire drill?" Irish asked from the back seat.

"Are they part of your vet clinic?" Mack said.

A chain of laughter erupted.

Jin shifted into drive as a dark rain cloud hurried south. Large raindrops rolled off the overhanging foliage. The winding driveway gleamed from the puddled water covering the brick pavers.

"The old fellow is John Edgar . . . Ah, we all call him 'Big John.' He's a permanent guest and a major financial contributor to Empyrean Gardens."

"How old is he?" Irish said.

"According to his medical history, around 100."

"He pretty spry for a hundred." Mack said.

"Yes, sometimes he's too spry as you can see."

"What does *permanent* guest mean?"

"He's our oldest guest and by guest I mean . . . When my father became ill I closed the vet clinic and we both moved here. I gutted one of the old warehouses on the riverfront and we moved in there until I finished building our house up on the banks," she pointed out her window, 'up there'. After we moved into the new house, I remodeled that warehouse into our medical center. The two existing warehouses are the ones that my great-grandfather converted into a convalescent and nursing home for seniors that couldn't afford medical treatment. Most of the patients, we now refer to as guests, have no family or a place to go after treatment; now they have Empyrean Gardens. I still treat some exotic animals from the zoo across the road, and of course we take care of the pets of older people who can't afford a vet."

"What does Em'pyr'ean mean?" Irish said.

"The highest heavens. Or in this case, 'heavenly gardens.'"

"Oh, that's pretty."

"How did you find Bear?" Mack asked.

"The story I got from the humane society was an old reclusive trotliner found him marooned on a sandbar in the middle of the Mississippi. The Louisiana SPCA called and said they found Bear tied to their front gate one morning with a note stuck under a rope around his neck. They asked if I would foster him until they found someone to adopt him. He was a mess; weighed about half of what he does now and looked like a small black bear. He was so matted. Eaten up with fleas, ticks and mosquito bites. I had to clip him down to the skin. He was lethargic, very sick with heartworms. There were times I didn't think he would make it. Then it was too late; I fell in love with him.

"He follows me everywhere. I thought of a microchip, but I didn't have a scanner. Besides, the odds were in my favor that he didn't have one. After he fully recovered and his coat grew out, I knew then that he was a full-blooded Bouvier, a very expensive dog that was probably micro-chipped. Nevertheless, I kept procrastinating until I was eaten up with guilt. Finally I took him to a vet I knew who had a scanner and when I saw that number pop up, I was sick inside."

"That was a good thing you did, thank you." Mack said. "A lot of people would never have taken the time to look for a microchip."

Jin came to a Y in the road and stopped. The brick paved road continued to the right, down toward the river. To the left was a new blacktop road, winding upward toward a manmade bluff with a wood carved sign mounted on a large cypress tree, 'Private Road-No Trespassing.'

"The brick road goes down to the converted warehouses along the river. The paved road goes up to my house."

A giant tortoise inched its way across the road in front of the Suburban, "Look Irish, there's my oldest resident, Abraham." Jin said.

"Daddy, he's bigger than the leatherback turtle we saw diving."

"How old is he?" Mack said.

"He's very old, not as old as the biblical Abraham, but older than Big John. He has cataracts and has lost most of his hearing; he and Bear are big pals."

They watched as Abraham crawled into a thicket of palmetto bushes.

"This is a large piece of property . . . how many acres all told?" Mack said.

Jin told them about her great-great-grandfather, Nicholas Girod, who was the 5th mayor of New Orleans in the early 1800's. He had made a lot of money in trading, marketing, and warehousing cotton and was a well-known philanthropist. When he died, part of his estate included the 126-acres here, plus over 1,000 feet of waterfront along the Mississippi River.

She nodded down toward the river, "Nicholas cleared a lot of land and used the cypress trees to build a large open-end building for the two cotton gins he had bought. The ginning business was a huge success, some old photos I have show the riverbanks overflowing with bales of cotton stacked on top of each other. He quickly realized the growing need for a construction company, and the first project for his newly created 'Southern Builders' was to design and build three long warehouses to store the cotton he ginned. The second project was the driving of pilings in the river to build the piers for docking the paddle wheelers so he could ship his cotton.

"Back then, cotton was king, the Southern states were providing two-thirds of the world's supply of cotton, and up to 80% of the crucial British market. New Orleans at the time was a major port and finance center for the cotton producing south, but unfortunately the Civil War dealt a deadly blow to that market.

"After years of slow recovery, my grandfather, Nicholas III, took the reins of the estate. The first order of business was a negotiated agreement with the Mayor of New Orleans and the city and county commissioners to build a much needed home for the aged on his vacant riverfront property in exchange for a lifetime tax-freeze; hence the Empyrean Gardens. The empty and spacious cotton warehouses were ideal for renovating into senior living; the tall ceilings, clerestory windows, and double-pitched skylights lent a sunny and airy atmosphere. That's enough history, let's go up to the house and get you two settled in before we go to dinner." Jin shifted into low drive and started up the tiered, serpentine paved road.

At the top of the bluff, Jin parked in the middle of the circular drive and Mack was first out of the Suburban. He stood looking up at a large A-framed cypress house with a cantilevered porch jutting out over a grove of trees and blooming shrubs. "You built this?" he asked.

"Well, not with my own hands, but I designed and supervised the construction. We used all reclaimed cypress, most of it stolen from the old shed covering the cotton gin."

"Look dad, a rainbow." Irish said.

They all turned and look out over the Mississippi River, a multicolored eyebrow that arched over a red ball of sun that sat on the river's horizon.

"Beautiful," Mack said. "Is this some kind of phenomenon?"

"It *is* beautiful. Look at all the colors," Jin said. "I've only seen pictures, but I think it's called a halo rainbow or a 22-degree halo. I can't remember the difference between the two."

They continued to watch as an elongated cloud fell onto the horizon blocking the halo and all but the rays of the setting sun.

"Oh shit," Irish said while fumbling with her cell phone. "I was going to take a picture and now it's gone."

"Watch your mouth, young lady."

Jin frowned at Mack's reproach.

"Sorry, Daddy, it just slipped out."

Mack used both hands as blinders while trying to focus on a large dark object protruding above the tree line. "What's that?" he said, pointing out toward the river.

"It looks like a smokestack, Daddy."

Mack looked back at Jin for an answer.

"We had better hurry if we are going to dinner, let me show you to your rooms."

Mack followed them up the steps onto the porch, then stopped and looked back at the top of the tree line. Mack agreed with Irish, it does look like a smokestack. *Strange, Jin had been talking freely and in great detail on other subjects but seemed to evade my question on the smokestack.*

CHAPTER 15

Crazy Ray sat at the kitchen table, edgy and impatient, waiting for a call from Vicente. He thought about calling him but didn't want to seem desperate. However, in reality, he was desperate. He checked the time on his phone again. Vicente said someone would call today . . . if interested. He's a drug dealer, why wouldn't he be interested? Although it was kind of a reverse deal, they normally would be shipping their drugs from Mexico to the U.S., but Crazy Ray figured it was an advantage for Vicente not having to cross the border with twenty-two pounds of heroin.

He needed this deal. He wanted to buy a place in the Keys, not Key West, way too expensive, but maybe Stock Island or Big Coppitt Key. Buy a good used boat and eat fresh fish with key limes, avocados, and fried plantains every night. The best time in his life was his trip to Fantasy Fest with Randy; they dined out every night, danced together, sunbathed in the nude, and fell in love.

The phone on the table started ringing. Crazy Ray saw the area code 832, sighed with relief and tapped the screen, "Hello?"

"Buena Dias, Senor Ray."

"Buena Dias, Vicente."

"My boss is very pleased with the SUV."

"Good."

"He liked it so much he's keeping it for himself."

"What about my second deal?"

"Si senor, a much bigger deal. He has a couple of questions, okay?"

"Fire away."

" Que? What do you mean fire away?"

"You know. Ask the questions."

"Oh, okay. My boss is curious about the sample you sent him and would like to know where you got it, how much do you have, and what is the price?"

"Vicente, I never reveal my sources. Did you test it?"

"I don't know, I just FedExed it to him overnight."

"You can tell him I have ten kilos to sell, all or none, for one million dollars."

"I will tell him but I think . . . too much money, senor."

"This is high-octane, not that black tar shit from Mexico. It's SEA purity, South East Asia 80 percent plus. He can sell it for four times that much."

"I will have to get back to you."

"When? Can't you call him now, I have other people interested."

"I'll see what I can do."

Crazy Ray started to say something when he heard the phone disconnect. Damn, did he screw the pooch, play it too cool? Did he need to start looking for another buyer?

CHAPTER 16

Girod's Restaurant was crowded with a long line waiting to get a table, but Jin, Mack, Irish, and Bear were ushered immediately through the crowd to a round table close to the kitchen. Bear pushed through the double swinging doors into the kitchen with cocky familiarity. The restaurant was large and airy with exposed wood rafters and old yellow pine floors. Jin stopped and chatted with friends at different tables, introducing Mack and Irish.

Between introductions, Mack whispered to Jin, "Are you in the restaurant business too?"

"My goodness no, it's my uncles, my dad's brother." She said.

Two large carafes of red wine and one white wine were on the table with a half-dozen glasses. The waiters were like water bugs, darting in and out of the busy kitchen, each one stopping to greet Jin's with a hug or a kiss and refilling their wine glass. Mack found himself alone and moved behind the table and continued to stand and wait while sipping on a glass of wine. He looked for Irish in the crowd but couldn't find her or Jin.

A waiter stopped with a tray of ramekins filled with tidbits of fried oysters, shrimp, and sea scallops and placed them on the table, "Compliments of Chef Jacques," he said.

The kitchen doors acted as a fan, wafting piquant aromas throughout the restaurant and igniting Mack's hunger pains. He decided he had waited long enough and started in on the appetizers. He heard his name called and with a mouth full of shrimp, turned and saw Jin at the kitchen door waving for him. He picked up his glass of wine and walked over to Jin and Irish standing inside the kitchen door.

"I want you to meet my Uncle Jacques," Jin nodded to a short man in a black Chef Coat walking toward him with a full head of white hair and a Van Dyke beard. "We are going to the table to replenish our stock," she held up her wine glass, "and to eat our soup. Jacques wants to show you his kitchen."

"It's turtle soup, Daddy." she raised the bowl, "Look, there's little turtles swimming in it," then laughed and kissed him on the cheek, "Later Daddy-O."

"Do I get a kiss too, Daddy?" Jin said, and quickly kissed him on the cheek and hurried to follow Irish out the door.

What doors a glass of wine will open . . . Mack thought.

"Welcome to my kitchen," Jacques said, wiping his hand with a bar towel. "You're a very poplar man."

"Thank you, Chef, sometimes that's not a good thing." They shook hands. "Your appetizers are delicious; seasoning and texture were spot on."

"You like Cajun food?"

"Yes, I do."

"Come, let me show off my kitchen while we have a quick tasting tour."

Jacques' first stop was at his dual zone, double-door wine refrigerator, one side for white wines and the other side for storing reds. Mack was more of a red wine person but Jacques removed a bottle of white Burgundy, a special gift from a wholesaler to celebrate the opening of his new kitchen. It was the best wine Mack had ever tasted, red or white. Jacques described it as 'light, crisp, and well balanced with a long lovely finish.' It was a perfect wine to soften the palate before tasting his Creole and Cajun cooking.

"This is an excellent wine. It's dry like a Chardonnay, but still light and crisp like you said."

"Very good, Mack, you have a taste for wines. It is a Batard-Montrachet from their Grand Cru vineyard in Burgundy, France, their grapes are 100 percent Chardonnay."

The all stainless steel kitchen was spotless with everyone dressed in white chef coats and hats. Mack lost count of the kitchen staff as he was introduced to the sous chef, sauté chef, grill chef, pastry chef, and salad chef, all working in perfect harmony like a well-oiled machine. Jacques stopped at the Line station and used a ladle to dip into a large pot of seafood Gumbo. Mack had a handful of tablespoons and filled one from the ladle, and then they marched down the line, from station to station, trying multiple dishes from rabbit and sausage Jambalaya to Crawfish Etouffee. The Blue Crab Beignets were Mack's favorite; a sweet, crispy fritter, with the perfect amount of heat, matched with Jacques special remoulade sauce.

The sous chef came hurrying over to Jacques and handed him a white apron, "I need you now, boss, the line is backing up."

Mack thanked Jacques and headed out the kitchen doors, Bear following. He could hear load music coming from the outside deck and patted Bear on the head, "Stay," he said and walked over to see if he could find Jin and Irish.

Jin and Irish were out on the floor dancing together and when they saw Mack, they came rushing over, "Daddy, it's a Zydeco band, come on and dance with us," Irish pulled on his arm.

"I don't know how to dance to that music."

"Ahhh, Daddy, you can dance to any music."

Jin pulled on his other arm and said, "You just shake your bootie."

"How much have you two had to drink?" Mack said.

"Not enough," they both said at the same time.

Laughing, the three of them hands together, boogied out to the middle of the dance floor.

Mack watched the slow-moving ceiling fan as it circulated the damp air from the half-opened window. He pulled the sheet up under his chin and waited for the next round of hooting calls from an owl just outside his window. Wide-awake, he rolled over to check the time on his phone; it was 3:20 a.m. He flopped back over on his pillow with his hands behind his head, thinking. He had a good time tonight, unexpected but very enjoyable. Irish had a wonderful time too, the food and wine were great, the Zydeco band was wild and entertaining, and while slow dancing with Jin, between the heavy breathing and closeness of their bodies, she left no doubt that her door would be open tonight if he was interested. He felt sure it was just the alcohol talking, but his experience had taught him that drunken words were sober thoughts. Did he really want to open that door, literally and figuratively? It had been a while since he had been with a woman, but no, they would be flying back to Key West later today. His days of one-night stands were in the past and he planned on leaving it there.

His stomach was churning from all the spicy food and way too much alcohol; he needed a Coke. He swung his feet off the bed and pulled on his jeans and crept down the stairs to the kitchen without shirt or shoes. There were only diet drinks in the fridge but in the pantry he found a regular Coke. He removed a glass from a cabinet, got ice from the freezer, and filled the glass with Coke. The fizz going down was like a fire extinguisher putting out a fire. He poured the rest of the Coke in his glass and started silently back up the stairs, stopping at Jin's door to listen. Good, no sounds, everything was quiet and undisturbed.

Mack finished his Coke sitting on the side of the bed, kicked his jeans to the floor and crawled between the sheets. His stomach was no longer growling, the owl was no longer hooting, and soon he was falling fast asleep . . . until he heard the bedroom door open.

"I heard you in the kitchen, are you ok?" Jin said.

He sat up and leaned back against the headboard. She was standing at the foot of the bed wrapped in a red robe.

"Sorry," Mack said. "I helped myself to a Coke from your kitchen to settle my stomach."

"That's okay, I wasn't asleep. I was thinking about what a good time I had tonight."

"It was fun and Irish had a good time too."

"You are a very good dancer, you've got rhythm."

"A good partner helps."

"Are you still planning on flying back to Key West today?"

"Yes, if the weather cooperates."

"Let's hope it pours down rain." She said. "You know, I would love for you and Irish to spend a couple or more days here?"

"We have to get back, I'm flying her to law school in California."

"Do you think I'm too old for you?"

"Too old for what?"

She didn't answer.

"No, of course not." Mack said. "I have no idea. I'm sure I'm older than you."

"You care to guess?" Jin untied her robe and let it drop to the floor. She cupped each breast in her hands, "These are mine, no silicone." She moved to the bed and sat beside him. She took his hand and placed it on her breast, holding it there.

"Yes . . . yes, I believe you."

"Your hand is so warm." She waited, then released his hand, and leaned over and kissed him on the lips, slow and lingering. Her long black hair created a curtain around them as her erect nipples brushed the hair on his naked chest.

Mack lay unresponsive, teetering.

She stood as if to leave but instead found the corner of the sheet and pulled it to the foot of the bed.

Mack laid spread eagle, buck-naked.

Jin stood at the foot of the bed; staring . . . she was no longer in doubt if he was interested.

There goes my no-more-one-night-stand all shot to hell. Mack said to himself.

CHAPTER 17

There are ten drug cartels in Mexico: Juarez Cartel, Gulf Cartel, and Jalisco New Generation Cartel, to name a few. These cartels take in over $29 billion dollars annually from US drug sales, and when a shipment of drugs is stolen, even as small as Tito's, the word spreads overnight to every cartel across the 31 states of Mexico.

Juan Carlos Acosta, capo of the United Ten Cartel and the largest and most powerful cartel in Mexico, had received an emergency call from his daughter, Maria del Carmen in Memphis. She was crying and in a panic that Tito was missing. He had not come home in two nights for the first time in their marriage, and hadn't answered his phone in the last 48 hours. Juan Carlos was aware Tito was missing. Jose Estrada, one of his lieutenants in charge of the Nuevo Laredo region, had reported a failed delivery of the heroin and that Tito was not returning his calls. The lieutenant was ordered to cross the border and standby at the Laredo Airport for one of their jets. It would be there in an hour to fly him to Memphis immediately. The missing drug information was already racing through the grapevine. Juan Carlos told his daughter there had been a bad storm in Mississippi and some cell towers were down and Tito probably decided to stay overnight at one of the casinos. He told her not to worry, he would find Tito and call her.

Juan Carlos knew Tito would not sign his own death warrant by stealing from his father-in-law. Someone had robbed and killed him or he had been kidnapped for ransom. It wasn't long before he got his first lead. Jose, the lieutenant he had sent to Memphis was at the West Houston Airport, a small exclusive FBO, one runway, 15 miles west of Houston. He had gotten a call while in-flight to Memphis from a local dealer in Houston that a small time car dealer named Vicente was searching for some partners to finance a million dollar buy of China White Heroin. Juan Carlos ordered him to take no reprisal, to stay in Houston until he had all the information he needed, and report back to him ASAP. Juan Carlos didn't hesitate, he ordered a second jet and sent Pedro Arellano, another of his lieutenants to Memphis.

Vicente was very cautious over the phone about meeting Jose. But after baiting Vicente with an offer to furnish the whole million dollars with a ten percent finder's fee, Vicente agreed to meet at a large Tex-Mex restaurant on Scott Street across from Yellowstone Park.

Vicente was a car dealer, not a drug dealer and never wanted to be. It was way too nerve-wracking and dangerous. Sure, over the many years of selling used cars, he had sold as much as a pound of marijuana from time to time or a little coke, mostly as an incentive or a convenience for his customers. But brokering 22 pounds of heroin was a different ball game. He was positive it had caused the recurrence of his old dormant bleeding ulcer. If his nerves could last a couple more days he could walk away with a hundred grand to boost his retirement plan. All he had to do was stay cool and close the deal today.

Like every Mexican living in the states bordering Mexico, Vicente had heard and read many stories of the murdering brutality of the United Ten Cartel. What he didn't know was the name of the cartel's new successor, Juan Carlos Acosta.

Patience was not a word in Jose's vocabulary, but instinct and street smarts were his life saving traits. He stood inside the restaurant's doors waiting for his eyes to adjust to the ambient light. He saw Vicente in a private booth in the rear and worked his way through the crowd, measuring his surroundings and each person in the restaurant.

"Buenas Dias, Jose."

Jose said nothing in response. He sat across from Vicente, vis-à-vis, reached inside his coat and removed a small automatic pistol with a silencer from his shoulder holster. With his left hand he shook out the fold of his cloth napkin and covered his right hand and pistol. He spoke in English with a soft tone,

"Vicente, are you carrying a weapon?"

"No." Vicente said.

"Stand up and lift your shirt."

Vicente complied, looking at the other customers, but no one was paying any attention.

"Now turn around. Okay, sit down and listen carefully." Jose leaned closer over the table. "If you don't tell me what I want to know, I will kill you first, right here inside this restaurant. Then I will drive to your house on Dogwood Street and cut off the head of your wife and mail it to your daughter in Phoenix."

Vicente tried to speak, but fear had locked up his brain and choked off his breathing.

"Hear me loud and clear so you will know who I work for. Juan Carlos Acosta is the supreme boss, Jefe de Jefes, of the United Ten Cartel. Tito, Juan Carlos' son-in-law is missing, his new, black Range Rover is missing, and his ten-kilos of heroin is missing, and all I have is *you*. Juan Carlos demands instant results. You understand?"

Vicente's eyes were bulging as he struggled to breath. *He knows where I live.*

The waiter placed a bowl of chips and salsa on the table and stood waiting to take their order. Jose shook his head.

Vicente took a deep breath and mumbled, "Mas tarde," and the waiter hurried to another table.

"Vicente, I have three questions; do you know a man named Tito, or have you ever heard that name?"

"No." Vicente started to say something else but Jose held up his hand and shook his head.

"Where did you get the Range Rover?"

"I bought it from a man named Ray Flynn, in Memphis, they call him Crazy Ray."

"Where are the ten-kilos of heroin?"

"I have not seen it but Flynn said he has it. He gave me a sample that I gave you. Please Senor Jose, do not harm my wife, I will tell you all I know. Here, take the keys to the Range Rover." Vicente reached for his keys.

Jose raised the napkin, the silencer protruding from underneath, and shook his head.

"I'm sorry, I'm sorry. I made a terrible mistake, I should never have gotten involved in this but I will do whatever you want me to do."

"How do you know this Crazy Ray Flynn?"

"I buy used cars from all over and a customer of mine from Jackson, Mississippi, named Tony, called me and gave me Flynn's number and said he had a high-end SUV he needed to move immediately. I talked to him on the phone, then met with him in Memphis, and bought the Range Rover.

"And the heroin?"

"That's when he gave me the sample and told me he had 22-pounds and wanted a million dollars for it."

"I am going outside to make a call and I want you to stay here while I'm gone. If you leave I will track you down and have no mercy while killing you." He got up and looked down at Vicente, "Relax, order something to eat."

Vicente watched Jose exit the front entrance. Many options flashed through his head, first was to run, but petrifying fear overpowered all options. He raised his hand and motioned to the waiter that he was ready to order."

Jose called Juan Carlos, and they spoke only in Spanish:

"I met with the man named Vicente, a small time thief, white hair, about 60, owns a used car lot. He's way over his head in this deal."

"Does he have the drugs?"

"No, but he's going to take me to the man that does, a Crazy Ray Flynn in Memphis."

"Did you bring enough cash with you?"

"Yes, I signed the book in the safe for 50k. I didn't know what all I would need."

"Do *not* let this fool get away from you."

"No way, Jefe. I know where he lives and I have been to his car lot, I will be very careful. Is Tito's SUV still missing?"

"Yes, why?"

"This Vicente fellow is driving a new, black Range Rover, with dealer tags."

CHAPTER 18

Mack woke up as if an alarm was going off. He sat up on the side of the bed to clear the heavy fog inside his skull. His eyes felt like they were glued shut. With all the alcohol in his system, he wasn't sure Jin had been in his room or he had been dreaming. He stood up, staggered, lost his balance, fell backward, bounced off the bed onto the floor. He laid flat on his back looking up at the ceiling. *What the hell just happened? Was he still drunk?* He ran down an imaginary checklist of his body parts to make sure he didn't break anything. He looked down and kicked over one of his worn cowboy boots. *Great boots, fit like a glove, but not made for running.* He needed a run to wash the alcohol poison from his system. The time and weather were perfect for a long run; second best would be a long walk.

Dressed, he stood on the porch looking up at the cloudless sky; the weatherman had missed his mark again.

"You wanna go on a long walk, show me around?" he said to Bear leaning against his leg. Bear was a puppy when Mack gave him to Irish for her birthday. His father and mother were champion Bouvier des Flanders with advanced degrees in tracking, obedience, and protection. At age 6 months, Bear was sent back to the Dutch breeder for the same Schutzhund training.

They walked down the paved driveway, Bear in front, looking back from time to time to make sure Mack was close behind. Mack stopped at one of the high points of the winding drive and watched the sky as it changed from nautical twilight to civil dawn. The stars appeared to be sliding off the edge of the earth as twilight climbed closer to the horizon. He smiled, remembering a whack on his knuckles with a wooden ruler by Sister Agnes George, followed by the biblical verse, "Be still, and know that I am God." The stillness and tranquility of Jin's 'heavenly gardens' was euphoric; no drugs or alcohol could produce such harmony between man and nature.

Within the changing light he noticed the development of a ghost-like object, silhouetted by the twilight, as it loomed above the treetops.

"Let's jog down to the river and do a little recon on that smokestack, big boy." Bear took off running, Mack followed, slowing his jog at each S-curve. At the end of the paved drive Bear waited for directions. Mack pointed left, down toward the river, and followed Bear.

Mack stopped in front of the three rough-sawn cypress framed buildings. The lights on the outside of the buildings were still burning and it was graveyard quiet, except for the humming of a mercury vapor light high on a concrete pole. There was no one in sight as they continued to walk toward the river, parallel to the buildings. A sign, *Medical Center,* was above the double doors of the first building. Mack was surprised at how big the cotton warehouses were, the quality of the remodeling, the blending of the covered cypress walkways from building to building, and how they unified the landscaping with the riverfront in the background; all first-class.

He passed the two senior-living warehouses and continued to check the treetops for a "smokestack" as Irish had called it. At the next curve, he noticed the trees on each side of the road were thicker and taller, with red and white signs, *Private Road No Trespassing* nailed to them. Halfway down the road Mack stopped when he saw Bear on his haunches next to a tall man with a black beard and long hair, standing in the middle of the road. He was dressed in hunting gear; a camouflaged 4WD Off-Road Jeep parked behind him.

Mack slowed his walk, assessing the situation . . . a heavy-duty 10' chain-link gate blocked the road; *Posted and Patrolled—No Trespassing* signs were wired to the gate.

As Mack got closer, he heard the low whirring of the two video cameras high on the gateposts. The guard, or whatever he was, stepped forward in a challenging manner, hands on his hips, and legs wide apart. Mack noted the holstered automatic pistol on the man's right hip.

Looks like a Glock . . . if he's a guard, what is he guarding?

Bear looked up at Mack, then the guard, back and forth. Feeling the tension, he ran to Mack and jumped on him barking and playing.

"You lost, pardner?" the man said.

"Not really, just out for a walk." Mack was right, a patch on his vest-pocket read Global Guardian.

"You must be a friend of Doc Jin, Bear don't take to no strangers."

"I'm no stranger; he's, my dog."

"Really? He's your dog . . . that's bullshit."

Careful Mack. This redneck is armed. And where is your Colt .45 . . . left in the Bonanza, dummy.

"You're up kind of early aren't you? What are you looking for? You a doctor?" The guard asked.

"No."

"Doesn't matter, you're off-limits. No one is allowed past this gate . . . *no one.*"

"Actually, I was looking for a smokestack-like object, is it close by?"

The man moved within a foot of Mack, his right hand resting on his gun hip, "You need to turn around and go back the way you came, *pardner.*" He turned his head and spit tobacco juice close to Mack's boots.

Mack could smell his stinking breath and refrained from shoving him backward. Instead, he snapped his fingers and Bear rushed to his left side at attention. His black eyes locked-in on the guard like a laser, his top lip rolled back, two long pointed fangs exposed.

The guard nodded his head a couple times and took a step back. Mack waited, then slowly backed up a few feet, turned and started back up the road. Bear matched him step for step.

At the top of the hill, Mack bent over with his hands on his knees and took a deep breath. *What the hell was that about? You know better, good way to get your ass shot.*

The lights were off on all the buildings now and the sun was climbing fast from the east. Mack stopped walking when he heard a light buzzing in the air, like bees swarming. He looked up and saw a drone hovering about 15 feet above him. He had never seen a drone except on TV and watched as it moved over the top of one of the buildings and hovered. Standing on the roof, waving at him was the old man with the white beard and long hair he had seen yesterday.

"Come on up," he shouted, pointing to the back of the building where there was a fire escape staircase. Bear raced up the back stairs as if he had been there many times and easily leaped over the short parapet wall onto the roof; Mack followed.

"You like coffee?" the old man asked.

Mack stepped over the parapet onto a grass rooftop. "Sure," he said.

The rooftop was a mini–Empyrean Garden in itself, with a long, copper gabled skylight surrounded by blooming flowers and potted palm trees.

"People around here call me Big John," the old man handed Mack a cup of coffee. He had on a pair of worn shorts, no shirt, and sandals. "I saw y'all drive in with Jin yesterday."

"Thanks, smells great." Mack took a sip of the coffee. "I'm Mack Shannon," they shook hands, *strong handshake for a hundred-year-old man.*

"Quite a gadget you got there," Mack pointed to the black drone.

"Here, feel this," he handed the drone to Mack. "It's less than 3 pounds, called a Quadcopter; four rotors, has a HD video camera mounted on it and will fly up to 70 mph. Amazon Prime Air is using a similar model now for their small package deliveries. I filmed you and Bear down at the gate with Hugo, the guard. Did he give you any trouble?"

"Tried to."

"Pay him no mind, he's sort of a Barney Fife type."

"What's he guarding?"

"It's Jin's medical research center, very private."

"Is that where I saw the smokestack?"

"What you saw was really a ship's funnel."

Mack stuck the drone out to hand it back to Big John.

"Hold on to it and I'll show you something." He picked up the remote control and tapped the screen and the four propellers started spinning and the drone rose from Mack's hand to about 10 feet above his head.

"Watch the monitor here," Big John said.

Mack watched on the screen as the drone raced down the road at treetop level, slowed and hovered at the gate that blocked the road, the camera rotated 360 degrees, but there was no Hugo. Mack could see the river on the screen as the drone climbed to 500 feet, and watched as it circled a long multilevel ship with a huge black funnel in the center.

"That's the floating research center, an international conglomerate of renowned doctors and scientists that Jin's brought together."

Big John operated the small joystick, slowly moving the drone over the top of the great white behemoth, 825 feet long from stem to stern. "It was a retired cruise ship and they gutted and refitted it withe latest medical and scientific research equipment. With worldwide investors the demand for top-level security was imperative due to the millions of dollars lost in corporate and industrial espionage and theft; hence, the ten-foot fence and the around-the-clock guards. The research ship has the highest rated and most complete IP unified security platform. It is wired with the latest high-tech cameras and theft-detections. It combines video management, access control, video analytics, intrusion alerts and more onto a single networked platform that can be accessed from anywhere, anytime, worldwide."

"Millions of dollars?"

"Yeah, that includes the gutting and transformation of the ship to a medical center. They have a couple of robots that cost over ten million dollars, and a super MRI for diagnostic imaging. I've only been inside the ship once that I can remember."

The drone camera zoomed in on a square red flag painted with a white crescent and a pentagon of five stars on each side of the funnel. Below the flag was a gold symbol of a snake wrapped around a rod with the letters FON at the bottom.

"Is that the ship's flag painted on the funnel?"

"It's the Civil Ensign of Singapore with the medical symbol, The Staff of Asclepius."

"What do the letters FON stand for?"

"Freedom of Navigation. Although it has never moved since it docked here years ago, it stays ready to sail to international waters at a moment's notice. The ship has a foreign registry, only subject to international laws, with exclusive jurisdiction over its ship and sailors, and all medical research operates under the laws of Singapore, 10,000 miles away."

Mack followed the drone as it moved to the rear of the ship, hovered, and focused on the name across the stern, GUANYIN, Ltd., and below that, SINGAPORE.

Big John tapped the screen and the drone's return-to-home feature took over and they watched as it flew back to the roof and hovered above them. "You see that small antenna over in the corner? That's a Wi-Fi docking station for drones. They call them UAV's, Unmanned Aerial Vehicle."

Mack watched as Big John's quadcopter descended onto the docking station. "What a gadget," Mack said. "No, I misspoke, gadget is not the right word, it is much more than that—this is revolutionary, I can think of a hundred uses already."

"Many companies have already developed their own drones, all sizes, from jumbo transports to insect drones the size of a fly."

"Really? Sounds like a great investment." Mack said.

"Other countries are flying commercial drones all over the place without restrictions, and our military flew over 3,400 'Lighting Bug' UAV missions as far back as 1964 over North Vietnam. The delay in the States is that the FAA has only approved certain cities and companies for testing commercial drone deliveries, like FedEx-Rapid, DHL-Parcelcopter, UPS-Zipline, Goggle-Wings. Even the Walmart-Whoosh is flying now."

"How can you fly your quadcopter then?"

"Mine's not commercial, not a delivery drone . . . yet. Commercial drones are under different rules and laws and compete with trains and trucks like Otto, the self-driving 18-wheeler. Trucks alone move 10-billion tons of freight a year. The big question now is, the skyway or the highway? But you're a pilot, you know the answer to that question. The sky is infinite."

Big John's phone dinged, indicating a text. He read the message and punched in a quick reply. "Jin is looking for you," he pointed to the road below. "I texted her that you were on your way."

CHAPTER 19

Vicente had just taken a bite from his empanada when he spotted Jose returning from outside the restaurant. Standing in front of the table, he watched Jose reach into his pocket and remove a twenty-dollar bill and placed it on the table and nodded his head toward the front door, "Let's go."

Vicente, looked down at his plate, then back up to Jose, "Go where?"

Jose picked up a fork and stabbed it into Vicente's empanada, "Vamonos!"

Vicente hurried through the crowd, Jose followed close behind.

Standing in the parking lot, Jose tossed Vicente the keys to the rental car. "You drive. I'm sure you know your way back to Memphis, right."

Vicente hesitated before pulling out onto Scott Street and looked over at Jose, "Can I call my wife?"

Jose, looking at a road map on his phone, said, "Take the 610 loop to I-10 east. Give me your phone. Once we're on I-10, I will call this Ray Flynn and you talk to him and set up the meeting."

Crazy Ray was pacing back and forth across the kitchen, his nerves frayed. He needed to get out of town as soon as possible, but had not heard a word from Vicente in 24 hours. Sitting on 22 pounds of stolen heroin was a dangerous problem he needed to solve immediately. Who else could he go to for a quick sale? Very few people had a million cash to pay to someone they never dealt with before, and if there was, he didn't know them. The bottom line was, he had run out of options and would sell it for half or less just to get rid of it. The sale of the SUV to Vicente was clean, no problems, what's holding up buying the heroin? Was it all BS about Vicente's boss? Was he just playing him? If not, why hasn't he called?

He sat down at the kitchen table, his head in his hand, and thought about calling Vicente. He heard the low vibrating tone of his Pax vaporizer; a signal to let him know the tiny oven was hot and ready to load. He opened a baggie half-full of marijuana, removed a small bud and packed it in the tiny oven. He took a long pull on the vaporizer, held it deep in his lungs, and leaned back with his eyes closed. Startled upright by a loud ring, he coughed out a cloud of smoke and groped for his phone. There was no name on the screen but he recognized the 832 area code of Houston.

"Hello."

"Senor Ray?"

"Yeah."

"This is Vicente."

"No shit, it's about time."

"I talked to my boss and he is interested and wants to meet right away."

"Has he got the money?"

"Yes."

"All of it?"

Si, Senor."

Jose whispered to Vicente, "Does he have the heroin?"

"Do you have the 10 packages with you, Senor?"

"Yes. When can we meet?"

"We can be there tomorrow."

"Who is we?"

"My boss, Jose, Senor."

"Okay, okay. Just you and . . . *Ho-za,* and no weapons, understand? Tomorrow, same place, same time."

"Si, si, Senor Ray. Hasta manana."

Crazy Ray stood up with a big smile on his face, and took another long hit from his pocket vaporizer. He let the smoke ease out from his nose, and then blew out a large smoke ring and followed it across the kitchen. He removed a beer from the refrigerator, opened it, held it high in the air and shouted, "YOU THE MAN!" Took a long drink and shouted again, "Ray Baby, You. Are. The. MAN!"

His exuberance was short-lived. What dominated his mind now was his meeting tomorrow with the two Mexicans. He sipped his beer as he stood in the doorway of his bedroom in deep thought, and stared at the packed bags ready to go at a moment's notice. He returned to the kitchen, tossed the beer can in the trash, and sat down at the table. What he needed was a foolproof plan for tomorrow; he had to make sure he was prepared for the unexpected—*sneaky spics*.

CHAPTER 20

Mack watched Jin's old Suburban wobble down the winding drive and stop at the fork in the road. Mack jogged to keep up with Bear as he raced to the truck anticipating a ride.

"Hop in you two, there's this food truck down the road that has the best coffee and makes fresh beignets every morning. I ordered a dozen for our breakfast."

Mack opened the back door for Bear, then climbed into the front and buckled up.

"I checked on Irish and she was still asleep. I didn't want to wake her." Jin said.

"Too much partying last night, you think?" The image of Jin's naked body flashed before Mack's eyes. He waited to see if Jin would say anything.

"So, you met my father, Big John?"

"Your father?"

"He didn't tell you?"

"No."

Jin quickly changed the subject. "I received a phone call this morning from Hugo, the guard on duty. He said you were looking for a smokestack?"

"Well, I . . ."

"Irish told me you were a Recon-Marine, and with my father being quite the reconnoiter with all his different drones, it was natural you two would meet each other. I trust he showed you the 'smokestack?'"

"He did . . . with his drone. And what I saw was very impressive, but he told me nothing about the kind of research you're doing?"

"Are you just curious or do you have other motives?"

"Sometimes I like to invest in developing ventures, especially after a multi-million dollar infusion."

"We try to keep a low profile: no advertising, no grants and no government funding. A totally independent and obscure operation."

"Why so mysterious?"

"With big money investors come demands. It's a race to beat death. And it's a 100-yard dash not a marathon. Our investors demand immediate solutions from our clinical trials, not years on a shelf waiting for FDA's approval."

"Are you circumventing the guidelines of the FDA?"

"Our guidelines are more stringent than the FDA's. But our primary market has not been the over three hundred million people in the USA, but the eight billion in other countries."

"But your research is being done here in the U.S., right?"

"No. We are a Singaporean company on a visa to the United States, conducting clinical studies to submit to the FDA. If challenged, we would weigh anchor and in a short time be in international waters."

"Your father mentioned 'medical' research. Is it for other diseases?"

"You don't give up, do you?"

Mack shrugged his shoulders and smiled.

Jin stopped for a red light. "Any disease that has to do with the brain, especially AD, Alzheimer Disease. China has twice as many people dying with AD as any other country in the world."

"That's over a billion people, right?"

"True, India and China both have over a billion people. We were very successful in China. But 90 percent of their elderly must be cared for by their families, it's the law. Old people cannot be admitted to a government nursing home if they still have living family members."

"Maybe I need to invest in nursing homes for AD?"

"Who's going to pay for their keep? Not India or the Chinese government. They don't have Medicare. China's economy is unraveling, their credit bubble has burst, and their growth in GDP is almost non-existent. Our nation's fiscal future is not looking any better with a debt if 28 trillion. The U.S. owes more than 1.2 trillion to Japan and 1.1 trillion to China.

"Is China's economy affecting your research?"

"No, but our investors expect us to pay our own way once our trials are approved."

"Have you found a cure?"

"Five years ago my father was bedridden, terminally ill with AD. It was the most wretched time of my life. It broke my heart to see this once powerful and beautiful man in diapers, withered down from 225 pounds to a 100-pound skeleton, with breathing tubes and IV's barely keeping him alive. I was hours away from writing a lethal prescription for him. We had many discussions about end-of-life care and he had signed an advance directive from the Death with Dignity Act explaining how he wanted to die."

"What happened?"

"I had read an article in a leading journal of the World Medical Association about a doctor in Singapore, a Hu Yang, who claimed to have cured numerous AD patients. I called him. I was desperate and grasping for straws. I left a message with his service and after not hearing from him, I wrote him off as a quack."

"Was he a quack?"

"He was just the opposite, more like Einstein. With a 14-hour time difference, I thought we would never talk. We finally met over the phone and he agreed to email me his CV that same day. He not only was an MD, but he graduated from Harvard with a Neuroscience and Behavioral degree. And he also has a PhD in Molecular Genetics and Genomics with over a hundred medical patents and scholarly publications. My first question was, if he would be interested in coming to the states and working for our research center? Serendipity. Fortunately for us, he was unhappily teaching post grad at the Singapore General Hospital and wanted to get back into research."

"Where is he now?" Mack asked.

"I hope back there," she nodded, smiling, "on the Quanyin doing research. We did a Zoom video interview and hired him immediately."

"Did Doctor Yang have a cure for AD?"

"You've seen Big John, what do you think?"

"I would never know anything was wrong with him. A hundred years old, he's a phenomenon. Why haven't you capitalized on this?"

"We have. That's how we've got our initial investors from other countries and are putting those profits into fast tracking Big John's trials. He was our star subject because he was in the last stages of AD. You have to remember, Alzheimer's disease does not kill you; it devastates the brain, destroys nerve connections from the buildup of plaques and tangles, specific proteins (beta-amyloid and tau) that cause brain cells to malfunction and die. He is still being treated, but his improvement is a major medical breakthrough. Not being able to swallow properly is particularly dangerous. The vast majority of those with Alzheimer's die from aspiration pneumonia — when food or liquid goes down the windpipe instead of the esophagus, causing damage or infection in the lungs that develops into pneumonia."

"I never thought of it that way." Mack said. "So, do you treat the pneumonia first or the brain?"

"We only had a short time in Big John's case, so we treated them both at the same time. The brain is the alpha and omega of the body, containing about 100 billion nerve cells, or neurons. Dr. Yang calls this dense, branching network a 'neuron forest.' The brain is under constant pressure making over 100 trillion calculations per second.

"Per second? How in the world do you find and treat that specific part of the brain? Is it with the million dollar machines Big John told me about?"

"You're a Marine. What is your saying, 'loose lips sink ships.' I need to have another talk with my Daddy."

"I notice this is the first time you referred to Big John as your father?"

"It wasn't easy. I've always called him Daddy, but our medical board thought it was best to avoid any confusion of nepotism or legalities between doctor and patient, especially during the FDA trials. Fortunately we are in phase-4, the last trails."

"Do you need any more investors, I would be interested?"

"You know better; I've already told you too much. It's enough that I'm dealing with the FDA. Now you want the SEC showing up at my doorstep waving their 'insider-trading act.'"

"Here we are." Jin slowed and pulled into a parking spot in front of a small food truck. "Let's see if our order is ready."

"Wait, let me give you some money . . ."

Jin was already out of the truck waving him off.

Mack and Jin stood on the tarmac and watched Irish do a pre-flight check on the V-tail Bonanza.

"Sure you won't stay another night or two?" Jin said, holding his hand. "I'll give you a tour of the ship and introduce you to doctor Yang."

"I'd love that," Mack nodded his head toward Irish. "But I've got to get that young lady to school in California."

"Will I see you again soon?"

"I hope so." Mack wanted to say, *come see me in Key West,* but from past experience had learned that was not a good idea until you find out if the relationship was more than just a fling. He liked to practice what Benjamin Franklin preached, *Guests, like fish, begin to smell after three days*.

They hugged, and with a light kiss said goodbye.

Mack walked to the airplane and helped Irish up from under the wing of the plane. "All clear?"

Irish showed Mack the gas strainer tube, "All clear, no water. Can I fly us home?"

"Sure, I'll get the tie downs, you get Bear in the back seat."

Bear barked and Mack and Irish waved goodbye as the plane taxied to the threshold of the runway.

"Lakefront Tower to Bonanza One Zero Seven Echo Sierra, cleared for takeoff on three six right."

CHAPTER 21

Vicente was driving north in Mississippi on I-55 and switched his lights to bright when he saw that the large green sign read SOUTHAVEN. Printed below the name was, *State Line Road Next Exit.* "This is where we get off," he said.

Jose sat up in his seat. "I want to check out where we are meeting before we go to the motel."

"It's just up ahead." Vicente turned onto the side road leading to the closed weigh station. The broken barricade was still half-standing and a long tree limb had fallen blocking the drive. The *No Trespassing* sign was face up under the limb. Vicente exited the car and pulled the tree limb out of the way and drove around the barricade. He stopped just short of the boarded up weigh station building.

"Pull around to the back, I want to see the whole place."

Vicente dodged some deep potholes as the high beam lights scanned the perimeter. "There's nothing back here, just overgrown woods."

"Yeah. Okay, let's check-in at the motel." Jose said.

It was ten o'clock in the morning when Crazy Ray heard the horn blow and hurried outside carrying a canvas shopping bag. Boone was waiting in his customized Hummer; painted flat black with dark tinted windows. Waiting behind them in a Chevy pickup were Boone's two brothers, Clyde and Lynn. Crazy Ray opened the trunk of the H2 and placed the shopping bag with ten bricks of heroin in the recessed floor and climbed in the front passenger seat.

"Everything copasetic?"

Mounted on the dashboard was an 8 x 12 inch LCD writing tablet. Boone removed the stylus pen and wrote, "Locked and loaded."

"Deer stands and weapons?"

He nodded his head and wrote, "2-stands and 2-M4's in the trunk, 2-Glock 9's, and 2-M4's in the back seat."

"You bring me a vest?"

Boone pointed to the back seat, opened his shirt and thumped his chest, showing Crazy Ray his Kevlar vest.

"You're a good man Boone, no matter what they say."

Boone nodded his head in agreement, a huge smile spread across his face.

Crazy Ray buckled his seat belt and said, "Let's ride."

Vicente poured Jose his third cup of coffee while sitting in the Quality Inn where they furnished a complimentary breakfast. "Are we waiting on someone?" Vicente asked.

Staring out the window, Jose frowned and shook his head. "Not your concern." He saw a red Dodge pickup with a matching camper turn into the parking lot and parked in front. A tall, broad-shouldered, Hispanic man eased himself from the car and entered the front door.

"Go check us out of this place." Jose said, and pushed a hundred dollar bill across the table.

On his way to the office, Vicente noticed the tall man standing in the doorway wearing a cowboy hat and boots. He watched the man turn and walk toward Jose.

"Buenos Dias, Roberto. You have any trouble finding this place?"

"No problem. Was that your man that just walked by?"

"Yeah. Sit down; I'll bring you up to date."

Roberto listened, them told Jose about his call from Juan Carlos in the middle of the night. "I didn't know what was going on; just that the boss's son-in-law was missing, and the shipment he had with him. My orders were to go to Culiacan International Airport immediately, one of our planes was waiting to fly me to Memphis. Then I got here I was to contact Pedro, who was guarding Tito's wife. After that I talked to a couple of local dealers, and then backtracked the last time Tito was seen; it was over in Arkansas at one of his food trucks. From then on, I ran into a dead end."

"No problem, I've found the *idiota* that's responsible, his name is Crazy Ray." Jose looked at his watch, "In less than an hour we'll know for sure. If it's not him, he'll spend a long time dying until I find Tito."

"Do we need any help; Pedro coming with us?"

"No, he's guarding Juan Carlos's daughter full time. I want you to go in your truck and I'll take the old man in my car. This Crazy Ray character is an amateur, in way over his head. You just back me up. Give me five minutes meeting with him and then come in roaring, and park right beside me. You carrying, right?"

Roberto looked around the room, and then lifted his jacket in front.

"44 mag?" Jose whispered.

Roberto smiled and lowered his jacket.

Boone stopped just short of the barricade and Crazy Ray got out of the Hummer. He had noticed the broken limb he had pulled from the woods and laid across the barricade yesterday had been moved to the side of the road. Someone was here last night . . . or could be waiting for them *now*. He walked to the pickup truck behind the Hummer and told Clyde and Lynn there may be trouble ahead, and to plug in their headsets and make sure their two-way radios were turned on. Back at the Hummer, Crazy Ray opened the rear door and removed one of the M4's, a bulletproof vest, a 9-mm Glock, and a walkie-talkie. While taking off his shirt and putting on the vest, he told Boone about the limb being moved and that the Mexicans may already be here, waiting for them. He climbed in the back seat and rested the barrel of the M4 on the window seal pointed at the boarded-up building. He pulled the charging handle back to make sure a round was in the chamber and moved the selector switch to a three-round burst. Boone scanned the wooded area as he drove to the left side of the building in first gear. Crazy Ray stuck his arm out the window and jabbed his finger a couple of times whispering over the radio mic for Clyde to take the right side of the building.

Crazy Ray adjusted his earbuds as he heard Clyde say, "All clear on this side."

Satisfied that the area was secure, Crazy Ray pointed out a small clearing in the woods for Clyde to hide their pickup, and then two trees, each across the parking area from the other, for Clyde and Lynn to install their folded deer stands.

Crazy Ray checked his time while he and Boone waited inside the Hummer for Vicente and his boss. They watched as Lynn helped the overweight Clyde climb up into his deer stand, handed him his M-4, and walked back across the field to his deer stand.

Crazy Ray ran through all the possible screw-ups. This deal *had* to come off flawless; he needed the money to get out of town, and to get setup in the Keys. He heard the static of a mic open and the whisper of Lynn,

"There's a car stopping at the barricade." He adjusted the scope on his M4. "I see two men in the front seat. They're pulling around the barricade now."

Crazy Ray stood behind the opened passenger door of the Hummer with the M4 on the seat beside him. Boone had installed lead panels from his junkyard in all the Hummer doors; panels salvaged from x-ray room doors in an old razed surgery center.

Crazy Ray had an earbud from his telephone in one ear and an earbud to his walkie-talkie in the other. He told Boone to leave the engine running.

"Hold up," Lynn shouted. "There's a truck. It's pulled to the side of the barricade, on the edge of the woods."

"How many in the truck?"

"I only see one person, the driver. He's wearing a cowboy hat."

I knew it, those sneaky bastards. Never trust a wetback. "Everybody listen up. Be alert, they're trying to rip us off. Remember, when I say *fire*, I want Clyde and Lynn to fire a three round burst warning shot across the parking lot. DON'T shoot anyone or anything, just walk the rounds across the asphalt to let them know you are here."

Clyde heard Crazy Ray, but couldn't hold it any longer. He had BPH, an enlarged prostate, and a small bladder. He knew not to wait or he would piss in his pants. Needing both hands, he had placed the M4 across the shooting rail of the deer stand, and fought with his pants zipper to get it out before he peed himself. Now, he waited and waited, drip by drip, as his bladder emptied.

Crazy Ray watched the dark sedan turn at the weigh-station building and drive toward the Hummer, and stopped about 40 feet in front of him. His phone started buzzing.

"Yeah?" Crazy Ray said.

"Senior Ray, is that you behind the door?"

"Who did you think it was, Pancho Villa? You got the money?"

"Si Senor. You have the heroin?"

"Yeah, I have it. Who's with you?"

"My boss, Jose, that is all."

"No one else, just the two of you?"

"Si, Senor Ray. Like we agreed, only two on each side, right?"

Lying bastard. "Okay, Vicente, here's how we are going to do this. Jose will stay in the car and my man will stay in the Hummer. You and I are going to meet half way in front of our cars and place the drugs and money on the ground in front of each other. You check mine and I check yours. If all is okay, I take the money, you take the drugs, and we both back away and leave, agreed?" Crazy Ray waited. He could hear mumbling.

"Okay, Senor Ray, we agree. You start walking."

Boone placed a Glock 9mm in the front passenger's seat next to the M4. Crazy Ray took the Glock and stuck it in his waistband.

"No, we walk together. Keep your phone on so we can talk. I'm stepping away from the Hummer now, you get out of the car and step to the side."

Crazy Ray stood away from the door of the Hummer with the canvas shopping bag at his side and watched Vicente exit and stand to the side of his car. "Where is the money?"

"In the back seat." Vicente opened the back door and removed a roller suitcase.

"Okay, let's walk," Crazy Ray counted, "One . . . two . . . three . . ."

They stopped in the middle of the parking area, equal distance from each car, face to face.

Crazy Ray sat the shopping bag down in front of him and said, "Check it out." As he reached to check the roller bag, he saw three things happened at once: Vicente pulled the roller bag away from him; Jose exited the passenger side of the car and was rushing toward him; and a speeding truck burst from behind the weigh station, rapidly closing in on him.

"Fire! Fire!" Crazy Ray shouted.

Lynn was waiting in the deer stand to hear Crazy Ray's words and had scoped out a spot on the pavement to shoot his 3-round burst, but when he heard Crazy Ray's shout, it startled him and he pulled the trigger, twice. Regardless, Crazy Ray's plan worked, everyone stopped dead still as the 6-rounds blew-up chunks of asphalt pavement in front of them.

What happen to Clyde? "Fire, damn you Clyde . . . FIRE!" Crazy Ray shouted in his mic again.

Clyde was trying to button his pants when he heard Crazy Ray shout the first time. Holding his pants with one hand, he hurriedly grabbed for his M4, stumbled, fell onto the shooting rail and watched as his M4 bounced from limb to limb until it reached the ground. He buckled his belt and hurried down the ladder, found his M4, and fired off a 3 round burst into the sky.

Roberto heard the automatic fire of the M4's and stopped his truck sideways, behind Jose's car, driver's side away from the fire. Ducking, he rushed from the truck to the tailgate and removed an AK-47 assault rifle with a 40 round magazine.

Jose had stopped, but was now walking toward Crazy Ray pointing a gun at him. Crazy Ray pulled his gun, grabbed Vicente and stuck the gun in his back and shouted, "Everybody back-off, we can still do this."

Jose opened fire on Vicente and his body sank from Crazy Ray's grip. Crazy Ray, in a maniacal charge, fired 3 rapid rounds at Jose, all 3 shots missed. Jose returned fire, emptying his gun into Crazy Ray.

From his deer stand, Lynn watched through his scope as Crazy Ray fell to the ground. He moved the crosshairs on Jose and pulled the trigger twice. Two of the six rounds hit—one in the gut, the other a deadly shot through the neck.

Boone was standing behind the opened door of the Hummer with Crazy Ray's M4 resting on the open widow. He watched through his scope as Roberto sneaked from the rear of his truck. He checked the selector switch making sure it was on 3-round burst and pulled the trigger, then pulled it again. Six rounds raked the side of the truck from bumper to bumper. Roberto squatted down behind his truck, held his AK-47 above his head and returned fire on full automatic, spraying everything in front of him.

Lynn couldn't get a shot at Roberto but fired 6 rounds into his truck.

Roberto, realizing he was outgunned, laid down a cover of fire and jumped into his truck.

Clyde, hearing all the shooting, stepped from the edge of the woods and saw the red truck racing across the parking lot in a hail of bullets. He didn't have time to use his scope, he just pointed his M4 at the truck and kept pulling the trigger. He followed the truck as it veered off the pavement and crashed into a large Pine tree.

"Careful, Clyde, he might not be dead," Lynn said, running up behind him.

"Oh, he's dead. Half his body is on the hood . . . through the windshield. Is Ray dead?"

"I saw Boone move him. What the hell happened, what went wrong?"

"A monumental screw-up, that's what. We need to get out of here now, let's get Boone."

Boone had Crazy Ray sitting up, his shirt and Kevlar vest removed. Lined across his chest were three, starburst indentions, each the size of a golf ball. Blood was dripping from his left tricep where a fourth bullet had glazed his arm and tore a chunk of meat.

"Damn man, you are one lucky dude. Look at the holes in that vest." Lynn said standing over Crazy Ray. "We thought you were dead for sure."

Boone tore the sleeve from Crazy Ray shirt and wrapped his arm. He motioned for the two brothers to help Crazy Ray to the Hummer.

"I'm okay." Crazy Ray said. "Get everything of ours loaded in the back of the hummer. We need to get out of here, *now*. How about the spic in the red truck, is he dead?"

"No more tacos for him." Clyde said.

"Make sure that suitcase and my shopping bag are in the Hummer. Everything else stays where it is. Boone, one of the bricks in the shopping bag is already opened. Take it out and spread some of the heroin on the ground next to Vicente." Crazy Ray said.

"Yeah, that way it'll looks like a drug deal gone wrong." Clyde said.

"No shit, Sherlock." Lynn said.

CHAPTER 22

Mack started leveling off the Beechcraft Bonanza from his climb and set the altimeter at 8,500 feet, the airspeed to 153 knots, and was setting the autopilot when Irish said; "You want your sandwich now?"

They had stopped by Manny's for two large cafe con leche and two hot pressed Cuban egg and cheese sandwiches.

"I'm going to sip on my coffee for a while first."

"This is *sooo* good, I'm going to miss this. Yours is going to get cold?"

"It's too early for me to eat."

"How far to New Orleans?"

"About four hours."

"Are we going to call Jin when we get there?"

"No, just a gas stop and probably pee with all this coffee."

"What's the next stop after that?"

"Amarillo. I figured we would spend the night there, and get an early start the next morning for Las Vegas, gas up there and fly the last leg into Palo Alto before dark."

"I'll fly the next leg . . . to Amarillo, I need the hours. Where is Amarillo anyway, in Texas?"

"You can't fly if you don't know where it is. It's in New Mexico."

"No it's not."

"How are you going to get in law school? You don't even know geography. Do they even teach it in school anymore?"

"No, I think it was grouped with Social Studies; I made an A-plus."

"Really? Do you have your log book with you?"

"Yes sir."

"Okay, I'll let you fly if you think you can find Amarillo."

"Have you ever been to Amarillo? Do you even know anyone that's been to Amarillo? Besides, what's my logbook got to do with me flying? Do you have *your* log book?"

"What do I need a log book for?"

"You're too much, Daddy." Irish stretched out her legs and propped her head deep into her down pillow against the door and seat, "Wake me before we get to New Orleans, I want to land the plane."

"Palo Alto Tower to Bonanza One Zero Seven Echo Sierra, you are clear to land on runway three one. Ground control is 125.0. Welcome to Palo Alto."

"Seven Echo Sierra, ground control 125.0. Thank you." Irish said, as she taxied toward the terminal building.

"Over there," Mack pointed, "next to that Cessna, that's transit parking." He started gathering all his maps and paperwork and stuffed them in his flight bag. The back seats and the rear compartment were stuffed with Irish's boxes and luggage. Most of her stuff had been shipped by FedEx and was waiting to be picked up. "How about you tie her down and unload the luggage while I close out the flight plan and check on our car."

Mack had ordered a convertible, but this was a small FBO with one runway and wasn't sure what he would get, or where it might be parked. Inside the terminal they couldn't have been more hospitable. They gave him the keys to a new red 840i BMW. The car rental had left, directions to their hotel, and told him to leave everything to them regarding the airplane.

Mack drove the bimmer onto the tarmac and helped Irish with the luggage.

"Wow. Daddy-o, now this is *some* wheels. Can I drive?"

"Sure."

"Where we staying?"

"The Garden Hotel."

"Is it a nice place?"

"It looked nice on the internet, kind of hippie-esque, Summer of Love, and all that."

"Oh boy. I can't wait."

"Now, now, don't prejudge something you've never seen."

"I'm not, I know *you*, Daddy. Your Marine requirements have always been minimal; clean, hot water, and a firm bed, that's it."

"What else do you need?"

With the trunk loaded, Mack gave Irish the directions he had written down and double-checked it with the GPS on his phone. She turned onto University, a tree-lined avenue that reminded him of his hometown Memphis; a city known for its canopy of prolific trees, and the hardwood capital of the world. One block off University, she pulled into the drive of The Garden Hotel. Irish said, "Holy Moly, Dad! If *this* is what you call Hippie-esque, count me in. You must have gotten a heck of a deal for us to stay here."

It was a small, luxurious boutique hotel. Its porte-cochere drive was paved with polished Saltillo tile and huge arches over a wide staircase led to the lobby. Two hotel staff members opened the car doors as Mack popped the trunk latch for them to remove the luggage. Irish gave them the keys to park the bimmer.

Their room was on the top floor, two queen size beds with a large balcony overlooking downtown Palo Alto and Stanford University, strategically located on its manicured 8,200-acre campus.

Irish's phone beeped a text and she was excited to see that it was from McKenzie O'Connor. "Dad, what should I call McKenzie O'Connor? She's sending me a text. I don't feel comfortable calling her McKenzie, yet, Ms. O'Connor seems a little formal since we've talked on the phone a couple of times."

"Call her Judge, especially when you are around other people; they like that. If not, she'll let you know what to call her. What does she want?"

Irish was reading the text. "She's inviting us to a small party, cocktail and hors d'oeuvres, she hosting after her speech tonight. Some important guest will be there she would like for me to meet. What should I say?"

"Say thank you, you will be there, and does the invite include your father?"

Irish texted the reply, and then read it back to Mack. He nodded his approval and Irish hit 'send.' Irish read McKenzie's immediate reply, "Absolutely, I look forward to seeing your father again."

"Where is the party?" Mack asked.

"It's here at this hotel, The Garden!" She looked up and saw his devious smile.

"*You* knew that all along, didn't you? You planned it. Hippie-esque, Summer of Love, all that malarkey, you are full of it. She's staying right here at this hotel, isn't she?"

"I didn't know she was having her cocktail party here."

"You knew she was staying here though. You called around to find out, didn't you? I'm going to pay you back for this." Irish said.

"Why? Aren't you glad we are staying here? It's costing me an arm and a leg."

"It is a grand hotel. Oh, *Daddy*, what am I going to wear?"

"Oh, *Irish*," Mack threw his hands in the air, "what am *I* going to wear?"

Mack and Irish walked into Stanford Law School to hear Federal Judge McKenzie O'Connor welcome the 192 freshmen to their first day of law school. The auditorium was filling up fast. Students, faculty, and some parents were still coming through the doors. Mack noticed the plush carpet, the multi-colored upholstered seats, and the dark walnut woodwork, all first-class. His overall impression of what he had seen walking through the campus was unrivaled, and why not, it was securely supported by a $22 billion dollar endowment. Money was of little concern.

Mack was looking for an aisle seat close to an exit door and stopped about halfway down next to two empty seats. No way was he going to be caught in any kind of crisis and not have a way out. He waited for Irish to go in first before he sat in the aisle seat and kissed her on the cheek as she passed in front of him, whispering how beautiful she looked in the black Chanel suit he had bought for her callback interviews. He was wearing a new navy blue cashmere blazer he had brought just in case of an invite like this. He was spoiled living in Key West. He couldn't remember the last time he had worn any kind of coat. But there was a plus side for wearing a coat; it made it easier to conceal his Baby Glock, holstered inside his waistband.

A tall, middle-aged blonde, with cropped hair, dressed in her academic gown and hood, walked to the podium and announced that she was the Dean of Stanford Law School (SLS). A red stole hung from her neck like a scarf with bold vertical black letters printed on the stole, BLACK LIVES MATTER. *What in the hell . . . ?*

She started talking about the growth of SLS and the accolades of female lawyers, their progress, and how of California's 20 law schools, a whopping 16 of those had more women JD enrollees than men. There was an immediate, spur-of-the-moment, standing applause. Irish pulled on

Mack's coat sleeve. He thought, *what have I done . . . I'm paying for this?* Then he remembered Justice Sandra Day O'Connor and Chief Justice William Rehnquist had both graduated from Stanford Law School. Unsure, he slowly stood. Looking down into the pleading blue eyes of his daughter, he thought, *why not . . . why the hell not?* What are those lyrics of Nina Simone's: *It's a new dawn. It's a new day. And this old world is a new world.* He started clapping in cadence with his daughter and Irish hugged his arm with a smile so wide, you'd have thought she had just passed the bar exam.

The Dean continued, "And it is my privilege tonight to introduce our guest speaker, please welcome one of our brightest trailblazers and greatest advocate in our field, the Honorable Judge McKenzie O'Connor."

McKenzie walked across the stage with a resolute persona, head high, and a long stride. Her walk reminded him of an article he had read about some sexpert who had a fairly easy time pinpointing women who can climax from a penis inside their vagina just by the way they walk. Turns out, that sexual response means you're more likely to have a flexible pelvis and backbone, and therefore a wider and more telltale stride. He wouldn't know, but now was sure curious to find out.

The bright red sleeves of her doctoral robe, like wings of an angel, flowed behind her. Irish whispered to Mack that the color red represented the school, Stanford, and the purple lining of her sleeves and the purple hood draped down her back, represented the school of law.

Mack said, "Wow. Cheeky." He winked, remembering it was one of the things he liked about McKenzie, bold and fearless. She always kept him on his toes, guessing.

McKenzie waited until the applause stopped and everyone was seated. After waiting a little longer, she started her speech, loud and clear,

"Sexual Harassment. Sexual Abuse. Sexual Assault."

Mack and Irish stood in the doorway of McKenzie's private cocktail party inside the conference room of The Garden Hotel. He did a quick guesstimate, 30 people, 10 men and maybe 20 women. Why? It was just a habit. The chairs had been removed from the circular conference table, which was now covered

with a cornucopia of food. A tall crystal vase was in the middle filled with long stem roses and a bartender was behind a portable bar in the corner.

"Mack Shannon?" Mack turned quickly, cautious to who would know his name. His reaction was the same as when he first met her; butterflies and tongue-tied. Only one other woman had ever made him feel this way . . . Irish's mother. Was it love or a warning? McKenzie waited, smiling at him. He couldn't think of what to say, unconsciously he stuck out his hand.

McKenzie stared at his hand. "I think we were close enough at one time for a hug." She wrapped her arms around him and whispered in his ear, "You look great. Thank you for the roses, they are lovely."

Mack gathered his wits. "After your speech, I wasn't sure a hug was appropriate."

"Why?"

"Oh, nothing. Forget I said that."

"No, really, I'd like to know why?"

"Men are in such precarious positions now days. In my case, I *wanted* to hug you, and then I remember the part of your speech about sexual assault? I *wanted* to tell you how beautiful you looked in your red academic robe. But then I thought, would that be sexual abuse? I haven't seen or spoken to you for a long time. Am I guilty of sexual harassment for sending you the two-dozen roses?"

"You must have hated my speech."

"No, it was a good speech. I agree with a lot of what you said, but it was a wee bit weighted."

"How do you figure?"

Mack hesitated, "I've said enough, I don't want to offend you."

"I won't be offended, please, it's refreshing to get a man's honest opinion now days."

"It wasn't just your speech, it was the whole ambiance."

"And?"

"The program started with a female Dean of Law School, praising all the females, and how the women now outnumber the men in 16 of the 20 law schools in California, and everyone gives her a standing ovation for that. Then, she introduces you, '*our* brightest trailblazer in *our* field.' I had a mental picture of 'Lady Justice' soaring across the fields, dispatching men—right and left—with her sword of authority. And then you started your speech—Sexual Harassment. Sexual Abuse. Sexual Assault. I was left wondering, do these women have fathers and sons. And how do the *males* in this auditorium feel and the male freshmen feel on their first day of law school?"

"My speech was for both sexes," McKenzie said in a heated voice. "For the brave women who have faced retaliation and lost their livelihood, that have been ostracized and banished, and for the predator males who are guilty of this barbarism."

"Guilty? Like the Duke Lacrosse Team rape case?" Mack fired back. *Damn, why did I say that?*

McKenzie moved a step forward with her hands on her hips.

"Uh, hello? Dad?" Irish said. "Are you going to introduce me?"

McKenzie backed away, "We can continue this later."

Mack was sure *he* didn't want to continue; he had said too much already.

McKenzie turned and put her arm around Irish, "We don't need an introduction, Irish. You are as beautiful now as you were when we first met at your house. Remember, for Beethoven's one-hundredth birthday celebration. Do you still play the piano?"

"Yes Ma'am. Oops, I forgot. I probably shouldn't say Ma'am out here. I read where some women are insulted by that, some Senator, I think."

"This is California, sweetie. Women out here get their panties in a wad over the slightest thing. I'm a Southerner, it's our culture, and to me it's a sign of good manners."

"I loved your speech, you laid out clear and legal boundaries."

Mack rolled his eyes and said, "I need a drink. Can I get you ladies something?"

McKenzie stuck her arm through Irish's, "Come, let me introduce you to some of your instructors."

Mack watched as they walked away, and turned toward the bar thinking, a double-scotch.

On his second scotch, Mack stood in the corner looking over the crowd for Irish and McKenzie. Some of the crowd had drifted out into the main lobby and he walked that way but still couldn't find them. He was tired, needed a shower, and decided to call it a night. His cell phone pinged as he exited the elevator on the fourth floor. It was a text from Irish, *"Where are you, Daddy?"*

"My room." He texted.

"Our room?" She texted with a smiley face, then a second text, *"I'm on my way up."*

Mack removed his blazer and walked out onto the balcony, his phone pinged again. He smiled as he read the text,

"I have a bottle of Dom and two glasses, you up for a nightcap on the rooftop garden?" MO.

"I am. Now?" Mack replied.

"Now!" McKenzie texted.

Her mysterious spontaneity was another admirable characteristic he admired. He was putting on his coat when Irish came through the door.

"Where are you going?" She said.

"Out for a smoke."

"You don't smoke!"

"Do you have to know everything?"

"I have to look after my Daddy."

"Rooftop." He pointed up. "The Judge summoned me."

He walked to the end of the hallway, up the steps, and open the door to the roof. The roof garden was a low-density woodland of full-grown trees in redwood planters. Long strings of fairy lights hung from tree to tree. Louvered deck lights lined the walkway as Mack made his way across the roof. He saw McKenzie standing under a redwood pergola covered with purple bougainvillea. She was dressed in a peasant skirt, sandals, and a matching off-shoulder blouse. The thin cotton gauze skirt was backlit by the moon, imprinting her long svelte legs up to her waist. He thought about her long stride.

"Good evening," she said. "Can I pour you a drink?" She held a bottle of champagne half out of the ice bucket. A warm breeze blew through the tinted mosquito net panels wrapped around the pergola.

"Let me," Mack took the bottle, tore off the foil, popped the cork and filled two flutes, "What should we toast to?"

"Forgive and forget."

"Forgive what?"

"I don't want you to think I have turned into some radical, leftwing male basher. I want us to be friends again, close friends, without confrontations. What you said made me think of my brothers, all fine men, and my father, without whose support and sacrifices, I wouldn't be here.

"And I thought about how you raised Irish by yourself, no easy task, and to everyone she meets it's immediately obvious what a great job you've done. And you did it without spoiling her—an iron fist in a velvet glove. I failed to take in to considerations all the good men out there, especially you. So, forgive and forget?"

"Wow!" Mack handed her a glass of bubbling champagne, "I'll toast to that." After a long swallow and a pause, McKenzie said, "Can I get a hug too?"

CHAPTER 23

Juan Carlos Acosta, his boat captain and fishing guide, Julio Cortez, and his two bodyguards had anchored over a secret "honey-hole" Julio reserved for special clients, especially Acosta, since he owned the half-million-dollar fishing boat they were on. Acosta, his helicopter pilot and the two bodyguards, had left Acosta's cliffhanging Sinaloa hacienda at dawn for a day of fishing in the estuary of the Sea of Cortez.

The sky was cloudless with a golden sun climbing fast from the east, the fish were biting, and Acosta was kicked back in his teakwood fighting chair. He watched his live bait thrashing about as the 41-foot Hatteras Sportfish trolled through the flat clear water. Acosta took a long pull on his favorite Black Dragon cigar and let the flavor of leather and a hint of earth roil over his taste buds and through the sensory glands of his olfactory.

The low ping of his sat phone broke the serenity. He removed the phone and read the three texted numbers, *"911"* from his daughter, Maria del Carmen. He switched the screen; entered a key for encoding a cipher that scrambled any listening, texting or imaging. He then texted his daughter, "Hola?" She texted him back asking him if it was safe to send him a picture.

"Si, esta bien." Acosta said, and waited for the photo to appear on his screen. Slowly, like a shade being pulled down over a window, large letters appeared on his sat phone screen, MEXICAN DRUG WAR PLAGUES THE MIDSOUTH.

The bold print was across the front page of The Commercial Appeal, the morning newspaper in Memphis. Numerous photos showed the bullet-riddled bodies of Vicente, Jose, and Roberto, splayed across the asphalt pavement, and the crashed truck and car pummeled with bullet holes.

Acosta exploded out of his fishing chair with a savage scream. He slammed his fishing gear to the deck, threw his thousand dollar freshly lit cigar over the fantail, and shouted, "Julio, vamonos! To shore . . . ahora!"

Acosta called his top lieutenant, his brother Ramón, and told him he would be at the airport in one hour, and ordered a meeting of the leaders of his cartel.

The helicopter hovered above the large white H painted on the helipad at

Culiacan International Airport. Acosta stared out the window at the flashing roof lights of the police cars waiting on the tarmac next to two black Suburban's. Acosta exited the helicopter and with a bodyguard on each side, hurried across the tarmac to his Suburban. The Suburban's followed the police escort as it turned onto Blvd Emiliano Zapata and raced into the city. Security guards had stopped the traffic at all four corners at the cross street of Ave Jesus Andrade, the two Suburban's turned into the underground parking of the headquarters of Acosta Enterprise's, a high-rise office building downtown.

The elevator stopped on the top floor and Acosta was the first off with his two bodyguards hurrying to keep up. One wall of the conference room was all glass, floor to ceiling, framing a panoramic view of the foothills of the Sierra Madre with its various deep canyons and the clear, shallow waters of the three rivers that ran through Culiacan. Everyone stood as Acosta entered the room.

Crazy Ray sat at his kitchen table smoking a joint and drinking a beer. He had been up all night, two nights in a row, from the pain of the gunshot wound in his arm. After dousing it with peroxide, he smeared a tube of antibiotic ointment over it, and wrapped it in gauze and duct tape. He agonized over taking a chance of going to the emergency room or getting out of town immediately. He yawned when he opened his mouth to down two painkillers with a swig of his beer. The last thing he needed was an amputated arm.

He stared at his luggage that had been packed for days as if there might be an answer inside. *Stupid wetbacks, tried to rip me off.* He kicked the canvas shopping bag beside his chair with the 22-pounds of heroin.

His cell phone rang; it was a 622 area code, Jackson, Mississippi. He thought of Tony, his old cellmate, but it wasn't his number. The hell with it, let it rang; no way he was answering any unknown numbers.

His phone pinged showing a message. He hit voicemail and was surprised to hear the voice of Tony, *"Man, I don't know if you are mixed up in that heroin shootout or not, but my phone has been ringing all night, half of Mexico is looking for you. Courtesy call, bro, you need to get out of Dodge, these are some pissed-off cartel hombres and they are coming for your ass, man."*

Crazy Ray's hand was shaking as he hit Call Back and got a recording, *"This number is no longer in service . . ."* He jumped up and slammed the phone down on the table, knocking his beer to the floor, and then kicked it across the room.

On the inside of the pantry door, hanging from a coat-hook by its sling, was the M4 assault rifle he had bought from Boone. He removed the M4 and three fully loaded 30-round magazines from a shelf and placed them on the kitchen table. He pressed the magazine release on the M4 and checked the mag to make sure it was fully loaded, jammed it back in, and checked to make sure there was one in the chamber.

He sat on the side of the bed yawning, his eyes heavy as he fought to stay awake a little longer to finish his final preparations. He checked his backpack with the $25,000 from the sale of the Land Rover, the $50,000 from the Mexicans, and the shopping bag full of heroin on the floor beside his bed. His Glock-17 with 3-mags was on his bedside table and his M2 was leaning against the shopping bag . . . let the *car'tel* come, I'm ready for them. They know nothing about me. They may know my name but not where I live. I'm out of here in the morning and they'll never find me . . .

He fell back across the bed, dead asleep.

Pedro was parked outside the chain link fence of the Memphis downtown airport. He was thinking about the power of a single hundred-dollar bill as he took the last hit from a roach he was smoking earlier. A quick flash of a hundred-dollar bill was like a shot of Pentothal when questioning the druggies that said they didn't know Tito. Soon there was a line waiting to tell him all he wanted to know and two names kept popping up, Crazy Ray Flynn and his friend Dago.

Pedro heard the low whine of a jet engine overhead and saw the small Citation Mustang, four passenger seats and approved for single-pilot operation, banking for a final approach. The downtown airport was an easy FBO to find from the sky—only one runway, running parallel next to the Mississippi River. He watched as the sun set on the west bank of the river, flipped what was left of the roach out the window, and turned the lights on as he eased the rental car through the open gate and out onto the tarmac. He waited till the small jet taxied up to the gas pumps, parked, and the door swung open. Pedro hurried over to the plane as Ramón Acosta, Juan Carlos' younger brother, carefully stepped down onto the tarmac carrying a briefcase.

"Look at those steps," Ramón said, as he handed his roller bag to Pedro, "they're like something you would buy at a Dollar Store, worst than that, it don't even have a toilet, just a slop jar and without a door . . . I'm going to take a piss." Pedro heard Ramón mumbling about a three million dollar airplane as he walked off towards the office.

On the drive to the motel, Pedro brought Ramón up to date. He told him there was a stakeout on the house where this Crazy Ray and Dago lived and wasn't sure it was the DEA or local police watching. Fortunately, there was a house for rent on the corner across the street and he rented it after paying the first and last month's rent plus a deposit. They had a perfect view of the front and one side of the house and there was parking in the back.

They had only seen Crazy Ray, tall and skinny with red hair, but no Dago or his truck. Dago's description was a big guy, over six feet, about 250 pounds, and drove a red pickup. They saw Crazy Ray a couple of times, followed him to a neighborhood store and talked to the clerk after he left. The clerk said *he* didn't call him *Crazy* Ray, but a lot of people did, and that Crazy Ray and Dago were regulars at the store and lived together down the street. He hadn't seen Dago in two or three days and clammed up when asked what Crazy Ray had bought. The clerk stared at me then looked at a video camera in the corner and asked if I wanted to buy something. I slid a Benjamin across the counter and he punched a couple of keys on his register and handed me a receipt: cigarettes, beer, newspaper, hydrogen peroxide, Betadine, and two rolls of gauze.

We figured he must have been wounded in the shootout and sure enough, I saw him about two hours ago, he came out of the house in a tee shirt with two bags and loaded them in the Beatle Volkswagen, his left arm was bandaged. We thought he might be getting ready to run, but no movement since then.

"Who's watching Maria?"

"We have a full time 24-hour guard service patrolling the grounds." Pedro said.

"So, these are the two bums Tito ratted out for a kidnapping charge?"

"That's the information I got, and three others confirmed it."

"I remember that name Crazy Ray, it was years ago. The DEA caught

Tito with a truckload of drugs, and the Feds gave him a stay-out-of-jail card to roll over on the kidnapping case."

"That was before my time."

"I told Juan Carlos back then, when you drop a dime on someone it always comes back to bite you in the ass. You know what he said about Tito?"

"What?"

"*Debil! Weak!* Ramón pointed to his temple . . . but what can he do?"

"Yeah, it's family." Pedro looked over and saw a grimace on Ramón's face, "What's wrong?" He asked.

"I don't like it that no one has seen this goon Dago, or his truck. Let's put another man over at Maria's, *inside* the house with her. I don't care how much hell she raises, if something happens to my niece, Juan Carlos is subject to kill both of us."

"She's not going to like it, but I'm with you, I'll do it right away."

"Just tell her it's only for a couple of days. This shootout at *O. K. Corral* has started a wildfire and its raging way too close to Juan Carlos, and his orders to me were to snuff it out, immediately. If I can't get them together, I'll do Crazy Ray while we've got him."

"What about the Feds, the stakeout?"

"Don't worry, I brought just what I need. They'll never know we were here."

"When do you want to do him?"

"Tonight."

Ramón sat upright abruptly thinking he had overslept. It was pitch dark and deadly quiet. He pushed himself out of the old recliner that was left in the rental house and look at his cell phone; the time was 2:55 a.m. He had set his alarm for 3 a.m. and now moved the alarm button to off. Why bother setting an alarm, he thought, he always woke up before it went off. Walking into the front room he saw Pedro looking through the window blinds with his binoculars, "Anything going on?"

"Nada. Our stakeout pals down the street changed shifts around midnight, but no changes at the house, not even a light on."

Ramón placed his roller-bag on the Formica bar top that separated the kitchen from the front room, unzipped the bag and folded the top back. "Let me see those binoculars."

Pedro handed Ramón the binoculars, "Wait for me, I got to pee and I don't want to miss this."

Ramón stuck the binoculars between the two opened slats in the blind and focused in on the driver of the stakeout car. He appeared to be sleeping, his head propped against the door window with a baseball style cap pulled down over his forehead. He moved the binoculars across the street and scanned the house, each window and door, and stopped on the silver painted gas meter piped up against the side of the house. One pipe went into the ground and another ran along the side of the house and entered the bottom of the chimney. He moved the binoculars up the chimney and focused in on the top; there was no chimney cap.

Pedro watched as Ramón removed each item from his roller bag placing them on the bar top. The first was two red bars of the plastic explosive Semtex, a little over two pounds, followed by a hybrid quadcopter drone, he called the Raven. He unfolded the four arms on the drone, turning each propeller making sure they were free, wiped the camera lens, and removed the transmitter with two joysticks for controls and a six by eight inch viewing screen.

"Semtex, isn't that dangerous stuff, like dynamite?" Pedro said.

"Kind of."

"I was thinking about that fifty grand and the ten kilos of heroin, that's a lot of money?"

"Not my concern." Ramón continued to unroll strips of duct tape, picked up the two bars of Semtex, taped them together, and inserted two pencil-size copper tubes into the bars.

"What are those?" Pedro asked.

"They're called Slappers, a new type of remote detonators." He opened the wire cage on the bottom of the drone and placed the two bars of Semtex. Closed the spring-loaded latch on the cage and nodded at a lone window facing the back of the house, "Open that window over there."

Holding the remote controller with both hands, Ramón flipped the power switch on and the Raven's small LED light came on, the motors started turning the four propellers, and Ramon hovered the drone about six-inches above the bar. He pushed the joystick forward and out the window it flew.

Pedro watched the iPad-like screen over Ramon's shoulder as the drone flew down the street, stopped above the stakeout car, and slowly descended hovering in front of the windshield. You could see all the features of the sleeping driver as Ramon pushed a button on the controller and the camera took a close-up picture.

"Wow, that's worth a little blackmail money." Pedro said.

"He won't be sleeping long." Ramon moved the two joysticks and the drone accelerated upward, raced across the sky and hovered about 30-feet above Crazy Ray's house. He adjusted the wide-angle lens on the camera, moved the controls to yaw, and watched the drone spin as it reconnoitered the surroundings of the house.

Being a gamer, Ramon was a natural when he switched to flying drones and had even raced one of his drones at the *World Drone Prix*, in Dubai, the world's biggest and most lucrative drone race. The total prize fund was $1 million US dollars and flying speeds in access of 120 mph.

Ramon, with great dexterity, hovered his custom made drone one foot above the chimney, flip the drop switch that opened the cage like bomb bay doors, and the two pounds of Semtex tumbled down the chimney. Ramon counted to three, "Bombs away" he said and pressed the remote detonator button on the transmitter.

They waited.

"What happened?" Pedro asked.

Ramon pressed the button again, the red power light flashed but no explosion. He walked across the room to the window closest to the house, pointed the transmitter in a direct line to the house across the street, and pushed the button for a third time. No blast.

"What's wrong, Ramon?"

"Don't know, but I've going to find out."

Pedro followed Ramon over to his roller bag and watched as he removed a wooden box with four nano-drones called Butterflies, each 9 cm, about 3.5 inches square. He took one out and placed it in the palm of his hand, checked the tiny HD camera lens and the four, less than an inch long, rotor blades. He attached his iPhone to the remote controller, opened the Butterfly app, and switch on the drone. With the miniature joystick he flew the Butterfly out the window, across the street, and stopped it hovering over the chimney.

"What are you doing with that?" Pedro asked.

"Watch." Ramon held his iPhone up so Pedro could see the Butterfly spinning in a yaw motion, and watched its slow descent into the dark chimney. Two LED lights came on and lit up the chimney as it spun downward in a circle of light and hovered two feet above where a damper should be. Resting deep into a batt of pink insulation, installed to completely seal off the hole where the old damper had been removed, were the two bars of red Semtex with the detonators still intact.

"Man! Look at that, this is *I Spy* stuff. You can see the smallest details."

"The government make some drones as small as a fly, you never know there in the room." Ramon hit the return-to-home button and watched as the Butterfly flew automatically back to the house, through the widow, and landed in his hand.

"What now?" Pedro asked.

"Now the payload." Ramon carefully removed a small triple-ought size capsule—one inch long—wrapped in a roll of cotton, and filled with nitroglycerin, absorbents, and a stabilizer. "Nitro. Extremely shock sensitive." Ramon said as he tore a paper straw in half, cautiously inserted the capsule in one end and sealed the end with small pieces of cotton. With the opened end, he poured in a teaspoon full of black gunpowder, stuck a slow-burning fuse in, packed it with cotton, and taped it to the Butterfly. "Hold out your hand," he said to Pedro. "It won't go off unless you drop it."

Pedro used both hands as he watched Ramon remove a small box of wooden matches. "You're not going to light the fuse while I'm holding it . . . "

"It's a slow burning fuse, 100 seconds. We have plenty of time." Ramon picked up the remote controller, flipped the power switch to on, turned off the drone's return-to-home button, set the stopwatch on his phone, and lit the fuse. With great care, he maneuvered the slow moving Butterfly across the room, out the window, and to the house across the street. He hovered the Butterfly with its burning fuse inches above the chimney and counted down to the last few seconds, "10, 9, 8, 7, 6," and on the count of 5, he flipped the power switch to off.

The Butterfly fell. In full autorotation it floated downward as the burning fuse set fire to the gunpowder that started a chain of explosives: the gunpowder setoff the nitro, the nitro ignited the Semtex, and the Semtex blew out the bottom of the chimney, the gas piping, and the gas meter, spewing natural gas throughout the house. The blast wave from the explosion raddled the windows and shook the floors of the house Ramon and Pedro were standing on.

Shocked and frozen in place from the power of the exploding gas, they watched as a second explosion blew out all the windows and doors of the house across the street. A roiling black cloud engulfed the house and mushroomed into the sky, raining debris up and down the street. When the cloud cleared, there was no house, just a flat field of debris.

"Let's get out of here." Pedro shouted.

"Not yet. Get everything of ours out of here, put it all in the car, and I mean everything. We'll leave when all the fire equipment, police, and ambulances get here. No one will even notice us."

On the way to the airport, Pedro asked, "Is the airport open this time of the morning?"

"I doubt it, why?"

"You just drive in and fly off?"

"Yeah, there's no tower."

"What keeps someone from stealing your plane?"

"Nothing, it's just like your car in a parking lot."

"How do you see when you take off and land?"

"PAL, pilot activated lights. I turn the runway lights on with my radio and they go off automatically 15 minutes later."

"What about Tito and this other guy, Dago?"

"Not my concern. Tito's money is gone, his drugs are gone, and his SUV is gone; 3 plus 1 is 4, Tito's gone, no matter how you add it up. If you find this Dago character, I'll come back."

They notice a white pickup truck parked under a streetlight when they pulled in the parking lot of the downtown airport. They watched as bundles of newspapers were being tossed to the ground while men, women, boys and girls hustled to get their papers for delivery.

A young Mexican girl saw Ramon opening the gate and shouted in Spanish, "Want to buy a paper mister, two bodies found in the river." She held up one of the papers she was wrapping.

Ramon was about to wave her off but the two bodies in the river perked his curiosity and he waved her over. He reached for the paper and she snatched it back.

"Two bucks, mister."

He smiled, gave her a five, and waved Pedro through the gate. Walking to the plane he unwrapped the paper and read the headlines,

TWO BODIES FOUND IN THE MISSISSIPPI RIVER

Turning to page two he found a small follow-up article,

Two male bodies were found early this morning floating in the Mississippi River tied together with a ski rope. One body was identified from his driver's license as Tito Estrada.

He looked up and saw Pedro loading his briefcase and roller bag into the plane and continued reading,

The second body is a white male, without any identification, with bleached hair and the name "Dago" tattooed on his forearm. If anyone has any information regarding this story please contact the Memphis Police Department or this newspaper.

Ramon stopped walking and stood next to a 55-gallon barrel painted yellow and marked trash. He was in deep thought for a few minutes, and then looked up at the sky. It was the break of dawn; the sun was peaking over the horizon and slowly erasing the stars from the skies. He made the sign of the cross, tossed the newspaper in the trash barrel and spoke to the heavens, "great day for flying."

"What's up, something in the paper?" Pedro asked Ramon as he walked up.

"Nada. Not my concern." He climbed the three steps and shut the door.

CHAPTER 24

Mack had checked out of the Garden Hotel and was ready to fly back to Key West. He was drinking coffee and waiting on Irish in the new, high-end, micro-grocery store on the Stanford campus right behind the Law School. She was next door at Munger Graduate Residence where she would live for the next three years.

He watched as two students raced to open the door, bowing, and showing off when they saw Irish. Mack had finally come to appreciate the fact that she was a grown woman now. People stopped and noticed her wherever she went, and with her the long blonde hair, sun-kissed skin, and blue eyes, she would soon be misjudged as a California girl.

"Your entourage?" Mack said.

Irish looked back at the two boys and waved. "Not my type. Like you, I'm picky."

"You want something to drink?"

"No thanks, Dad, I've got to run to the library. They have some used law books that I need for my classes and they are in big demand." She pulled him up from his chair, "Come on, I got time to walk you to your car."

Mack drove into the Palo Alto Airport parking lot, parked in a reserved space for return rental cars, and while inside check the weather again. While walking to his plane his phone rang and on the screen he saw the name McKenzie O'Connor, he smiled, eager to talk to her again. "Good morning," he said.

"Good morning, to you. Have you left yet?"

"I'm standing in front of my plane as we speak. Are you still at the airport, is something wrong?"

"Yes, my plane was delayed and now we were just notified the flight has been cancelled and there's not another flight out of here till tomorrow?"

"My offer to fly you home is still open."

"Are you sure?"

"Of course, just know that it's a 12 hour flight, 1,800 miles to Memphis. My little puddle jumper cruises at 180 mph. Your commercial flight is over three times faster.

"More time for us to spend together."

Ooh-rah. My exact thought. "Are you still at the San Jose Airport?"

"Yes. I checked and they have a shuttle leaving here for Stanford in thirty minutes, I can take that."

"No, no, I'll pick you up there. Let me find out where you can meet me and I'll call you right back."

Mack called San Jose Airport and got the number of Signature Flight Support, a small upscale FBO. He called McKenzie back and told her to go to Terminal-A at the information kiosk, and a driver from Signature will meet you there and shuttle you across the airfield to their offices. Wait there and I'll park out front and come get you.

"San Jose Tower, Bonanza One Zero Seven Echo Sierra, you are clear to land on runway two seven left."

"Bonanza One Zero Seven Echo Sierra, landing on two seven left."

"Bonanza Echo Sierra contact ground 121.9."

"121.9, Bonanza Echo Sierra."

Ground control cleared Mack to taxi across two runways to the FBO. He parked the plane and as he walked to the office he saw McKenzie walking to meet him. She was dressed in tight fitting jean, a light pink sweater, and running shoes pulling a roller bag. He thought of the old saying, *'She'd look good in anything, even a potato sack.'*

Mack knew that McKenzie was everything he could ever want corporeally, from head to toe, but were they compatible, like-minded? They had not spent a lot of time together and never had sex with each other. It had been many years since Mack flew her down to Key West for Fantasy Fest and they ran into her husband with his male lover; what a fiasco that was. There was no better way to find out if they were a match than being encapsulated in a metal tube for 12 hours or more.

"That was quick." She said walking up to Mack.

"A few of the advantages of a small plane."

"Nice plane, is it new?"

"No, it's an old classic, completely restored; engine, electronics, interior, and new paint."

"Beautiful, it reminds me of my Porsche.

"I hope you don't mind, I changed into something more comfortable."

Mack hiked up his jeans, "I'm all about comfort. Did you go to ladies room?"

Puzzled, she asked, "You mean to change?"

"No," he nodded to the plane. "No toilet, no place to pull over and stop. A few of the disadvantages."

"I'm good." She grabbed his arm and pulled him toward the plane singing and humming,

We're off to see the Wizard
The wonderful Wizard of Oz
We hear he is a whiz of a wiz
If ever a wiz there was . . .

Mack leveled the plane off at 9,500 feet, set the airspeed at 160 knots, and made adjustments to his storm-cope. "I filed a flight plan at Palo Alto before I left and there radar showed a heavy storm will be pushing us all the way to Santa Fe." Mack pointed to his storm-scope, which was painting green, yellow, and red splotches. "Hopefully we can stay out in front of it."

"What happens if we can't?"

"We land, or go around it."

"This is cool, my first time in a small plane, you get to see everything"

"Well, let's hope we have a lot more 'first times' together. Would you like to fly the plane?"

"Can I?"

"Sure, put your hands on the yoke, grip it lightly, it's similar to a steering wheel. When I move it you can feel the reaction of the airplane. Let's say we get a call from ATC, Air Traffic Control, to go to 10,000 feet. We pull back slowly and watch the altimeters there on the instrument panel move from 9,500 to 10,000 feet." Mack took his hands off the yoke. "Now I want you to slowly push the yoke forward and the nose will drop a little until we reach

9,500 feet again and we level off."

"Oh, how was that?"

"Good, now, we get another call from ATC to change our heading from 112 degrees to 90 degrees. We were pointed toward Santa Fe, now we turn a little left toward Denver." Mack leaned forward and tapped on the Heading Indicator. "This is similar to a compass, now bring us back to Santa Fe, a heading of 112 degrees.

"Great, that's it." Mack raised his hands. "You are flying the plane now. I'm going in the back and take a nap, wake me if you need anything."

"No you're not! Don't you dare leave me."

"Okay, you keep flying and I'll go over a couple of things you'll need to know if I have a heart attack while flying."

"Don't say things like that. Do you have a bad heart?"

"No, fortunately I'm very healthy. How about you?"

"What do you think?"

"If looks is any measure I'd say you where top-shelf."

McKenzie reached over and squeezed his hand, "Good answer. My last physical I passed with flying colors, and my Doc said, 'compared to his other patients my age, I could pass for 20 years younger.'"

"How old are you?"

"Really? I would have thought you knew better than to ask that. Let's just say I'm younger than you are."

"Touché!"

"I have a question, how do planes keep from running into each other?"

"Watch you altimeter, you're climbing, keep it at 9,500. In general aviation, not passenger airlines or transports like FedEx, it's like driving a car except we're layered at different elevations. We are flying VFR, Visual Flight Rules, that means we have to always be able to see the ground and continuously looking for other planes." He pointed to the compass like Heading Indicator on the instrument panel again, "The rule for how high to fly is simple, if you are flying anywhere between 000-degrees north to 179-degrees south, you must fly an *odd*-thousand plus 500 feet, like 3,500 feet, 5,500 feet, or 7,500 feet. If another plane is coming toward us, 180 degrees to 359 degrees, they must fly an *even*-thousand plus 500, like 4,500, 6,500, or 8,500.

"What? Say that again, I don't understand."

"What direction are we flying now?" Mack pointed to the Heading Indicator, "The little plane's nose on the indicator is pointed to what number?"

"112?"

"Right, so that number is between zero and 179 degrees. Now, what altitude are we flying?" Mack pointed to the Altimeter.

"9,500 feet."

"Right. So we are flying an odd thousand, 9,000 plus 500 feet. This simple rule will keep planes flying opposite directions separated by 1,000 feet. An easy way to remember is 'Odd North East.'"

"I love this, it's like being on a magic carpet, you can see everything, and your plane is just like my little Porsche, sensitive to the touch and fast."

"You're a natural. I've never seen anyone fly so straight and level the first time with the controls. If you want, you can land it in Santa Fe when we stop for gas."

"I'm game if you are."

Mack noticed her fingertips were whitening as she griped the yoke. "Relax." He pushed the button for the autopilot to take over and put his hand on hers, "You can take a break now, it will fly itself."

"Wow," She stretched her fingers. "I didn't know I was so tense. Your hand is so warm. Why hasn't a good-looking man like you remarried?"

"Why hasn't a good-looking women like you remarried?"

"You first."

"At this age it's hard to find someone compatible."

"What are you looking for?"

"Well, I'm really not looking per se, it's way too much trouble. What's the saying, 'Being with no one is better than being with the wrong one. Sometimes those who fly alone are the ones with the strongest wings.'"

"But you're not flying alone today."

"You are an exception."

"Thank you, kind sir. So, you would never marry again?"

"I wouldn't say that, but the pickings are slim. What about you, why haven't you remarried?"

"I would like to find *someone*. I get tired of going places by myself. Most of the men I meet are married, and what's left is too young, too old, misogynistic, drinks too much, between jobs, overweight smoker, unkempt and unhealthy and with ED."

"That sounds like my history with women, except you left out one four letter word, *sane*."

"I know, sometimes I feel like an alien from another planet. It's sad, makes me sound like a prima donna, that I'm some perfect Barbie doll. But the facts are, those are my minimum requirements to date, and I'm willing to go DUTCH."

"I'm not married, I don't smoke, and I drink very little. I'm not overweight, I shower regularly and brush my teeth twice a day, and it's been awhile but I'm sure I don't suffer from ED."

McKenzie laughed and leaned over and kissed him on his cheek, "That's why I'm here."

"Santa Fe Tower, Bonanza One Zero Seven Echo Sierra you are clear to land on runway two zero."

"Bonanza One Zero Seven Echo Sierra, landing on two zero."

"Bonanza Echo Sierra contact ground 121.7."

"Bonanza Echo Sierra 121.7."

Dark clouds were overhead and raindrops started peppering the windshield. "Okay, the airfield is a little under 7,000 feet elevation, the rain is no problem, but at this altitude there's a pretty good crosswind blowing. When you turn on final approach you will feel the crosswind and you'll need to crab the plane all the way down to the landing zone. We can't land the plane sideways so just before touchdown, you'll push your right rudder pedal to line the plane up with the runway centerline for landing. Do you want me to land it or you want to try it yourself?"

"No, I got it as long as you . . . what do you call it, cover me?"

"No, but that would nice." Mack laughed, "The word is 'shadow.'"

"Aw, shucks." McKenzie said with a wicked smile.

Mack's hands *shadowed* the yoke lightly in case he had to take over immediately. "You're doing great, that was a nice turn. You are on final approach now, you see the runway?"

"Yes."

He pointed to the throttle, "Cut your speed a little and keep the nose of the plane pointed at the number 20 on the runway . . . that's good. You're lined up perfect. Now I want you to use the trim for the decent and glide right to the number 20 for touchdown.

"Let's slow it up a little more, add 20 degrees of flaps," Mack pointed to the handle for the flaps, "the first notch."

"I'm trying to hold it on the runway number, but the wind keeps blowing me off course."

"That's the crosswinds, slowly dip your wing into it a little . . . hold it there, now push your right rudder to line up with the centerline."

McKenzie overshot the runway's second set of landing zone markers, about 800 feet in front of the runway number 20, then one wheel touched down on the runway and the plane bounced back into the air crabbing almost sideways as it past the aiming point landing markers. "Push your right rudder pedal." The airplane corrected itself back to the centerline and hovered a little before dropping about five feet onto the runway.

Mack switched the radio to ground control and pointed for McKenzie to taxi toward the man standing under an umbrella in front of the FBO waving. As they both hurried from the plane the roiling black clouds above opened up with thunder and lightning and a downpour of blowing rain.

Inside, standing at the counter, Mack order gas and checked the weather while McKenzie headed for the ladies room. Mack scanned the pilot's weather forecast for Santa Fe and it was marked "NF," meaning weather was "no factor." There was, however, a notice of an area of isolated thunderstorms moving up from the Gulf.

"I'm ready when you are," McKenzie said as she bounced into the pilot's lounge.

"Bad news, that thunderstorm that was pushing us is scheduled to collide with a strong storm moving up from the Gulf of Mexico within the hour. The weather forecast is for severe weather, possible large hail over Santa Fe and the surrounding area for the next 12 hours. We're socked in. I'm going next door to check and see if they have any hangar space to park the plane. You want to wait in here?"

"Sure," McKenzie said. She watched Mack leave, removed her cell phone and sat in one of the recliners. She opened Google search and typed in hotels in Santa Fe. Scrolling down she stopped on a five-star rated B&B and opened their website:

A rich history resides at The Black Horse Inn. Created by noted poet, translator and essayist, Walter Brenner. He created his rambling adobe villa, constructed in Spanish-Pueblo Revival style, from a core of rooms that date to the early 1800's. It is now considered one of Santa Fe's most important historical estates. With its signature portico, towering pine trees, magnificent rock terraces, and lush gardens filled with lilacs, wild roses, and other flowers, the Inn offers guests a bucolic retreat close to the center of Santa Fe. Brenner was famous—or infamous—for the riotous parties he hosted in this estate.

They had one room available for the night, a suite with a king size bed. She had her credit card out and was reading the number before he was ready.

"Ms. O'Connor, if you are at the airport we have a driver dropping off a couple of guest in about ten minutes and we can have her pick you up?"

"Thank you so much, you are a sweetie." McKenzie said. She thought she heard the whispered response,

"Yes . . . I know."

McKenzie opened her briefcase, stuffed her wallet back in and removed a windbreaker. She stood as Mack hurried out of the rain into the pilot's lounge.

"The temperature's dropping. I got the plane in a hangar, now we need to find *us* a hangar for the night."

"No problem, I found us a place, my treat. A pink Jeep will be here in ten minutes to pick us up."

Mack took her windbreaker and held it for her to slip on. "A pink jeep?"

McKenzie shrugged her shoulders and zipped up the jacket, "That's what 'Charlie' the gatekeeper said."

The door opened to the pilot's lounge and a small young girl entered with an umbrella, "Ms. O'Connor?"

"Yes."

"I'm here to take you to the inn."

McKenzie sat in the front seat next to the driver, who was sitting on a foam cushion, stretching her torso to see over the steering wheel. During the drive she welcomed them to the Black Horse Inn, introduced herself as Erin, and said she lived with her father, Charlie, and that he and his partner, Alan, were the owners of the Inn.

"Are you in school, Erin?" Mack said.

"I home study online." She turned off the main road onto a steep gravel road. She stomped the clutch and jerked the floor shift down into first gear as the jeep tried to skid off the road.

"How old are you," Mack said.

"How old do you think I am?" Erin said as she strained to see through the rain beating against the windshield as she shifted into second gear.

McKenzie turned to the backseat, "Mack, let her drive."

"I'm fifteen." Erin said, dodging a pothole.

McKenzie double-checked to make sure her seatbelt was securely fastened.

After about a mile of in and out turns through a grove of tall pine trees, Erin eased the jeep under the porte-cochere were her father stood waiting on the steps. He opened the door for McKenzie, "Welcome, Ms. O'Connor to The Black Horse Inn on this cold, rainy night."

McKenzie felt the rich and cozy ambiance immediately as she walked through the double doors into what seemed like someone's private living room. With low, round wood beam ceilings, soft recessed lighting, and a wide stone fireplace with burning logs, it was living up to its five-star rating.

After checking in, Charlie led them down a hallway to the Cantina, "Your suite will be ready within minutes, we are making sure everything is being refreshed. The first drink is on the house. The bartender is gone for the night, but I make a mean martini?"

The Cantina was recessed two steps lower than the hallway. A long wooden bar with a copper top stretched from one wall to the other. Charlie stoked the dwindling fire in the fireplace and placed a small log on the ignited embers.

"I need a drink after that landing," McKenzie said. "Make mine a double and very dry, please."

"It wasn't that bad, you made it down on the first try." Mack said.

"Martini, Mack?" Charlie said.

"You got a single malt?"

"Macallan?"

"Yes sir-re, I'll pay for a double."

"It's all on the house. Neat?"

"Neat," Mack said. "Pour one for yourself on me, and please join us." Mack sat on the couch with McKenzie in front of the fireplace.

Charlie placed their drinks on the coffee table in front of them with a cheese plate, toasted pita bread, some hummus, and a sundry of vegetable sticks. He sat in a stuffed chair at the end of the couch and lifted his drink, "Cheers."

"Wow! I needed that," McKenzie said after a hefty swallow. "Perfect martini."

After a short period of chitchat, they were shocked to find that Charlie was from Memphis, and that Erin was born there. Small world, they all agreed. Charlie fixed them another round of drinks and told them about owning a small beauty shop in Memphis and a half interest in a late night gay bar called the Rainbow Lounge.

"Dad." They all turned to see Erin standing in the doorway with an oversized golf umbrellas as tall as she was. "Their suite's ready. I'll walk them up, it's still raining hard."

Inside their small adobe cottage the Spanish-Pueblo style continued. The concrete floors were stained in a buckskin design, resembling worn leather. The burning logs sent a warm glow across the room and highlighted the colorful and vibrant reds, turquoise, and gold colored Aztec area rugs that donned the floors.

"Another wood burning fireplace, I've never seen so many fireplaces; nice touch though." McKenzie said.

"It's all original." Mack said staring at the king-size bed, "the only way to heat the places back then."

"Their website said it was built in the early 1800's. I wonder what they did for air conditioning?" McKenzie said from the bathroom while turning on the faucets of the vintage claw-foot tub. She screwed the top off a small sample bottle of lavender bubble bath, poured some in her hand, smelled it and emptied the bottle into the running water. She heard Mack mumble something and walked back into the bedroom carrying two terrycloth robes. He was still standing in the same place staring at the king-size bed. She imagined what he was thinking.

"This was the only room they had for the night. I don't see a bundling board," she said smiling, "We'll just have to be on the honor system." She sat on the side of the bed with her back to him, removed her running shoes and socks, her sweater and bra, and stood to slowly work her jeans down over her hips. "I'm going to take a hot bath."

Mack watched her shapely hips swaying as she walked to the bathroom dragging her robe. She left the door partially opened. His imagination was on a roller coaster of fantasies.

Should he just barge right in? Is the half-open door an invitation? Are you becoming a hoary old man? Grow some balls big boy and remember what Mark Twain said: "Twenty years from now you will be more disappointed by the things you didn't do than by the ones you did do."

Mack kicked off his shoes, stripped down to bareness, grabbed the white robe and charged to the bathroom. Just short of the door he stopped, turned back and tossed the robe on the bed, walked over to the kitchenette and removed two splits of champagne from the mini-fridge. Standing in front of the half-opened bathroom door, a bottle of champagne in each hand, he eased the door open with his foot and stepped inside.

McKenzie was sunk down into the tub to her neck, covered with Vita bubbles. She sat up and scanned Mack from head to toes, "My, my, my . . . this is what I call first-class room service."

CHAPTER 25

At 9,500 feet altitude, a cruising speed of 160 knots, and a heading of 90-degrees, Mack followed I-40 to Memphis. The bright sun had warmed up the cockpit and the steady hum of the engine had lulled McKenzie into a deep sleep. Mack pushed his sunglasses back on his head and studied McKenzie's face, not a wrinkle or a blemish. Very little makeup, that "peaches and cream" look, a real asset for someone her age. He leaned over perusing around her ear and forehead for signs of surgery. A minty and citrusy smell lured him in closer, his nose almost touching while his hot breathe wafted over her face.

Her eyes popped opened, "What!" she said, growling at him like prey.

He jerked back from her. "What?" he said.

"What were you doing?"

"Admiring your beauty."

"Really?"

"Really."

She sat up rubbing her eyes, "That sun was so warm it put me right to sleep. Did you get sleepy?"

"Yes, but your snoring kept me awake."

She punched him on the shoulder, "I don't snore. How long have I been sleeping?"

"A couple hours."

"No wonder, you kept me up all night."

"You complaining?"

"Nooo. You were . . . it was . . . memorable."

"Memorable? That's it?"

"As was breakfast this morning."

"Are you talking about the food or something else?"

"What do you think?" She reached over and squeezed his inner thigh, "You were very altruistic. I'm still basking in the afterglow from last night and this morning. How about you?"

"How about me what? Memorable? Altruistic? That sounds a little dispassionate don't you think?"

"Well shoot, I was hoping you enjoyed it as much as I did? Did I misread those primal sounds coming from you last night?"

"No, of course not. You were everything I fantasied about, a real wild woman. You have it all; you're beautiful, have a great body, super intelligent, and with all that you are a sex goddess. I'm still in shock, why am I so lucky? With all the available men out there, you chose me?"

"Okay, okay, enough of your Irish malarkey."

"I meant every word."

"Did you really fantasize about me? What was your fantasy?"

"Black leather mask, a whip, handcuffs . . . things like that."

"No!"

"Look," Mack pointed straight ahead. "Thar she blows, the mighty Mississippi River. We'll have to land at Memphis International; the small downtown airport is closed due to runway repairs. You want to take a shot of landing at a busy airport?"

"Sure, why not."

"I got the radio, you take the controls."

"Memphis approach, Bonanza one zero seven echo sierra, I have the airport in sight."

"Bonanza echo sierra, Memphis approach, cleared visual approach for runway one eight Charlie, traffic one o'clock five miles west bound, American Airbus five two eight delta november descending through 6,000."

"Memphis approach, I have the American Airbus in sight."

"Bonanza echo sierra, you are six miles out, turn left to a heading of two three zero to join Delta triple seven. Follow that traffic, caution wake turbulence, clear visual approach for runway one eight Charlie, contact Memphis tower one one niner point seven."

"Memphis approach, Bonanza echo sierra following Delta triple seven to runway one eight Charlie, Memphis tower one one niner point seven."

"Better let me take the controls, we may have some wake turbulence from that big boy in front of us." Mack switched the radio frequency to Memphis tower.

"Memphis tower, Bonanza echo sierra following Delta triple seven traffic to land on one eight Charlie."

"What's wake turbulence?" McKenzie asked.

"It's what trails behind an airplanes after a landing or taking off. The big body airplanes, what they call "heavy" aircraft, like the triple seven in front of us, generate a strong rotating air mass from both wingtips, sometimes a whirlwind turbulence that's equal to a tornado."

"Why not wait till it's out of the way?"

"Busy airport. With all the FedEx planes mixed in with the commercial flights, doesn't take long for them to get backed up."

"Bonanza echo sierra you are clear to land behind Delta triple seven on one eight Charlie. You need to tighten it up, you are lagging too far behind."

"Memphis Tower, Bonanza echo sierra using caution to avoid wake turbulence."

"Close it up to two miles Grandpa, you're not the only one landing today, there's a line of planes sequenced behind you on final."

"Damn it, he's pushing me."

"Can't we go around?" McKenzie said.

Mack pushed the nose down and closed within two mile of the triple seven.

"Memphis Tower, Bonanza echo closing to two miles. I think I'm too close."

Mack figured he would maintain his altitude, set the trim on a steep glideslope, and land a little hot in front of where the Airbus touched down and avoid its turbulence.

He watched as the triple seven glided pass the threshold landing marker, pass the first and second touchdown zone, and finally landed on the last touchdown marker on the runway.

Not good. The triple seven ate up too much runway for Mack to land in front of where it touched down and it was too late for a go-around. The gray wake turbulence from Delta triple seven filled the sky in front of Mack, he shouted, "HOLD ON!"

The wind-force was like a car smashing into a concrete wall at a 100 mph. The old plane shook and rattled as if coming apart, but it held together as Mack fought to keep it in the air. It was like a small bird caught in the middle of a tornado, tossed and slammed in different directions. The vortices pushed the nose of the plane straight up, lifting it over a thousand feet then rolled it upside down, over and over as the blast of the stall horn and McKenzie's screams filled the cabin. Mack lost all control of the plane, his body frozen, his arms and legs pinioned in place due to the G-force as the plane went into a death spiral, a corkscrewing dive toward the earth.

To keep from passing out, he had to get the blood that was forced to his legs back up to his brain again. This is where working out regularly paid its dividends. He squeezed his core muscles and the muscles in his legs as hard as he could, and sucked in sharp breaths every three seconds, forcing the blood back to his upper body. Now, with the fog clearing from his brain, he had to focus on getting out of this spin. He was not going back to Irish with his mutilated body stuffed in a plastic bag.

All his years of flying, and years of hands-on flight training from Sargent Buck Jones, his Marine mentor, raced through his mind like a spinning rolodex that stopped on the acronym PARE. A memory aid from NASA Technical Standards for spin recovery:

P-for Power. Mack cut the power to idle.

A-for Ailerons. He forced the yoke till the ailerons where neutral.

R-for Rudder. He held the right rudder peddle to the floor.

E-for Elevator. Mack shoved the yoke forward.

The plane stopped its rotation in clear skies with less than 500 feet from the ground. The vortices dissipated. Mack found the horizon, raised his landing gear, and shoved the throttle to maximum power while pulling back on the yoke as hard as he could, but careful not to stall the plane. At 100 feet from crashing, he recovered to a level attitude and immediately climbed to 1,000 feet.

He looked over at McKenzie, the blood was drained from her face and tears were on her cheeks. "You okay, kiddo?"

"Can I breathe now?" She squeezed his arm, "Hell of fight there, cowboy. You saved our bacon."

"Bonanza echo sierra, Memphis Tower, is you plane damaged, can you land?"

Mack's first thought was how he was going to kill a specific air traffic controller, but this was not the same controller, this was a female. Over the open airways was not the time for invective accusations, but he would find this controller, and they would have more than just a little talk.

"Memphis Tower, Bonanza echo, all is well. You got a place for me to land this bird?"

"Yes sir. Glad you're okay, and sorry about that turbulence. All traffic is in a holding pattern and you are clear to land on runway one eight Charlie. Contact ground control at 121.90.

"Memphis Tower, Bonanza echo landing on runway one eight Charlie. 121.90 ground."

CHAPTER 26

She could feel the soft hair from his chest against her back. She loved it that he slept in the spooning position with both arms wrapped around her, like a butterfly in a cocoon. His warm body radiating enough heat that she needed no covers. She moved his hand under her arm and placed it over her breast and pushed her bottom closer into his cupped pelvis. He stirred, turned a little, and draped his leg over hers. She felt his hardness between her legs.

Loud thunder woke her as rain and sleet slashed against the window. She sat up half-asleep, reached over feeling for Mack, but that side of the bed was cold and empty. Was she having a lucid dream? She pummeled her king-size pillow and fell back on to it dragging the covers with her. She pulled her legs up in the fetal position, her hands between her legs, and was shocked to feel wetness in her panties. *Wow. Nocturnal emissions . . . it had been years.*

McKenzie pulled the covers tight around her, closed her eyes, and tried to recreate the dream.

Mack had just landed his plane at Miami International Airport and was parking it at the FBO, Signature Flight Support, when his cell phone ranged. "Good morning, beautiful."

"Now that's the way I like to hear you answer the phone. Where are you?"

"Miami airport."

"I had a wonderful dream about you this morning . . . about us."

"You're still in the bed?"

"I'm luxuriating, trying to revive that dream."

"Must have been a good one?"

"Much more than good, you've spoiled me. I need you here to warm my bed, it's freezing. There's a foot of snow on the ground."

"I'm on my way. Uh-oh, my shuttle's here, I've got to run. I'll call you when I land at LaGuardia. Oh, I knew there was something else I wanted to tell you."

"What?"

"When I left Key West this morning it was 78 degrees."

"You are a mean man, Mack Shannon."

Mack tossed his flight jacket in the seat behind the driver, placed his roller bag in the luggage carrier, and hung his garment bag on the grab bar overhead. He told the shuttle driver he was flying Delta, and before taking his seat he sniffed his garment bag to see if his tux inside still had any lingering odors. It was practically a new tux and had been sealed for the past year in the dry cleaners plastic cover. He had sprayed it with Febreze and hung it outsize to air the mothball smell.

Mack's cell phone signaled a text and on the screen flashed a green shamrock emoji. His daughter Irish: "Where are you, Daddy?"

"Miami, Delta Airlines, waiting on my plane. Where are you?"

"On top of the world . . . 130 feet above the Pacific Ocean."

"The Ferris Wheel at the Sana Monica Beach Pier, right?"

"You're so smart, you know everything."

"I wouldn't say everything."

"How did you know?"

"I bribed a Leprechaun with a cup of gold coins to follow you everywhere."

"No Daddy, really, how did you know?"

"You told me you and your friend were driving down to her parents' house in Santa Monica and you said you were 130 feet over the Pacific Ocean. I've been on that Ferris wheel a couple of times before you were born."

"It's so beautiful, Daddy. It's about 80 degrees, sunny, and I can see all of the beach, north, south, and way out into the ocean. You know there's a snow storm in New York?"

"That's what I hear."

"What are you wearing?"

"Leather coat, jeans, cowboy boots . . . "

"That's not enough clothes, Daddy, you'll freeze."

"I'm not working outside in the weather, Irish, just walking to the subway and the train."

"Are you excited about seeing McKenzie?"

"Yes."

"You don't sound excited. You have your tux and shoes?"

"I have my tux, my tux shirt, and my bow tie. "

"Daddy, what about your tux shoes, tell me you're not wearing your cowboy boots with your tux?"

"What's wrong with that, they're black alligators, they're dressy, very tony."

"Not with a tux. Daddy, you're in New York, the fashion capital, everyone will be dressed to the tees New Years Eve."

"I'm not a New Yorker, Sweetheart, I'm a Southerner. I'm wearing my black gators. At $1,000 each, I'll be the best dressed at the party."

"You're right, Daddy, my bad. You are the most handsome man I know. I love you."

"I love you too. Got to run, the planes boarding. Be safe, there's lots of kooks out there."

Three hours later, Mack's nonstop flight touched down at LaGuardia. Immediately, he was caught up in the foot traffic without knowing if he was going in the right direction. He worked himself through the crowd and stood against the wall to get his bearing. People were rushing by in both directions, a blur, and speaking in different languages. He remembered reading as many as 800 languages are spoken in New York City and it was the most linguistically diverse city in the world with more than 3.2 million residents born outside the United States. *So much for immigration,* he thought.

He saw the directional arrow pointing down the escalator for luggage. He had no luggage, just carry-on, but knew it was the way to exit the airport. He saw an opening in the flow of traffic and jumped in.

He stood outside under a canopy and put his leather jacket on. People continued to bump into him without an apology. He placed his garment bag over the top of his roller bag and opened a subway map he'd picked up at a Kiosk inside. Busses, cabbies, trucks and cars roared past him, five lanes in one direction. Shouts, horns, sirens, and whistles filled the air. With all the hustle and bustle there was something magnetic about New York City. The energy was contagious and electrifying, percolating 24/7 at an unsettling level. Mack loved this change of pace from laid back Key West. He was thinking about getting back in the rat race . . .

"Can I help you, sir?"

"What?" Mack said to a tall dark man wearing a suit and a turban. He nodded to Mack's map.

"Oh, yeah, thanks." Mack pointed to the map, "It says here to catch bus Q70 from the airport to Woodside and . . ."

The man leaned in to look at Mack's map. "What is your destination, sir?"

Mack recognized the pleasing aroma of cloves. Instead of breath mints, his Aunt Irish always sucked on whole cloves. "I'm headed to East Hampton."

The man pointed to a yellow sign about 20 feet away, "That's where you catch the Q70 to Woodside Station. Come, first you must buy a Metro Card at the vending machine. There is one just inside the door." He walked Mack inside. "The busses are very clean, most are new, and they run about every 15 minutes."

Mack inserted a $5.00 bill in the machine and the man continued talking. "Very easy direction, the Q70's is a short ride to Woodside Station. There, you will buy a ticket and board the train on the Long Island Rail Road to East Hampton. You will have one transfer at Jamaica Station. "

As they walk back outside to the bus stop, Mack said, "No subway? Someone told me to take the subway."

"No subway. Bus, then train." The man half-bowed, "There is your bus now. Have a safe trip and travel with God's guidance."

"Thank you, sir." Mack said.

It was a short bus ride to 61st Street-Woodside. Mack exited the bus, crossed the street, and climbed the steps to the train platform. His train ticket to East Hampton was $21 bucks. Thirty minutes after he bought his ticket the train rolled in on one of their six tracks. The next stop was Jamaica Station, the busiest railroad station in North America. Mack hurried off the train, worked himself through the horde of people whizzing back and forth, and found the two-hour train ride to East Hampton. Now, relaxed on board, his race to make connections from airplane, to bus, to train had been an enjoyable adventure, and a drastic difference from his laid back lifestyle in Key West. Everyone he had encountered had been helpful and friendly; contrary to what he had been led to believe.

He took a deep breath, slowly exhaled, and closed his eyes to the hypnotic clicking of the iron wheels on the railroad tracks. Half asleep, his subconscious checked off the announcements of the small hamlets along the Atlantic Ocean: Wantagh, Massapequa, Babylon, Bridgehampton, etc. There was very little time to board or depart the train at each stop, so Mack had imprinted Southampton Station in his psyche, the last hamlet before East Hampton.

Mack stood when he heard the call for East Hampton Station and searched for McKenzie out the window as the train slowed along the platform. He picked up his luggage and waited for the door to open. Big snowflakes swirled like a swarm of white butterflies as the train hurriedly departed the station. He zipped up his flight jacket, turned up the collar, and waited under the covered platform standing in calf-deep snowdrifts. It was quiet and serene, no sounds except for the wind. He checked his phone for the time and realized he was about 15 minutes late. The few cars in the parking lot were unrecognizable, just mounds of snow. As he started to call McKenzie, he saw a long black Suburban limo pull into the parking lot and stop at the foot of the platform steps. McKenzie bounded out the front passenger door waving at Mack. She was wearing a pink toboggan hat and fur top boot as she pushed through the snow and up the steps to greet him. She grabbed him in a big bear hug, her faced pressed against his chest.

"Oh, Mack, I've missed you so much."

Mack relished every minute of her affection. He felt that McKenzie truly cared for him. It was a good feeling, one he hadn't trusted or enjoyed in a long time. He felt he could relax now and reciprocate without any guarded moments.

"I'm sorry I'm late. The roads are a mess, but isn't it beautiful?"

"Not as beautiful as you are." He laid his garment bag over his luggage and took her face in his hands and kissed her softly on the lips. Her toboggan fell from her head and her long red hair covered the snow on her shoulders.

"Ah, keep talking sweet man, I love it." She took his garment bag, "Let's get back to the house, there's more snow coming, can you believe that."

The driver, a towering black man with grey in his hair and beard, waited at the bottom of the steps and took the garment bag and Mack's roller bag. He noticed the small scarlet and gold wing patch on Mack's flight jacket, "Semper Fi, bro."

"Mack, this is Henry, he owns the limousine service and was kind enough to work hauling all of us around on New Year's Eve."

They shook hands, "Air wing?" Henry said.

"Yeah, 1st Marine Aircraft Wing helicopters. You?

"1st Battalion, 9th Division. Di bo chet."

"The 1/9." *The Walking Dead.* "Semper Fi, my brother." Mack patted him on the back, remembering their battalion had lost over 700 Marines in Vietnam.

Henry plowed through the snow carrying the roller bag under his arm and opened the rear door placing the luggage inside.

McKenzie noticed Mack staring at the Pirelli snow tires on the SUV as he climbed into the back seat.

"All this snow and ice is dangerous to drive in," She said. "And with guest coming in from all over, John and Martha felt it would be safer in the Suburban."

Mack said, "Nice," patting the heated seat as McKenzie snuggled close to him holding his hand. "Tell me about John and Martha," Mack whispered over the soft music playing in the front seat. "I know you told me she was a judge and a longtime friend. What about John? What's there last name?"

"Her name is Martha Moses, she kept her family name. His name is John Whitmore. Martha inherited her great-grandfather's walk-out-the-backdoor to the Atlantic beach house."

"Are other guests staying in the house?"

"There are some relatives and one other couple. Most are staying at the Inn's and B&B's around Main Street. Why do you ask?"

"Just curious."

"Martha is no longer the Chief Judge of the state Court of Appeals. Next week she is being sworn in as the Attorney General of New York, a hellish job in a historically corrupt New York State government. We grew to be great friends while rooming together in college and law school."

McKenzie took the end of her scarf and wiped Mack's face from the melting snow dripping from his thick hair.

"And what does Mr. Whitmore do?" Mack said.

"You will like John. He's a little older than Martha, but they are still lovebirds after twenty-five years. He's the founder, chairman, and CEO of RedRock, Inc., an investment management corporation."

Mack nodded slightly.

"You've heard of them?" McKenzie said.

"Yeah, they are one of the largest money-management company in the America."

"In the world. The largest public company in the world."

"Does John manage your assets?"

"To John, my assets are like a grain of sand in the Sahara. RedRock is a growth machine. If you look at its stock performance, it's up 3800 percent and has $6.3 trillion assets under *John Whitmore to Martha Moses to McKenzie O'Connor could change her financial status for life.*"

Mack could smell the ocean as the limo turn onto Gracie Lane. Every house appeared to have a swimming pool and a tennis court.

McKenzie whispered that Gracie was Martha's great grandmother's name. The lane was lined with tall Maple trees and Christmas tree shaped Cedars that dead-ended at a large stone archway with opened gates; the beginning of Martha and John's property. The hundred-year-old house, about two football field lengths from the archway, was perched on an elevated foundation. The Shingle Style design, three-stories high, was built to endure the whipping winds of Nor Easters. The weatherworn cedar siding, wraparound balcony, and a nearly 360-degree view of the ocean, enriched the natural beauty of seaside living.

Henry stopped the Suburban in front of the wide steps leading up to the house. Two women stood at the top, waiting for them under the covered porch.

"Quite a pad," Mack said, looking up at the house."

"Shhh," McKenzie elbowed him in the ribs.

Mack whispered, "Which one is Martha, the blond?"

McKenzie nodded.

"And the little Asian woman behind her?"

"Her PA, Mika."

"Personal Assistant?"

"Private Assistant."

"What's the difference?"

"Hush. Come on." McKenzie grabbed his arm as they cautiously climbed the snow-covered steps sprinkled with sand.

CHAPTER 27

It was 7:00 a.m. and New Year's Eve. Mack hurried down the stairs dressed in sweat pants, a hooded sweatshirt, and running shoes. He eased himself out the backdoor and down the brick walkway to the beach. The sun was still low but fully risen without a cloud in the sky. Snow was still on the ground but not on the beach. The tide was rising with long slow swells packing the sand along the water's edge. Mack stretched each leg with his foot propped on a redwood bench connected to an enclosed beach shower. He set the timer on his phone, and took off on a slow jog.

Last night, with McKenzie wrapped in his arms, Mack drifted in and out of sleep due to three words heavy on his mind. After an interlude of lovemaking and in her afterglow, McKenzie whispered in Mack's ear, "I love you."

When there was a problem, something weighing on his mind, he could always work out a solution with a long run. His feelings toward McKenzie had deepened, and occupied a great deal of his attention. He had been single for a long time and had learned to live alone, moderately happy. He was healthy, debt free, and had budgeted from his investments enough income to live comfortably, without working, the rest of his life. He had a house in Key West that was paid for. He had a boat, an airplane, a 1973 Volkswagen Thing convertible, and his favorite mode of transportation, his Conch Cruiser bicycle with a large basket. His standard dress was sandals, shorts, and t-shirt. He could be in the ocean fishing or diving, or on the city courts playing tennis in five minutes. He had everything a man could want, just as he had planned. Yet, now more than ever, he longed for a woman, not just *any* woman, but someone special. Was McKenzie O'Connor that woman? If so, why didn't he respond in kind when she said she loved him?

Mack slowed his jog and checked his time, 31 minutes. He turned and started back to the house.

Sitting out by the pool in Key West after he had got back from California, Mack reminisced about how he had drawn a line down the middle of a blank piece of paper. On one side he had listed all the 'positive' things about McKenzie, like: very pretty, intelligent, great body, affectionate, funny, age compatible, good lover, fashionable . . . he had listed close to 20 things. Strangely, when it came to the 'negative' side of the page, he could not think of one thing he didn't like about her.

He looked up at the skyline and saw the roof of the three-story house, about a half-mile away. He started picking up his speed and was in a full sprint when he reached the walkway to the house. Breathing deep, with the warm sun on his face, he watched the tide roll in. His hands were freezing as he fumbled with his phone to check his time—fifty-seven minutes. *Just under a ten-minute mile, not bad for an ole man with a bad knee.*

Parked in the driveway was a panel truck with the name, Heavenly Caters painted on the side. Inside the house was a beehive of activity, everyone preparing for the New Years Eve party. Surely, McKenzie was up and about.

Across the kitchen, Martha waved him over holding up a coffee cup.

"Good morning," she said. "Coffee?"

"Thank you."

"Help yourself to the cream and sugar. Did you have a good run?"

"Great. It was beautiful on the beach; the sun's bright and warm, lots of vitamin-D."

"McKenzie hasn't come down yet, you want to take a cup up to her?"

"Sure, she loves coffee. I'll be back down after a quick shower if you need help with anything."

Mack hurried up the steps, careful not to spill the coffee, and entered the dark bedroom. McKenzie was under a pile of covers, all you could see was her long red hair spread out over the top of the white comforter. He set the coffee on the bedside table, lifted the covers, eased his body up close spooning behind her, and whispered,

"Wake up, wake up, Sleeping Beauty, the sun is shining."

McKenzie stirred, rolled over and crawled on top straddling him, like on a horse. She took his face in her hands and kissed his cheeks, his forehead, and a long kiss on the mouth. Suddenly, she jerked upright, both hands on his chest, "Is that coffee I smell?"

"Yes, but right now I have something else in mind."

"Can I have a sip of my coffee first?"

Mack stood in the corner of the glassed-in porch off the kitchen. He sipped on his scotch and watched the waves crash onto the beach as a large floodlight mounted on the outside shower illuminated the beachfront. A bar was setup at the other end of the room and the guests were mingling in and out of the kitchen. Mack had made a rough estimate of about 30 guests, all in formal dress. He felt a little uptight in his tux, but his comfortable "gators" and his second scotch balanced his anxiety.

"Mind if I join you, Mack?"

"No sir, not at all."

John Whitmore looked to be in his late sixties. "I think I've gained a little weight since I last wore this monkey suit." He said as he unbuttoned his tux coat.

Mack didn't think so. Whitmore was short, maybe five foot seven, lean body, with short gray hair and a neatly trimmed beard; very distinguished looking. Mack liked him immediately when they first met earlier.

"I know what you mean, I had to air the moth ball smell out of mine."

" Sorry, I had to rush off earlier."

"No problem. A company as large as yours, I'm sure is a 24/7 job."

"McKenzie tells me you owned a pretty big company yourself."

"No, no, nothing like yours. I followed your portfolio for years and invested in RedRock's offshore funds, the Global Funds, and some GIS Investment Series. I made money on those funds and they are still paying good dividends every year. Thank you, John." Mack smiled.

"Your welcome, I have some of those funds myself. So, you are retired now, living in Key West? How's that going, you're a little young aren't you?"

"Sometimes I'm bored, miss the action, but there's—'no stress in Key West.'"

They both laugh.

"You should come visit, it was 78 degrees there yesterday. Do you like to fish?" Mack said.

"Yes, like a lot of New Yorkers, I love to fish."

"Then come on down, let me reciprocate your hospitality. I guarantee you a full ice chest of fish to take back with you."

"I might take you up on that. McKenzie speaks very highly of you and your daughter."

"McKenzie is top shelf for sure, a real sweet lady. I don't know what she sees in me, but I'm crazy about her." Mack looked over John's shoulder and saw McKenzie walking down the hallway toward him and watched closely when a tall man stepped in front of her. She tried to step around him, but he grabbed her arm and pulled her back.

When John saw the look on Mack's face, he turned to see what distracted his attention, "Oh, that's Niles, an old friend of McKenzie's."

Mack stepped around John, "Excuse me a minute," and walked directly to the hallway. Niles's back was facing him as he poked him hard in the middle of his back, "Is there a problem here?" Mack said.

Niles jerked around, "I say old fellow, that hurt. I don't see where that's any concern of yours."

McKenzie moved in fast between the two, "Mack, this is Niles Ainsworth a longtime friend of mine. Niles, this is Mack Shannon, my guest from Key West, Florida."

Her guest! That's what I am to her? Mack thought.

"A good old boy from down south, huh? Welcome to the big city." Niles stuck out his hand to shake.

Good old boy my ass. What's with the British accent, you pretentious prick. Mack stared at his hand; pushed closer, glaring at him vis-à-vis. Toxic vapors surrounded his aura, ready to explode.

McKenzie hurriedly took Mack's arm. "Let's go talk to John." She guided him across the kitchen, and about halfway stopped, her hands on her hips, "That wasn't very nice."

"No, it wasn't. He's lucky I didn't smash his face for calling me boy."

"Mack! Please, why so volatile?"

"Sorry, I was a little mad when I saw him jerk you by the arm . . . "

"He's harmless. Plus, I don't need your help, I can take care of myself." She stalked off leaving him in the middle of the kitchen.

Should I go after her?

The hell with it, I'm just her 'guest'. I'll get me another scotch and go find someone else to violate.

Mack heard a faint sound of a bell and saw Martha walking through the rooms with a small dinner bell announcing it was time to eat. He followed her into a decorated dining room where a long table was brimming with a cornucopia of every food imaginable. Mack was starving. He placed his empty scotch glass on a tray and started loading his plate when he felt someone watching him. On the other side of the table he saw McKenzie staring at him with a big smile on her face, her plate overflowing with food. *Great, she's no longer pissed.*

She nodded toward a bay window at the end of the room where they could sit and eat. Mack's plate looked like he was feeding a family of five as he followed McKenzie to the bay window.

"You going to eat all that?" She said.

Mack fired back. "Huh, look at your plate that's enough for both of us."

"It *all* looked so good, I wanted to try everything. I vacillated whether to wait and come back with another plate or take a little taste of each now. Every time I choose to come back the very dish I wanted is gone."

"And we don't even have dessert yet." Mack said.

A server stopped in front of them with a tray filled with glasses of champagne. Mack took two glasses, handing one to McKenzie.

"I really shouldn't. I've had enough." McKenzie said.

"Me too, but we've got to have champagne to bring in the New Year.. How about we wait till the ball drops and we'll make the toast together." Mack set the two glasses of champagne on the windowsill.

McKenzie leaned over and gave Mack a quick kiss, and whispered, "And we can sleep late in the morning."

After eating, Mack gathered up the two plates and glasses to take to the kitchen.

McKenzie placed the knives, forks, and napkins on the plates. "Good, while you're doing that I will get us some party hats and horns. It's almost that time for the New Year. I will meet you back here."

Mack returned to the bay window but McKenzie wasn't there. It was getting close to midnight. He picked up the two glasses of champagne and walked through the crowd looking for her. He searched the dining room, the kitchen, even the outside patio. The music stopped and everyone started shouting the countdown: "10 . . . 9 . . . 8 . . . 7 . . ." Mack hurried through the crowd, stopped and stuck his head in the walk-in pantry off the kitchen, "6 . . . 5 . . . 4 . . ." the countdown continued, "3 . . . 2 . . . 1 . . . Happy New Year!"

There were shouts and lots of laughter. Someone turned up the TV as the ball dropped on Times Square and 'Auld Lang Syne' boomed through the house. Everyone was kissing and hugging, blowing their party horns, streamers flying across the room, and colorful top hats thrown to the ceilings.

Mack stopped at a door off the hallway that was partly open. He edged the door open wider with his foot and was immediately stunned, as if struck by a bolt of lightning. The noise throughout the house was deafening, but Mack heard no sounds as he stared at McKenzie sitting on top of a washing machine. Niles Ainsworth stood between her open legs, wrapped in her arms, as they kissed the New Year in.

He stood in the doorway watching, unnoticed. The two glasses of champagne slipped from his hands shattering on the floor. Rage battled with his bleeding heart . . . he bent over choking back bitter bile.

He staggered backward out of the room.

CHAPTER 28

McKenzie, a little woozy, aware she had had too much to drink, pushed Niles away and eased herself off the wash machine. "Where are you going?" Niles said.

"Damn! I've got to find Mack."

She stopped when she saw the two broken champagne glasses scattered in the doorway and hurried to the bay window, Mack was not there. She worked her way through the boisterous crowd, searching from room to room. *That was stupid of me, how could I forget Mack? He will be furious with me for not bringing in the New Year together.*

After checking each room a second time, she stood in the kitchen digging in her purse for her phone to call him. She dialed his number but it went direct to voice mail. Where could he be? Maybe he went to their room looking for me? She rushed up the stairs and opened the door, certain he'd be there: No Mack. No clothes. No luggage. *What the hell! He's gone?* She thought about why would he leave . . . and remembered the two broken champagne glasses. One broken glass she could understand, but two, in the same place . . . it was Mack. He saw Niles and I. "Damn! Damn! Damn!" She said out loud. "Damn *him* and that Irish temper!"

But where could he go this time of night? Is he walking in the freezing snow? She found Martha and asked if she had seen Mack and told her that his clothes and suitcase were gone. They found John and he said he saw Mack a short while ago walking through the crowd with a couple of glasses of champagne.

Martha walked into the kitchen and asked Mika. Mika told her she last saw Mr. Shannon, maybe 15-minutes ago, upstairs talking to Henry and then Henry put his coat on and went out the front door.

"Call Henry, get him on the phone for me." Martha waited while Mika called, but there was no answer.

Mack hurried up the steps and stopped when he saw Henry standing at the top watching the festivities below. "I need your help."

"You got it bro, whatever you need." He followed Mack to his room watching him rip off his coat.

"I'm out-of-here." Mack threw his coat on the bed and started changing clothes. "Can you get me a ride to LaGuardia, or is there a place I can stay till morning?"

Henry watch Mack ball up his tux coat, pants, and shirt, and stuffed them in his roller bag.

"I doubt if there's any vacancies in town, everything was pretty booked up in advance. But if you want to take the train back to the city there's one that leaves Montauk at 0142 and stops at East Hampton Station, we can make that one."

"That's what I want."

"You ready to go now?"

"Right now."

"Let me tell Mr. Whitmore I'm leaving."

"I'd rather no one know I'm leaving." Mack folded his garment bag and stuck it in the side pocket of his suitcase, and picked up his phone and pressed the off button until it shut down.

"Sure, I'll be back before anyone will need me. There's a back staircase that lead to the basement with a door to the outside, I'll meet you there with the Suburban."

Henry was waiting with the SUV running when Mack climbed the icy steps from the basement. A freezing Arctic wind blasted him as he tossed his roller bag in the back seat. He turned up the collar on his flight jacket, opened the front door, and climbed in the bucket seat already warm. He noticed the digital outside temperature reading on the dashboard, 21 degrees. Another reason to get out of Dodge; he hated cold weather, unless of course, he was skiing.

Two hours later Mack stepped off the train at Woodside Station in Queens. He followed the exit signs down the stairs to ground level and flagged a taxi to LaGuardia.

No one was at the Delta counter. Mack searched the electronic departure schedule and spotted a non-stop flight to Memphis leaving gate C13 at 06:30. Once through security, he stopped at McDonald's for a large coffee and made his way through C terminal to gate 13. He kicked back in one of the seats against the wall, sipped his coffee, and tried to relax. But he couldn't stop thinking about McKenzie: *Did I overreact . . . running away like a spurned teenager? Was some part of this my fault? Should I call her?*

He had forgotten that his phone was off. Had McKenzie called? As he waited for the phone to reboot, he hoped she had left some kind of explanation or at least an apology. There were three calls from McKenzie, about thirty-minutes apart, but no messages.

Too self-centered to apologize . . . the hell with her! He shoved the phone back in his jacket pocket. It was her fault. He did nothing to provoke such disrespect. Was there a character flaw he missed? Did she have a weakness to succumb to flattery and excessive praise?

But why show me all that attention? The sweetness and affection and most important, why would she say, 'I love you?' Was it all just BS? He removed the phone from his pocket to check his voicemail again—nothing. He flinched when the phone buzzed in his hand, indicated two voicemails; one from Irish who had called a little after midnight. She, and a crowd in the background, all shouted Happy New Year. The second voicemail, an unexpected one, was from Jin, "Come see me, handsome! Happy New Year!" He remembered a saying but not who wrote it, "Cry a river, build a bridge, and get over it." Maybe New Orleans was just what he needed?

"Why would Mack leave like that, you think he had an emergency?" Martha asked McKenzie.

"No, I'm sure he saw Niles and me in the laundry room."

"What the hell were you doing in the laundry room with that loser?"

"I thought Niles was a friend of yours?"

"No, not a friend, maybe a court jester."

"He had hung some mistletoe over the doorway and pulled me in for a kiss."

"Sounds like him," Martha said. "What are you going to do about Mack? I thought you guys were a perfect match. He seemed crazy about you. You do care about him don't you?"

"I do . . . a lot. I don't know what to think now."

"What do you mean you don't know? Didn't you lose him once before when he flew you down to his house in Key West in his private jet? You have finally met a man you can't push around. Baby, at our age, men like him are few and far between. He's gorgeously handsome and obviously loaded . . . here's what I'd do, call him and apologize. I know that's hard for you to do, it's hard for all of us to say 'I screwed up.' Tell him you were drunk; tell him whatever it takes to get him back. 'I apologize' it's just two words that could change your whole life.

"I did call him . . ."

The next day, while the Delta flight 3359 nonstop to Memphis lifted off the LGA runway, McKenzie was having deep, irrepressible thoughts about Mack. She knew he had checked his phone by now and saw that she had called him. Why hadn't he called her back? What she did wasn't that bad? For God's sake she wasn't sleeping with Niles; she just kissed him . . . and it was New Years Eve. Why such a drastic reaction, was he that insecure?

"Excuse me, would you care for something to drink?" A flight attendant interrupted McKenzie thoughts.

"Yes, thank you. Do you have a single malt scotch?"

"I have a 12 year old Glenlivet."

"Good. Neat, with a cup of ice, please."

McKenzie opened the miniature bottle and pored half of it in the plastic cup, dropped two cubes of ice in, swirled it around, nosed it, and took a long sip. A buzz went off indicating a text message, it was Abby Jones, her secretary: *"Kevin O'Shea insisted on picking you up at the airport, he said it was urgent that he talk with you. Do you still want me to pick you up?"*

McKenzie texted, *"No. I'll call you after I talk with him. Did he mention what the urgency was about?"*

"I asked, he wouldn't elaborate."

"Okay."

Mack dominated her thoughts. She reclined her seat and her mind drifted back to when they had first met. It was a wonderful party at his house to celebrate Beethoven's 125th birthday. The thirty acres he lived on were manicured to perfection, as was his house, a unique design furnished with eclectic and rare pieces.

His grand entrance to the party that day was a low flyover in his helicopter, but she didn't meet him till later and when she did, she thought she would need a defibrillator to jumpstart her heart again. It was a powerful mixture of fear and thrill like the first time she jumped out of an airplane, skydiving. The French have a special saying for such a meeting "coup de foudre" (love at first sight). Danger was written all over him—beware, irresistible sexual magnetism, strong and infectious.

She mixed another drink, emptying the small bottle in her cup, and adding two cubes of ice to open up the whisky or 'wake up the fairies' as her father use to say. She rolled the single malt over her tongue and palate and felt the hot liquid warm her blood, ending with a slight sweet taste.

Why did she play around with Niles? It was senseless. She knew Mack was already suspicious. Was she trying to make him jealous, teasing him? Whatever-she screwed that up. They had an unspoken agreement; they used each other. He was a stand-in when she needed an escort, a date. Mack was right, he had sized Niles up instantly: he was a pretentious narcissist.

She ended up most of the time paying the tab herself.

I'm not calling Mack. If he cares enough about me as much as he claims, he'll call me.

It was 10 a.m. and 78 degrees as Mack walked across the tarmac to his plane at the Miami Airport. After filing his flight plan, paying his bill for parking and topping off his gas tanks, he was still ambivalent about flying across the Gulf to see Jin.

He removed the chock blocks, the tie downs, and taxied over to runway 27 while still weighing his destination, New Orleans or home to Key West. He could always change his flight plan once in the air.

As his classic Bonanza, one of his favorite gifts of all times, lifted off the runway there was a hard trade wind that kept pushing the nose of the plane southwest. That's all it took, Mack believed in a sixth sense, it had served him well and saved his life a couple of times. He reached over to the instrument panel and wiped his finger across the GPS screen and tapped in 'Conch Republic.' It was almost 700 miles to New Orleans, way too far after flying all morning. He wanted to go home and could be there in less than an hour. Home was his respite, his Shangri-La, he had redesigned it that way: an eight-foot privacy hedge around the property, a pool, and a verdant garden that was full and lush with every tropical plant you could think of. The lot was small but he had made it a realm of harmony between man and nature to forget your troubles. He could swim, lay in the sun and read, ride his bike to play tennis, drive 'The Thing' his VW convertible to the boat docks, fish, and dive, all within one mile of his house. What more could a man want? The hell with women, nothing but trouble, always trouble.

The weather was clear skies all the way to Key West. He would call Jin when he got home.

Pulling her roller bag, McKenzie hurried down the arrival passageway until she reached the main terminal of the Memphis International Airport. Standing in the middle of the three-story atrium she scanned the area looking for O'Shea.

They made eye contact at the same time as he stepped off the escalator with his boyish, almost seductive smile on his face. Dressed in dark blue, almost black uniform with four bright stars on his shirt collar, he was an eye-catcher, a centerfold for male testosterone.

McKenzie was smiling too. She didn't know why, it was instinctive, a warm secure feeling of protection, he was like a big brother always there when needed. Yet, it was a little more than that. For years they had an esoteric agreement, unwritten and unspoken, as sex buddies, friends-with-benefits. She knew he was a confirmed bachelor and she had a choice, give him up or learn to accept him without any commitments. Why punish yourself, he was a great lover, what was wrong with having a loyal friend and hooking-up when needed. She had sent out what he joking referred to as the "Bat-Signal" (a distress signal summoning the superhero Batman) when in need and he always responded. Much better than her vibrator, she thought.

"Welcome home pretty lady, and Happy New Year." Kevin O'Shea wrapped his arms around her with a tight hug.

She gently pushed him away. She had fallen hard for Mack and she couldn't think of anyone else. Plus, she didn't believe in public display of affection. Although, Mack had his moments of PDA and she never remembered pushing him away or being embarrassed. The truth was, she blossomed when it happened with Mack.

"Happy New Year to you too. Wow, is that another star on your collar?"

"Yeah, promoted to Deputy Director, the old Deputy died from a heart attack."

"Congratulations . . . I guess."

O'Shea took her roller bag, "You know the Police Department, it's like ice cream, you're in flavor one year and out the next."

"What's the urgency you needed to talked to me about?" She wasn't sure that there was one; maybe he was just sending *her* a Bat-Signal.

"One of my men got a text from a snitch late last night that protesters would be picketing the Federal Building in the morning, your name was mentioned."

"My name? For what?"

" I don't know, I thought you might have some idea? A case you've got coming up or any kind of threats or disputes?"

"No, nothing controversial that would create a protest. You sure my names was used?"

"I'm not sure of anything, it's all hearsay at this point."

"Do you know who's doing the protesting, what group or name of the protesters?"

"I've got some of my people looking into it and I have two men assigned to you in the morning, just in case." His cell phone started ringing. "Hold on, maybe this is some more information.

"O'Shea." He listened, "Okay, keep me abreast." He turned to McKenzie. "They've talked with the NAACP and they are not involved. They think it might be the BLM group, Black Lives Matter."

"Is it a black protest?"

"Probably—they are checking all angles."

"Can you drop me off at my office, I need to search this out. I don't want to get caught with egg on my face in the morning."

McKenzie greeted the screeners in the Federal Building as she hurried through security and onto the elevator. Strange—just for a moment she stood staring at the buttons but couldn't remember what floor her office was on.

She knew she had a corner office with a panoramic view of downtown Memphis, the Mississippi River, and West Memphis Arkansas. She slowly dragged her finger down the numbers and stopped at 10. That's it, 10th floor and pushed the button.

Abby looked surprised when she walked in, "I knew it! You couldn't stay away from the office another day could you?"

Abby Jones had been McKenzie's right-hand woman for almost twenty-years. First when McKenzie's worked in a large law firm and Abby was a runner in the secretary pool. Then she took Abby with her when she was elected Chancellor and paid ten-grand for her to get her paralegal certificate.

"Tell me all about the New Year's party, did you have a great time?" Abby said. Then she noticed the seriousness on McKenzie's face. "What's wrong honey, what happened? Is it O'Shea?"

Abby followed McKenzie into her office, "No." McKenzie said, setting behind her desk.

"Nothing has happened yet. O'Shea got a tip that some protestors were going to march here at the Federal Building tomorrow. He said my name was mentioned in the protest."

"What?"

"That's all he knows. Can you think of anything we've done or fail to do that would generate a protest?"

"No, nothing. Are they sure you are involved?"

"I don't know. Maybe you could check with some of your contacts. O'Shea said it's not the NAACP, and he's checking on Black Lives Matter."

"Let me make some calls." Abby said.

A couple of hours later, Abby tapped on the door and walked in McKenzie's office. "Does the name Auburn Calloway ring a bell?"

"No, should it?"

"I just got a call back from my friend at Tennessee Permits and Licenses. A group by the name of Black Criminal Justice (BCJ) was granted a demonstration permit to protest the life sentence of this Calloway fellow."

"A life sentence?"

"He hijacked a FedEx plane here in Memphis."

"When was that?"

Abby read from her handful of pages, "Back in 1994, April 7th. I googled his name and all kinds of information came up." She handed her copies of articles she had printed off from The Commercial Appeal, USA TODAY, Newswire, and Free Republic. There's a highly rated book on Amazon called 'Hijack' written by a Memphian, Dave Hirschman, that tells the whole story. I checked the library and the Novel bookstore and both have copies."

"I think I remember that case, wasn't that in Julia Gibbons' court?"

"Yes, is she still alive?"

"Oh yeah, she was a tough lady, paved a smooth road for a lot of women in law." McKenzie stared at Abby in deep thought. "I tell you what, just in case, how about calling downstairs to records and get us a copy of the trial transcript while I look over these pages."

McKenzie started speed-reading down the middle of each page then slowed her reading and half-whispered some of the important facts:

On April 7, 1994, Auburn Calloway, a 42 year-old off-duty Flight Engineer hitched a ride in the jump-seat on FedEx Flight 705, a DC-10 cargo plane bound for San Jose, California and back to Memphis the same day.

As the wide-body plane climbed to 19,000 feet, Calloway opened his carry-on bag, a guitar case, and inside was four hammers of different sizes, a speargun, and a diver's knife. He removed the largest claw hammer and eased behind the Flight Engineer seated behind the cockpit and landed numerous blows to his head.

The co-pilot turned immediately on hearing the commotion behind him and was hit with a savage blow to the head shattering the left side of his skull driving bone chips into his brain and severed his temporal artery. With each heartbeat, blood gushed from the torn artery. A deep half-moon gash was carved above his right eye where his face had collided against a sharp metal corner of the instrument panel.

"My God!" McKenzie said out loud. She took a deep breath and continued reading:

Calloway immediately tuned on the captain who was still buckled-in and defenseless. Swinging from behind, Calloway delivered one devastating blow after another to the captain's head; one nearly severed his right ear knocking his glasses across the cockpit.

There was a light knock on the door and Abby stuck her head in, "I'm going to run down to records, they have a copy of the transcript ready for me to pick up."

"Okay," McKenzie said without looking up and then she shouted, "Lock the door."

She continued to read:

Realizing all three were still alive, Calloway retreated from the cockpit back to his guitar case, removed his speargun and rushed back to the cockpit shouting, "Sit down, sit down, all of ya! Get back to your seats, this is a real gun, I'll kill ya!"

The Flight Engineer grabbed the speargun as Calloway pointed it in the captain's face. The co-pilot jerked the yoke back, pointing the nose of the plane straight up throwing the pilot, the flight engineer, and Calloway from the cockpit pass the galley onto the deck of the airplane.

A fierce battle for control pursued as the three men rolled back and forth on the bloody deck shouting and screaming. Calloway managed to grab the hammer once more and strike the captain again. The captain shouted for the copilot to put the plane in autopilot and come help as Calloway sank his teeth into the left shoulder of the flight engineer. Bleeding profusely and with his last drop of strength, the captain wrestled the hammer from Calloway's hand and struck him until Calloway stopped moving.

McKenzie stopped reading. Unaware she had been holding her breath, she leaned back and exhaled and took in a deep breath. "This is unbelievable," she said to herself, but could not stop reading:

The copilot gripped the speargun as he left his seat and hurried to the back and kept it pointed at Calloway while the captain made his way back to land the plane. But paralysis had set in left arm and side making the speargun slip from his grip, then Calloway, faking unconsciousness, took that opportunity to renewed his attacked. The only thing the two seriously injured men could do was throw all their weight onto Calloway to try to keep him pinned down.

McKenzie heard the door open and looked up to see Abby standing with her arms wrapped around two stuffed expandable legal folders. "I got the trial transcript, it's a lot—"

"Hold tight, let me finish this page."

Abby place the two folders of transcripts on McKenzie's credenza while she continued reading:

With a full load of over 37,000 gallons of jet fuel, this white missile-like plane was what Callaway was trying to pilot into FedEx's main hub killing hundreds of fellow employees, destroying a multimillion dollar plane, all in hopes his family would collect on a $2.5 million life insurance policy provided by Federal Express.

At 300 feet above the ground, weighing 600,000 pounds, and with full flaps extended and landing gear down, the pilot hit the runway hard and rolled safely to a stop with less than

900 feet left in front of him.

McKenzie picked up the pages she was reading and stacked them together, "What a horrific tragedy, it's like something out of a Stephen King novel." McKenzie handed the stack of articles back to Abby.

"I copied Calloway's appeal thinking you might want to read that as well." Abby said.

"You know, I don't want to spend too much time on this, it may not even involve me. We don't know what they want."

"But we do know there is a permit issued for a demonstration and they're protesting because of Auburn Calloway's incarceration."

"True. Let me read over the appeal and we'll wait and see what tomorrow brings."

Abby dug the copy of the appeal out of one of the folders and gave it to McKenzie. "Do you want me to read these articles while you're reading the appeal?"

"Wouldn't hurt, I might have missed something." McKenzie started reading:

United States of America, Plaintiff-appellee, v. Auburn Calloway,
Defendant-appellant, 116 F.3d 1129 (6th Cir. 1997)
US Court of Appeals for the Sixth Circuit - 116 F.3d 1129 (6th Cir. 1997)
Argued Dec. 2, 1960.
Decided June 20, 1997. Rehearing and Suggestion for Rehearing En Banc
Denied July 25, 1997.

John T. Fowlkes, Assistant U.S. Atty., (argued and briefed), Office of the U.S.
Attorney, Memphis, TN, for Plaintiff-Appellee.
Robert C. Brooks (argued and briefed), Memphis, TN, for Defendant-Appellant.
Auburn Calloway, Atlanta, GA, pro se.
Before: LIVELY, NELSON, and RYAN, Circuit Judges
Convicted on federal charges of attempted aircraft piracy and interference with flight crewmembers, defendant Auburn Calloway received concurrent sentences of life imprisonment. On appeal, Mr. Calloway presents six assignments of error: (1) the district court erred in refusing to suppress certain evidence; (2) the evidence as a whole was insufficient to support the conviction for attempted aircraft piracy; (3) the district court's jury instructions constructively amended the indictment; (4) the jury was not properly instructed on the wrongful intent element

of the offense of attempted aircraft piracy; (5) the conviction for interference with flight crew members must be vacated as a lesser-included offense of attempted aircraft piracy; and (6) the district court erred in departing upward from the applicable sentencing guideline range.

The government concedes that interference with flight crewmembers is a lesser-included offense of attempted aircraft piracy. We shall vacate the interference conviction on the strength of that concession. We find no other reversible error, and the conviction and life sentence for attempted aircraft piracy will be affirmed.

The conviction on Count II of the indictment (interference with flight crew members) is VACATED, and the conviction and sentence on Count I of the indictment (attempted aircraft piracy) are AFFIRMED.

Well, that's says it all, McKenzie thought. There's no way I could be involved. He's had a trial; he's had an appeal, a rehearing that was denied July 25, 1997 and there was no cause for a mistrial due to racial bias of jury selection. In one of the articles she read there were 10-African-Americans and 2- whites on the jury, nine women and three men. The jury foreman was also African American as was both, the prosecuting attorney and the defense attorney, as was the psychiatrist, the main expert for the prosecution. Of course, some judges now are letting mass murderers and child molester out of prison for good behavior.

She cleared her desk gathering her papers in a neat stacks, checked her desk calendar and made a mental note she had a preliminary hearing on a mergers and acquisition case at 2:00 p.m. tomorrow.

She stood to leave and tilted forward a little, lightheaded and unbalanced. What the hell was that? She closed her eyes, took a deep breath while moving her head left and right and walked into Abby's office.

"If you don't need me for anything I'm going home."

"You okay?"

"Yes, just a little tired from the travel."

"A good night sleep in your own bed and you'll feel better. I'll see you in the morning."

McKenzie stopped at the door and looking back said, "Anything important on the calendar for tomorrow?"

Abby checked her calendar, "Just that M & A preliminary hearing at 2 o'clock."

"Okay."

CHAPTER 29

McKenzie turned south on 2nd street and checked her rearview mirror to see if the black sedan was still following her. She knew it was one of O'Shea's men because he had been parked in front of her house all night. She thought it was a little overkill but he was adamant, he told her to stick to judging and let him do the policing.

She put her right blinker on as she turned into the underground parking at the Federal Building and stopped as a U.S. Marshal walked over to her. She lowered her window, "Good morning . . ." *What is his name?* He had been greeting her every morning for over 10 years?

"Morning Judge," He watched the black sedan that was following her pull to the side apron and park with the motor running.

"How's Margret doing?" *How can I remember his wife's name and not his?*

"Not too good. The oncologist told her yesterday they found more cancer and would have to take her other breasts."

John, that's his name. "Oh, John, I'm so sorry. If there is anything I can do please let me know?"

"Just pray that they will get it all this time."

"I'll ask Father O'Brien to say a special prayer for her, Sunday," McKenzie said and then drove inside to her reserved parking space.

John tipped his hat, then walked over to the sedan to chitchat. Most Marshals, like John, were retired policemen supplementing their pension.

"Anything happening with the protesters?" The driver asked.

"Naw, looks like a mixed bag of young and old, black and white, all's peaceful so far."

"Okay, Johnny, be careful." The driver backed the sedan out onto Second Street and drove off.

Abby was looking out the window with her military binoculars someone gave her to watch the river traffic from time to time. She turned when she heard the door open and McKenzie walked into her office, "Quick, come look," she said.

McKenzie took the binoculars and focused below on the large plaza. She saw groups of people milling around, two men in suits giving out signs, newscasters with their cameramen and then a school bus pulled up an unloaded 50 to 60 people. She watched as a dark sedan pulled up short of the plaza and stopped in front of the police barricades. The driver, a huge man wearing dark sunglasses hurried to open the back door. McKenzie followed a woman wearing a hijab as she walked across the middle of the plaza, and then handed the binoculars to Abby.

"See if you know that women wearing the hijab?"

Abby focused the binoculars, "I do know her. She calls herself Amala Kahn." She adjusted the binoculars for a closer look. "Her name was Wilma Wilson when we went to college together years ago at Lemoyne-Owen, she was beautiful. The last I heard she moved to New York to be a model, then married a rich Iranian and they live in Dubai."

McKenzie took the binoculars for another look. "Is she white?"

"Mostly, she's mixed, has that creamy milk chocolate skin we all envy, I believe her mother is white."

"You think she's part of this protest?"

"Why else would she be here? She was somewhat of a rebel in school."

McKenzie handed the binoculars back and walked into her office.

Abby followed. "Did you get a good night sleep?"

"You were right. There's nothing like your own bed."

"Oh, I found something else on that Auburn Calloway, he wrote a letter to President Obama asking for clemency. It's in that folder on your desk."

McKenzie opened the folder. "Obviously, that didn't work out."

"I couldn't find any record that the President even acknowledge the receipt of his letter."

The office phone started ringing and at the same time someone was knocking on the locked office door. Abby answered the phone first, "Judge O'Conner's office, hold please." She turned and saw a dark shadow through the top half of the opaque glass door. She knew that security had posted extra Marshals at the screening machines and was not allowing anyone in the building today that didn't work there, in other words 'No Visitors.'

"Who's there?" She asked.

"O'Shea."

Abby picked up the folder with all the clippings on the hijacking of the FedEx plane and opened the door. Deputy Director O'Shea walked into the office and Abby gave him the folder, nodded towards McKenzie's office, and turned back to the phone. "Hello, sorry to put you on hold, how can I help you?"

"Could I speak with Judge O'Connor please?"

"She has someone in her office, who's calling?"

"Amala Kahn, I'm . . ."

"Hello, Wilma."

"Who is this?"

"Abby Jones, do you remember me? We went to college together for a short time."

"Yes, yes I do, how are you Abby? You were a year ahead of me. I always admired you."

"Really?"

"You were the class president and always dressed so nice and had such perfect diction. I use to practice speaking just like you."

"Thank you, that's sweet of you to say."

"Are you a lawyer now, working for Judge O'Connor?"

"I'm her paralegal, have been for the last twenty years."

"Oh, are we that old?" Amala said.

"Watch out girl that's not old. You never go by Wilma anymore?"

"No, not for years. I married a Muslim and he wanted me to change my name. I loved him and I never like 'Wilma' so it was no problem for me, and it was good branding for my modeling career. My husband always quoted the Qur'an when the name change came up, he would say: *In the name of Allah, Most Gracious, Most Merciful, Proclaim your real parentage. That will be more equitable in the sight of Allah.*'"

"Amala is a pretty name. Would you like to leave a message for Judge O'Connor?"

"Thank you, Abby. I am downstairs at the screening machine and the guards tell me no visitors are allowed today. I have come from New York today just to see her and would like to talk to the Judge today. Can you help me, I don't mind waiting?"

"Please hold, let me see if I can interrupt her."

McKenzie was dubious about getting involved personally with this woman and her organization. But she had always made herself available to the public to explain the law when possible. Years ago, she remembered reading an article titled Classification of Elected and Appointed Officials: *The courts have generally held that anyone who exercises significant authority pursuant to public laws is a public officer. This includes any official who administers or enforces public laws, whether the individual is elected by the public or appointed to an office.*

O'Shea looked up from reading the articles on Auburn Calloway and suggested that if she agreed to meet with this woman it should be with her alone; no reporters, no bodyguards, no associates.

"Okay, let's see what the lady wants."

"You think you should tape this meeting?" Abby said.

"No. Call down to the marshal's office and have her escorted up here alone and have her wait in your office until I've read his clemency letter."

After Abby shut the door to McKenzie's office, O'Shea with the open folder in his hand said, "I remember this hijacking, I was working that day and we listened to our dispatcher on the radio as they tried to land the plane."

"I remembered it too, but had no idea of the gruesome tragedy those pilots went through. Let me read this letter real quick."

"How about reading it out loud?"

"Why don't you come over here and read over my shoulder?"

O'Shea walked over behind her desk as she removed the letter from the folder:

January 6, 2017
Dear President Obama:

I am a 65-year-old African-American veteran of the U.S. Navy, [honorably] discharged in 1982. I held a top-secret security clearance for nuclear weapons training. I am now the founder of Veteran Community Mentors and author of its Mission Statement (enclosed). I cannot accomplish the mission unless I receive a sentence commutation from you.

I hope that you are concerned that after serving my country from 1976 until 1982, I was convicted and sentenced to life imprisonment without parole possibility having no prior criminal history except for a few traffic violations. No one was killed in the incident for which I was incarcerated where I brought 4

*hammers, cartons of nails, $700 in cash, an uncharged pneumatic speargun which
could not have been fired, along with other personal paraphernalia on board
a FedEx cargo flight that I had been scheduled to fly the previous and subsequent
days. Although I incurred the most serious injuries in the fracas, I took full
responsibility and apologized to my fellow crewmembers in a letter that was
published in the local newspaper. I derived no possible benefit from my conduct,
which makes what I did a self-victimizing "crime" with no criminal intent. The
trial judge, a conservative Republican who removed my case from a rotating docket
which would have sent it to the late District Court Judge Jerome Turner (a
liberal), instructed the jury with a "general intent" instead of the legally required
"specific intent" mens rea element. That was enough to get a guilty verdict instead
of a not guilty by reason of insanity verdict, which would have allowed me to
receive treatment and be released long ago.*

*The most important question now remaining is whether (A) justice and (B) the
public welfare is better served by your exercising your power of clemency in my
particular case. The answer to (A) is provided by law professor Kenneth Gallant.
The answer to (B) is given by my Mission Statement
at VeteranCommunityMentors.org and by my good conduct record for more than
two decades of imprisonment. Mercy is yours to grant or deny.*

*President Ford defended his pardon of Richard Nixon by advising the American
people to consider how much Nixon had already suffered as a result of his crimes.
Ford said "I feel that Richard Nixon and his loved ones have suffered enough
and will continue to suffer no matter what I do, no matter what we, as a great and
good nation, can do together."(see "Someone Must Write, the End." Newsweek,
Sept. 16, 1974, 22). This is where you can direct any naysayers and clemency
critics.*

*I hope you agree that it's time for reciprocity for your clemency, which you will get
from me and other incarcerated veteran clemency recipients who, like me, dedicate
themselves to pursuing a rescue effort in economically and socially beleaguered
communities across the United States.*

*I go beyond my request that you grant my clemency with immediate release, and
commutations for honorably discharged veterans, by asking that you also stand*

beside us, shoulder to shoulder, in places like Chicago, when we make our presence known. With you standing there with us, no one will doubt our legitimacy nor oppose our mission!

What matters most is that there are good people who have served our country honorably and sacrificially in every branch of the U.S. military, but have also suffered misfortunes under the criminal justice system. From the highest general to the lowest private, we have all served and suffered in one way or another.

I believe that incarcerated U.S. veterans deserve clemency despite having no assistance from a "Clemency Project" like that, which has helped nonviolent drug offenders.

I will close by reminding you that we all love you and your family out here in common-class America. I hope you will reciprocate our love for you with love and mercy toward incarcerated veterans and our families.

Thank you in advance for your personal consideration of this clemency request.

God Bless You,
Auburn Calloway

"Was Obama president in 2017?" O'Shea said.

"This letter was written on January 6, 2017, Obama was still President. The Constitution specifies that the term of every U. S. President begin at noon on January 20. Now hush and let me think."

"He's a spineless bastard that got what he deserved. He calls what he did an 'incident' and a 'fracas'." O'Shea leaned over and underlined with his finger and read each word: *I derived no possible benefit from my conduct, which makes what I did a self-victimizing "crime" with no criminal intent.* "No criminal intent my ass. He was going to crash a multi-million dollar airplane into FedEx's main hub killing hundreds of his fellow employees including the three pilots. They should have burned his ass in the chair."

"Kevin!" She gave him a dirty look. "Please."

The red light on McKenzie's desk phone blinked.

"You want me to stay while she's in here?" O'Shea said.

"Can you wait in Abby's office? I don't foresee any trouble."

O'Shea couldn't take his eyes off Amala and caught her eying him as he took a chair directly across from her. O'Shea had never married, but had been with a lot of women in his lifetime, some were real beauties. But never had he seen a woman with such flawless features. He wondered if she had a body to match that face. Is it true that Muslin women didn't shave under their arms and legs? Ugh—that would be tragic.

O'Shea saw Amala staring at the gun on his hip.

"Hello," she said. "Are you here to arrest me?" Her smile was warm and unguarded.

O'Shea, always quick with a snappy retort, was so stunned that this goddess would even speak to him, couldn't think of a thing to say, he stared lock jawed.

"Oh, I'm sorry Amala, this is Deputy Director Kevin O'Shea, a friend of Judge O'Conner," Abby added. "Kevin, this is Amala Kahn, we went to school together." Abby's phone buzzed.

"Amala, the judge will see you now, go right in."

O'Shea, studied her body as she walk into McKenzie office and wonder if a Muslin would go out with a Catholic?

When McKenzie's door shut, Abby said, "Shame on you."

"What? What did I do?"

"You know exactly what I'm talking about."

"She's gorgeous, how can anyone *not* stare? Is she married?"

"Yes!"

"You think Muslim women buzz their hair like Catholic nuns do?"

Abby just shook her head and said, "Men."

McKenzie was standing up when Amala came in. "Have a seat please, Ms. Kahn. It is Ms., right." *God, she's beautiful as Abby said . . . got to be close to my age and not a wrinkle anywhere.*

"Thank you, but please call me Amala." She waited till McKenzie was seated behind her desk before she sat in one of the two chairs.

"What can I do for you, Amala?"

Amala pushed the hijab back off her head; the scarf rested on her shoulders, the dark hair a soft frame accentuating her beauty.

"Did Abby tell you we were classmates in college?"

"She did. She said you were beautiful and a professional model."

"I appreciate the compliment," Amala smiled. "She's too kind."

"I disagree."

"Well, thank you. You are quite beautiful yourself."

"Now who's being flattered? But thank you anyway?"

There was a long silence. "Then I'm afraid you have made a fruitless trip down from New York."

"Why do you say that?"

"From all that I've read, Auburn Calloway has exhausted every possible means of a release from prison. I have no authority in his case unless there was a new appeal, which the Appellate Court has already denied. "

A smile broke out on Amala's face her eyes sparkling.

McKenzie's Irish temper snapped. "Did I say something *funny!*"

"Judge O'Connor, please, I'm so sorry, I wouldn't offend you for anything in the world. It's just that I have no idea who Auburn Calloway is . . ."

"You're not with the protest marchers on the plaza?"

"No ma'am, I'm not."

"That is funny."

They both laughed.

"Now I'm almost afraid to ask; why are you here?"

"Six years ago my father was sentences to 12-years in prison for transporting and selling marijuana. He goes before the parole board this month and I was praying you might write a reference letter recommending his release. We've been estranged all this time and we are trying to get back together. I spoke with the prison warden and he said my father has been an exemplary prisoner. He's in his sixties now, a diabetic, and not in good health."

"I'm sorry, but why me? I was a Chancery Judge back then and only heard civil cases, never criminal. It would be better to talk to the judge who heard his case."

"I tried but he died two years ago. My grandmother worked for doctor Winchester in his pain clinic and always talked about what a fair and righteous person you were. I didn't know anyone else in the legal business to talk to."

"Your grandmother worked for my husband?"

"Clara Mae Wilson?"

"Oh my God. She was the sweetest woman, Randolph loved her to death."

"She was like a mother to me."

"I'm so sorry I missed her funeral. Maybe I can help your father. Is he in the State Penitentiary, up at Fort Pillow?"

"Is that the one in Henning, Tennessee?"

"Yes, it's the same. I'll need his full name, his social security number and date of birth?"

"William Albert Wilson . . . let me look in my phone for his social security number."

McKenzie dropped her pen and bent over quickly to stop it from rolling under her desk. When she lifted her head, her face had turned a pale white. She dropped the pen again and grabbed the edge of her desk, the side of her face flat against the desktop. She struggled as the room started spinning and held on to the desk with a life-saving grip as if she was in the vortex of a tornado, "Oh my God!" She moaned.

Amala jumped up and rushed to Abby's office, "Hurry! Something is wrong with the Judge."

O'Shea was the first into McKenzie's office with Abby right behind him. They found her on her knees vomiting violently into a plastic wastebasket.

"What happened?" O'Shea shouted at Amala as he kneeled beside McKenzie.

"I don't know. We were talking and she fell forward grabbing onto the desk and crying out as if she was falling."

Abby hurried with a wet face towel from the private bathroom in McKenzie's office and wiped her face with it.

After O'Shea checked her vitals and questioned her, he lifted her back in her chair.

McKenzie handed Abby the face towel, "Can you wet that again for me and get me one of those small cokes from the mini fridge to settle my stomach?"

"We need to take you to the emergency room," O'Shea said.

"No, no. I'm okay."

"Oh, thank God, I was so afraid." Amala said.

Abby handed McKenzie the wet towel and the coke.

"This happened once years ago." She took a big swallow of coke, "but I didn't throw up then. It's vertigo, I've researched it and lucky for me it lasts only a few minutes."

"What caused the vertigo?" Abby said.

"I was bent over and jerked my head up too quick I guess. There are these tiny crystals, calcium particles, that build up in the inner ear and they get displaced and roll around touching sensitive nerve endings inside that causes vertigo."

"Are you sure you don't want me to call doctor Franklin just to talk to?" Abby said.

"No, there's nothing they can do. In a few minutes I'm going to do some exercises that will send those little crystals back where they belong.

"Amala, I apologize for this. If you will leave your number with Abby, I will check on your father and get back with you."

"I'm so sorry this happened to you. I'll pray for a speedy recovery."

"Kevin, Ms. Kahn is not with the protesters. Will you escort her down to the plaza and to her car?" McKenzie motioned Abby to shut her door.

Abby followed O'Shea and Amala to her office shutting the door behind her. Amala turned and hugged Abby. "You have my number now so please call me if you come to New York. I hope the Judge can write the letter for my father and I will be back in Memphis next month for his parole hearing."

Abby opened the door to McKenzie's office and found her lying on the floor on her right side with her head tilted at an angle.

"Are you all right?"

"Wait." McKenzie said.

Abby watched as McKenzie sat up and switched sides doing the same exercise. Then she sat up cross-legged and rolled her eyes up and down.

"I've got to do this three times."

"Can I talk while you're doing them?"

"Yes."

"That's all you have to do, these exercises?"

McKenzie nodded her head.

"How strange. I wonder who thought of that?" Abby sat in one of the chairs to watch. "So, your instinct was right. Amala had nothing to do with the protesters or Auburn Galloway?"

"Nothing whatsoever; she never heard of him. I felt like an idiot. I went on and on about this Galloway guy and she just sat there with a smile on her face. I like her. She's as sweet as she is pretty."

"She really is. Was there something you wanted me to do for her father?"

McKenzie was on her side again. "Yes, write a letter of recommendation for her father to the parole board for me to sign. There's information on her father, William Wilson, on my desk."

CHAPTER 30

As the door closed on the elevator, O'Shea thought to himself, now would be a great time for the elevator to get stuck between floors. "Are you not allowed to show your hair in public?" He asked Amala.

"It's a personal choice for me."

"Why would you cover up such pretty hair?"

"Thank you. According to some, the veil has been used as a way of curbing male sexual desire."

"Really! Does it work?"

Amala smiled. "I don't know. You would have to answer that."

"It doesn't curb any desire for me, if anything it enhances the desire. You know, the unknown . . . the mystery."

"That nice of you to say. The covering of the head and body predates Islam. Jewish, Christians and Hindu women have also covered their head at various times in history and in different parts of the world."

"I never thought about that. But I remember my mother would never go to mass without a scarf on her head."

"I lived many years in Dubai with my husband who was a Muslin from Iran. He was in the import and export business and we traveled a lot in Muslin countries, and out of respect I dressed accordingly."

"What did your husband import and export?"

"He owned a fleet of ocean freighters and had long-term contracts with the government of Dubai and other countries with multi seaports along the Persian Gulf, Arabian Sea, and the Red Sea."

"You speak of your husband as in the past, are you divorced?"

"My husband was killed in a water accident three-years ago."

"A shipping accident?"

"No. We were at a friend's beach house for an outdoor wedding and it was the day before the wedding, a lot of drinking and celebrating. The father of the bride, a close friend of my husband, took him out for a ride on his new high-powered Sea-Doo. A 15-year old kid in his father's cigarette boat with his girlfriend was racing another boat and came from behind a rock formation and broadsided the Sea-Doo killing them both instantly. Witnesses confirmed he was traveling at over 70 miles an hour."

"I'm so sorry, what a tragic accident."

The elevator door opened on the main floor and O'Shea walked over and opened the double doors to the plaza. The protesters, over a hundred now, were walking back and forth in front of the doors with their signs.

"Where are you parked? I'll walk you to your car."

"I took an Uber from the airport. I can call for one again."

"No. I can take you in my car. What hotel are you staying in?"

"I made reservations at The Peabody."

Amala saw some of the protesters stop and were staring at them. "Are you sure it's okay? I've never been in a police car before."

"Don't worry, I won't put you in the back seat. Just kidding, it's an unmarked car. We can walk to the underground parking."

"Is Dubai in Saudi Arabia?"

"No it's in UAE, United Arab Emirates. Emirates are like our states, Dubai is one of only seven . . ."

They were at the corner of the building when O'Shea felt something hit hard on his shoulder knocking him sideways. He turned back quickly when he heard Amala scream and saw her fall to the ground. A large brick had ricocheted off his shoulder and hit her in the back.

O'Shea dropped to his knees to check on Amala. He looked out over the protesters to see who threw the brick and saw a large black man with deadlocks breaking from the crowd and running toward him. O'Shea stood and drew his gun. The man stopped 20 feet away, threw up both hands, and shouted "POLICE! UNDERCOVER!" The man slowly lifted a lanyard from his neck with a gold police badge hanging from the end.

O'Shea holstered his weapon and motioned him to come help.

"Detective Newcomb, Director," the undercover officer introduced himself.

The two of them turned her over and found her unconscious. He looked up at Newcomb and said, "Call an ambulance." With a fire station only two blocks away, he could hear the siren and knew they were minutes away.

"Did you see who threw the brick?" O'Shea said.

"Yeah, my partner Harris got him. I came running when I heard the scream."

O'Shea heard shouting and looked up and saw a homeless looking guy with a long pony tail pushing a fat white kid toward them. The kid was shouting about the handcuffs being too tight behind his back.

"Director, this is my partner, Harris and this is the little shit that threw the brick," Newcomb said.

O'Shea stood up and grabbed the front of the kid's shirt. "You see what you did?" pointing to Amala. "You could have killed her."

The kid spit at O'Shea and screamed, "FUCK YOU, PIG!" and tried to pull away.

O'Shea jerked him close and with his other hand dug his fingertips deep into his Adam's apple. "Say that again, you pimple faced little bastard and I'll tear your throat out."

Newcomb grabbed O'Shea and whispered, "Director," and nodded toward a crowd that had their phones out taking videos.

Harris jerked the handcuffs hard and the kid shouted in pain.

O'Shea pointed to his shoulder where the brick had torn his shirt. "Book him for assault with a deadly weapon on a police officer and on an innocent-bystander, Amala Kahn."

O'Shea heard Amala moan and saw she had opened her eyes and was trying to speak. He kneeled down and took her hand and leaned over to hear what she was saying.

"Kevin . . . please don't leave me."

She remembered my name. O'Shea squeezed her hand as she lost consciousness again. He waved at the two paramedics unloading their gurney to hurry. All four helped lift her onto the gurney and O'Shea hurried to his car to follow the paramedics to the hospital.

O'Shea had been waiting over three hours in the Emergency Room while they ran test on Amala. Finely, he saw a doctor walking down the hallway toward him. He stood as the doctor introduced himself.

"Director O'Shea, I'm doctor Kumar." He was tall, young looking, with grey streaks through his dark hair. He spoke with an English accent. "Ms. Kahn has regained consciousness and is setting up in bed. She has a sprained wrist from breaking her fall. And she has a high temperature so we tested her for Covid and found her to be positive."

"Can I see her?"

"Yes, she's in our trauma area, I'll show you."

Mack picked up Amala's satchel-bag he had carried from the ambulance and followed Dr. Kumar.

"Ms. Kahn told me she was a New York model and was here on business just for today. I plan to release her today but she will have to be quarantined for 7 days."

"Thanks Doc." He turned to leave.

"Hold on there, Director. You need to be tested for Covid too." Kumar opened a drawer and put on a pair of surgical gloves and with a cotton swab took a sample from O'Shea's nose.

The door opened and a nurse rushed in, "Dr. Kumar, a bad auto accident, they are bringing them in to ER now."

"I'll have the nurse bring your discharge papers to sign."

"Oh, you brought my satchel. Thank you, I couldn't remember where I left it." She unzipped the top and hurriedly searched the inside. "It's not here, my purse is not in here."

"Did you have another purse?"

"Yes, a clutch purse, a small purse that I had my phone and wallet in with my ID, credit cards, and money."

"I picked your big bag up from the sidewalk when they loaded you on the gurney. I didn't see your phone or a small purse."

She rose to get out of bed, but fell back dizzy. "I've got to find that purse, I have everything in there."

Do you think you might've left it in Judge O'Connor's office?"

"No."

"Don't worry, we will find it. Do you remember what happened?"

"No. I remember we were walking on the plaza and the next thing I knew I woke up here with a brace on my wrist and pain in my back. I do remember you holding my hand and talking to me."

"I'm sorry, some piece-of-shit kid tossed a brick at me and it bounced off me and hit you. We did catch him and took him to jail."

A nurse tapped on the door and came in with the paper work. Amala gave her all the information and signed the release papers. The nurse went over the things not to do, i.e., no travel for a week and get lots of rest. Oh, by the way, that's for both of you. Director, you tested positive too."

She then helped Amala out of the bed. When she stood, her legs gave way and she lost her balance. O'Shea was quick to grab her and helped the nurse get her into the wheelchair.

Outside the emergency room, O'Shea's car was parked in a no-parking zone. He opened the door and helped her in.

"Where are you taking me?"

"Where do you want to go?"

"I don't know, I was just thinking about that."

"I've been thinking about that too. You trust me don't you?"

"Of course. You are here to 'protect and serve,' right?"

You betcha, if you let me. "Right. First, let's stop by the Peabody and I can get you checked out. You can't stay there by yourself."

"I haven't checked in yet. I came to see Judge O'Connor direct from the airport. My return flight back to New York is tomorrow."

"Okay, I can call and cancel both your reservations. I don't know about you but I'm starving. I know this place that's famous for its breakfast that has a drive-through; buttermilk biscuits and milk gravy, grits, smoked maple-bacon, and eggs that will melt in your mouth and the best café-con-leche in town. We can get two orders to go and I want to show you this place you can stay a week or more till you recuperate. It's quiet and peaceful, bucolic like." He looked over at her to see if she was surprised with the word 'bucolic.' There was no reaction. "A-ha, I gotcha with that word didn't I?"

"Pastoral, rustic, country."

"How did you know that? Somebody called my place bucolic and I had never heard that word before. I thought it was a disease of some kind."

"I like to work crossword puzzles."

O'Shea had picked up the two orders of breakfast and had been driving on a country road for about 20 minutes when he turned onto a steep, newly asphalted driveway covered with overhanging tree branches. Two large magnolia trees guarded the entrance. He pushed the remote button over his sun visor and waited for the gates to open.

There was a lot of loud barking and Amala saw a bunch of mixed bred dogs running down the driveway. At the top of the hill waiting like the king-of-the-jungle, ready for friend or foe was Brutus, a 135-pound Bloodhound with ears almost touching the ground. Standing between Brutus's front legs was Snow, a solid white teacup Chihuahua.

Amala looked frightened. He assured her they were his security system and all bark and no bite except snow. He was born without vocal cords but would bite if he didn't like you. O'Shea drove by the big house, past the large garage, and stopped in front of a renovated log cabin. He hurried around to open the door for Amala and helped her inside the cabin. He told her about when he first bought the property that he lived in the one room cabin while he built his house up on the knoll. When his mother died, he moved his father into the cabin so he could watch over him. His father died one year later. He took two years to remodel the inside then the outside. No expense was spared.

He pointed out the walnut floors, the pecky cypress walls, the cedar beamed ceiling, and the many casement windows. He proudly stated that he had cut all the wood on the cabin from his 360 acres. "Now isn't this better than being alone in The Peabody Hotel?"

"Oh . . . Kevin, it's beautiful. Thank you." She threw her arms around him. "I love it."

He could feel the beat of her heart and her warm thighs pressed against his.

"The sun is shining, let's eat our breakfast out on the front porch and then I'll show you my house."

CHAPTER 31

Mack and Bear walked over to Smathers Beach before starting their run and let Bear do his business. Mack wanted to check if the large white sign was still there. The sign with its red letters and black skull and crossbones warned of deadly bacteria in the water. In early December water testing showed off-the-chart numbers for fecal contaminants. The sign was gone but no one was in the water. Rotten seaweed had washed up on the beach and covered the first 20 feet out to the water's edge. There was a front-end loader and dump truck fighting the invasion of the pungent, slimy Sargassum. It smelled like a sulfur pit. Bear loved to chase the sandpipers and gulls out into the water but the smell was so bad he wouldn't go near the surface.

After running halfway around the island, Mack stopped at the corner of First Street and Truman and checked his time, his heart rate, and the mileage on his new Apple Watch that Irish had sent him for his birthday. He had been running a little over an hour now averaging a 10-minute mile. He had settled on this running speed years ago when he first started running with Bear. It was a good speed for both of them to keep their heart rate up and the fat off. The sun was great. He felt like he was on a slow rotisserie, his body browning on all sides, the sweat glistening as it ran down his body soaking his running shorts.

Walking down Truman to cool down, he couldn't decide whether to go straight home and jump in the pool or treat himself to a grande café con leche at Sandy's. He turned on White Street. Life is short; he *might* even get an egg, sausage and cheese sandwich with his coffee. Plus, they always had a dog biscuit for Bear and there was that pretty little Cuban girl.

Later, Mack sat on the side of the pool cooling his feet dangling in the water while sipping on his coffee. Bear was stretched out half submerged on the first step in the pool. He had passed on the Cuban girl—too young—even though she kept smiling at him with that seductive look. He wasn't sure she spoke English, most of the time he only heard Spanish at the café and his Spanish was limited to maybe 50 words. If that wasn't enough, he had just read an article in yesterday's local paper, The Citizen, that 65 million

Americans have an *incurable* STD and 20 million new cases are reported each year. Half of these infections are among people ages 15 to 24. Yes, he was horny, and that young milk chocolate, green eyed, Cubanelle pepper tested his resolve, but no thank you little Cuban girl—I'll swim alone.

From the ocean, one block over, a strong wind worked its way through the eight foot tall Ficus hedge that bordered his property and rustled the tops of the palm trees shaking little black seeds into the pool. He stood and pushed his running shorts down, kicked them to the side, and dove into the deep end of the pool. The cold water was a refreshing shock to his body as he swam back underwater to the other end of the pool. When he surfaced, he heard his watch buzz and his cell phone on the deck chair ringing and hurried from the pool hoping it was McKenzie. It was Jin; he never did return her call wishing him a happy new year.

"Dr. Jin."

"What's wrong, you don't love me anymore?"

"I'm sorry, I've been out of town. I meant to call you back."

"That's been over a month ago."

"I know. I know . . . I owe you one."

"Good, can I collect now?"

Mack was hesitant to respond.

"Mack, I'm not trying to trap you into anything. This Tuesday is the beginning of Mardi Gras and there are great parties every night. What do you say?"

"Let me think about it."

"No. Just hop in that little puddle-jumper of yours and come see me. I'll pick you up at Lakefront airport."

Mack didn't need to think about it, it was just what he needed to get his mind off McKenzie. "Okay. I'll call you tomorrow when I'm in the air."

"Mack, one more favor . . . bring my dog for a visit."

"You know he loves to fly. He's here beside me, you want to ask him?"

Mack, flying at 1,000 feet, banked his Bonanza on a left turn for a final approach to the Lakefront Airport, five miles from downtown New Orleans. The airport would be hard to miss with their runways jutting out into Lake

Pontchartrain and The Causeway twin bridges stretching 23 miles across the lake.

Mack was clear to land and cut his speed, lowered his flaps and touched down on runway 18-R. He taxied across the tarmac in the direction where he remembered the General Aviation building was but the building was no longer there. It had been two, maybe three years since he and Irish flew in to pick up Bear. He radioed ground control and at the same time he saw a lineman about a 100-yards away waving at him in front of the new Signature FBO building.

After parking the plane he removed his roller bag and backpack and called for Bear who eagerly jumped from the plane instead of using the short steps.

"Damn!" Shouted the lineman as he came up from chocking the wheels and bumped his head under the wing when he saw Bear. "Scared the shit out of me. I thought it was a bear. What kind of dog is that?"

"A Bouvier." Mack said as he hooked a leash to Bear's collar and noticed he was a little anxious and pulling away from him. Mack turned to see what was upsetting him and saw this woman from a distance walking toward him. Could that be Jin? If so, what a transition! No longer a carefree hippie with unkempt long black hair, no makeup, and worn-out running shoes. This new makeover was right out of a high-fashion magazine. Her long hair had been cut short, real short, in a pixie cut and she was dressed in black designer skinny jeans with a tight pullover sweater that showed off her curvaceous runners body.

Bear looked up at Mack, his nose twitching. Mack nodded, "Go." Bear bolted in a full run and Jin grabbed him with both arms around his huge chest.

Mack looked over at the lineman. "Thanks for tying her down. And would you make sure whoever gases her up that they fill the two auxiliary tanks?"

Mack walked over to Jin, "Look at you, what a change. Just stunning, right out of Vogue."

Jin wrapped her arms around him. "Thank you."

"I like your haircut."

"Do you really?"

"You look ten years younger."

She gave him a quick kiss. "I'm glad you like it."

Bear kept pushing against Jin's leg until she picked up his leash, "You ready to go for a ride big boy?" She looked at Mack, "Are you hungry?"

"I'm starved."

"I've got some fresh shrimp and smoked salmon at home or we can go by uncle Girod's restaurant for some Cajun food."

"I'm not really dressed for going out. The shrimp and salmon sound good."

Jin looked at Mack's jeans, his gator cowboy boots, and the soft leather flight jacket over his denim shirt. She grabbed him by the arm, "Come on, you look great, and I love the way you dress, but we can go to the house, that way we can talk."

In the parking lot, Jin unsnapped the leash from Bear's collar and punched her key fob. Down the row of cars, Mack saw the tailgate open on a shiny black Mercedes G Wagon. Bear saw it too and took off running and leaped into the back, happily barking.

Mack noticed the AMG G63 badge, which added a luxury package and a twin-turbo V-8 engine to the G Wagon boosting the price close to two hundred thousand, a lot of money for an SUV. He opened the door and scanned the plush interior, "Wow, this is first class."

"A gift from the board members and merging partners."

"Nice gift. A big change from that old Suburban."

"Don't talk bad about her; she was my best ever. Over 250-thousand miles and still runs like a Swiss watch. The ASPCA was ecstatic when I gave her to them." She turned off Morrison Road onto I-10.

"Why are you staring at me?" Jin asked.

Mack smiled, "I'm real curious; why the big change? I mean, I love it, but did you have an epiphany or something?"

"Yes, I did. Something wonderful happened that made me reevaluate my whole lifestyle and my way of thinking. I'll tell you about it when we get to the house."

After a long ride along the Mississippi River, Jin turned on Nashville Ave and then drove to the end of Terminal Drive. She stopped at a stone archway with double gates covered with ivy and pushed a button above her rear view mirror.

Mack watched the gates open inward. "Well, Empyrean Gardens hasn't changed, it's as beautiful as I remember."

"No, not the gardens, but there have been some changes. We've built a new road and a large new entrance about a half-a-mile down the main road that leads to the two new medical research buildings. Empyrean Gardens are no longer connected to the medical center."

Bear started barking as the gates closed. "Is it okay to let Bear out, he probably wants to look for his old buddy, Abraham. You remember Abraham, the big tortoise?"

"Sure, let him out. He needs to run."

Jin stopped where the Y in the road used to be and pressed the trunk release. Bear leaped out running with his nose to the ground. Mack noticed the brick road that ran down to the river was no longer there; flowered plants and trees had replaced the brick road.

Jin turned up the serpentine drive slowing at each elbow turn till she reached the top where her house sat cantilevered out over the river bluff. Mack could see the panoramic view of the river now with the treetops of cypress, oak, and sycamore covering the hillside. Jin parked in the circle drive.

"Why don't you rest out here on the porch while I make us some lunch."

"You need some help?"

"No thanks, it won't take but a few minutes."

A nice breeze was blowing carrying the smell of burning wood. Mack needed to relax. He wasn't sure if this was a good move or not. He took a deep breath and kicked back in one of the wicker chairs with his feet on the porch railing. He could hear Jin talking to someone inside, her housekeeper he thought.

Jin came out with an ice bucket of champagne and two crystal flutes.

"Will you pop the cork and pour us a drink and I'll bring the food out?"

"My pleasure." Mack loved champagne. It was an adventure, always a new experience with each bottle, like turning the first page of a new book.

He removed the bottle and read the label, 'Pol Roger.' Good champagne, not that expensive, supposedly Churchill's top pick, and the official bubbly at Harry and Meghan's wedding. Mack pointed the bottle toward the yard as he unscrewed the top and the cork shot over the porch railing. He filled the two glasses and sipped the bubbles from his glass as Jin came out with a large tray of shrimp cocktail, smoke salmon with cream cheese, sliced tomatoes and onions, capers and Parisian Toast.

"That looks great, I'm starved." Mack picked up both flutes and handed one to Jin, "A toast to the new Jin." They touched glasses and took a drink. "Now you can tell me about your metamorphosis?"

"Can I fix you a plate?"

"Sure, thanks."

"There were two things that changed my life," Jin handed a plate of food to Mack.

"One was business and one was personal and they happened at the same time. We had investors for the purchase of the cruise ship and converting it as a Research Center. Shortly after that we remodeled the two warehouses to nursing/convalescing homes. Then we hired more doctors, technicians, and bought equipment and our overhead rapidly rose above our income. We were in a financial crisis. So we merged with ECHO, one of the largest full-service contract research organizations (CRO) in the world."

Bear came running up the steps two at a time with his tongue hanging out. "Let me get the boy some water," Jin said.

Bear laid his big head in Mack's lap. "Did you have a good run? Did you find your old buddy, Abraham?" Mack scratched behind Bear's ears.

Jin sat the pan of water on the other side of the porch and Bear rushed over and started lapping up the water eagerly.

Jin looked at Mack, "Let's see, where was I? I won't bore you with all the people we talked to; the private equity groups, the venture capital firms, etc. They vetted us and we them. Every board member agreed that the best deal was with ECHO. They had the money and the promotional skills, and we had the product. It has turned out to be an excellent marriage."

Jin handed Mack the brochure she had left out to show him, "You can look it over when you have time."

Mack opened the high-end cover with multi-colored lettering and read the first paragraph:

'Based on your internal project requirements and budget, ECHO provides integrated services and customized solutions that support the optimal allocation and use of your resources. Our offer covers the entire spectrum of clinical development, such as project management, clinical monitoring, data management, statistics and site management. In addition, we offer specialized services such as targeted regulatory interpretation; regulatory strategy consultation; medical support in specialist areas; key opinion leader (KOL) consulting; and medical statistics support during the formation of preliminary strategies for clinical research projects. These offerings can help you develop an optimal clinical research protocol and product development strategy for all markets.' "Sounds like a good company."

"I was trying to be the CEO and CFO, and I was terrible at both. But at the time we were trying to save money, plus, no one else wanted the job. I'm happy now, in the lab full time, working normal hours, and finally getting commensurate pay."

"Good for you. Getting your business organized is as important as your personal life."

"In most cases I would agree, but in my case the change in my personal life was more important than my business."

"Did you get married?" Mack said.

"God no."

"What then? Was it a good thing or bad?"

Jin removed the bottle of champagne and refilled their glasses. "At first it was bad, a shocking detection—I was devastated."

Mack asked, "Was it cancer?"

"Hold you horses. No, it's not cancer."

"Well, what then?"

"Mack, please, no interruptions, okay?"

"Okay, I'm sorry."

"What was so devastating, especially at my age," Jin took a big swallow of her champagne emptying her glass and moved her chair closer to Mack, "I found out I was pregnant."

Mack opened his mouth to say something, but remained silent.

"I was born and baptized a Catholic; I had no choice in that. But after years of college and with agnostic and atheist professors, I drifted away from the Catholic Church. When I thought of an abortion, all that Catholic teaching came back to remind me I would be murdering a human living in my body. This was a gift from God and every night I was on my knees begging God to forgive me for even thinking about an abortion.

"I never knew about babies, never held one or wanted one. I recognized early that I didn't have that maternal instinct, or the time required to be a mother. While pregnant I would think back about your relationship with Irish, how much you loved her and how much she relied on you. It changed my way of thinking. I had nothing in my life but my work. I was alone and wanted someone to love. And as each day passed, I could feel him growing inside of me. What a miraculous sensation.

"I hadn't heard from you in over two years and didn't know if I was just a one-night-stand or what. I have never been in love. I've been smitten a couple of times but never in love, not the kind like the great poets write about. My focus has always been this burning desire for knowledge. I'm not looking for a husband or even a lover as much as I like sex, so you can relax. At this age, we both are set in our ways and have our priorities. So, I make no demands on you, physically, emotionally, or financially. He is the love of my life now and I have more money than I will ever spend to take care of him. You have a right to know you have a son. I would like for this triangle between us to be nothing less than a loving and long-lasting friendship. My offer to you is that you can be a part of his life or not. You have an open door policy—you can see him anytime you want. You are a good man Mack, intelligent, with lots of street smarts, and I want him to learn from you and be a part of your life. There was no way God wasn't a part of sending this child to us.

"If you want to meet your son, Nicholas Shannon Girod, he's playing with his nanny upstairs. I'm afraid he's picked up the nickname, Niko. I know this is a shock to you as it was to me and to get involved is a major responsibility. Remember, you don't have to open that door, we can get back in that wagon and drive you back to the airport and all this never happened."

Mack stood up, his hands on his hips with a blank face. He reached for the ice bucket and filled his glass with champagne and chugged the whole glass. "Sorry, I'm a little stunned. This is not what I expected." He flopped down in his chair. "I need to think about this before I say anything."

"You might be thinking, is this my child?" Jin said. "The truth is you were the first man I had sex with in over two years and no one since then. I'm not bragging or complaining—it's just the facts. And if you add the time I spend in the lab, the time I spend with Nicholas, and my age, there's no time or desire for a relationship. Regardless, when you see him there's no denying that he is your child."

Thoughts were bouncing around in Mack's head, and Jin was right, his first thought was 'is this my child?' But why would she lie, she's not asking for anything from me.

What would Irish think? He thought about the past twenty-five years of his life raising her by himself. Would she think he was too old? Was he too old? Those were some tough times for sure, but he never regretted a minute of time with her. She had taught him as much as he had taught her. She would love having a little brother.

What about his freedom? Would he still be able to come and go without feeling shackled? He never felt that way with Irish, why would he with Niko.

His love for McKenzie was just starting to bloom—or was it? What would she think?

Who cares? You haven't heard from her since you caught her with that shithead Niles in the laundry room New Years Eve. Are you going to seek everyone's opinion on what you should do?

What do *you* want? Listen to what your heart is telling you. *Your* blood is pumping through that boy's heart.

Mack stood up again. He was pissed at himself for all the wavering. *I love kids,* he said to himself, *and secretly I've always wanted a son.*

"Thank you, Jin," Mack said as he leaned over and kissed the back of her hand. "You are a wonderful woman, highly intelligent with a great love for helping people. I'm proud I'm the father of your son. I would love to meet Niko."

Jin sobbed as she wiped the tears with both hands running down her cheeks.

CHAPTER 32

Kevin O'Shea was a pet lover and had a menagerie of dogs, cats, a raccoon, two flying squirrels, chickens, rabbits, guinea fowls, wild turkey, and two goats. Everyone in the area was aware that O'Shea's 360-acre property was a drop-off for unwanted pets. Once or twice a month, O'Shea would find a new addition in a box, a cage, or just let loose on the property. If needed, he would nurse them back to health and look for a responsible owner.

O'Shea looked behind him at the covey of animals following him as he carried two 5-gallon buckets of feed down the frost covered pathway to the lake. Yesterday morning, Amala watched from the front porch and called out, 'Hey, Dr. Doolittle.'

It was breaking dawn and the sunrays reflected off the lake and broke through the naked trees limb by limb. A misty fog floated over the lake as a family of ducks rushed to the sound of crunching leaves, cutting an arrowhead formation through the water.

O'Shea stopped at the water's edge and filled the mini-feeders and a long food trough. With a sack of birdseed and duck pellets, he walked out onto the small wooden dock and filled the birdfeeders and broadcast the pellets out over the lake.

O'Shea sat on the dock railing watching the animals eat. He was amazed at how they all got along, sometimes a growl or a peck but never a fight. This was his favorite time of day. He turned the collar up on his coat to block a cold gust moving across the lake and thought about Amala. He had taken a week of sick leave and was due back to work tomorrow. Amala had spent every night in his house and in his bed, seven of the most wonderful nights of his life.

The first night she was there. It was late and he was in bed when she knocked on his door. She was afraid, saying that something was clawing on the cabin roof and then scratching at her door. He offered her his guest bedroom but she declined. 'I don't want to sleep by myself tonight.'

Never had he been with a woman that was so perfect for him. Not only did she have a beautiful face, but also her body was flawless and she had this sweet, affectionate personality, always positive and happy. With all those attributes there was one more that was 'top shelf.' Sex with her was a wild adventure, an all-night exotic exploration, exhausting yet unforgettable. A treasure he did not want to squander.

O'Shea had a lot on his mind as he walked back up the trail to his house. Last night, the end of their quarantine, Amala told him she had to get back to New York, that she had a big modeling job coming up and she needed the money. He didn't want her to leave. He was afraid she would never come back.

He had never been married or even in love, not the kind of love he was feeling now. Being with someone like her was his lifetime fantasy, a dream and desire he had longed for and almost given up on. He had made up his mind as he walked up the steps to the house. He was tired of living alone. He needed to find a ring before asking her 'the big question'. He opened the door and hung his coat on a hook.

Amala was on the house phone and hurriedly hung up the phone when O'Shea walked into the room. She had on a pair of his jogger pants and a T-shirt with no bra. He could see her small, perky nipples imprinted through the shirt. There was something much more enticing about that look than bare breasts. Hers were implants but they were soft and natural feeling, not like some that were oversized and felt like baseballs. At her age, there was nothing wrong with regular visits to the surgeon for a little nip and tuck, and Botox injections. You don't look that perfect without it.

"I hope you don't mind but I had to make a couple of calls to New York. If there are any charges, let me know and I will reimburse you."

"Don't be silly. Make all the calls you want." He put his arms around her with a big hug, then lowered his head and blew a hot kiss on one of her nipples."

The phone rang. O'Shea hesitated, then picked it up.

She punched him on the arm, frowning.

He listened for a while and said, "Great, thank you," and hung up. "A lady found your small purse under a bench on the plaza and gave it to one of the marshals in the office building and he gave it to a police detective. One of my men patrolling this section is bringing it to the house. Now, aren't you glad I answered the phone?"

"Oh, all praise to Allah and Director O'Shea." She threw her arms around him, "I was dreading having to get new ID's and losing the contacts on my phone." She gave him a soft kiss on his lips.

He lifted her T-shirt over her head and kissed both breasts.

She moaned while tearing at his shirt and kissing him wildly on his mouth, neck, and the nipples of his chest.

He reached down between their pressing bodies and pulled the drawstring on her sweatpants. As they fell to the floor, she stepped out of them and kicked them to the side. She was wearing no panties and she could fell the burning heat from his hard body.

They both fought to unbuckle his belt and shoved his pants and underwear below his knees. He took her hand and turned her toward the bedroom, but she resisted and pulled him stumbling back into the living room. She stopped and bent over the large arm at the end of the couch, her beautiful heart-shaped bottom stuck up in the air, then turned her head to him and playfully slapped one of her butt cheeks—"I want you now, *right now!*"

It was late afternoon and O'Shea had been at his desk since early morning when his secretary buzzed his phone once again.

"There's a man named Lucky Goldstein on line one, says you are expecting his call?"

"Thanks Irene, I'll take it." O'Shea stared at the blinking light and thought, *with all his years on the police department, he knew as many criminals as non-criminals. Goldstein was marginal.*

He picked up the receiver and could hear bells and whistles going off and loud music, like a room filled with pinball machines. "Where are you?"

"Down at the casino in Tunica . . . Horseshoe." Lucky said.

"Hang up and go outside, I'll call you."

Lucky answered on the first ring, "I've got you taken care of, Chief."

"How did you know it was me?" O'Shea's number was blocked on all calls.

"You said you would call right back. I'm not doing anything illegal, you know."

"No, you're not."

"You remember back in the old days when you were a beat cop what you would say about me?"

"What's that?"

"If Lucky Goldstein couldn't find it or fix it, then forget it. Well, I haven't lost my touch. I found just what you're looking for. It's a beautiful, brilliant, solitary three carat Marquise cut diamond mounted on a six prong Tiffany platinum ring."

"How much?"

"Kevin, it's a steal—I ain't lying."

"How much, Lucky?"

"Fifteen big ones."

"What? I told you seven was my limit. I'm not paying 15 thousand for a ring. You think I'm crazy? Regardless, that sounds cheap for a three-carat solitaire. You trying to sell me something hot?"

"Kevin, how long have you known me? You think *I'm* crazy? I'm going to sell the Chief of Police hot jewelry?"

"*Director* of Police."

"Okay. I checked everything out before I called you, and I found . . ."

"Who has the ring now and where did they get it?"

"Are you going to let me finish?"

"Okay, sorry, go ahead."

"The real beauty in all this is that it has a GIA Diamond Dossier."

"What's that?"

"It's a grading report. The diamond has a microscopic laser inscription number on the girdle."

"What the hell is a girdle?"

"It's a very thin line that separates the crown, the top of the diamond, from the pavilion, the bottom of the diamond. Think of a belt around your waist."

"And what is this GIA report?"

"I have a copy of the report, it grades the diamond on 4C's: carat weight, color, clarity, and the cut."

"Who has the diamond now?"

"Jeremy Jones, a high roller from Las Vegas. He won it in a poker game and now needs the money to pay off the casino down here. He's willing to drive up there with me and we can meet at Goodman's Jewelers over on Madison. That way you can have Mr. Goodman check out the grading for you."

"I'm not paying fifteen thousand for a diamond."

"Jones is hurting, Kevin. There's room for negotiating. Just look at the diamond first. I'll bet it's worth twice that much."

Two hours later O'Shea was in Goodman's office in the back of his store while Lucky and the owner of the diamond waited outside. Goodman unwrapped the white parcel paper and the diamond was huge and like Lucky said, beautiful and brilliant. This was an eye-catcher and O'Shea made up his mind immediately. He was going to buy this di0amond for Amala no matter what. Goodman verified the diamond was GIA graded and he estimated retail value was $30,000, maybe as high as $35,000.

O'Shea and Jones stood outside in the parking lot, and then started walking toward the rear of the building. O'Shea asked what was the least he would sell the diamond for? Jones said he wouldn't let it go for less than $14,000 . . . "rock bottom," he said.

They turned and started back to the front of the store. O'Shea brought up the fact that he had told Lucky that the most he could afford was $7,000.

They stood at the front of the store, Jones looking down at his shoes with a frown on his face. "All right, $13,000 and not a penny less."

Lucky got out of the car thinking the deal was settled but watched as O'Shea touched Jones's elbow and turned him toward the rear of the store. He shook his head as the two moseyed back down the parking lot again, O'Shea with his arm over the shoulder of the shorter man. He leaned against the car and watched as the two stopped at the rear corner of the building and saw O'Shea remove a small stack of money and handed it to Jones. Jones hesitated, then stepped back and shook his head. O'Shea stuck the money back in his coat and started walking away. "Damn," Lucky said aloud. "No deal."

Halfway to the front of the store, O'Shea heard his name called and turned to see Jones hurrying to catch up with him.

"Okay, okay. I'll take the ten grand."

It was already dark outside when O'Shea pulled out from the underground parking onto Second Street. He had been trying to leave his office earlier but between the many phone calls, including the mayor's office and the new president of the police union, he was lucky to be leaving now. His last call before leaving the office was to Amala but there was no answer, so he left a message that he was on his way home and was bringing her a big surprise. At the first red light, he reached over on the passenger seat and picked up a small leather box. Inside, pressed deep into the soft black velvet, the diamond sparkled like the brightest star in the midnight sky. He smiled with excitement and eager anticipation of Amala's reaction to the ring and to his proposal. The first thing he noticed when he turned into his driveway was that the gates were open. He stopped just inside the gates, lowered the driver's side window, and listened. Where were his dogs, his outside alarm system. He cut the engine, put the ring box in his coat pocket, and stood outside the car until his eyes adjusted to the darkness. He removed his 9mm from his holster and started walking just inside the woods that lined the driveway. At the top of the driveway, he scanned all three buildings, stopping immediately at the main house. A chill ran down his back as his eyes froze on the front door standing wide open. There were no lights on in the house. He thought about calling for backup but decided to wait.

He fired up a bullet prayer, *Heavenly Father or Allah, please let me find Amala safe and uninjured.*

Moving slowly, he silently crept to the rear of the house and entered through the back door. He waited in the darkness but all he could hear was a hooting owl from outside. He moved from room to room turning on the lights but found nothing missing or ransacked. *Where is Amala?* He holstered his pistol and sat down to call her again. This time he got a recording, 'I'm sorry, you have reached a number that has been disconnected or is no longer in service.' He called the number again and got the same recording. Fear and anger raced through his mind.

He hurried to the bedroom and checked the closet, her satchel purse and coat were gone as were her jeans and undergarments she had in the dresser. He rushed to the bathroom, bumping against the doorframe and almost tripping, and found her electric toothbrush he had bought her was gone. He kicked the door shut and saw the door-hanging organizer where she kept her little red bag with all her toiletries and it was gone.

He sat on the toilet with his face in both hands, trying to fight the negative thoughts burning in his skull. *Maybe she had some kind of family emergency. Bullshit, she would have called.* He stood up; *I know one damn way to find out,* he thought, as he headed for the door and stopped immediately on hearing movement in the hallway. He waited at the door with his gun drawn as the sound came closer.

Walking in the doorway with big bloodshot eyes, saggy jowls, and long ears was Brutus, his big Bloodhound. He wasn't much of a guard dog but was just what O'Shea needed now as he sat on the floor and hugged the huge bundle of love, slobber and all. "You didn't run off with all the others? Where's your buddy, Snow?"

At the sound of his name the tiny Chihuahua tiptoed around the corner like a lost child. O'Shea picked him up and held him in the palm of his hand and let him lick the side of his face.

"You know, boys, us sitting around here pissing and moaning will get us nowhere. Let's find out what happened here today."

O'Shea marched out of the house to the garage, his two trusted soldiers right in line behind him. Inside, he opened the door to the small mechanical room and removed the tape from the video security camera and hurried back to the house.

Sitting in front of the monitor, he inserted the tape and watched the time sequence rewind. He stopped the tape when he saw the two of them on the porch that morning at 7:40 a.m., the time he left for work. He pushed the play button and watched as she waved and blew him kisses as he drove down the driveway.

Fast-forwarding the tape, he stopped it again when the gate camera showed a dark Honda Pilot coming up the drive to the front of the house. The time was 9:21 a.m. O'Shea watched as an older black man with gray hair climbed out of the backseat and the camera moved to the front porch and filmed Amala rushing down the steps wearing her hijab and carrying her satchel purse and coat. The two of them embraced and hurried into the back seat. *Damn her.*

The SUV turned around in the yard and headed down the drive. O'Shea stopped the tape, enlarged a still shot of the license plate, and made a mental note of the small sign in the back window, Uber.

O'Shea stood up and looked down at his two pals, "Okay boys, now we know that the deceitful, lying, Mata Hari has skipped out. Let's find out where." The two dogs followed O'Shea down the hallway and watched as he pulled down the attic staircase and climbed the ladder. Since her cell phone was lost, she would have to use the house phone that had a private number and one he seldom used.

Years ago after his first assignment to the undercover unit of the Vice Squad, he decided to tape all his telephone conversations, especially after he had received some questionable orders from a few of the Executive Command Staff and conversations with other known and unknown individuals and later some politicians.

He walked down the center of the attic and stopped in front of a wooden box between two floor joists. O'Shea reached inside the box and unplugged the tape recorder and carried it downstairs. At his desk in his den he plugged in the recorder and watched the date and time counter as he rewound the microcassette. He stopped the rewind on the date he brought her home from the hospital which was Thursday, seven days ago.

THURSDAY: No taped recordings.

FRIDAY: There was a call from Amala to Judge O'Connor's office and she talked with Abby about Judge O'Connor's attack of vertigo. Then, the real reason for her call: 'Had the judge sent the letter of recommendation for her father to the Parole Board at the State Penitentiary?' Abby said she had faxed the letter first thing that morning.

TUESDAY: It was 7 a.m. O'Shea would have been outside feeding his animals when this unknown phone number came in. It was her father on a burner phone letting her know the parole board had granted his release and that this phone number would be good for five days, then the number would be burned. He would be free Monday and had to get off the phone now. If they caught him, it could violate the conditions of his release.

FRIDAY: The timer stopped on 7 a.m. again. Amala had O'Shea's schedule down pat and this time she had made the call to her father. He told her he would get an Uber ride to Memphis Monday, about an hour's drive, with a cellmate that was being released on the same date and to be ready for him to pick her up around 9:30 a.m. 'Do you have any cash?' he asks. She said she had credit cards and something better than cash. Her next call was to Delta Airlines to charge two tickets one-way to New York City departing Memphis at 11:46 a.m.

Better than cash? He sat at his desk thinking, *what the hell is better than cash?* Then it hit him like a punch to the head. He jumped up and hurried to his bedroom, opened the top drawer of his chest-on-chest dresser and saw that the small padded mail envelope was empty. *The dirty bitch.* He jerked the drawer out and through it across the room, socks flying everywhere. His two dogs took off scrambling to another room.

She had stolen his two, 1854-0 and 1856-0, brilliant uncirculated $20 Liberty gold coins he had just bought through the mail to complete his collection. *Stupid, stupid, stupid—a real show off.* He had planned to take the coins that same morning to the safe deposit box. But he had to boast about his 167-year-old gold coins. And then, in haste, left them in the drawer. *I'll catch her, he swore. This is a felony theft and I'll haul her ass back to Memphis myself and throw the thieving little con artist in jail.*

The next morning, O'Shea sat in Judge O'Connor's outer office waiting while the judge was on the phone. O'Shea had received a call from Abby that O'Connor needed to see him ASAP. Abby had whispered to him that all hell had broken loose over the release of William (Willie) Wilson, Amala's father, from prison. The judge had been on a conference call the last thirty minutes with the governor and the Executive Director of the Parole Board.

Abby's desk phone buzzed. It was O'Connor calling both of them into her office.

"Have a seat. What a shit storm we're in. I can hardly sit. My ass is so raw from the governor chewing on it. You may not know this but Governor Edwards, whom I've been on the phone with, and the president, are best friends and hunting buddies. That friendship had a lot to do with my appointment as a federal judge."

"Does the president know about Wilson being paroled and why would he care?" Abby said.

"Because Willie Wilson is dead."

"WHAT?" Abby and O'Shea said at the same time.

"It's on the front page of the New York Times this morning." Reading from her cell phone, 'Harlem Shoot Out. A long awaited undercover drug bust went down in Harlem late last night killing three, one an undercover policeman.'

"The article goes on to say that William Wilson, a Tennessee prisoner out on parole less than a day, was shot and killed in the home of his brother, an infamous kingpin drug dealer."

"Did Wilson kill the policeman?"

"Don't know, but the press is all over this 'early release' of Wilson. Unfortunately, according to the prison warden, Wilson was a troublemaker, not the ideal prisoner Amala praised him to be."

"Was Amala mentioned in the article? They flew to New York together." O'Shea said.

"How do you know that?" O'Conner said.

O'Shea tells his story from the beginning, leaving out his amorous attachment and his purchase of the diamond ring. "I had no idea she was a grafter; she played me like a fiddle. Not only did she rip me off, stealing my six thousand dollar coins, she hit me up for a loan of a thousand cash until she could replace her lost ID." His phone buzzed signifying a text. Abby and O'Connor watched the expression on O'Shea's face turn to rage, then with a guttural growl, "I swear to God, I'm going to track that thieving bitch to the four corners of the earth and drag her ass back to Memphis."

"What now?" O'Connor said.

"The text is from VISA fraud. It says 'Did you just charge 768.00 USD at Delta Air for two first class tickets, Memphis to New York? Press1 if yes, or 2 if no.'

"They send me this now? It's a little late, you think?" O'Shea said as his phone buzzed again. "I'll be damned." He read the second text message aloud, 'Did you just charge 3,805 USD at Emirates Air, for one business class ticket, New York to Dubai? Press 1 if yes, or 2 if no.'

"You had better call and cancel that credit card right now." Abby said.

"Hold on everybody. Let me tell you where we're going with this debacle. Obviously, Amala, or whatever her name is, duped all of us. The governor has gotten calls already this morning from the Nashville news media asking questions about Wilson's early release and the shootout. The governor and the director of the parole board are close friends and with over 500 shootings in NYC so far this year and a shortage of policemen, they feel that if ignored this shooting will evaporate and be forgotten. So far, so good. I have had no calls from any local media. Let's keep it that way. Do *not* talk to anyone about this."

O'Connor stood. "I've got a doctor's appointment in twenty-five minutes." She stuffed some folders in her briefcase and stopped at the door. "Kevin, I'm sorry, but you are going to have to suck it up and cut your losses. Can you imagine the headlines across the national television news if the media got hold of this?"

'Kevin O'Shea, Director of Memphis Police Department
Hoodwinked by Muslim Femme Fatale, Amala Kahn'

And the subheading would go on to say 'her father, Willie Williams, whose recent early release from prison is questionable, was killed in a New York City drug bust.'

"Y'all call me if you need me . . . remember, no press. And Kevin, I know it's an expensive lesson, but best you stick with rescuing homeless animals and shun treacherous females."

CHAPTER 33

"Okay, you three sleepyheads, wake up." Jin, dressed in two-piece silk pajamas, nudged Bear with her foot as he looked up from the end of the bed. Three-year-old Niko, his long black hair spread out across Mack's chest, didn't move.

Mack raised his head, "I smell coffee."

Jin placed the tray of two steaming coffees with four heavily powdered sugar beignets on the nightstand. Mack lifted Niko to the side and took a pillow and leaned back against the headboard. "That boy was all over this bed last night."

"Tell me about it, I had to go sleep in the other bedroom, both of you were rolling and kicking me all night. Move over," Jin said, as she crawled into the bed. "I guess I'll need to get a king size bed."

Niko looked up, "Mama, I got to pee-pee."

"Come on, I'll take you." Jin said.

"I'll take him," Mack said, "I got to go myself." Mack sat on the side of the bed and pointed to his back, "Hop on." Niko bounced up and down like a bronco.

"I got to pee-pee." Niko laughed holding onto Mack's neck.

"When are you going to cut this boys hair?" Mack shouted from the bathroom.

"I'm not." Jin shouted. "Your phone's ringing."

"They can leave a message. Hey . . . this boy has a hard-on."

"That's normal."

"He's peeing all over the toilet. He's got more pressure than a fire hose."

"You've got to hold it for him."

"Me? You want me to hold his pecker?"

"Yes, it won't bite you."

"Too late, he's finished."

"Ok, show him how you make bubbles when you pee and make sure you show him how to wipe when you finish."

"Wipe what?"

"Take the toilet paper and wipe the pee pee from his tee tee."

"Men don't wipe their pecker, they just shake the dribble off." Mack said walking back to the bedroom.

"I didn't hear the faucet running, did you wash your hands?"

"I didn't 'pee pee' on my hands and my pecker was clean enough for you last night."

"Mack!"

"Let me ask you something, you ever seen a roll of toilet paper next to a urinal?"

"I'm just trying to teach my son sanitary habits."

"Good, you teach him your way and since he's half mine, I'll teach him my way."

"What's a hard-on?" Niko said.

Mack picked Niko up and tossed him onto the bed, pulled his tighty-whities down and said, "Look, that's *my* son, he still has a hard-on."

They all laughed as Niko started jumping up and down.

Mack's phone was ringing again and he showed Jin that it was his daughter, Irish. He had told Jin he wanted to wait to tell Irish in person that she has a little brother, so he pointed to Niko, shook his head, put his finger to his lips and walked outside on the balcony.

"Hello stranger, I thought you had forgotten your old man."

"That dog hunts both ways, Daddy-O."

"Touché."

"Daddy, I miss you so much. When are you coming out here to see me?"

"Soon. You tell me when you're free. You still working those long hours?"

"I love my job. I have a great secretary and they pay me the big bucks to work those long hours. Have you heard from McKenzie O'Conner?"

"No, why?"

"I thought you two were going hot and heavy. You're not still holding a grudge from that New Years Eve party are you?"

"I'd rather not talk about her."

"Daddy, that's been over a year ago, you're too big of a man to act like that."

Mack didn't say anything.

"I know, none of my business. I'm sorry. But one of the reasons I called was about her. You know I'm on the alumna committee of the law school and they know I'm from Memphis and that McKenzie is from Memphis and that over the years we've worked together on numerous programs. The committee asked me to see if I can get her to speak at this year's law graduation like she did at my first day of law school. I called her direct number last week and left my name and number on a recording and she didn't call me back. I called again this morning and the call rolled over to a lady that answered 'Federal Courts.' She said she was not allowed to give out any information about the judges. I asked her could I speak with Abby, her secretary and she said she thought Abby was on vacation. I told her why I was calling and she grudgingly told me Judge O'Conner was on sick-leave."

Mack's heart skipped a couple of beats. He took a deep breath. "What do you want *me* to do about it?"

"Oh Dad, don't be such a hard ass. I know how much you care about her."

"I didn't say I didn't care . . . did you call her cell phone?"

"I did and left a message. That's not like her. She always returned my calls. I'm really worried, Daddy. You know she has no family."

"I know. I'll track her down, I promise. I'll call you as soon as I find out what's going on."

"Thanks, Daddy. I love you."

"I love you too."

Jin walked out onto the balcony. "Everything all right?"

Mack told her about Irish's call. That a close friend of theirs in Memphis was sick, lived alone, had no family, and no one was answering the phone. He needed to make a couple of phone calls first. But he may have to fly up to Memphis, a two-hour flight, to make sure everything was okay. He asked if Bear could stay with them a couple of days while he was gone. And while gone, he wanted Jin to think about letting Niko fly back with him to Key West for a week or two.

Mack, flying VFR in his V-tail Bonanza, broke through some scattered clouds into a beautiful blue sky and leveled off at 4,500 feet. The weather forecast was for clear skies with 10 mph wind out of the southwest. He set his speed at 175 knots, about 200 mph, and dialed his magnetic compass to 350

degrees—almost due north. The Mississippi River was on his left and I-55 on his right all the way to Memphis. He could fly it blindfolded.

Mack thought about Jin, Niko, and Bear standing side by side on the tarmac waving goodbye as he taxied out to the runway. Jin had snapped a couple of pictures of him and Niko out on the wing of the plane and one with Niko standing in the left seat holding on to the yoke. Being the father of Niko, life would be different now. Unlike his raising Irish alone, he would be raising Niko with Jin.

What would Irish think about having a little brother?

His phone started ringing and he saw Tom O'Brien's name flash on the cell phone screen. He had called O'Brien before leaving and left a message asking about McKenzie being on sick leave and was it serious? He had received a text saying he was at the hospital with her now and her condition was serious and he would call him back within the hour.

"Tom?" Mack answered the phone. O'Brien had insisted on not using his title of Bishop or Father any longer, just Tom.

"Mack, where are you?" He could hear the airplane engine humming.

"When you texted me that McKenzie was very sick, I decided to fly up to see her." Mack looked at his sectional map and out the left side of his window at the river. "I'm just north of Vicksburg and Jackson, about an hour from Memphis. I was already in New Orleans when I called you. How is she?"

"They are still running tests but I'm afraid it's serious, we'll talk when you get here. I can pick you up. Are you landing at the downtown airport?"

"Yes, Dewitt Spain. Thanks, Tom. I should be there in one hour."

Mack thought, *was it cancer or did she have a heart attack*? He meant to ask what hospital she was in. Probably Winchester Clinic named after her late husband.

Mack taxied the plane up to one of the tie downs and saw O'Brien walking across the tarmac. He was bent over a little more than the last time he saw him and walking a little slower. He looked good for his age though. He remembered sending him a card for his 75th birthday a couple of years ago. He was dressed in a pair of khakis and a sweater over a polo shirt, with a ball cap and sunglasses.

Mack was right; McKenzie was in Winchester Clinic. O'Brien carefully maneuvered his long vintage Cadillac, a gift from an older lady of his parish that could no longer drive, along the serpentine Riverside Drive while explaining what he knew about McKenzie's illness.

"I didn't want to tell you over the phone but she is in a hepatic coma."

"A coma? How? Why?"

"She had an attack of vertigo in her office and fell hitting her head on the corner of the desk. She assured Abby and O'Shea that she was okay and that she had had vertigo before and knew how to get over it. Two hours later Abby found her unconscious on the floor and called the fire department paramedics. They transported her to Winchester Clinic and she is in ICU."

Inside Winchester Clinic they walked side by side down the long hallway to the ICU. O'Brien acknowledged greetings from nurses and doctors. He waited outside the ICU room while Mack entered and stood over her bed, studying her condition. A mask covered her nose and mouth. A long twisted hose, like a tree snake, ran from her mask to the IV pole and to a ventilator. A gravity nutrition bag and various tubes hung from the IV pole and he counted four large monitoring screens.

He took her hand that didn't have an IV catheter inserted and held it in his palm and covered it with his other hand. He bent over and in a soft voice whispered, "I love you. I've always loved you from the first time I looked into those deep green eyes. Do you remember, at Beethoven's birthday party? My heartbeat must have shot up to 200. I froze standing there and felt like an idiot, mumbling my words. I know, I never told you this but as I look at you now, my heart cries out to you. I promise with all that is within me, I will never leave you again." He bent over and kissed her hand.

"Sir, you are not supposed to be in here unless you are a family member." A young woman dressed in light blue scrubs stood in the doorway, O'Brien standing behind her.

Mack continued to hold McKenzie's hand.

"I'm the PA in charge of the ICU. Are you related to Judge O'Connor?"

Before Mack could answer, O'Brien jumped in and said, "Yes, he is."

"Oh, is he her husband?"

O'Brien nodded.

"I'm sorry Mister O'Connor, my name is Katie and I've been taking care of your wife. We have been dialing down the amount of oxygen on the ventilator; slowly weaning her off the machine and I'm here to take her off the ventilator."

"Should I leave?"

"No, you can stay. I heard you talking to her and the latest research shows a coma patient may benefit from the familiar voice of a loved one. It may help awaken the unconscious brain and speed recovery." Katie said as she carefully removed the mask while studying the breathing monitor.

"Is she breathing on her own now?" Mack said.

"Yes" She read from the monitor, "blood pressure, pulse rate and respiration rate all in the normal range."

"Does that mean she might come out of her coma soon?" Mack said.

"With her good readings, yes, but with a coma you never know."

Mack removed a hundred dollar bill from his pocket and put it in Katie's hand. "I appreciate you taking such good care of her."

"Katie handed the money back to Mack. "Mister O'Connor, I appreciate it but I can't take your money . . ."

"Why not? You deserve it; I insist."

"Well, thank you so much." She look around outside the room stuck the money in her pocket.

"You are more than welcome. Do you think I could stay the night in case she wakes up? I could read to her."

"I'll see about a more comfortable chair for you." Katie said as she walked out the door.

"Do you want me to stay with you?" O'Brien said.

"No, I'll walk with you to the car to get my toothbrush out of my backpack."

"Okay, I'll come by in the morning around eight or eight-thirty. There is no need to walk me back to the car. You stay here with McKenzie and I'll bring your toothbrush. Anything else you want from your backpack?"

"On second thought, just bring me the backpack. It has my shaving kit and Kindle so I can read to McKenzie."

Three hours had passed with nurses and techs in and out but none questioned his presence in the ICU. Mack had stopped reading from his Kindle each time someone came into the room. Katie had brought him a tray of food for dinner, which was quite good. He guessed that was why they had the moniker of a boutique clinic. After eating he dosed off to the humming of the machines.

When Mack awoke, he checked his phone and saw a text from O'Brian, "Mack, my older brother, James, in a nursing home in Richmond had a heart attack. I'm at the airport now and flying up to be with him. Please keep me informed on the condition of McKenzie. I'll call you sometime tomorrow."

"Tom, I'm sorry about your brother. I hope he okay when you get there. If you need anything call me." Mack returned Tom's text.

The room was dark except for a dim wall light. He walked over to McKenzie's bed where the light glowed and listened to her breathing; she looked as if she were asleep. He took her hand and said, "Maybe you are tired of me reading but I know how much you love Walter Benton and I want to finish the last verse I was reading to you before I nodded off to sleep; it's so apropos to us.

Were I Pygmalion or God
I would make you exactly as you are . . . in all dimensions.
From your warm hair to your intimate toes would you be wholly in your own image.
I would change nothing, add or take away.
The same full red flower would model for your mouth —
And from the same seashore
Would I bring the small translucent earshapes of your ears?"

He leaned over and kissed her ear and whispered, "I would give anything to write like him. He expresses his love so openly, with passion and rare beauty. When I read his words, I think only of you."

He stood, stretched his back but still held her hand and continued to talk to her. "The clinic here is taking great care of you, real VIP treatment. They have taken the ventilator off and you are breathing with ease. A nursing assistant came in and brushed your hair and gave you a sponge bath; I promise I didn't watch. You look like 'Sleeping Beauty' now with your beautiful long red hair spread out over the white pillow. Each feature on your lovely face is perfectly formed . . ." He traced her nose with his finger and then her lips. "Your lips are like Benton said, the petals of a full red flower."

Mack quickly backed away from the bed when one of the monitors started beeping and then multiple sensors stared going off. The door opened, the lights came on, and Katie rushed in with another nurse behind her. Katie reached up to the heart rate monitor and turned the beeping sound off. The other nurse re-taped the IV catheter on top of McKenzie's hand. The other sensors stopped beeping.

Mack stood back in a corner with a concerned look on his face. *Did he cause the machines to go off when he touched her face?*

"Nothing to worry about Mr. O'Connor; just the machines doing their job alerting us." Katie said as she walked out the glass sliding door.

Mack walked over to McKenzie's bed and took her hand and said, "I'm right here if you need me. I'll be here all night." He kissed her hand, said goodnight and walked over and stretched out in his reclining chair and soon was fast asleep.

Mack first thought he was having a bad dream when he awoke to shouts, screams, and machines beeping and bells ringing. The room was filled with nurses and assistances swarming around McKenzie's bed. He was shocked when he stood up and saw McKenzie sitting upright shouting 'Where am I? Let me out of here!' She was flinging her arms, fighting the nurses, and had ripped the catheter from her hand and pulled the breathing tube from her nose.

One of the nurses walked over to Mack and with her hand on his elbow asked him to wait outside in the waiting room.

Mack checked the time on his cell phone. He had been in the waiting room for almost an hour watching people going in and out of McKenzie's ICU room. He stood when he saw Katie walking toward him.

"How is she? Is she out of her coma?" Mack asked.

"We have her settled down now. She was agitated and confused—typical reaction of a patient coming out of a coma. It might be helpful for her recovery to see someone familiar. If you would like to see her, you can go in now."

Katie leaned over McKenzie's bed, Mack standing behind her. "Judge, your husband is here to see you. He's been here all night watching over you." Katie moved to the foot of the bed. Mack took McKenzie's hand and in a soft voice said, "McKenzie, it's me, Mack."

Mack saw the look of terror cross her face and then she snatched her hand away with a scream of horror. "Get away . . . get away from me. Who are you? Don't you touch me!"

CHAPTER 34

As far back as he could remember, Mack never ran from a problem. The Marine Corp strengthened that trait even more forcefully. Yet, here he was flying back to Key West as fast as he could with a short stop in New Orleans to pick up Niko and Bear. Running back to his little hideaway, his Shangri-La. He would never forget the look of revulsion on McKenzie's face when she screamed, 'Don't you touch me!'

She couldn't have hurt him more if she had stabbed him in the heart with a hunting knife. He had been single for many years and had resolved to stay that way . . . until he met her. From the first day to this very moment, he knew that she was the perfect woman for him and that he could not spend the rest of his life without her. But not now, not after the pure hate and vitriol he saw on her face.

It's a long flight from Memphis to Key West flying a single engine plane. But at 7,500 feet and clear skies, there are very few distractions. This allows you plenty of time to think—introspectively. Why did he let himself get so deeply involved? Was it a sign of weakness, stamped in his DNA as far back as Adam and Eve? He certainly wasn't unhappy being alone. He answered to no one, went anywhere he wanted and at any time. He had planned his life that way. Like Solomon said, "whatever his heart desired."

The Bonanza coughed twice, then—dead silence. The prop was still turning, windmilling, but the engine had stopped. Mack immediately switched from the left main gas tank to the right main tank and turned on the fuel auxiliary pump. Nothing. Damn, maybe a vapor lock? The running propeller should have started the engine on its own. *Move on Mack. Think fast. Check airspeed.* Mack pitched the nose up with the trim and cut the speed to 65 knots for the best glide speed while keeping the ball in the middle of the turn indicator. *Move on Mack. Find a place to land.* He had less than ten minutes to land this baby safely. He had flown this route many times and knew there were no airports or private airstrips within that time limit. He scanned the horizon left and right looking for an open field. He had been following I-55 but there was a lot of traffic, plus wires and road signs . . . it was an option though. He checked his speed and altitude and turned the nose a little to line up with the forward moving traffic on the interstate.

He ducked his head and threw up his arm instinctively when he heard the roar of the big Pratt and Whitney engine as a crop dusting plane blew by him. *Damn, that was close. Where did he come from?* Mack watched as the plane dove under a power line and sprayed a cornfield at about eight feet above the corn. He checked his altitude; he was 3,000 feet and dropping fast. He changed his mind; he would rather land in a cornfield than take his chances of a dead-stick landing on the interstate.

He saw a field straight ahead that he could easily reach and lined up the plane with the rows of corn that were about five feet high. No reason to lower the wheels, this would be a belly landing. He tightened his seatbelt, cracked the door open, turned the ignition switch off, and the fuel pump and the carb heat. The last thing he wanted now was the plane to start up.

He heard the crop duster again and looked to his left and saw the pilot, wearing dark sunglass and a baseball cap, waving and pointing downward to follow him.

Mack looked in all directions but failed to see a landing strip. The crop duster had to have a runway to take off and land. How did he miss seeing it? Was he too far away? He checked his airspeed and altitude again. He was flying, well not flying but gliding, at 65 knots and had dropped to 2,000 feet. Time to make a decision . . . he turned the nose of his plane and followed the crop duster that was now out in front of and below him. He had to maintain the same glide slope—speed, ball, and altitude. He searched the horizon to see where the crop duster was taking him and at the same time picked two cornfields, one close by and one farther out, for alternate landing sites. He watched as the crop duster turned and headed for a large section of trees on a hillside. Oh shit. He wasn't sure he had enough altitude to clear those treetops. He was committed now; too late to change. Focus on the treetops.

He watched as the crop duster cleared the treetops and then fell out of sight. What the hell, where did it go? He rolled the trim wheel a couple of notches to move the nose up to help him clear the treetops while watching his air speed indicator. The last thing he wanted was the plane to stall over a forest of mature trees. Then he saw it . . . the crop duster had landed in a deep valley and was taxiing off the end of a grass airstrip.

God is good . . . thank you Lord. Once he had cleared the treetops, there was a sheer drop-off of 1,000 feet. The problem now was he had too much speed.

To try to spiral down without any power this low was too risky. He lined up his approach, pointing the nose of the plane short of the threshold of the airstrip while lowering his landing gear and his flaps. Both cut his airspeed. He was going to need the entire airstrip and more. He saw the orange windsock on a flagpole and it was hanging halfway, indicating a 12-knot wind that he would be landing into. That added another step to cutting his airspeed. Still, he was going too fast. He started a forward slip, crabbing the plane sideways to the airstrip to create more drag. The plane slowed to 60 knots. Mack worked the rudder pedals till the nose of the plane was lined up with the middle of the landing strip and pulled back on the yoke. The plane flared, the blast of the stall horn filled the cockpit as Mack held the nose up and the plane floated till both wheels touched the grass. Then a couple of bounces and the nose wheel was down. He got the plane stopped just short of the end of the airstrip.

He released the seatbelt buckle, leaned back and took a couple of deep breaths. No injuries and no damage to the plane. He had an immediate urge to pee. He pushed the door open, stepped out onto the wing, and jumped to the ground hurrying to get his pants unzipped.

He looked over the wing of his plane and saw the pilot from the crop duster running toward him. *I hope he doesn't mind me peeing on his grass strip.*

"Hey, you okay?" Mack heard the crop duster as he came around from the rear of the plane. "Oops. Sorry about that."

"No problem." Mack said as he turned his back while he finished, "couldn't hold it any longer."

"I know the feeling."

Strange voice Mack thought. He turned as he zipped up his fly. "Thanks for . . ." He stopped mid-sentence. They stood staring at each other . . . then Mack said, "I'm so sorry," looking down at where he had peed. "I had no idea."

"When you gotta go, you gottta go. I'm Gina Garcia," she stuck out her hand, and then pulled it back. "On second thought we better wait till we wash up."

They both laughed.

"Mack Shannon." Mack said pulling his hand back. *Pretty teeth,* he thought. But what was most notable was the olive tee-shirt with *U.S. Marines* printed in black letters and of course the tight jeans outlining a perfectly heart shaped derriere. "Thanks for guiding me to your airstrip."

"Great landing. Did you run out of gas?"

"No. A vapor lock I think or could be the booster pump. My right main is full but it wouldn't switch over. I had picked out one of your cornfields to belly land when you waved me to follow you."

"Nice bird, I would hate to see her busted up."

"Yeah, well, you saved that from happening. It's an old plane but still has great bones." Mack nodded his head toward her shirt, "Were you in the Corps?"

"Yeah, aviation. How about you?"

"Semper Fi. Were you a pilot?"

"Yes. Were you?"

"No. Force Recon."

"Badass Marine, huh?" Gina said.

Mack remembered what his Aunt Irish told him years ago when he was all gung-ho about the Corps; 'The Corps is not your career—it's a stopgap, that's all. Stay focused on your life's future and don't get caught up playing Marine.' But the Corps had its own plans. Once he signed those papers, he gave up total control of his life for the next 4 years. In retrospect, it was the best experience in his life, but his Aunt Irish was right. As much as he loved it, a career in the Marine Corps was not for him.

"I thought all Marines were badass." Mack said.

Gina laughed "True. Where were you headed?"

"Home. Key West."

"A real conch, huh?"

"Not a native, but I've had a house there for a long time."

"I love Key West, great party town, but I hear it's changed a lot now."

"Yeah, what hasn't?"

"True, some good and some bad. Come on, let's get the tractor and pull that pretty girl in the hangar and see what the trouble is."

Mack walked from around the back of the plane and saw a large man dressed in jeans and a sleeveless shirt with bulging biceps and one arm covered in tattoos from shoulder to wrist, walking toward them. He walked slowly across the field with the help of a cane, each step carefully planted.

"That's my Daddy," Gina nodded toward her father. "He retired as Sergeant Major Of The Marine Corps."

Mack turned and in a low voice said, "Now that's a *badass* Marine. There's only one of those."

They all stopped in the middle of the field. "Daddy, this is Mack Shannon. He's from Key West and a Force Recon Marine."

"Oorah, Sergeant Major," Mack said.

"Oorah. Call me Brock." He stuck out his hand. His speech was slow. "No damage to your plane, huh?"

"None, thanks to your daughter." His grip was strong.

"Great looking plane. I know they stopped making the V-tail in the early 80's but yours looks like a showroom model."

"Thanks. It's a 79, V35B, 300 horsepower. It's a one owner. An old country doctor in Mississippi who kept it parked in his barn most of the time. A close friend gave it to me when we retired a shared business. Buck Jones, you might have run across him. He was a Master Gunnery Sergeant in the Corps."

"No, the name is not familiar. A nice gift though."

"I can't believe that plane is over 40 years old; it looks new." Gina said.

"I've kept it up over the years: new paint job, latest avionics, and all new custom upholstery."

Mack's phone rang and he saw Irish's name on the screen. "It's my daughter, excuse me." Mack turned and walked away a few feet.

"Hi, baby girl."

"Daddy, you said you were going to call me about Judge O'Connor. Did you find out anything? Is she sick?"

"She is in the hospital and was in a coma."

"Oh my God. What happened? Was there an accident?"

"She fell and hit her head."

"Oh, Daddy, I feel so sorry for her. What can I do?"

"Don't worry, she's getting first class care at the Winchester Clinic, named after her late husband."

"Where are you now?"

"You're not going to believe where I am. I'm in the middle of a cornfield somewhere south of McComb, Mississippi. My plane malfunctioned and I had to land on a private airstrip."

"Are you all right?"

"Yep. No damage to the plane or me. We're pulling the plane into the hangar to see what caused the failure and hopefully we can find a part for whatever needs to be replaced before dark."

"Dad, that plane is going to kill you yet. It's too old, you are always replacing parts."

"I'm old too. Should I not get a new knee or a heart stent when needed? Just fold my tent and stop living? I love flying and I'm going to fly till I die."

"I know Daddy. But I don't know what I would do if I lost you."

"I promise you, I'm not going anywhere."

"Where were you headed before the crash?"

"It wasn't a crash, honey, just a forced landing. I was on my way to Jin's in New Orleans."

"Why aren't you with McKenzie?"

"I was. I was in her room with her all night until she woke up the next morning from her coma. But she was frightened by my presence and screamed at me to get away from her. She was terrified with me being in the room."

"Daddy, temporary loss of memory is normal for someone coming out of a coma. You can't leave her there by herself."

"She's not by herself. Father O'Brien is with her."

"Daddy! You're dating both these women at the same time. You are just asking for trouble."

"I'm not dating either one of them." Mack heard the tractor and looked back to see Gina backing the tractor up to the plane.

"Look, I've got to get back to my plane. I'll call you when I'm back in the air. Love you."

"Love you too, Daddy. Be careful."

Mack helped Gina hook up the tractor to the plane and walked behind it to the hangar. Sergeant Brock and another man had pushed the tall hangar door open as Gina pulled the plane inside. A mechanic was quick to roll his ladder over and had the cowling up in a short time. A couple of men in the hangar came over to admire the V-tail.

It didn't take long for the mechanic to confirm Mack's latest diagnosis of a bad fuel pump. Gina and Mack sat outside the hangar on a wooden bench while she called Air Parts Locator Services and found the fuel pump.

"It's your lucky day." Gina said. "They have one. It's a rebuilt pump and they will deliver it the first thing in the morning by a FedEx drone." She handed Mack's credit card back. "It was $386.00 including shipping."

"Thank you. Now, is there a motel close by that I can stay the night?"

"Yes." She pointed to the three-story house across the road and up on a hill. "We have an extra bedroom next to mine upstairs but we'll have to share the bathroom between the bedrooms." She wiggled her eyebrows up and down with a seductive smile.

Mack watched Gina as she walked back into the hangar with both hands in her back pockets. He thought of the old saying, 'Many a true word is spoken in jest.' She turned and looked back to see if he was watching. Her Marine tee shirt was pulled tight, one nipple protruded just under the *U. S.* and the other under *Marines . . .* yes, he was watching.

He heard what sounded like a ship's bell ringing in the distance. Mack stood up as Sergeant Brock and Gina rolled out of the hangar in a golf cart.

"That's mama ringing the bell for supper. Hop on the back for the best meal you ever had." Gina said.

Gina was right. The food was great and plenty of it but it was hard to enjoy. Gina, with her shoe off, kept rubbing his leg up and down under the table. That came to a sudden stop when the swinging door to the kitchen opened and the most attractive woman Mack had seen in a long time walked in. She was tall and lean like a runway model, dressed in a 3-piece custom suit. Her name was Bobbie. She walked over and patted Gina's mother on the back. "Sorry I'm late, mama."

Mack thought, *this couldn't be Gina's sister; she's a black woman . . . unless she's adopted.* But that question was soon answered when Bobbie walked around the table and kissed Gina on the lips.

"Who's our guest, Gina?" Bobbie said, staring across the table at Mack with both hands on Gina's shoulders.

"This is Mack Shannon." Gina said. "His plane lost its fuel pump and he was forced to land on our airstrip. Mack, this is Bobbie Lang."

Bobbie reached across the table to shake Mack's hand, "Nice to meet you Mack Shannon. Gina is my wife."

Mack had played poker all his life and had learned to keep a straight face no matter if he was holding four of a kind or a royal flush. He wasn't sure he met the challenge this time though. But one thing he was sure of and made a mental note to do was to lock the doors to his bedroom tonight.

Mack was up early sitting on the porch steps drinking coffee. He had received a text that his fuel pump was being delivered at 7:45 a.m. Mack's watch buzzed and he tapped the screen and saw the drone on his GPS flying across the cornfields. The drone slowed down, hovered about 25 feet above the front yard, lowered the tether to the ground and automatically released the package. Mack hurried to the hangar with the package under his arm.

Mack helped the mechanic install the fuel pump and buttoned up the cowling. "Let's pull it outside, crank her up and see if she'll run" the mechanic said. Mack backed the tractor in and pulled the plane from the hangar. The mechanic stood outside at the wing tip with a thumb pointed up as Mack hit the starter button. The engine started immediately and Mack adjusted the throttle to 1000 RPM. He looked out the windshield and saw Gina driving down to the hangar in the golf cart. He shut the plane down and climbed down on the wing to meet her. He walked over to the mechanic to thank him and handed him two one hundred dollar bills. He raised both hands and stepped back refusing the money and told Mack the Garcia's paid him a good salary. Mack rolled up both the bills and stuck them in the mechanic's shirt pocket. "Have a good dinner on me."

"Hey Marine, you weren't going to leave without saying goodbye, were you?" Gina said as she pulled up beside him in the golf cart.

"No, of course not. Your dad said you were still asleep."

"I was in the shower. I know you said you had to get back to Key West right away, but I wanted to apologize for Bobbie popping off last night with that 'she's my wife.' She has to tell everyone that we are married. She is very insecure and sometimes I think she enjoys watching the shock effect it has on people."

"To each his own." Mack said.

She handed Mack a paper bag, "I put in a couple of buttered biscuits and a hot coffee for your trip. Give me a hug." She put her arms around him and whispered, "Maybe soon I can sneak off and drive down to Key West and we can party . . . just the two of us."

Mack looked up at the house and saw Bobbie standing on the porch looking through a pair of binoculars.

He hurried to the cockpit of his plane.

CHAPTER 35

Mack had called ahead of time and asked Jin if she could bring Nico and Bear to meet him at the Lakefront Airport so he could get to Key West before dark. He did not tell her why he was a day late to pick up Nico. If she knew that he had to make an emergency landing, she might refuse to let Nico fly with him.

Taxiing the plane across taxiway Foxtrot to Flightline First, he saw Jin, Nico, and Bear standing in front of the FBO. *The ideal nuclear family. Is that what you want at this age, to start all over again?* Mack thought.

He stepped out on the wing of the plane and waved at Nico running toward him shouting Papa, Papa, with Bear right behind him.

Yeah, that answered that question. I mean, what's more important than your own child.

Mack jumped onto the tarmac and picked up Nico in his arms and spun him around and around singing Nico, Nico, Nico.

Bear jumped and barked, bumping his head into Mack's leg as Jin walked over to them, "Hey, save some of that for me."

Mack put Nico down and picked up Jin and swung her around and around singing out, Jin, Jin, Jin. When Mack stopped, Jin wrapped both arms around his neck and kissed him long and hard, then whispered, "You may not want to hear this but I think I'm falling in love with you."

Mack was saved from responding by the gas truck driver when he blew his horn, stuck his bandana wrapped head out the window and shouted, "Hey lover boy, you need gas?"

"Yeah," Mack shouted back. "I'm not staying, I'm leaving in a few minutes. Can you top off both tanks?"

The truck driver nodded and stuck his hand out the window with his thumb up as he moved the tanker to the front of Mack's plane.

"Are you sure you can't stay an hour or so?" Jin said.

"I'd love to but I need to get back to Key West before dark. There's a storm brewing in the gulf and I want to be home before it moves into the Keys."

"Let me get Nico's bag for you. I made some sandwiches and cupcakes for you all."

"You don't need any clothes for that boy, just shorts and flip-flops. We're going to be in the water most of the time."

"You know he doesn't swim and you have to watch him closely, he's an adventurous little thing. I've got sunscreen in his bag and you will have to be careful, Mack, his young skin will burn in minutes down there."

I've rescued him just in time. Mack said to himself as they all walked back to Jin's car and got Nico's bag and the sandwiches. Jin stayed with the car and waved goodbye as Mack hurried to catch Nico and Bear running back to the plane. The last thing he heard was 'Don't cut that boys hair.'

Mack signed the credit card reader for the gas and helped Nico buckle up in the copilot seat. Bear was already stretched out in the back seat on his favorite beach towel as Mack taxied over to the shorter runway, 36R, for takeoff. Mack looked over at Nico as the plane's wheels lifted off the runway. The enlarged pupils in his moon-shape eyes showed bewilderment and fear. Mack started singing his piecemeal rendition of different services' songs:

Up, up and away
In my beautiful plane
We can sing a song and sail along the silver sky
For we can fly, we can fly.

Off we go into the wild blue yonder,
High in the sky
We can fly

If the Army and the Navy
Ever look on Heaven's scenes;
They will find the streets are guarded
By United States Marines.

We can fly, we can fly.

Every time Mack shouted 'We can fly, we can fly,' he put both thumbs under his armpits and flapped his 'wings.' He watched a small grin grow into a large smile and heard a light giggle from Nico.

"Okay. Here's the deal, Lucille. Every time I sing 'We can fly, we can fly,' I want you to sing out 'We can fly, we can fly,' and you have to flap your wings with me. Okay, here we go. Loud now, let me hear you." Mack had Nico laughing and singing as he flipped the landing gear switch up and set his altimeter to 5,500 feet.

Flying VFR (visual flight rule), and now at 7,500 feet, Mack kept a constant outlook for air traffic, weather, and the Florida coastline. Nico had crawled over to the backseat with Bear and both were sound asleep. Nico was hugging his baby pillow with one arm and the other was wrapped around Bear. The vanilla icing from the cupcake that he had been eating was still on his face. Mack checked his storm scope, which was good for 30 miles out and the sky looked good all the way home to Key West.

Mack reached back and shook Nico's leg, "You want to see where we live?" He switched the radio frequency. "Key West approach . . . Bonanza 107 Echo Sierra . . . 20 miles northeast at 3500 . . . inbound for landing at Key West International with Bravo."

"Bonanza 107 Echo Sierra approach . . . radar contact, altitude indicates 3500. Contact Key West International tower, 118 point 2"

"7 Echo Sierra, 118 point 2. Thank you."

"Bonanza 107 Echo Sierra . . . Key West Tower . . . 10 miles northeast with inbound for landing with information Bravo."

"Key West Tower to Bonanza 107 Echo Sierra, enter right downwind, runway two niner. Is that you Mack?"

"Key West tower, affirmative Marcella . . . 107 Echo Sierra . . . right downwind for two niner."

"107 Echo Sierra clear to land. Cervezas at the Parrot? I'll pick you up at your plane."

Mack heard someone key their mic "Hey Bonanza, I'll take that offer if you can't."

Another keyed mic "Ditto for me too, I'm landing right behind you."

Mack felt something pushing his shoulder. He rolled over and stared into the face of a furry monster trying to lick his face. It was time to let Bear out to do his business. He sat up and looked over at Nico who was sound asleep hugging his pillow. He was a big hit at the Green Parrot last night sitting on top of the bar eating popcorn and throwing some to Bear. Mack stood, lost his balance and sat back on the bed. *Wow. What was that?* They left early last night and he had only two beers. He tried to stand again and swayed a little, pitched and rolled, like trying to set his inner gyro to even flight. After a minute or so he felt okay. Was it an ear infection? He looked down at his left hand and his little finger was waving at him. He sat down again and lifted his hand and stared at the tremor in his little finger. *What the hell is causing that? That's the second time this has happened. I must be sleeping on my hand and pinching a nerve?* He stood up again and was fine. He held both hands out in front of him and there were no tremors in his hands or fingers.

He let Bear out, went to the bathroom himself, and walked back to the bedroom and picked up Nico and walked outside to the pool. He entered at the shallow end of the pool and lowered Nico into the water waist high while holding him under both arms. Nico's eyes popped opened and he started kicking and squirming.

"Easy big boy, we're in the pool and I'm going to sit you on the first step and you watch me, okay?" Mack pushed back from the steps and ducked his head underwater with his eyes open, smiling up at Nico.

"I'm going to swim to the deep end and back underwater." Mack pointed to the other end of the pool and took off underwater.

Nico was standing up on the steps holding out his arms when Mack surfaced and grabbed Nico under each arm and pulled him around and around in a circle. Mack took an exaggerated deep breath and jumped up and down under the water while holding Nico above the water.

"Now, take a deep breath, we are going under the water together on three." Mack knew that drowning was the leading cause of death in ages 1-4 and his top priority was to teach Nico how to swim like a fish. Mack counted 1, 2, 3 and they slowly submerged. He remembered when Irish was in diapers and he taught her how to swim and that babies have a diving reflex that automatically holds their breath. They did this numerous times until he had Nico opening his eyes underwater and floating on his back. Before the day was over, Mack was pushing Nico to the bottom of the shallow end of the pool picking up coins Mack had thrown in.

Mack sat on the side of the pool looking at the notes he had numbered on his phone. He had listed all the things he wanted to accomplish with Nico in the two weeks he had him:

TEACH HIM:

1. How to swim.
2. How to ride a bike.
3. How to snorkel, how to dive with a hookah and a small air tank in the pool & hopefully in open water.
4. How to bait his hook & catch a fish.

Nico came running over to Mack, "Papa, Papa, I got to pee-pee."

"Okay, kick those tighty-whities off." Mack pulled them down to his ankles and Nico stepped out of them holding on to Mack's head. "Now, go over there and water the bushes."

Mack followed his little white butt as he hurried over to the bushes and sprayed every bush he could. *That butt is going be as brown as a berry when he leaves here.*

It had been a couple of months since Mack had flown Nico back to Jin. She had called them every day when he was in Key West. Now, it had almost become a ritual that Nico called Mack to tell him about his day and that he loved his Papa. Strangely, while talking to Nico, he had not heard from Jin. When he ask Nico about his mother he would say she was working and the Nanny was watching him. The last he heard from Jin was a text that she and Nico were looking forward to some warm weather and would fly down to Irish's upcoming birthday. Mack had sent Irish a plane ticket to Key West for her birthday.

It was another beautiful day in paradise. Mack was reclined in one of his redwood chaise lounge chairs by the pool, drinking café con leche, and reading the Key West Citizen morning paper. Now that Nico was back in NOLA, Mack could sleep with all the windows and doors open and not worry about Nico wandering off into the pool. The patio glass pocket doors opened all the rooms on the south side of the house to the pool, including the kitchen, living room, and the master bedroom and bath. The ceiling fans carried the cool salty ocean breeze throughout the house.

Mack dropped the newspaper onto the pool deck, leaned his head back on the soft cushion, took a long deep breath and closed his eyes. *This is the good life. Just what he had planned and worked so hard for. So, stop with the A-type personality, get off the power train, and just kick back and savor every minute of your freedom.*

Irish had spent most of her life in and out of Key West and was pretty much on her own now; half island girl (conch) and half cosmopolitan girl. He would do the same with Nico. Jin was totally involved with her research and assured him he could have Nico as often as he wanted.

Mack heard someone whistle, and then "Hello."

He sat up in his chair and looked up in the tall coconut palm. "Hey Paddy, what's up? You want something to eat." Mack went to the kitchen and got a hand full of peanuts in the shell and half of a pomegranate. A beautiful green Amazon parrot was sitting on the back of his lounge chair when he came back to the pool.

"Paddy, me boy, where you been." He held out a single peanut. "Hey Mack." Paddy said and took the peanut in his beak.

At one time Paddy was someone's pet and escaped his cage or they moved away and let him loose. He stopped by Mack's house two or three times a week. Paddy shrieked and whistled and said "Nico."

"Nico's gone, Paddy, he'll be back soon." Mack held the half-eaten pomegranate in his hand as Paddy sat on his arm picking out the seeds. This was his favorite fruit.

The back gate bell rang.

"Nico's gone. Doorbell. Doorbell." Paddy shrieked.

"Fausto's, Senor Shannon." Mack heard Carlos shout from the back gate. He walked to the bedroom and fished a five-dollar bill from his money clip and opened the back gate.

"Thanks, Carlos." Mack handed him the five and took the box of groceries and deli sandwich's he had ordered earlier.

As he walked across the patio, he saw Paddy fly back up to the palm tree. He stepped up into the kitchen and tripped when his flip-flop caught the edge of the step. The box of groceries went flying across the room. He tried to catch the box but fell hard, head first, into the glass patio door. Blood splattered everywhere. He grabbed his forehead just above his eyebrow and the blood ran through his fingers like a busted water pipe. He rolled over on his back, took a deep breath, and did a mental assessment of his circumstances. He didn't have any broken bones, just a cracked head. He had face planted right into the glass door, failed to throw up his hands or arms to break the fall. What happened to his 'great' reflexes?

He sat up. The bathroom was right next to where he had fallen, so he pushed himself up and staggered to the sink as blood ran down his face and bare chest. He washed his face with cold water and pressed a washcloth hard against the cut to stop the bleeding. Looking in the mirror, he removed the washcloth and saw a five-inch, half-moon cut between his right eyebrow and hairline. He unrolled a handful of toilet paper, stuffed it over the cut and wrapped a face towel over that. He pressed hard on the towel but the blood was still flowing freely, soaking through the towel. If he hadn't seen the cut himself, he would have thought it was a cut artery. He needed to get to an emergency room and remembered seeing the Urgent Care out on North Roosevelt, next to the US Customs, in an old Pizza Hut building. He grabbed the keys for his Volkswagen Thing and a clean shirt and headed for the back gate.

After a CT scan and 12 stitches, Mack stopped by the Green Parrot Bar for a single malt scotch to wash down some Tylenol and antibiotics the Doc had given him. It was dark when he left the Green Parrot. He had a nice buzz with only two drinks. He drove along Atlantic Boulevard with the top down. The sky was a kind of soft blue, full of stars and a bright yellow moon that looked like van Gogh had painted. Mack turned on Reynolds Street passing the Casa Marina and stopped at the corner of Waddell. He took a deep breath and inhaled the pungent smell of herbs and spices from Louie's Backyard and realized he hadn't eaten since early morning.

He turned left, drove to the end of Waddell and parked. He walked past the front of Louie's and down a walkway on the west side. He could hear the waves washing against the pilings of the After Deck Bar, cantilevered out over the ocean. He saw his favorite bartender, Reva, and she pointed to a bar high table in the corner by the handrail.

"Hey, handsome, what happened?" She nodded to the bandage on his forehead.

"I tripped wearing flip-flops and fell face first going from the pool to the kitchen."

"Are you all right? I'm off work in 30 minutes and could follow you home and make you forget you ever had that boo boo."

"I'm sure you could and I'd love it, but that 250 pound cop boyfriend you live with would put another boo boo on the other side of my head."

She laughed.

"You got any fresh fish left?"

"I could get them to make you a Grouper sandwich?"

"Perfect, and press it with everything on it. And how about a small bowl of Conch Chowder with a cold Silver Heineken?"

"You got it handsome."

CHAPTER 36

Mack stood and adjusted the lounge chair in the upright position. The sun had moved and it was time to get some sun on the front of his body. He leaned back, closed his eyes and thought about the much-used axiom Conchs say about Key West, 'another day in paradise.' And it was. The temperature was about 75 degrees, a clear blue sky with a bright sun, and a sea breeze fanning the palms around the pool. But the added attraction that completed this tropical picture of paradise was the nude, golden brown beauty, standing at the end of the pool.

About two weeks ago while Mack was swimming laps in the pool, he heard a loud ooga bike horn outside his back gate. With a towel wrapped around his naked body he opened the gate to find the sexy young green-eyed Cuban girl from Sandy's Café with two large cafes con leche and what turned out to be a pressed egg, sausage, and cheese sandwich in her bike basket.

"Buenos dias."

"Buenos dias," Mack mumbled, somewhat off-guard at seeing her this close vis-à-vis.

"I brought you breakfast."

She speaks English. Great. He smiled and stepped back to let her walk her bike inside. "And what do I owe this fortunate occasion to?"

She pushed her kickstand down, turned and stepped up close to him. She was small but had a great body. He remembered Irish had told him her name was unusual . . . started with an S . . . Savanna, that's right.

"Is your daughter McKenzie here? She is so sweet and friendly and speaks very good Spanish. I haven't seen her in a while."

"No, she living full time in California now."

"I don't remember who wrote this but it was something I liked and memorized in school, *If something one wishes to be done cannot be commanded done, one must find another way to achieve one's goal.'* Your smile has been haunting me for weeks and every time you stopped to buy coffee, I hoped you would say something to me. I couldn't command you, so bringing you breakfast was my way of achieving my goal—to meet you."

And that's how it all started. She was not as young as he had thought, she even had a small child the same age as Nico, his name was Charlie, and he loved to swim in Mack's pool. But being truthful, Mack knew she was too young for him. Certainly not the *socially acceptable minimum age,* i.e., *the half your age plus seven rule.* She was, as some would describe, drop-dead gorgeous. He had never been with anyone that beautiful and sometimes thought 'why me.' But the fact that she was young and playful was contagious, and Mack found himself laughing more and happier than he had been in years. Added to all that, her affection had his libido at its highest level.

Now, here she was at his pool of her own accord, bold, naked, and uninhibited. She was laughing in mid-air as she did a 'cannonball' jump into the pool trying to get him wet. She swam the full length of the pool underwater and exploded like a sea nymph from the deep, her long black hair covering her face and splashing him with water.

"Come on, lazy, get in the pool." She said.

Mack stood completely naked with both hands on his hips like Superman.

She put each index finger in her mouth and blew a long wolf whistle then laugh and splashed him with water.

Mack stepped down to the first step and his phone started ringing. He held up one finger at Savanna. He picked up his phone and saw it was his daughter calling. Looking back at Savanna, he said, "It's my daughter, I've got to take this call," and walked into the enclosed patio.

"What's up baby girl?"

"Not much daddio. Just getting packed to come see the number one man in my life."

"I better be number one."

"You will always be my number one, but I have met someone important and I want you to meet him too. Would you mind if he came with me to celebrate my birthday?"

"What's his name? What does he do? How old is he?"

"William Silverstone. Everyone calls him Will. He's a yacht builder here in California and he is eight years older than me."

"What kind of name is Silverstone? Is he Jewish?"

"No Daddy, he's a Christian and his family is from England. Now, is it okay if I bring him?"

Of course, honey, the more the merrier. It's your birthday, you can bring anyone you want."

"What did you buy me for my birthday?"

"It's a secret."

"Give me a hint."

"I thought you liked surprises."

"I do, and I have a big surprise for you too."

"And what might that be?"

"Oh no. We both will have to wait."

"Okay, I'll still pick you up Friday at the airport, 1:30?"

"Yes sir. I love you and can't wait to see you."

"Bye, darling. I love you too."

As Mack walked back to the pool his phone started to ring again. He looked at the screen and saw a picture of Nico. He looked over at Savanna standing on the side of the pool with a towel wrapped around her waist with both hands on her hips and a big scowl on her face. He held up one finger again and said, "I'll be just a minute."

Mack turned and walked back to the patio.

"Hey little man, you got a haircut." Mack was looking at him on FaceTime.

"Papa, I see you."

"I know, I see you too. You coming to see me?"

Mack could hear Nico's mother in the background tell him what to say. "Yes sir, Friday."

"You're flying all by yourself, like a big boy."

Jin took over the phone. "Mack, I changed my mind. I couldn't let him fly down by himself, even with an attendant, he's just too young. I'm going to fly down with him if that's okay? You did invite me, remember? And there is something we seriously need to talk about."

Mack heard the gate bell jingle and turned to see Savanna leaving. She gave him the bird, waving her middle finger. Back to Jin, he said, "Sure . . . sure I remember."

He heard Savanna's farewell shot, four loud blasts of her ooga bike horn. He smiled, *fiery Cuban women. He loved it.*

"Great. The more the merrier," he said. "I'll pick you both up at the airport Friday morning."

Mack turned off Bertha Street onto A1A along the ocean side with the top down on his VW Thing. Bear was sitting in the front seat, his head hanging out the window. The sun was bright and a good breeze was blowing across Smathers beach. He saw two windsurfers racing each other as he turned into the airport. He looked up when he heard the big jet engines roar overhead and stop to watch the Jet Blue airplane land on the runway right on time.

Mack stood outside at the gate chatting with a ticket agent as the plane taxied to a stop. Jin held Nico's hand as they stepped off the mobile ladder onto the tarmac. The ticket agent opened the gate and nodded to Mack when she saw Nico running towards them shouting Papa, Papa. Mack's heart swelled and it was hard for him to swallow as he grabbed Nico and swung him around and around singing Nico, Nico, Nico. He was so proud of this son of his. He put Nico on his shoulders and his arm around Jin and they walked out to the car. Bear let out a long wolf call when he saw Mack carrying Nico on his shoulders. The back seats were laid flat and Mack pointed and Bear jumped into the back as he lowered Nico on top of him. Nico grasped two hands of fur as they wrestled---rolling in the back seats, Bear growling and Nico laughing.

Mack stopped by Five Brothers Grocery on Southard Street to pick up lunch for the three of them: two Cuban Mix (ham, pork, salami, cheese, lettuce, tomato, pickles, mayo & mustard) pressed on Cuban bread, a hamburger for Nico and a pork bone for Bear.

After a long swim in the pool, Jin suggested a short siesta. Mack hinted his king size bed to Jin, but she thought she should sleep with Nico in one of the other bedrooms. What was that all about? Damn, with trying to figure women out.

Mack couldn't sleep and it was time for him to pick up Irish and her boyfriend. He looked in the back bedroom and Nico and Jin were still asleep. He was running a little late and hurried to the airport a short distance from the house. When he turned onto Faraldo Circle the airport traffic was backed up in front of American Airlines. As the cars moved forward he saw Irish standing by her roller bag waving at him. Standing beside her was a tall man, tanned with light blonde hair. Mack double-parked and jumped out of the car as Irish rushed over and Mack grabbed her in a bear hug. She introduced William Silverstone and he said to Mack, "I've heard lots of stories about you,

Mr. Shannon and it's a pleasure to finally meet you."

Mack hurried to put the back seats up for William to sit and their luggage. As they drove around the circle Irish said, "Oh Daddy, I left something at the airport can you go back around?"

"Sure honey, what did you forget?"

"It's my surprise for you, remember? Just pull over and I'll hop out and be right back."

Mack moved into a parking spot as a car pulled out just past the American Airlines entrance. Irish jumped out before the car completely stopped. Mack looked back and watched her go through the American Airlines doors and then looked at William in the back seat.

William shrugged his shoulders as if he didn't know anything about what was going on.

They both sat without saying anything, just waiting on Irish. Mack was in deep thought about his surprise for Irish and trusted his judgment that she would love little Nico like he did.

Mack felt the air around him changing and watched a dark cloud block out the sun. A cold chill ran down his back signaling a warning. He looked around quickly and outside the passenger side door was the most frightening, yet magnificent surprise he could ever imagine. McKenzie O'Connor stared down at him with those piercing green eyes and that beautiful smile he had dreamed of many nights. He was frozen in his seat, speechless. This couldn't be real . . . was this a hologram?

Then Irish walked up beside her, killing the illusion, as they locked arms and shouted together, "Surprise!"

Seeing the look on her father's face, Irish said, "Daddy, are you okay?"

Mack waited, trying to slow his rapid heartbeat. "Your surprise could give someone a heart attack."

"You're a Marine. You're too tough to have a heart attack." Irish said, handing William McKenzie's luggage. "I'll ride in the back and you ride up front." Irish said to McKenzie.

Mack shifted into first gear and as he pulled out onto highway A1A, McKenzie put her hand over his as it rested on the floor shifter. *Oh my God.* Her touch sent a shock through his body like a cattle prod. He then realized what a volatile gamble he was taking by bringing McKenzie home while Jin was there waiting for him.

Mack drove the VW into the carport and cut the engine. He heard Nico laughing and shouting in the swimming pool. Jin had told him she had forgotten her swimsuit and Nico never wore a swimsuit in the pool. *Please Lord don't let them be swimming naked. I've got more than I can handle now.*

Mack took McKenzie's luggage from behind the back seats and Irish and William got theirs as Mack opened the gate and they all walked into the pool area.

"Papa, Papa!" Nico came running across the pool deck naked as the day he was born. Everyone stopped and stared.

Jin was standing with a beach towel wrapped around her.

McKenzie's eyes had dilated into two large black-green dots. She was stunned.

Irish, with both hands on her hips stared at her father while he held Nico in his arms. "Is *this* my surprise?"

"This is my son, Nico. He is part of your surprise. Nico, this is your sister, Irish."

Jin hurried over and took Nico from Mack. "Let me put some pants on this boy." Jin put her arm around Irish and kissed her on the cheek. "You look as beautiful as ever. Come with me to the back bedroom while I get the boy dressed and we can talk. Mack, show your guests around."

McKenzie sat on a patio couch by herself.

Mack looked over at William and shrugged, "Not the way I meant for this to happen. I need a drink, you want one?"

"Sure."

In the back bedroom, as Jin dressed Nico, she explained to Irish how she was never on the pill. "While I was in med school, I had a lot of missed periods and a lot of stress, which caused an ovulation disorder. My gynecologist had told me I probably couldn't get pregnant. Well, they forget to tell your father that. In retrospect, it's the best thing that ever happened to me. I love your father but knew he didn't want to get married. I always felt there was someone else but I never knew who until I saw McKenzie, that is her name, right?"

"Yes, McKenzie O'Connor. Isn't she beautiful? She's a federal judge."

"I had heard her name before, from Mack, I think." She looked at Nico. "At first, I was going to let Nico fly to Key West by himself but I changed my mind for two reasons. One, he was too young, even with the Unaccompanied

Minor Service. The other reason, I wanted to tell Mack that I had met someone else. Tell him, face to face, not over the phone or texting. He's a neurosurgeon at our facilities. I hired him and now he has asked me to marry him." She lifted her hand to show her the large diamond engagement ring.

"Have you told Mack yet?"

"No. I haven't had time."

"Good. Can I tell McKenzie. I know she will be relieved to know that he is not married or involved with someone."

"Just make sure Mack is not around. I don't want him to hear this second hand. On second thought, I'll talked to him now. Can you take sleepyhead here with you and ask Mack to come back here to see me?"

Nico was stretched out on the bed half asleep. Irish sat on the edge of the bed patting her back to Nico. "All right little brother, this stagecoach pulls out of this station at the count of three."

Nico was up and on her back at the count of two. He whispered in her ear as he rode out the door. "Are you really my sister?"

"We got the same daddy, that makes us brother and sister."

"I love you sister."

"I love you little brother."

Mack excused himself from McKenzie and Will who were in deep conversation and hardly looked up. He hadn't had any time to talk with McKenzie alone, but first, he needed to talk to Jin, ASAP. He owed her that much and more. He smiled when he saw Irish skipping down the hallway with Nico bouncing up and down on her back. "Whoooa there, cowgirl, where are you riding off too?" Mack said.

"Looking for you, Sheriff. I have a warrant for your arrest."

"For what, what have I done now?"

"Missing in action."

"Hi Papa, look at me. I'm riding a horsey."

"Yeah, big guy on a big horse." He stared at Irish. "Well, what do you think?"

Irish tilted her head as if asking a question.

"About that cowboy riding your back."

"Oh Daddy, he's beautiful. Did you think I wouldn't like him?"

"You never know. Admittedly, I was a little scared."

"You, scared, no way. But you better go see Jin, she asked me to find you."

"She did? I was on my way to see her. Oh, I'm going to dread this. Is she upset?"

"No, Daddy. She is a wonderful woman and the mother of my little brother." She bounced Nico up and down on her shoulders.

Mack kissed Irish and then kissed Nico. He turned and hurried to see Jin but stopped when he overheard Nico, just above a whisper, say to Irish, "I am not going to tell Mommy that Daddy kissed you."

Irish walked out by the pool and over to where Will and McKenzie were still talking. She turned her back to Will and neighed like a horse, "Sir William, take this cowboy off my back and watch him closely." She grabbed McKenzie by the arm, "Come, lets walk and talk."

Irish led McKenzie around the side of the house through a thick growth of plants, shrubs, and trees. Many of them in bloom like the pink, yellow, and red hibiscus, the frangipani, the Royal Poinciana, and the multi colors of bougainvillea growing wild everywhere. A constant sea breeze carried a piquant fragrant throughout the house. A large Cork tree, rare in Key West, had grown up wild in the front yard. Portugal is the largest producer of corks, some 30-million a day for champagne and other wines.

Irish and McKenzie sat on an old shipbuilder's bench under the Cork tree. Irish held McKenzie's hand. "I'm so glad that you and my dad are going to be together again. I've always thought you two were a perfect match, that is, if you can harness those Irish tempers."

"Look who's calling the kettle black. No my dear, you are right. He's a lovey man, a very independent man. But he's always projected an attitude of not having a need for anyone. That scared me. I've missed him greatly, and I know now that I don't want to live without him. However, it's like now, here I am uninvited, in his house with his wife or girlfriend and their child. I feel so uncomfortable, I'm scared, and I want to leave."

"Don't you even think about that. I'm not supposed to tell you this yet, but I believe it's okay because Jin is talking to Mack now. Jin told me she met a doctor at her clinic and that she is engaged to be married. Believe me, you are the only woman he has ever been in love with."

"Oh, if that were only true."

"Listen, I know my Daddy better than anyone. I've known every woman he's dated since I was born and you are *it*, lady."

Irish watched as all the fear and stored anxiety drained from McKenzie's face and a beautiful smile blossomed like a bright sunshine after a dark storm.

McKenzie put her arms around Irish and kissed both her cheeks twice, "I love you to death." Irish and McKenzie walked back to the pool arm in arm.

Mack, Jin, and Will were sitting on the edge of the pool with their bare feet in the water watching Nico and Bear swim up and down the pool.

Irish stood at the end of the pool, "Can we all have a seat on the patio, I need to say something important."

Jin picked up Nico, wrapped him in a towel and sat on one of the couches. Will took McKenzie's hand and they sat on one of the other couch. Irish walked over and took Will's hand and guided him to a chair and took Mack's hand and walked him to the couch with McKenzie.

"Today is my birthday and I thank God I'm with all the people I love. I want this to be one of the happiest days of my life. There is a lot of tension in the air, not caused by one person, but a buildup of unexplained circumstances. I want to try to clear the air."

In the carport there was a loud blast of an ooga bike horn followed by the ringing of the gate bell. Everyone turned and looked as the gate swung open and little four year Charlie came running toward Mack, his beautiful young Cuban mother, Savanna, right behind him pushing her bike inside and calling out, "Mack, surprise, surprise!"

Everyone turned and stared at Mack. McKenzie pulled Mack over in a tight squeeze and whispered in his ear, "Please, Johnny Appleseed, tell me that one is not yours too?"

Mack closed his eyes, *Oh, God, what are you doing to me?*

CHAPTER 37

I rish walked over and put her arms around Savanna and squeezed her like a little sister. "Savanna, so good to see you again, is this your little boy?"

"Yes, his name is Charlie."

Irish took her hand and said, "Come, let me introduce you to everyone. I'm sorry, I don't remember your last name?"

Mack didn't know her last name either. He stood frozen in place, mummified with all this conflict. Thank God for Irish.

"De la Cruz." Savanna said.

"What a pretty name." They stopped in front of Jin. "Savanna De la Cruz, this is Dr. Jin Girod and her son, Nico from New Orleans and this is William Silverstone, my boyfriend from Pacifica, California." They turned toward Mack holding Charlie in one arm and McKenzie was holding Mack's other arm.

"Savanna, this is McKenzie O'Conner, Mack's friend from Memphis." Savanna's black eyes, like burning lasers, cut into Mack's brain. He watched as her hot Cuban blood boiled and a small crease around her mouth grew into a snarl like a rabid dog.

Mack moved one step back, his leg hitting the couch, as Savanna leaped forward and snatched Charlie from his arms and hissed, "You bastard!"

Mack could smell the lingering vapors of sulfuric acid, like a dragon's breath, as he watched Savanna storm out the gate dragging her bike in one hand and Charlie in the other.

It was deadly still. The ocean breeze had even stopped, and no one said a word. Mack finally said, "I'm sorry, I didn't plan for any of this to happen, but it is what it is, and like Irish suggested, I do think it has 'cleared the air.' All the cards are on the table, if anyone has anything to say, now is the time to speak up."

Mack looked around waiting. "Okay, I made reservations for Irish's birthday dinner at the Sea Breeze, a new restaurant on the island of Sunset Key, just across from Mallory Dock. If we hurry to the marina, my boat is ready and we can be there in time for sunset."

After a second round of cocktails, everyone was laughing and cheerful.

Mack excused himself from the table to steal off to make a phone call. The delivery service assured him his daughter's birthday present would be there waiting for them when they got home tonight and agreed to text Mack when it was delivered.

All the waiters and the owner gathered around the table singing happy birthday as the chef carried a large cake from the kitchen with 30 burning candles and placed it in the middle of the table. Everyone in the restaurant was singing now. Mack had ordered a bottle of Remy Martin XO and was pouring drinks for a toast. He stood at the end of the table raising his glass.

"Irish, my daughter, you are awesome. When I look at you and how you've grown, I feel so proud. It's not just the beauty in your face, but your shining spirit that lights up my world! I don't know where the time has gone or when yesterday became today, but each time I think of the joy you are in my life, all that comes to mind is 'You are awesome.' Happy Birthday." Everyone shouted, "Hear! Hear!"

Mack held the boat steady as they all climbed in. No lights were needed because there was a full moon surrounded by a sky full of sparkling stars that lit up the restaurant and the boat dock. Mack pushed the boat away from the dock and jumped in as Irish cranked up the two 200hp Mercury outboard motors, backed out into open water, and flipped on the navigation lights. She eased the two throttles forward till she cleared the no wake area and then full throttle pointed the bow toward Fleming Key Cut.

Mack heard the text tone signal on his phone and read the text, "Delivery complete. Looks great. Happy Birthday to your daughter."

Mack stopped the VW about 3-car lengths from the front of the house and turned his headlights on bright. They all stared at a huge cardboard box about 15ft long, 10ft wide, and 6ft tall. A red ribbon was painted horizontally and vertically across the front and on the ends with a large red papier-mache bow on top. The back was opened and pressed against the tall stucco wall. Mack turned to the back seat and said to Irish, "Happy Birthday Baby Girl."

Irish stood up on the back seat with both hands over her mouth, "Daddy, what have you done?"

Mack got out of the car and started to lift Irish from the back seat, "Let's go find out."

"No, no, Daddy. I need to take a picture first." Irish removed her phone and took a couple of pictures and told her Daddy to stand in front and took a couple more. They all stood up in the car and started taking pictures of the box and with Irish and Mack in front of the box. Mack picked up Irish and sat her on the hood of the VW and got Will to stand at the end of the box while he stood at the opposite end. A latch was on the front of the box at the top. Mack counted to three and Will and Mack released the latch at the same time and the front of the box and the sides fell to the ground.

Irish let out a loud scream as the high beam lights magnified the brilliant red shine of a new Mercedes Benz SL convertible. Everyone took photos of Mack handing Irish the keys to the car and then her radiant smile sitting behind the wheel.

The next morning at the airport, Mack hugged and kissed Jin and Nico goodbye. Jin took Mack's face in her hands, "I want you to know I will always love you and would have married *you*, but that was not in your cards. In a way, we are married. Nico is my wedding ring and will always be there to remind me of my love for you." Tears were in her eyes as she took Nico hand and hurried across the tarmac to their plane to New Orleans.

Mack stopped at Sandy's for four grande café con leches and to see Savanna. She was not at work yet, so he drew a big smiley face on a napkin with her name on the outside and handed it to the girl that waited on him along with a ten-dollar bill.

Irish and Will were busy packing for their flight back to San Francisco. He gave them their coffee, then walked across the house and eased open the door of the master bedroom and closed it behind him. McKenzie was still asleep with a black mask covering her eyes. He sat on the edge of the bed staring down at her soft red hair spread out over the white silk covered pillow. He put her coffee on the bed side table and removed the top from his taking a sip and inhaling the strong aroma of the Cuban coffee.

He thought about their long bike ride along the beach last night after everyone had gone to bed. They ended up on a bench at the end of White Street Pier under a full moon with waves splashing against the pilings. This was the first time they had been alone together and McKenzie said she wanted to talk about their relationship.

Mack protested. "Let's not wash dirty laundry, let's start a new relationship without any past."

"No." McKenzie said. "Let's start with what your daughter recommended, clear the air."

Two tough women, Mack thought. He would have to learn to back off a little from his strong opinions.

"I'm going to start from the beginning.' McKenzie said. "I had heard a lot about you before we met, and none of it was good."

"You can't believe every. . ."

"Please, Mack.' She squeezed his hand. 'Let me finish without any interruptions. I've never told you how deeply I feel about you. The first time I met you in person was at your home at Shamrock to celebrate the 125th birthday of the Beethoven Club. I was with Father O'Brien. Only when the president of the club, Lucile Ludwig, I'll never forget her name, introduced you did I put two and two together; that I was a guest at the home of the man I had signed a warrant for his arrest.

"It was hard for me to believe that such a well-spoken, good looking, and obviously wealthy man was the same drunk Irishman on a bulldozer at Arthur's restaurant."

"I wasn't drunk."

McKenzie put her finger against Mack's lips.

"Later that night on the rooftop, sipping your cognac, we watched as a warm breeze pushed a cloud across the sitting sun leaving reddish-orange striations in the sky. It was a perfect night for romance. We shook hands agreeing to call each other by our first names, but you kept holding my hand, never letting it go. I certainly didn't want you to let it go. The heat from your hand shot through me was like an IV into my libido. I was sweating embarrassingly with tremors and my legs weakening. Never had I felt this way before. You kept holding on; it was scary. All my life I have studied and trained myself to be independent and self-supporting, but I kept holding on to your hands." She took both his hands in hers, "That, Mr. Shannon, is how it was and how it is now. I never want to let them go."

McKenzie rolled over on her back, removed her eye mask and smiled, "Is that my coffee I smell?"

Mack helped her sit up and put a pillow behind her back. He kissed her lips twice, the second kiss much longer. He removed the top from her coffee and handed it to her. "Careful, it's hot."

She took a long slow sip. "Ahh, now and forever, this is my two favorite things to wake up to, your hot kisses and hot coffee."

After her second drink of coffee, Mack took her cup and sat it on the side table next to his. He slowly folded the sheet down from where she had covered herself and unbuttoned her pajama top. She leaned forward sliding both arms from her sleeves and grabbed Mack's head pulling it to her heaving chest. Mack's mouth covered one breast then the other, his tongue circling the areola over and over till her nipples were hard and erect.

McKenzie kicked back the covers and slid down from the headboard moaning as Mack sucked on her bulging nipples. Breathing hard, he painted a wet track with his tongue down the curvatures of her body, stopping at her sunken navel. He raised his head and stared down at her naked body; no pajama bottoms, no panties. Nothing awakened his desire more than her lily-white belly that cradled the contrasting red fluff that stored the fire between her thighs.

McKenzie ran her fingers through Mack's hair, pushing his head down as she arched her back.

There was a loud knock on Mack's bedroom door, "Hey Daddy-o, we're ready to go to the airport; don't want to be late."

Mack sprang upright, instinctively praying Irish wouldn't open the door. He threw the covers over McKenzie and said, "McKenzie's getting dressed. Give us five minutes."

At the airport Irish hugged Mack with tears in her eyes. "Please Daddy, come see us. Pacifica is just 10 miles from San Francisco Airport and bring McKenzie with you. We have plenty of room and we are right on the ocean front. Thank you so much for my beautiful car. It's what I always wanted, the color and everything."

"Don't forget NEXUS is shipping your car and it should be there by the end of this week. I'll text you the tracking number." Mack and McKenzie waved at Irish and Will as they walked across the tarmac to their plane.

Back in the VW Thing, Mack pulled out from the airport turning right onto A1A. McKenzie leaned over and ran her hand up his thigh. "You know what I want to do now?"

"Duh . . . I have no idea."

McKenzie pinched the inside of his thigh.

"Ouch, that hurt. I'm glad you weren't aiming a little higher." Mack turned right on Bertha Street.

"Don't you worry, I'll take care of that when we get to the house."

Mack leaned over to kiss McKenzie and a black blur covered the left side of his face just before a powerful explosion into the left side of his door. He felt his hands tear away from the steering wheel as the VW Thing jumped the curb, flying across the corner and slammed into a concrete power pole. The last thing Mack heard was a scream from McKenzie as his body sailed through the air crashing into a chain link fence . . . headfirst.

On the opposite corner, standing by his bicycle, was Ben Perez a Key West policeman on the Bicycle Unit. He immediately called the fire department for help and for an Emergency Medical Services ambulance as he ran across the street triaging as quickly as he could. The young girl that ran the stop sign on the black scooter was dead, her helmet shattered, her neck twisted at an odd angle. The scooter was still imbedded in to the front seat of the car. He stopped and checked her pulse to make sure, then hurried to the woman crying out inside the car. Blood was all over her face from her head hitting the windshield. He took a towel from his back pocket and wiped the blood from her eyes and asked if she was hurt anywhere. Her safety belt was still on but she was pinned in from the dashboard in her lap and the driver's seat pinned against her arm. She said her arm and her knee were hurting. Her arm was pinned against the door and he could see the bone of her forearm sticking through the skin. He heard the siren of the fire department and told her help was on the way and they would have her out in a few minutes. Perez ran over to check on the driver pinned against the fence. He saw him ejected over the hood of the car like a missile, and heard the force of his head hitting the fence. No one could live through that; he must not have been wearing his seat belt. He wasn't breathing and he couldn't find a pulse. *Damn, part of the wire fence was embedded in his bleeding skull.* Checking him over again, he saw the man's little finger moving up and down and shouted at the EMT, who had just pulled up, to bring some oxygen. The captain on the fire truck came running up and Perez told him he would need the 'jaws of life' to cut the woman out of the car and that she had a compound fracture to her right forearm and maybe her knee as well.

The EMT came running up and shouted, "Who needs the oxygen?"

Perez pointed to the man against the fence and said, "He's barely breathing, his head is imbedded in the chain link fence and they'll need bolt cutters before they can move him. Make sure no one removes that wire. They'll have to transport him with the wire still in his head."

Perez heard screaming and crying and saw a young girl running up as one of the EMT's was covering the dead girl's body in the middle of the street with a white sheet.

Perez ran over and put his arm around the girl and led her over to a bus bench. "Did you know the girl in the street?"

"Is she dead?"

"I'm afraid so."

She was trembling and sobbing. "Oh my God! How am I going to tell her mother."

"I'll take care of that if you want." Perez pulled a notebook and pen from his belt. "Can you tell me her name?" He waited for her. "Take a couple of deep breaths; it'll help you."

"Shelby White. I didn't know her that well. We had just met at school, both freshmen at Ole Miss and came down here for a short vacation. She wanted to race scooters and I told her no; it was too dangerous. She was looking back at me, waving to come on when she ran into the car"

She continued to talk, on and on, maybe a little in shock or just plain scared. Perez listened, writing down what was important for his report.

"Had you been drinking?"

"You mean last night?"

Perez waited, staring at her.

"Could we get in trouble?"

"I think your friend, Ms. White, is no longer worried about that."

"We did have too much to drink last night . . ."

" And what about today? This morning?"

He looked up when he heard the siren of the last ambulance leaving and saw the Chief of Police walking toward him.

CHAPTER 38

*A*m I dead?

Mack wasn't sure. He remembered *some* things. He remembered a saw cutting into his skull and someone calling for irrigation and suction to wash the blood clot away. Were you supposed to remember things if you were dead? How were you to know? He was in no pain, just ink-black darkness and deadly silence.

Irish and Will were in the Intensive Care Unit (ICU) waiting room of the ECHO RESEARCH AND SURGERY CENTER in New Orleans. They stood and watched as a nurse pushed a stretcher down the long white hallway. Mack was sitting upright on the stretcher. An oxygen mask covered his nose and mouth and his head was wrapped in heavy gauze. Walking behind the stretcher were Dr. Devi Shah and Dr. Jin Girod.

Tears were streaming down Irish's face as they all watched the nurse push Mack into the ICU room. Jin hugged Irish and told her the operation was a success. She introduced Dr. Devi Shah as Dev, the neurosurgeon who operated on Mack and as her fiancée.

"Your father did great." Dr. Shah said. "He's tough like Jin said. We were lucky to get him here as fast as we did; it made a lot of difference. He should make a speedy recovery without any complications."

"Look," Jin said, as they all turned and saw McKenzie in a wheelchair being pushed toward them. Her face was marked with numerous red abrasions from the broken glass. She had a cast on her right forearm and her right knee had multiple stitches from the impact of the dashboard.

Irish walked over and put her arm around McKenzie's back, "I'm so sorry. Are you in any pain?"

"Other than a face that looks like a dart board, a broken wing, and only one wheel," she lifted up her arm cast and nodded to her bandaged knee, "I'm okay."

"Do you remember what happened?"

"Not really. I was half-conscious the whole time but I couldn't see anything. There was blood all in my eyes and I couldn't move to wipe my face. In the ambulance they told me someone on a motorcycle ran into us; it felt more like a bulldozer. I do remember the EMT putting my arm in an air-splint and us waiting on a jet to fly Mack here in New Orleans. I don't know how that happened."

"The EMT called me after getting my number from Mack's wallet," Irish said. "I told them NO surgery. Do nothing unless it's a dire emergency. I would call them back with instructions immediately. I called Jin and she took over and called the Key West hospital and ordered the jet ambulance."

Jin walked over and Irish looked toward the ICU room, "Can I see my Daddy?"

"Let's ask the doctor." Jin said.

They all followed Dr. Shah into the ICU room. It was cold and dark. Mack was still sitting upright. Tubes and wires running in all directions.

Irish was holding his hand, the one that had an IV catheter inserted on top, trying to hold back the tears. "Why is he sitting up instead of lying down? Is he conscious?"

Dr. Shah put his arm around Irish's shoulder, "We're keeping him upright to decrease intracranial pressure after his surgery. I have him heavily sedated to keep him relaxed, to control the pain, and to decrease swelling in the brain. Don't worry, we have him under excellent care."

Six months later.

Mack, McKenzie, and Bear walked along the wide sidewalk at Smathers Beach. They were excited, jabbering about the trips they were going to take now that Mack had recovered and McKenzie had retired.

Mack was wearing a baseball cap to cover his scarred head until his hair grew back.

McKenzie's cast had been removed and the stiches in her knee had dissolved. They had been walking every day since their return from the hospital and had almost fully recovered from their injuries, except for a couple of small problems. Mack had been having some headaches that were bothering him a little. He was waiting for a follow up appointment with Dr. Shah before they started on their first trip.

They agreed to take turns picking out different destinations and McKenzie wanted Mack to go first. He suggested they visit Irish out in

California, and then take a slow drive along the oceanfront, down highway one. They could stay a couple of nights in Carmel, play a round of golf at Pebble Beach and then eat dinner at Clint Eastwood's restaurant alfresco.

McKenzie agreed with that. She loved golf and like Mack, she had never played Pebble Beach.

"Okay, it's your turn now." Mack said.

Both had picked a book a week and read to each other every night since the accident.

Mostly, it was McKenzie reading to Mack, to helped his cognitive processes and to go to sleep each night and sometimes on the beach or out by the pool. The latest book she was reading was on Mack's Kindle and it was his all-time favorite, 'Into Africa.' McKenzie loved it too. They hadn't watched TV in weeks.

So, her choice of their next vacation was to go to Africa.

Mack frowned. He loved Africa . . . vicariously. He reminded her of all the kidnappings and beheadings from that part of the country. Different terrorist groups had expanded and consolidated their African operations according to an article Mack had read in Jihad Analytics.

The attacks claimed by the group called the Islamic State (IS) since the beginning of 2022 were carried out in 10 African countries. Not only in West Africa but in Mozambique and in some of the most visited safari countries like Tanzania and Kenya.

The article went on to say that terrorists are very likely to carry out attacks in South Africa. The main threat is from extremists linked to Daesh. In February two South African-British nationals were kidnapped and killed.

"But I read in this month's travel magazine and this couple said their trip was completely safe."

Mack open Google on his phone, typed in a couple of words and handed McKenzie his phone.

McKenzie read:

February 9, 2023
Security Alert for U. S. Citizens
U.S. EMBASSY NAIROBI

Location: High traffic areas frequented by foreigners and tourists in Nairobi and elsewhere in Kenya.

Event: Locations frequented by U.S. citizens and other foreigners and tourists in Nairobi and elsewhere in Kenya continue to be attractive targets to terrorists planning to conduct potentially imminent attacks. Terrorist groups could attack with little or no warning, targeting airports, hotels, embassies, restaurants, malls and markets, schools, police stations, places of worship, and other places frequented by foreigners and tourists. The U.S. government may have very limited ability to step in should travelers' safety or security be at risk, according to the State Department.

"Well, kidnapping could happen anywhere. There's probably were more kidnappings in Memphis than in Kenya last year." McKenzie said.

"Get real. You can't be serious?"

McKenzie opened Google on her phone and typed in a few words and handed her phone to him.

Mack read:

WREG-TV NEWS CHANNEL 3
Memphis, TN
More than 100 kidnappings reported in Memphis in 2023

Two arrested in Saddle Creek kidnapping attempt
MEMPHIS, Tenn. – The men charged with trying to kidnap a woman in Germantown in December also face a litany of other federal charges, showing an alleged crime spree 10 days before the attempted kidnapping.

One of the suspects also faces three charges of aggravated rape and aggravated kidnapping in Memphis in August.

According to federal documents, the two men, Adrian Pegues and Malik Malone, face a 10-count federal indictment that includes the attempted kidnapping of a woman near her car on Dec. 30 outside a store at Saddle Creek.

By: Stacy Jacobson – Posted Mar 3, 2023 / 04:41 PM CST

McKenzie's phone started ringing; she looked at her screen and saw the name Jin Girod.

Mack looked over at McKenzie.

"It's Jin," she whispered, as if Jin could hear her.

"Well, answer it," Mack whispered back, smiling.

"Hello, Jin?"

"Hi McKenzie, how are you doing? Your arm, okay?"

"I'm fine. You all did a great job. It's like it never happened. How's Nico?"

"He's growing like a weed, a wild weed."

"Give him a big kiss for me and his Papa just blew him one too. He's standing right beside me, did you want to talk to him?"

"Not now. Can he hear me talking?"

She turned her back to Mack and walked away a few steps. "No."

"Dev found something on Mack's MRI he doesn't like. Have you noticed anything different about him? Headaches, tremors, loss of balance?"

"No . . . not really. Well. Now that I think of it, he's been having some headaches and he's a little dizzy when he first stands up, but Dev told him that was to be expected. Oh, he did fall awhile back and had 12 stitches above his eyebrow. What did Dev see on the MRI?"

"It's not just his MRI, it's a combination of things, most important is observation. Remember the physical and cognitive examination where Dev tested Mack's movements and reactions, his walking and finger tapping.

"Can you two come up this week? You can stay with us."

"Let me talk to Mack and I will call you back right away."

Mack laid flat on his back with both arms pressed tight against his body, his head in a headrest strapped down with a flexible restraint to help keep the head from moving during the scan.

Everything in the room, the ceiling, the floor and the walls was covered with white tile. It was very cold as the trolley rolled him into the chamber of the MRI machine. He was thinking of those sliding drawers of wall coolers at the morgue when the explosion of sounds started: bells ringing, horns blowing, sirens screaming. Mack thought, *wasn't it enough that you had to lie still in this tomb for 30 to 40 minutes. You would think by now that for a machine that cost a couple of million dollars they would have eliminated the sounds that would terrify most first-*

timers.

Late that afternoon as Mack and McKenzie waited in an exam room there was a tap on the door. Drs. Dev Shah and Jin Girod walked into the room. Dev placed his iPad and cell phone on the exam table next to where Mack was sitting in a chair. He then pulled up a chair beside him and took his hand, "How are you feeling big guy?"

Mack noticed Dev slide his other hand up the inside of his wrist checking his heart rate as they talked.

"I'm okay. I've been walking a lot and lifting light weights a little to get back in shape."

"Good, that's very good."

Come on Doc, I'm a big boy; tell me what you found on the brain scan.

Jin and McKenzie stood in the back corner of the room. Jin had her arm around McKenzie.

"Are you up for a couple of short tests to help me support my diagnosis?"

"Sure, whatever it takes."

"I want you to cross your arms over your chest, stand up and sit down three times, not slow and not fast, just normal."

"That was good. Now, I want you to close your eyes and count backwards from 100 in increments of seven." Dev looked down at his cell phone.

"Let's see . . ." Mack said. "7 from 100 is 93. 7 from 93 is ah . . . 87, no 86. 7 from 86 is 79. 7 from 79 is 72. 7 from 72 is . . . let's see . . . ahhh."

"Mack," Dev put his hand on Mack's hand. "That's good. Let me show you something."

Dev tapped on his phone camera icon then started the video and handed it to Mack.

Mack watched the video of his thumb and index finger uncontrollably tapping his chair arm while listening to his voice struggling to count backwards. He looked up at Dev.

"Those are tremors, Mack. One of the main symptoms of Parkinson's disease."

"Are you saying I have Parkinson's disease?"

"Yes, I'm afraid so. All the symptoms point in that direction."

McKenzie groaned and quickly covered her mouth with both hands to keep from screaming; tears cascaded over her fingers. Thoughts raced through her mind of her suffering grandfather who had this incurable, slow crippling disease that continuously eats away the dopamine in your brain that controls movement and coordination.

Mack, with his trained poker-face, showed no emotions, "Could you be making a mistake with your diagnosis?"

"Possible. It's not an easy disease to identify but I'm confident in my diagnosis. Yet, you are certainly free to get a second opinion. I can recommend a couple of experts for you to see. Regardless, I won't stop treating you. As long as you need me, I will be your doctor and help you along the way. This is the beginning of a long journey, not the end."

"Thank you, Dev. I'm sorry, I didn't mean to question your judgement, but overall, I feel great." He held both hands out in front of him which were steady and unmoving. "There are no tremors in my hands or any other parts of my body."

"We caught it early and what you saw on my phone we call *resting tremors.*"

"What is Parkinson's disease and what causes it?"

"In medical speak they refer to it as PD. It is a neurodegenerative disorder that affects predominately the dopamine-producing neurons in a specific area of the brain called substantia nigra or known in Latin as the black substance. It is estimated that a person must lose approximately 80 percent of the dopamine producing cells in that part of the brain and this cell loss always occurs before the symptoms. This morning, the DaTscan test you had, provided us with more detailed pictures of my diagnosis."

There was a soft knock on the door and a nurse stuck her head in the room. "Dr. Shah, there is an emergency call for you in level 4 operating room."

Dev stood up.

"You need me?" Jin asked.

"I'll let you know."

After Dev left the room, Mack said, "I hope I didn't offend Dev . . ."

"No. Not at all. Dev is the most caring and dedicated man I've ever known." She sat in the same chair that Dev was sitting in across from Mack.

"Dev has devoted most of his practice to Parkinson's Disease, clinical and research. He is the Director of Movement Disorder and Neurorestoration here at ECHO. He not only has an M.D. in neurosurgery but a Ph.D. in Neuroscience and has an active science lab here in our research department.

Believe me, if you looked the world over, you could not find a better doctor to treat you. A lot of our other doctors here tease me about hiring him for his looks but I hired him for his knowledge and experience."

"Is there a cure for Parkinson?" Mack asked.

She reached out and took Mack's hands in hers and almost said *Mack, my darling*. "No Mack, there is no cure, not yet. But Parkinson's disease (PD) is one of the most treatable of all neurological conditions. Medical treatment increases longevity and allows most people with PD to remain active and productive for many years."

"How many years?" Mack asked.

"It's different for each person." She squeezed his hands. "You're strong and take good care of yourself. You should have a long life. Any day now, with world-wide research rapidly gaining ground, we could have a cure."

Jin's phone vibrated. She looked at her screen and said, "I'll be right back."

Mack asked when Jin left, "You think they're shorthanded?"

"No, I think it's just Dev. When Jin called, she said Dev would work you in. He's booked 6-months in advance."

"Oh." Mack sat in deep thought, and then said, "Well, this will change a lot of things. You certainly didn't bargain for this."

"No, it will not! It won't change a damn thing. You listen to me, Mr. Mack Shannon," she held his face in her hands. "Look at me . . . I love you. Nothing else matters. We are going to be together forever. I'm not losing you again. Get that in your thick Irish head."

"You better be careful what you say, you may not know what you are signing up for."

"I've been careful all my life but now, at my age, we are going to do things and go places we've never been or done before. You are the only thing important in my life and I'm going to take care of you till you die or I die."

Mack stood up and wrapped his arms around her, "How could I say no to that."

"I'm not the only one that loves you either."

"What do you mean?"

"Jin. She still loves you."

"Does that bother you?"

"Not in the least. If something happened to me, I know you would be taken care of."

The door opened and Dev and Jin walked in, Dev with a small white paper bag in his hand. They smiled when they saw Mack kissing McKenzie. Dev looked over at Jin, "I told you we should have knocked."

Dev handed Mack the bag, "Here are some samples till you pick up the prescription I ordered at Publix in the Key West Plaza. A big positive, Mack, is now that we know it's Parkinson; we can treat it. Remember, timing is very important when taking these dopamine drugs. I want to see you again in three months."

"Maybe in three months ya'll could take a break and come down and visit us." McKenzie said. "We could all go out in the boat and get you a bunch of lobsters and fish to take back home. You could leave Nico with us for a month or so."

"Oh Dev, it would be so good for us to get away from here for a week."

"Let's wait and see how Mack reacts to the medicine before we make any plans."

What does that mean? Mack thought.

CHAPTER 39

Mack, sitting out by the pool with Bear beside him in the shade, was reading:

'How do you know if you have Parkinson's disease?

In the early stages of Parkinson's disease, your face may show little or no expression. Your arms may not swing when you walk. Your speech may become soft or slurred. Dysphagia; involves a complex sequence of movements and it is no surprise that PD affects swallowing. Aspiration pneumonia is the number one killer in PD.

And of course, the one symptom that is most notable to the uninformed, as Michael Okun, M.D. explained, is tremors. As far back as 1541 in Shakespeare's Henry VI: "Why dost thou quiver, man?" The character in the story responded by stating "the palsy and not the fear provokes me." Parkinson's disease symptoms worsen as your condition progresses over time.'

Mack read everything he could get his hands on regarding PD and McKenzie read them too, and many times they alternated reading to each other.

Dev lived up to his commitment: *As long as you need me, I will be your doctor and help you along the way.* He sent Mack the latest medical trial results of PD, articles from Randomized Controlled Trials (RCT) and journals from PubMed Central (PMC). They had telemedicine videos, numerous emails, and texts.

There was a stack of books Mack had collected and some he was still reading and some he used for references. One of his favorite books, especially for references, was from the neurologist, J. Eric Ahlskog, M.D., Ph.D. 'The New Parkinson's Disease Treatment Book.'

Another superbly written book, translated in 23 languages, was 'Parkinson's Treatment: 10 Secrets to a Happier Life' by a world's authority on PD treatment; Michael S. Okun, M.D.

Mack was entertained, informed and educated by the many books of Michael J. Fox's 32-years' experience living with PD. He was diagnosed at the young age of 29.

Mack stood with sweat running off his body. He stepped around the two

15 pound dumbbells, careful of his of growing loss of balance, then onto the steps and into the pool.

Nico ran down the jet bridge squeezing his present and shouting "Papa, Papa," when he saw his father. A most attractive, young, dark haired flight attendant walked close behind Nico pulling his small roller bag. Mack picked Nico up and whirled him around kissing him over and over.

"Papa, look. I brought you a present."

"Well, I guess I don't have to see any ID that you are Mack Shannon, Nico's father." said the flight attendant.

"Papa, your present," holding it up to Mack.

"Thank you, big boy. You flew all this way by yourself."

Mack took out his driver's license to show her his ID with a $50 dollar bill on top.

She deftly lifted the driver's license leaving the $50 in his hand. Her deep brown eyes demanding his attention. "Thank you, but Nico was a delight and so smart and polite. I thought he was twice his age."

"He gets that from his mother."

"Hmm, modesty and good looking. I'm staying at the Casa Marina. Maybe you could come by later and we could use that $50 on drinks. My name is Camila Todd, my friends call me CT."

"Papa, where is MO?" Nico said.

"Uh oh, is that his mother?"

Mack leaned over and kissed her on her cheek and whispered, "Thank you CT for looking after my son. Maybe at another time." Mack stuck his present under his arm, grabbed the roller bag and in his other hand took Nico as they walked down the jet way.

"When did you start calling McKenzie MO?" Mack asked.

"When we talked on the phone, she told me to call her that. Papa, open your present."

"Can't it wait till we get to the car?"

Nico stopped, they were in the waiting room now, and Nico looked up at Mack with disappointment.

"Okay, big boy."

"It's from Dev; he asked me to make sure I gave it to you."

Mack tore the paper off and looked at a small wooden plank, puzzled. Then turned it over and read aloud the axiom burned in the wood *"Lack of activity destroys the good condition of every human being, while movement and methodical physical exercise save and preserve it."*

PLATO.

Dev was an ardent proponent of exercise for all his patients and had told Mack to never stop exercising.

"What does that mean, Papa, and who is Play . . . toe?"

"Dr. Dev wants all his patients to exercise. We will put this up on the wall in the kitchen to remind us to run, swim, and lift weights every day." Mack put the plank under his arm and took Nico by the hand again and started walking. "Plato was a Greek philosopher from over 2,000 years ago. In today's time we would think of him as a teacher, a professor in a collage, teaching philosophy which in Greek means 'love of wisdom.' Like you, he loved to read and study. We will talk more about him later."

Mack's right hand and arm, the one holding Nico's hand, started jerking and shaking uncontrollably. He stopped and stared at his hand pulling Nico back and forth. People stopped when they heard Nico shouting "Papa, Papa, stop."

Mack shoved the roller bag to the floor and with his left hand grabbed his right arm and hand, forcing it against his body until it stopped jerking. He kneeled down on the floor in front of Nico still holding his right hand and arm.

"Papa, did I do something wrong?" Nico had a frightened look on his face.

Mack thought *my God what in the world is happening to me.* "No son, you did nothing wrong." He tried to let go of his right arm and hand but it was still shaking.

"Damn!" I'm scaring my own son. I can't even put my arm around him.

Mack spoke softly. "You know Dr. Dev is treating me for a sickness, what they call Parkinson's disease. It's like when you get sick, sometimes you throw up, or pee in your pants. You have no control. This sickness is a movement disorder. Sometimes I have no control over my hands and now it's moved to my arm. But Dr. Dev is going to fix me up, give me the right medicine."

"I can carry my bag," Nico said.

"I know you can, son. Let's see if this old hand is tired of shaking." Mack cautiously released his left arm and lifted his right arm and closed and opened his hand. He pulled Nico close to him. "I didn't mean to scare you. Are you okay?"

"Yes sir. Are you okay?"

"Yes sir, I'm good to go." Mack stood up and grabbed Nico's bag in his right hand this time and took Nico's hand with his left hand. Some people were still staring as they walked by.

"Let's get out of this place."

Mack, shuffling his feet, stumbled on the threshold between the carpet and mosaic tile floor, righted himself, and paused for a moment. "I'm okay," he said, looking down at Nico.

Lift your feet, dummy and watch where your step.

Mack was still out by the pool reading when he heard McKenzie singing *"Yippie-yi-yo- I'm an old cowhand from the Rio Grande,* she came galloping out of the patio in her bikini to the pool deck with Nico on her back, *and I learned to ride before I learned to stand.* She jumped into the pool, Nico holding onto McKenzie's long red hair, both yelling *Yippie-yi-yo.*

"Well, I guess they finished their siesta," Mack said to Bear standing beside him now.

McKenzie started putting Nico down for a nap from 1 to 2 pm every day and got in the habit of lying down cuddled with him and falling asleep. They tried to get Mack to take a siesta with them but as soon as he laid down, his mind started spinning like a pinwheel on a racing bicycle.

He placed a bookmarker in the book he was reading and jumped into the pool. Bear stood poolside watching closely. McKenzie dove underwater grabbing Mack by the ankle shaking him like a shark. Mack thrashed the water wildly with both hands shouting SHARK! SHARK!

Nico, kicking hard, and with a little help from Mack, pushed him on his back across the pool to the steps. Nico turned when he heard the sound from the movie Jaws, "dum-dum, dum-dum, DUM-DUM." McKenzie, now under water with her one hand above the water acting as a dorsal fin, raced toward Mack to finish him off. Nico moved quickly up the steps and to the side of the pool and jumped onto McKenzie's back. They rolled over and over fighting each other to the bottom of the pool until McKenzie broke loose and swam to the far end of the pool. Nico swam to the steps and helped his father out of the pool. He stood with both arms above his head flexing his small biceps shouting "dum-dum, dum-dum, DUM-DUM."

They all sat on the pool steps, Nico in the water between McKenzie's legs and Bear stretched out on the first step. They were drinking McKenzie's favorite smoothie, a mixture of fresh passion fruit, mangos and key limes; the sun hot on their tanned bodies.

"I just love our life here," McKenzie leaned over and kissed Mack on the lips "and I love this little man here as if he were my own child," she ruffled Nico's hair.

"What do you say, Nico?" Mack asked.

"What?" Nico asked. "Oh, I love you too, Daddy."

Mack frowned, and pushed Nico's head underwater.

Nico came up gasping for air. "I was just kidding." He turned and put his arms around McKenzie and hugged and kissed her and shouted, "I . . . LOVE . . . MO!"

Mack stood up when he heard the gate bell rang and walked over and opened the gate.

Charlie jumped into his arms and hugged Mack. Savanna was picking up Nico to take him and Charlie to the Regal Key West movie house on Roosevelt to see Disney's latest movie, Peter Pan and Wendy.

Months ago Mack had stopped by Sandy's Café to talk with Savanna one more time. They had sat under the large Banyan tree across the street. Mack convinced Savanna not to break off their friendship, that it would be better to have a platonic relationship. Savanna never knew her father and her mother lived in Cuba with her 4th husband. Charlie's father was a college student on spring break and was no more than a passing ship in the night. Savanna had forgotten his name.

Mack assured her he had no ulterior motive and that he was in love with McKenzie but was committed to helping her and Charlie when they needed someone.

He always remembered that in his younger days many mentors helped him along the way, his Aunt Irish, the most important one. She was a strict disciplinarian and taught him that history always repeated itself and if you wanted to know the future, there was no better history book than the Holy Bible. She laid out a great plan for him to follow; the life of King Solomon, from the beginning to the end. The last thing she insisted upon was for him to memorize Hebrews 13:16 "And do not forget to do good and to share with others, for with such sacrifices God is pleased."

McKenzie waved goodbye to them from the steps of the pool and Mack locked the gate behind them and jumped into the pool. McKenzie sat on the second step in the pool leaning back, the lower part of her body underwater as she watched Mack swim to her underwater. She parted her legs as he got closer until his head wedged against both her thighs. With both hands she pulled his head in closer and arched her back above the water. She moaned as Mack blew hot air into her pussycat as she called it. Mack picked her up and bent her over the edge of the pool, unsnapped the back of her bikini top and tossed it over his shoulder. He then pushed her bikini bottom down over her hips as she kicked frantically. He tore at his bathing suit, stomping with both feet to get it off. He then mounted her from the back, sliding both hands under her arms caressing her swollen breast and erect nipples. Like two wild animals fighting, Mack with one foot on the second step and the other on the bottom of the pool, McKenzie, her hands behind her pushing and clawing the cheeks of Mack's butt; howling and screaming, could be heard a block away. Three pieces of swimwear floated lazily to the other end of the pool disappearing into the skimmer.

Mack and McKenzie, languished, naked, floating side by side on their rubber rafts holding hands in an exhausted afterglow. The swaying rafts, the hot Key West sun combined with the cool ocean breeze, induced a tranquilizing effect, leaving them semiconscious.

"I love you," McKenzie said.

After a long pause, Mack mumbled, "I love you too."

"You are a great lover." McKenzie said.

After another long pause. "You are too," Mack slurred.

"I want to make love again." McKenzie said.

After a very long pause, Mack said, "No way. I can't get it up again."

"Don't you worry about that old man, that's my job." She released his hand and grabbed the side of his raft and turned it over.

Mack flailed in the water like he was drowning, then sunk to the bottom. With both knees bent he pushed off, exploding upward, crashing into

McKenzie's raft sending her high into the air. He grabbed her in mid-air and put her in a tight bear hug, "I'll make you think 'old man.'" At the same time, the alarm went off on Mack's watch reminding him to take his 3 pm Parkinson medication.

"Saved by the bell, lover boy." McKenzie said. "I'll get your pills."

The gate bell starting ringing. Bear raced out of the kitchen, across the patio to the gate while McKenzie grabbed two towels throwing one to Mack as he hurried out of the pool. "Let the kids in while I dry off," she said heading for the bathroom. "Don't think this gets you off, buddy. I want a raincheck."

Mack stood watching McKenzie as he wrapped the towel around his waist. There's not another woman her age that looks that good. He was a lucky man. She was beautiful, intelligent, and amorously lustful. She took care of his every need. He loved her more than he could ever express. There was no doubt in his mind he had made . . . 'the right choice.'

The gate bell rang again. He hurried to open the gate. The boys rushed to the pool pulling off their shirts, kicking off their shoes, and short pants, and jumped into the pool in their tighty whities.

"Papa, come swim with us." Nico shouted.

Charlie, holding onto the side of the pool next to the skimmer, pulled out Mack's bathing suit and held it up in the air giggling.

Savanna stared at the towel around Mack, smiling "Well, aren't you going in?"

McKenzie came out of the bathroom in shorts and a sleeveless top.

Charlie threw Mack's bathing suit to Nico and pulled McKenzie's bikini from the skimmer waving it around and around laughing.

Savanna walked over and snatched the bathing suit from Charlie's hand giving him a threatening look. Savanna walked over and handed McKenzie her bathing suit. "I'm sorry, boys will be boys. They had a good time at the movies and Charlie wants Nico to spend the night with him tonight."

Both boys came running over to McKenzie saying, "Please, please."

McKenzie looked over at Mack for an answer and mouthed, *'raincheck.'*

Savanna looked puzzled. I'll bring him back in the morning around nine."

Mack nodded his approval.

Later that night on the flat roof of the patio, McKenzie laid in the arms of Mack on a queen size blow-up mattress with silk sheets and down pillows. There were no lights except the full moon and a dark blue sky full of brilliant stars shining down on two nude bodies. Mack was on his back, McKenzie across his chest. She listened to the rhythmic beat of his heart alternating with the palm fronds knocking against one another as the treetops swayed back and forth.

"What time is your flight in the morning?" Mack asked.

"What flight?"

"Ha ha. You know what flight."

"I don't want to go."

"I don't want you to go."

"Why don't you come with me."

"We've already talked about that. How long do you think you'll be gone?"

"I don't know. It's a complicated case. Plus, I've got that trouble with my condo."

"Why don't you sell it."

"Not yet. It's nice to have when we are in Memphis and it has a beautiful view of the river."

Most of the day, off and on, McKenzie had been reading the trial transcripts and the written briefs from the appellant, Federal Express and the appellee, Memphis-Shelby County Airport Authority. There would be a panel of three judges, McKenzie would preside as the chief judge. There would be no additional evidence allowed and no jury or witnesses at the hearing.

When McKenzie retired, she agreed to hear appeal cases part-time and would continue to receive her full salary for life.

A pounding headache woke Mack up. He sat up and looked over at McKenzie, she was curled up and wrapped in the sheet. Mack looked at his watch but it was just a blur. He tried to get up but was too dizzy. His head was throbbing with every beat of his heart. He scooted off the edge of the mattress and pulled on a vent pipe to stand. He waited till he was balanced and worked his way over to the ladder and climbed down to the pool deck. He started toward the bathroom but didn't make it. He puked violently, splattering the pool deck with one convulsion after the other. He sat on the lounge chair with his head in his hands. *What the hell is going on? I never have headaches. Thank God the pounding in my head has stopped.*

He looked at his watch; it was 2:20 am. He stood, no problem with his balance or blurred vision, walked over and turned on the outside faucet. He stood over the pool trench drain, turned on the nozzle of the water hose to a fine mist and sprayed the top of his head letting the cold water run over his body. He changed the nozzle to a full stream and washed the vomit from the pool deck into the drain.

He dried himself and slowly climbed the ladder back to the rooftop and laid down next to McKenzie.

"You okay?" She asked.

"Yes, just had to pee."

She rolled over with her arm across his chest again covering both of them with the silk sheet.

At the airport the next morning, Mack held McKenzie's hand as they walked to the gate of Delta Airlines. They kissed and waved goodbye and she climbed the steps and boarded the plane.

A few hours later Mack was back at the airport again with Nico in his lap crying as they waited for his plane back to New Orleans.

"I don't want to go Papa; I want to stay here with you."

"What about all your friends from school, especially your little girl friend down the street? What's her name, Ava?"

Nico stopped crying and wiped the tears from his eyes. "No, it's Avery, and she's not my girlfriend."

"Oh, sorry about that. You sure talked to her a long time over the phone last night." Mack saw three flight attendants walking toward them.

"Well, look who's here. Hello Nico, you get to board the plane first, you ready?" CT asked. She stared at Mack, then a big smile, "I saw Nico's name on the board and volunteered to watch over him on this flight. I will be staying at the Casa Marina again on my return flight, maybe we could meet for a drink at the bar around seven."

Mack shook his head, "I'd love to, CT, but I'm seriously involved with someone. He kissed and hugged Nico and gave CT a bag of four books. "He likes to read."

"Great, so do I."

Mack waved goodbye as he watched them walk across the tarmac and up the steps into the plane.

At home, Mack walked into an empty house; no kids, no women, just peaceful silence.

He had mixed emotions. He had lived a lot of his life alone and grown to enjoy the solitude. He felt a little guilty now as he meandered across the patio and around the pool, settling in his lounge chair. He realized how much he missed being by himself. He certainly loved McKenzie, Irish, and his son, but full time, 24/7? That was the question. Of course, he was older now and had more patience. The real question he asked himself was could he do without McKenzie? The answer was immediate, hell no. He had finally met someone he really loved and he was planning on spending the rest of his life with, and that was that.

His right leg jumped. How strange. He stared at the leg. This had never happened before.

There, it jumped again, about a foot above the chair then started shaking. First his little finger then his hand and arm, now his leg. *What the hell?* Was his body taking over his brain? He had no control, it was as if the lower part of his body from waist down was in the other lounge chair next to him. The electrical wiring from his brain to his leg had short circuited. Other parts of his brain were working fine because at the same time he was fighting panic and fear. Weird thoughts flashed in his mind: *his aunt Irish wringing a chicken's head off in her hand and watching the chicken flopping all over the back yard. And back in the orphanage, a classmate in the fifth grade having an epileptic seizure. He fell to the floor unconscious, muscles convulsing, body jerking and his eyeballs rolling back in his head.*

Then he remembered reading something about on and off periods. He realized he had missed his scheduled time to take his carbidopa/levodopa medicine. He reached into his right pocket to get the small pill box but his leg was shaking so hard he couldn't get his hand in his pocket. He threw his left leg on top of his right leg and hurried to get the pills out. He removed a double dose and swallowed them immediately as his right leg stated kicking up again. This was the gift that keeps on taking. But, like a miracle, the medicine broke through the brain barrier and the kicking and shaking stopped.

CHAPTER 40

'Lev'o'dopa-induced Dys'ki'ne'sia (LID): is a form of dyskinesia associated with levodopa used to treat Parkinson's disease. It often involves hyperkinetic movements, including chorea, dystonia, and athetosis. In the context of PD, dyskinesia is often the result of long-term dopamine therapy.'

Mack continued to read about dyskinesia but had to stop to look up hyperkinetic movements.

Damn! Mack didn't know what to think. Dev would tell him one thing then he would read something different. Dev told him he had not been taking levodopa long enough for it to cause dyskinesia. Plus, he said he had patients that had been taking levodopa, the gold standard for PD, for the past 20 years. None had ever had dyskinesia. How confusing is that? He was curious to see what Dev was going to say when he told him about his jumping leg. One thing for sure, he knew the disease was incurable, everything he read and researched confirmed that. If this was a life sentence; he was not going to live the end of his life with these kinds of disabling attacks. All his life he had tried to live with integrity and dignity and if he couldn't continue to live like that, then it was time to go. He had lived a good life, no, a great life, leaving nothing from A to Z unexplored. He didn't want to wait till he was unable to make his own decisions.

From the day we are born we all have an expiration date stamped on us somewhere.

Unquestionably, we all are going to die, some early and some late. Who, more than yourself has the right to determine how and when you die. Why would anyone want to spend the end part of their life in a broken body; like a string-marionette, with no control over your movements. You're not the same person; so why would anyone want to be around you, especially in public. There was never a warning when an outbreak would occur, you could be anywhere, like at the airport with Nico and everyone gawking and backing away as if you had a deadly contagion. What kind of quality of life was that. One day you're a strong, virile, manly man, and the next day you are a shaking, jerking, amnesic cripple. Already, Mack had noticed some of his friends had stop calling or coming by. It was degrading and humiliating and was only going to get worse.

He needed to prepare for the worst.

Mack had read about Death with Dignity, a national leader in end-of-life advocacy and Physician-assisted suicide, and the different life-ending drugs you could take to end your life peacefully.

In one case a toxicologist in Iowa, a veterinarian, a pharmacologist, and a couple of anesthesiologists met to decide. The group had three main criteria. They wanted "a drug that would: number one, put a patient to sleep and keep them asleep; and, number two, make sure there was no pain involved; and number three, ensure that they would die, and, hopefully, die relatively quickly."

Plus, it had to be cheap. They aimed for $500 a dose.

For years, the two barbiturates widely considered the best drugs for hastening death in terminally ill patients were pentobarbital and secobarbital. These medications were painless, fast- acting, and relatively affordable. And of course, like Aunt Irish, morphine is commonly used to hasten death.

Mack was sure that Dev would help him get the right prescription. He had always been extra friendly to Mack and accommodating. He looked down at the screen of his phone as it vibrated, it was like his phone was reading his mind; it was Dev returning his call.

Mack sat inside Dev's office waiting and listening to the thunder and heavy rain. He watched the electrical storm through the office window, lightning burst across the darkened overcast skies. He was glad he didn't fly his plane to New Orleans.

After their short phone conversation yesterday, when Mack told him about his leg jumping and his loss of balance, his headaches and throwing up, Dev told him to come to New Orleans ASAP and *do not* fly his plane or drive his car.

He hadn't seen Dev yet, his morning was spent taking an MRI scan of his brain, blood work, and waiting; mostly waiting. Mack turned when he heard the door open and Dev hurried into the room. He was in black surgical scrubs and a black surgical cap pulled down to the top of his eyebrows and tied in the back. Mack stood up and Dev shook his hand, his other hand was on Mack's shoulder.

"Sorry about keeping you waiting, we had a problem in surgery, we lost power while I was operating and had to stop until the backup generators kicked in." Dev sat in a chair across from Mack, not behind his desk.

"I never thought about that. Does that happen often? How long does it take for the generators to kick in?"

"Most of the time, not long. But let's talk about you, how do you feel?"

"Strangely, I feel pretty good. Except when I have one of those episodes; tremors, my jumping leg and most recent, those debilitating headaches."

"When did the headaches start and how long did they last?"

"The first one was about a month ago, not long, but this last one almost sent me to the emergency room. Did anything show up on the MRI?"

"I'm waiting on that now. The radiologist, Dr. Osteen, is bringing the film to my office shortly and we'll all look at it together."

"Do you think the headaches and dizziness is caused by my PD? And the jumping leg . . . what's that all about? I read that it was dyskinesia."

"The headaches and loss of balance typically are not a symptom of PD. The jumping leg could be a damaged or a trapped nerve, we'll know more when we look at the MRI."

"There's something I want to ask you to do for me."

"Sure Mack," Dev leaned over and put his hand on Mack's knee, "what do you need?"

"I feel like a cripple, Dev. From all that I've read about PD and what you've told me there is no cure and every day this disease continues to suck the life out of me. I don't want to live out the rest of my life like that, it's embarrassing and humiliating to have to have someone wipe my ass, change my diaper, and wipe the slobber from my mouth. I've lived a good life, with honor and dignity and I want to die that same way. I have been reading about the Death with Dignity Act, they advocate for the fundamental freedom of choice in end-of-life options for all. They clearly outline the process by which individuals may obtain life-ending medications. The medications most often used were propofol 98.5%, midazolam 91.4%, and rocuronium 90.8%. The median time from the first injection until death was 9 minutes. I need you to write that prescription for me."

Dev got up and walked behind his desk and leaned over with his hands on top. "So, let me see if I have this right. You want me to kill you, right?"

"I . . ."

"No." Dev said forcibly, "*You* listen to me." He sat in his chair. "Do you know how many years I spent studying to become a neurosurgeon . . . 17 years of doing without. No 40-hour weeks either, most of the time 80-hours. No weekends off, no vacations, barely enough money to live on and a half million dollars of loans to pay off.

"I was not an erudite, studying didn't come easy. I had many tutors and many hours in the library. In my four years of college I had to take tough courses; chemistry, mathematics, biology, physics, and had to make top grades to get in the best med school. Four years of med school and seven years of surgical residencies and add on another two-year fellowship. Some of my patients wait months, some over a year, for me to operate, to save their life or extend it. I'm a surgeon, Mack. I save lives for a living. That's my job. I don't murder my patients."

Mack stood up, red-faced, flushed.

Dev stood too, "You talk about being a cripple. What about that Marine buddy of yours at the VA, with both arms blown off at the elbows and one leg blown off above the knee. *He* is a cripple. You are nowhere close to being a cripple."

Mack stepped forward with a menacing stare at Dev. He trembled, then staggered, his eyes closing as his body crumbled to the floor.

There was a knock on the door and Dr. Osteen walked in.

They both rushed to Mack.

Mack woke up in a dark hospital room. He looked down at an IV taped to the top of his hand.

There was a knock on the door and Dr. Dev walked in. "How you feeling? Here, let me raise you up." Dev hit the remote button and the top half of the bed stopped at a 45-degree angle. "You, okay?"

"Yeah."

"You remember what happened?"

"I remember being in your office. What am I doing here?"

"Medical term, orthostatic hypotension, you fainted. You had me worried there for a while."

"What caused me to pass out?"

"Low blood pressure, your BP was 70/40. It's another side effect of Parkinson disease, when you stand too quickly. Also, it could be caused by your PD meds, levodopa especially."

Mack held up his hand with the IV. "What's this?"

"Saline. Salt helps raise low blood pressure. Do you remember what we were talking about just before you collapsed?"

"We were waiting on the results of my MRI."

"Yes, that's true, but I'm talking about when you asked me to write you a prescription to hasten your death."

"You turned me down."

"I did. But after studying the MRI images and reading the radiologist's report, there's some good news and bad news from that report."

"Is that why you said 'You had me worried there for a while.'"

"Partly. Your symptoms were very similar to a recurrent brain tumor. The good news is there were no signs of the old tumor. The bad news is, when I ordered the MRI, I included a scan of your midbrain, specifically the substantia nigra, which showed a rapid depletion of dopamine. This is very unusual. It could be the cause of your dyskinesia and the acceleration of the disease. We need to do something immediately."

"Is it that serious?"

"Yes. The depletion rate of dopamine is faster than the accumulation."

"Is there anything we can do?"

"Yes, there is a new procedure if you're willing to gamble, gamble your life that is, and I assume you are since earlier you wanted me to write you a deadly prescription."

"It's not like I want to die, I want to live with as much quality as I can for as long as I can. I could care less about the odds as long as there is the slightest chance of a cure, you can count me in 100%. What's the new procedure?"

"While Nico was staying with you and McKenzie, Jin and I flew to Australia. I was honored to be invited to participate in an updated surgical trial for Parkinson's disease. We operated on four patients while I was there, two in the morning session and two in the afternoon.

"The consortium has been tracking the four patients and they are improving with no negative side effects. However, a year ago this procedure was a complete failure and ended in a tragedy for all four patients. Remember, these were all volunteers in the last stages of PD knowing the odds were not in their favor.”

“What happened to them.”

“Two died and the other two were left with brain damage.”

“But in this latest trial all four were successful, right?”

“It’s too soon to say for sure. You must remember it was only four individuals out of thousands, that’s not good odds. This upcoming trial will have 25 patients, I can try to get you in for those trials.”

“Will you be doing the surgery?”

“Yes, I will assist Dr. Audrey Livermore, the chief surgeon.”

“A woman brain surgeon?”

“Does it matter?”

“No, not at all.”

“In my opinion she’s the best there is.”

“This would be in Australia?”

“Yes.”

“Well, it is what it is. I’ve made life changing gambles most of my life. What the hell, it’s all a roll of the dice.”

Dev’s phone rang. He saw it was Jin. “Hello, Dr. Jin, this is Dr. Dev your personal caretaker.”

“Oh yeah, well I’m lonely. You better get home and do your caretaking. Are you with Mack?”

“Yes dear.”

“Tell him to call McKenzie ASAP. She’s worried about him and hasn’t heard from him in two days and knew nothing about his condition and him coming to see you . . . you men!”

“Yes dear.”

“Don’t be cute. You two come home now and stop by Smokey’s and pick up a 3-pound order of barbeque ribs, and a 3-pound brisket with beans, slaw, corn on the cob and banana pudding. I don’t feel like cooking tonight. And hurry home, I’m hungry and horny.”

At 40,000 feet and traveling at 650 mph you would think that wherever you are going you would get there in a short period of time; 16-hours nonstop is not a short period of time.

It was dark inside the combined two suite cabins of the Singapore Airlines Airbus except for the reading lamp above Mack's recliner chair. He stopped reading and looked over at McKenzie sleeping soundly in the double bed. He was glad he upgraded to cabin class. It made the 16-hour flight much more tolerable. Across the aisle Irish and Dev had separate single bed cabins. It was an expensive upgrade, $48,000 for the four round trip tickets, but what was money to Mack now? He may not even be alive after this surgery. He had been reading the research papers Dev gave him of the past two trial operations and the odds of success were not in his favor. His eyelids were heavy; he could read no more. He removed his pants and shirt, turned the reading light out and slipped between the sheets moving close to McKenzie.

A long black Toyota Sequoia waited for them outside the Sydney Kingsford Smith Airport with the name Westmead Institute for Medical Research painted on the door in small letters. While the driver was loading the luggage, Dev said, "Would you mind driving by the Opera House to show my friends?"

"No problem, mate. How 'bout I drive over the Harbor Bridge on the way, you know it's the widest steel bridge in the world."

"Sure, that would be something else for them to see."

Westmead was about 16 miles west of Sydney in a large medical district. The driver pointed out the numerous medical buildings as he drove through the maze of streets. In one block alone there were four different hospitals. The driver turned and stopped in front of the 175 Hotel Westmead. After checking in and getting settled, Dev and Mack walked across the street for a scheduled meeting with the surgical team at Westmead Institute for Medical Research.

Dev opened the door for Mack and they walked into the Anatomy Lecture Theater. It was a bowl-shaped auditorium with steep seats looking down onto a circular stage and a theater shared with the University of Sydney Medical School at the University of Sydney and the Westmead Hospital, a major teaching hospital in Sydney. A large 20' projector screen stretched across the wall above the stage.

Professor Nathan O'Reilly, CEO of Western Sydney Local Health

District, stepped behind the podium as the lights blinked off and on. "If all of you will please have a seat, we will get started with our program." O'Reilly went on continuing to introduce dignitaries and concluded with a glowing introduction of the chief surgeon, Dr. Audrey Livermore.

Dr. Livermore was 47 years old, unmarried, with an athletic body, short dark auburn man-style haircut. She was one of the top brain surgeons in the world. Eighty percent of her time she would be dressed in pink scrubs but this evening she was dressed in white pants with a light pink cashmere sweater. "Welcome everyone." She waited, looking up scanning the crowd with a smile. "We are very excited about the latest results of our research trials for a possible cure of Parkinson's Disease. You may have notice I didn't say treatment of Parkinson's. We have many medical, surgical, and behavioral symptomatic treatments but no cure. Here at the Institute, we are focusing 100% on eradication of this crippling disease. This will be our third trial.

"Westmead Institute for Medical Research is just one spoke in the large wheel of Professor O'Reilly's Western Sydney Local Health District, which covers over 780 square kilometers. WSLHD is a leader in clinical services, research and education providing a diverse range of public healthcare services across more than 70 sites including Westmead, Auburn, Cumberland, Blacktown and Mount Druitt hospitals as well as a network of comprehensive integrated care and community-based services. The primary purpose of all these 70 sites comes down to one word . . . TEACH."

Mack was impressed. Enough to let her drill a hole in his head and dig around in his brain? He was glad Dev would be there. That upped the odds a little. Mack overheard someone wish Dr. Audrey Livermore a happy birthday and mentioned to Dev that he would like to take everyone out to dinner to celebrate.

It was late afternoon; they were all at the elevated polished brass bar in the world renowned Bennelong Restaurant, waiting for their reserved table. The golden glow of the lamps complemented the brass tones throughout the interior detailing and set the ambiance for the restaurant. Mack had ordered a bottle of vintage champagne and they were making a toast when everyone at the bar started singing happy birthday. Mack ordered a couple more bottles of champagne for everyone at the bar.

The restaurant was embedded in dramatic continuum of one of the vast 14 shell roofs of the Sydney Opera House. If all the shells were combined it would be a perfect sphere. Mack stared up at the vast ribbed-cage vaulted ceiling with each precast rafter resting on the steel framing of the glass curtain wall. The massive glass wall, from floor to ceiling, outlined a majestic panoramic view of the Sydney Business District and the Harbor Bridge.

The waiter walked them to a choice table against the glass wall. It cost Mack fifty bucks, anywhere else it would have been twenty. The lights dimmed inside as they were seated and on the outside, like magic, as if someone flipped a switch, all the lights on the zigzag buildings of the business district came flashing on, one after the other igniting the skyline in multiple colors.

Mack, who was still standing, reached over the back of McKenzie's chair, took her hand and guided her to him. They embraced as if to dance. Mack whispered, "Look, it's *Twilight Time.*"

All along the Harbor Bridge and over the top of the 450-foot arch large yellow lights splashed across the blue-black sky.

McKenzie put both her arms around Mack's neck and kissed him long and slow and then in a low voice she sang, '*Heavenly shades of night are falling, it's twilight time.*' She led him in a slow dance turn. "You *remembered* my favorite song we danced to in Key West."

'*When purple-colored curtains mark the end of day I'll hear you my dear, at twilight time.*' Mack whispered the second verse.

They turned when they heard Dev, Irish, and Audrey clapping their hands. "What are you two celebrating?" Dev asked.

Mack looked over at McKenzie, she shrugged. Mack threw both arms out wide and nodded toward the sky, "Look . . . van Gogh's The Starry Night."

CHAPTER 41

Irish hurried across the street carrying two café lattes from Starbucks. She hadn't realized that Aussie's loved their coffee as much or more than Americans. There was a line out the door waiting to order their favorite, café latte. She had just got a text from McKenzie that Mack's doctor was in the preop holding area and was on her way to their room. The door to Mack's room was propped open and Irish walked in and saw Dr. Audrey leaning over Mack's bed holding his hand.

She turned, smiling at Irish, "Is one of those for me?"

Like her father, not to be one-upped, she fired back smiling, "Both of them are yours if it elevates your dexterity while operating on my daddy."

"Your father beat you to it," She squeezed his hand, "anybody that takes me out to fine dining and keeps my glass filled with Krug Champagne has my complete, and undivided attention."

Everyone turned to see a huge black man, an aboriginal, his body blocking the doorway. McKenzie backed away from the door.

"Ah, our concertmaster of this ensemble. Everyone, this Dr. Koori our anesthesiologist and my right hand in surgery." Dr. Audrey said taking his arm and pulling him inside. "Don't let his size scare you he's as gentle as a koala bear."

Dr. Koori walked over to Mack, "How you feeling Mr. Shannon? If you're a little anxious I can give you something now."

Mack shook his head. "Thanks, I'm okay."

Dr. Koori asked him a few more questions, checked his oxygen level and his blood pressure and nodded to Dr. Audrey.

The head surgical nurse walked in and said, "OR is waiting on us. Everyone ready?"

McKenzie hurried over to the bed, leaned over and kissed Mack with tears in her eyes.

The nurse raised the bed railings and moved to the head of the roller bed and started pushing but stopped when Mack called out, "Hold it!"

Startled, everyone stared at Mack. He leaned forward, "I would like to talk to Dr. Audrey alone. If all of you would wait outside for a few minutes, please."

Dr. Dev looked at Dr. Audrey and got no reaction. He shrugged his shoulders and walked over to the door.

Irish walked over to the bed and put her arm around Mack's shoulder and whispered, "You okay, Daddy?"

"I'm fine, Baby."

Everyone filed out of the room one by one with Dev closing the door behind him.

Dr. Audrey moved over to the bed. "You a little apprehensive, Mack?"

"No. I have some more questions before I get a hole drilled in my head. We talked a little about it but not in details that I remember. Dev has talked to me a little and of course I heard your lecture at the auditorium. I'm not questioning your qualifications. It's like Dev said, and I believe it to be the truth, you are the best. To me, you seem to be a straight shooter, my kind of person, and if you could explain to me in layman's terms, sort of a CliffsNotes play-by-play of the surgery and the odds of living, dying, or permanent damage, I would appreciate it."

Dr. Audrey pulled a chair up along the side of the bed. "We will have to hurry, we are holding up a lot of people, Mack.

"I assume you know quite a bit about PD already, so I will focus just on the surgery, Trifecta-4, phase 4 clinical trial. So, here at Westmead Institute our research team has developed a cure for PD. We started with a . . . let's say, a cocktail, better yet, using your Marine vernacular, we will call it a small bomb. We filled it with major drugs, chemicals, and other bioactive materials and to make it even smaller we burned it into a gas and encapsulated it inside microbubbles."

"What are microbubbles?" Mack asked.

"Microbubbles are minuscule, between 1 to 10 microns and in this case are used as carriers to the substantia nigra, our destination, located in the midbrain. Under the exposure of sufficiently high-amplitude ultrasound, these targeted microbubbles rupture, spewing the bioactive materials contained in its encapsulating layer, to targeted cells or tissues and penetrating even into the small blood capillaries.

"Okay, we built the bomb, now we have two more important things to do; a way to deliver the bomb and a way to circumvent the barricade blocking our delivery. The 'barricade' is the blood-brain barrier (BBB), which is a microscopic structure that shields the brain from the vast majority of circulating drugs, and microorganisms, such as bacteria, fungi, viruses, or parasites, that may be circulating in the bloodstream. Unfortunately, it also stops the repertoire of drugs that can be used to treat Parkinson's diseases. In our in-depth study it showed that the fusion of focused ultrasound with a microbubble contrast agent opened the BBB and then the ultrasound is used to burst the microbubble, causing site-specific delivery of the bioactive material. Microbubbles work by resonating in an ultrasound beam, rapidly contracting and expanding in response to the pressure changes of the sound wave."

"That's intense. How long is the operation?" Mack said.

"We have no choice. The opening of the blood-brain barrier is short-lived and most of the blood-brain barrier is closed within one hour."

"If these microbubbles are in the micron sizes, how can you see them inside the brain?"

"Brain mapping. It's akin to fingerprinting or GPS. We have approximately 86 billion neurons in our brain, woven together by an estimated 100 trillion connections, or synapses. It's a daunting task to understand the details of how those cells work. We took the image of your MRI and marked it up like a roadmap with a red line to your substantia nigra. A monitor in the operating room combines two cameras with advanced image processing giving us a 3D TV-screen view of the mapping of your brain in very fine details that are magnified during surgery."

"I have one more request and they can roll me out of here. If something goes wrong in this operation, don't wake me up. I know all of Australia has passed the voluntary assisted dying, the VAD law, and I would like to take advantage of it."

Dr. Audrey didn't say anything but did nod.

Many thoughts raced through Mack's mind as he was rolled down the all-white tile corridor, the overhead lights clicked by one after the other. The double doors to the OR opened automatically and the freezing cold sent a shiver down his spine. His immediate thought was the morgue, live meat, or dead meat, which would he be. Inside the OR Mack was shifted from his roller bed onto the operating table. The lights in the OR room were so bright he had to close his eyes. After a few minutes he opened his eyes, and the room was dark except for the light directly over the operating table and at least 30 to 40 eyes were staring down from the circular balcony above. He heard Dr. Koori whisper, "Mack, we have a lot of pretty med students looking down at you, so you'd better behave, no farting. Dr. Audrey is about to attach the Leksell frame to your head but first I'm going to give you a little general anesthesia. What's that old saying you have in the states, 'See you later alligator.'"

Mack thought he could feel the stereotactic arc frame pins being screwed into his head, but his thought was short-lived. As the first drop of propofol raced into his circulatory system, up his arm, in and out of his heart and into his brain, a euphoric magic carpet appeared. There was no steering wheel, gas pedals or brakes; Mack was just along for the ride.

As Mack soared over the Rocky Mountains through snowflakes as big as butterflies, he heard John Denver,

> *He climbed cathedral mountains, he saw silver clouds below*
> *He saw everything as far as you can see*
> *Rocky Mountain High*

He hovered at the top of Aspen Mountain, 11,200 feet, then floated down through silver snow clouds into the cavernous bowl of North Star run and schussed downhill through deep powder leaving a large rooster tail behind him as snow crystals covered his face and head. When he approached the intersection of Gentleman's Ridge the carpet turned southeast, crossing New Mexico, Texas, and into the Gulf of Mexico following 25-degree north latitude toward Key West.

The carpet moved like a surfboard over the clear turquoise water of the Florida Keys. It stopped and hovered over Jewfish Basin, Mack's favorite honey hole for fishing and lobstering. He wiped the saltwater from his face just before the carpet dove to the bottom of the bowl-shaped coral reef. The visibility was unlimited as the carpet glided around the coral reefs that provided habitat for a large variety of multi-color marine life, including various sponges, oysters, clams, crabs, sea urchins, and many species of fish. Mack watched a huge slow moving jewfish swim out of the seagrass and dive under a coral head. There was a deep sea-shelf on the outer edge of the reef with a drop off into dark waters of over 300 feet.

The carpet floated on top of this shelf while Mack watched a collection of fish. Two large silver barracudas drifted in place stalking prey. He looked down and saw a long cloud of sand and had counted over 30 lobsters, single file, scurrying across the bottom when suddenly the sun was blacked out. At first, he thought jewfish; some weigh up to 800 pounds, or a leatherback turtle weighing over twice that much. Then something slammed into him like a loaded dump truck pushing him along the bottom. He couldn't see for all the stirring of sand but soon felt the pressure of 50 rows of serrated teeth into his hip. When the sandstorm cleared, he saw that a bull shark had him in his mouth and was dragging him off the sea-shelf and down into the dark waters of the deep drop off. Mack pounded the shark's head over and over with his fists and tried to gouge his eyes out. The shark, undeterred, shook him like a rag doll dragging him deeper and deeper down the drop off.

Dr. Audrey secured the last screw into the bone flap covering the hole in Mack's skull and backed away as Dr. Dev pulled the skin flap over the skull and started stitching. A light applause started at one end of the balcony and worked its way around the building to a crescendo. The lights were turned on in the balcony as Mack was wheeled out of the OR and down the corridor into an ICU room where McKenzie and Irish were waiting.

Mack was upright in the bed, semiconscious, with a large bandage around his head. Irish cried out with a low moan and tears in her eyes seeing all the tubes and wires hooked up to her daddy. He looked more like he was dying than recovering. One of the monitors showed his heart rate, breathing, blood pressure, intracranial pressure, and cerebral perfusion pressure. A tube through his mouth was to help with breathing and suctioning, and another one through his nose into his stomach to suction the stomach and provide liquid formula. An ICP monitored a tube placed into the top of his brain through a small hole in his skull to measure the amount of pressure inside the brain. An IV catheter allowed fluids, nutrients, and medicine to be given directly into a vein. The last tube was a Foley catheter hanging out the end of his penis.

The door opened and Dr. Audrey and Dr. Dev walked in the room smiling. Mack opened his eyes. Dr. Dev said, "Why so sad?" looking at Irish and McKenzie's sad faces.

"Mack did great. The operation was a total success, not one problem. We will get rid of most of this equipment in a couple of days when we move him to a private room." Dr. Audrey said.

"Ah, he's awake." Dr. Dev said walking over to Mack's bedside. "How do you feel big guy?"

Mack just stared at Dev.

Dev took his hand and said, "Look around the room. You see McKenzie and Irish? Squeeze my hand if you see them."

Mack's eyes scanned the room, and he squeezed his hand.

"Good. Do you know what day this is?"

Mack nodded.

"Is it Thursday?"

Mack shook his head slowly.

"Friday?"

Mack squeezed his hand.

"Good. You are doing great. Are you in any pain?"

Mack shook his head.

"Good. Just rest and we will be back tomorrow to take some pictures and get you moved out of here."

Mack closed his eyes and faded into deep sleep.

They all walked out of the room, Dr. Dev closing the door behind them.

Later that evening, Dr. Audrey, Dr. Dev, McKenzie, and Irish were enjoying a light celebratory dinner over the success of Mack's surgery when Dr. Audrey got a vibrating text,

EMERGENCY! CALL 61 2 9240 8000 ASAP. Dr. Audrey stood up, "Please excuse me, I have to make a call." Almost immediately she was back at the table. "I have to go, it's an emergency. Dr. Dev, you want to ride with me."

McKenzie asked, "Is it Mack?"

"I'm afraid so."

"What's wrong?" Irish said.

"You two go, I'll take care of the check. Irish and I will follow right behind you." McKenzie said.

Dr. Audrey and Dr. Dev hurried into Mack's ICU room. The first thing Dr. Audrey looked at was the intracranial pressure (ICP) monitor that measured the pressure inside the skull. It was high, 31 mm Hg, which indicated one of two things, brain bleed or infection. Dr. Dev suggested a CT scan and one was ordered immediately.

Dr. Audrey's surgical nurse, Mia, told her the alarm on the ICP monitor went off and when they got to his room, he was conscious and complaining about a severe headache.

The door opened and two CT techs rolled in with a portable head CT scanner and started hooking it up.

Drs. Audrey and Dev stood staring at the CT monitor as it scanned sliced images of the brain. They both looked at each other when certain slices started showing bright white . . . blood.

"Damn. Brain hemorrhage. A hematoma." Dr. Audrey said under her breath. "Mia, call down and get an OR ready. Stat!" The ICU room exploded into hyperactivity. Equipment was unplugged, tubes removed, Mack was rolled out the door first with Drs. Audrey and Dev following.

McKenzie and Irish stopped when they saw the whole surgical team coming toward them in the corridor. Dev held back and led them into a private room.

"What's wrong? Where are you taking him?" Irish said.

"We're taking him back into surgery."

"Is it serious?" McKenzie said."

"I'm afraid so." If you go to the waiting room, I'll make sure someone will keep you up to date on how he's doing. I must go now." Dev hurried out of the room and down the corridor.

In the operating room, Dev was on one side of the table and Audrey on the other. She understood that a brain hemorrhage can cause death within 12–24 hours if the bleeding is extensive and rapid. A decision had to be made immediately; open the brain again or minimally invasive. She knew the latest data suggested that the three-needle minimally invasive stereotactic puncture could effectively remove the hematoma, reduce ICP, decrease the degree of brain damage, and improve prognosis.

"Okay, minimally invasive. I need the stereotactic (a three-dimensional coordinate system combined with CT scanning to precisely locate the targets deep within the brain). I need the disposable intracranial hematoma removal package." She read from a list on one of the monitors. "Everything, the full package: ICP monitoring sensor and ICP monitor, miniature skull drill, cerebral drainage bag, silicone syringe, disposable applicator, urokinase injection, urapidil injection, nitroglycerin injection, compound mannitol injection, glycerol, fructose injection, 2% lidocaine hydrochloride injection, and 0.9% sodium chloride injection. Stat."

Dev focused on fitting the location framework on Mack's head (the stereotactic) while Audrey set up the CT scan and printed in actual size. Using the CT scan, the coordinates of the intracranial hematoma and puncture sites were determined without damaging the functional areas. Dr. Koori, the anesthesiologist, then administered at the puncture point local anesthesia before surgery. The skull was punctured by an intraosseous drill-needle under the guidance of the stereotactic instrument, and an ICP sensor probe with a drainage tube was inserted slightly into the anterior horn of the lateral ventricle opposite the hematoma to monitor ICP and drain cerebrospinal fluid that the brain floated in. Dr. Audrey inserted this first needle. Dr. Dev inserted the second needle in the upper lateral edge of the hematoma or in the anterior horn of the lateral ventricle opposite the hematoma to monitor ICP. The third puncture needle was inserted by Dr. Audrey slightly into the upper and lower parts of the hematoma respectively.

The drainage tube clip was opened, and the liquid hematoma was slowly aspirated with a syringe connected to the drainage tube. Before removing the syringe from the drainage tube, the clip was closed to prevent air from entering the cranial cavity. In the next step, a pipeline with a drainage device was connected after suction of the liquid hematoma. Because hematomas are usually partially solid, they needed to determine whether urokinase should be injected to liquefy and drain the residual hematoma. Urokinase dosage was chosen, 20,000 IU mixed with saline was injected. After urokinase injection, the drainage tube was clamped and reopened two hours later. The aspiration was stopped when the ICP returned to a normal low limit.

Now all anyone could do was wait for the outcome. One-third of patients will survive with good recovery; one-third will survive with a disability; and one-third will die.

CHAPTER 42

Mack woke up sweating. The intense Key West sun had moved under the umbrella. He eased off the red wood lounge chair and sat on the first step of the pool. The water was cool to his hot body as he slowly scooted off the steps until he was totally submerged. He swam underwater to the deep end of the pool and back. When he surfaced, he heard something splash into the water, he turn and saw floating on the water a black baseball style hat with a golden eagle, globe, and anchor and in red letters, U.S. Marine Corps.

"You know what Dr. Dev said about covering that bald head of yours." McKenzie said standing at the edge of the pool in shorts, a sleeveless olive-green t-shirt with U.S. Marines printed in black letters across the chest, and an identical hat like she threw to Mack.

Mack rubbed the stubs of hair on his head. "It's growing back fast. It's a race between my beard and my head. You sure you want me to grow a beard?"

"I love a beard on you. It makes you look . . . debonair."

The surgical nurse had shaved part of his head before the operation and half a head of hair with a half-moon scar looked ridiculous.

McKenzie bought some hair clippers and gave him a buzz cut.

"You want some company?" She said.

Mack reached over and grabbed her ankle and tried to pull her in but she was too quick turning her foot and pulling away. She backed away a few steps standing between the lanai and the pool shaking her index finger side to side like a metronome. She reached back and pulled a chair from the lanai dragging it out onto the pool deck. She picked up her cell phone and tapped the screen until a deep, gravelly voice with sultry background music drifted across the pool. It was Joe Cocker singing *'You can take your hat off.'*

"Baby, take off your coat
Real slow."

McKenzie's svelte body moved with perfect symmetry to every beat and sound as she slowly turned her back to Mack and removed her shirt throwing it over her head into the pool.

"And take off your shoes
I'll take off your shoes."

McKenzie turned to the left kicking off one flip-flop into the pool and back to the right kicking the other flip-flop into the pool all in rhythm with the music.

"Baby take off your dress
Yes. Yes, yes."

McKenzie, with lingering and measured movement, turned around facing Mack and slowly removed her black lace bra and tossed it into the pool. She lifted both breasts, cupping them in each hand and moving them in sync with the music.

"You can leave your hat on
You can leave your hat on"

She continued her slow dance, her hands squeezing her breasts then sliding them down creasing each side of her body. One hand falling inside the top of her shorts.

"Come over here
Stand on that chair
Yeah, that's right."

She stood on the chair, unbuttoned her shorts and kicked them into the pool.

"Sweet darling
You can keep your hat on."

McKenzie swayed side to side to the music as she moved to the edge of the pool looking down at Mack. Inch by inch she pushed her panties down stepping one leg out then the other. Mack thought to himself, was there anything more beautiful than her flaming red bush framed by her snow-white skin. He reached up, took her hand and walked her to the shallow end of the pool and lifted her off the edge into the knee-deep water. They kissed, her lips hot and swollen. He could feel her erect nipples against his bare chest. As they both fought to get his bathing suit off McKenzie's hat fell into the water. Her long red hair tumbled to her shoulders and down her back. As the music faded, Mack heard the last words of Joe Cocker,

"Put it my way
You can leave your hat on
You can leave your hat on now."

Mack was busy in the kitchen making McKenzie's favorite breakfast; a bowl of vanilla Greek yogurt with blueberries, strawberries, raspberries, slivered almonds, crumbled walnuts, and sprinkled with spicy and sweet ground Cassia cinnamon. He had cut a large blooming yellow hibiscus out by the pool and placed it on top of the yogurt. The espresso machine pinged and Mack poured two cups of Cuban Café Bustelo topped with frothing milk. He placed all this on a wooden tray and carried it into the bedroom.

"I could smell that coffee all the way from the kitchen." McKenzie said as she sat up in the bed.

Mack sat the tray on her lap and picked up a pillow and placed it behind her back.

"Wow! Oh, Mack. The flower is so beautiful. What do I owe all this too?"

"For every striptease dance like last night you get breakfast in bed."

"It's a deal." She picked up a pillow and leaned it against the headboard and patted the bed. "Here, lover man, right beside me." She sipped his steaming coffee before handing it to him. "This is a lifesaver; you have me addicted to this Cuban coffee."

Mack moved closer putting his arm around her back. "Are you addicted to anything else?"

"Hmmm, let me think." She put her thumb under her chin and closed her eyes.

He leaned over and pinched one of her nipples.

"Oh. Do that again." She gasped. "They are so sensitive. You have triggered every erogenous zone in my body, some I didn't even know I had. I've never been so happy. Not that I was unhappy, just never thought at this stage of my life that I would find someone that I could love so deeply."

Mack rolled off the side of the bed onto his knees. He opened the drawer of the bedside table and took out a small gold wrapped box and leaned across the bed and handed it to her.

She put the tray on the floor next to her side of the bed and dove across the bed on her stomach face to face with Mack. She juggled the box, "Now, what could this be?" She shook it, smelled it, tossed it in her hand. "A watch, a bracelet . . ."

"Just open the thing."

"Okay, okay . . ." She tore into the package, the paper, then lifted the top off, turned it upside down and out dropped a small red velvet jewelry box. She looked over at Mack but there was no expression. It couldn't be what she was thinking. He said many times he would never marry again. *STOP IT! It's not going to ever happen.*

Mack grabbed the box from her hand.

She shrieked, not knowing what was happening.

He opened the top and handed it to her.

She was in shock. She couldn't breathe. Her heart stopped pumping blood to her brain. Her head dropped face down into a pillow.

Mack tapped her on the head with the box. "Hello? Hello? There's another part to this."

She lifted her head. Tears running down both cheeks.

Mack took the ring out of the box, the large round ideal cut solitaire diamond sparkled with brilliance as if it were on fire. He was still on his knees, "I had a long speech ready, but the bottom line is . . . will you marry me?" He took her hand and slipped the ring on her fourth finger of the left hand.

She sat up, scooted to the edge of the bed, wrapped her legs around his chest and took his face in both hands, "Never, never in my whole life could anything be more important to me than being married to you. You have stolen my heart forever Mack Shannon." She leaned down and kissed him. Mack could taste her salty tears on his lips.

Dr. Dev told Mack he could now run as far as he could, but to make sure to start slow and stretch first. Bear usually set the pace for Mack's running time, about a 12-minute mile for the first mile, then a 11-minute mile, then the 3rd mile was a 10-minute mile, Mack's favorite pace. He felt like he could run forever at that pace. They were running on the beach side of A1A just past the airport when his phone rang. He looked at his screen and saw it was McKenzie. He stopped running, "Hello sweetie."

"Hi baby. Whatcha doin'?"

"Just passed the airport, Bear and I are out for a little run."

"You be careful; don't overdo it."

"No problem, I'm feeling great. You in Memphis?"

"I'm outside the airport waiting on an Uber. I wish I was running with you and Bear, I miss you already."

"What time is your appointment with the real estate lady?"

Now that Mack and McKenzie were getting married, she was selling her condo in Memphis. "Two o'clock."

"You still think you can get everything wrapped up in a week?"

"I hope so. I don't want to be away from you any longer than I have to. I've got to find a moving company and someone to clean up afterwards. Darling, I think this is my Uber ride pulling up. I'll call you later. I love you."

"I love you too."

An older model black Chevy Suburban with an Uber sign on the bottom of the windshield stopped in front of McKenzie. The driver got out, introduced himself, put her luggage in the back and opened the backseat door for her.

As the Suburban moved onto I-240, McKenzie kept trying to remember if she had met the driver, Robert, before. She caught him looking in the rear-view mirror and said, "Excuse me, have we met before?"

"No ma'am, I don't think so."

It was my brother, Otis, you're thinking of. You sent him to jail for protecting his nine-year-old son. How many more innocent people have you sent to jail since then.

"Are you from Memphis?" McKenzie asked.

"Born and raised. How about you?"

"Yes, born and raised, but I'm moving to Key West and getting married." She held up her hand to show her ring. *I shouldn't have done that. Good way to lose a finger.*

"Congratulations." *The sooner you leave the better.* "Is he from Key West?"

"He lives in Key West but he's from Memphis too."

"What does he do to make a living in Key West."

He's just being friendly. Don't be so suspicious. "He's retired, we both are. He was in the construction business in Memphis."

"Really. I worked in construction for years in Memphis, maybe I know him."

"Mack Shannon, he owned the company."

You can bet your white ass I know him. "No, I don't know the name."

Robert turned onto I-55 that took him to downtown. Then he crossed Crump Boulevard onto Riverside Drive and turned right onto Beale Street. McKenzie's high-rise condo was on the corner overlooking the Mississippi River. Robert pulled around the circular drive and stopped under the front door canopy. He pushed the trunk release and the overhead rear door opened and then opened the door for McKenzie and removed her luggage handing them to the doorman.

McKenzie and Robert turned at the same time when they heard someone shout her name. A tall man with long hair came running up to McKenzie, grabbed her and whirled her around and around.

"You're as beautiful as ever." He said, kissing her.

McKenzie smiled, "You scared me to death, Niles. What in the world are you doing here in Memphis."

"I came to see you." He picked up his roller bag, took her arm pulling her up the steps,

"Wait." She turned toward Robert as she opened her purse and gave him a twenty-dollar tip.

Robert stood watching them climb the steps following the doorman into the main atrium. He spit on the steps, *skag whore.*

"How did you find me and know that I would be home today?" McKenzie asked Niles as the elevator climbed to the top floor.

"I'm interviewing for a job here with International Paper and Martha Moses gave me your address. I talked to the real estate lady downstairs, Vickie Johnson, and she told me you were coming home today."

McKenzie's phone started ringing as she opened the door to her condo, it was Vickie Johnson returning her call. "Hi Vickie, I was calling you to see if you knew of anyone to help me pack up everything for the movers and maybe someone that might be interested in buying some of my furniture?"

Niles sat his roller bag against the wall in the living room and stared at the panoramic view of the Mississippi River and the heavy traffic coming and going across the Memphis-Arkansas Bridge.

"You want something to drink?" McKenzie said as she placed her phone on the bar. She opened the refrigerator, took out a bottle of Chardonnay and poured herself a drink.

Niles hesitated, "Some water maybe. What a magnificent view. Why are you selling this place?"

"I'm moving to Key West. I'm getting married," she showed him her ring. Quickly, she jerked her hand down. *You got to stop that.*

No reaction. He sat on the couch, downtrodden. "I'm in trouble, McKenzie. I need your help."

"What's wrong, Niles?" She handed him his water and sat in the chair next to him.

"I lost my job over two years ago after 16 years. They said it was attrition because of Covid but I think it was something else. Regardless, I didn't have enough money to fight them. Every day I looked for a job . . . sent out a hundred resumés. Did you know it's impossible for a middle-aged white male to find a job nowadays. Anyway, I got depressed, started drinking and couldn't stop. Spent all my savings. I was so addicted that I sold my car for a case of Vodka. The police found me in an alley almost dead and took me to the hospital. When I got out and went back to my apartment, I was locked out. All my furniture and clothes were in the street." He choked up, McKenzie thought he was going to cry,

"Oh, Niles, I'm so sorry. What can I do to help?"

"I'm sober now. I haven't had a drink in seven months. I stayed at the Salvation Army last night and yesterday I went to two AA meetings. If I could stay here with you till Monday when I have my interview with International Paper and if you could loan me a little money to get a haircut and buy a suit I saw at the Salvation Army that would be a great help."

"Niles, you know I will help you all I can but I'm getting married to Mack Shannon, you remember him? If he found out you stayed the night here, he would kill us both. Well, maybe not kill me, but I wouldn't want to find out."

"It's only till Monday, three nights. I know it's only a one bedroom, but I could sleep on the couch or on the floor, no one would ever know. I could pay back the money you loan me by doing all your packing and moving. You know I was a Logistics Specialist all those years and that's the same job I'm interviewing for with IP."

"Let me think about it. You want something to eat?"

CHAPTER 43

Robert turned off North Second Street onto Luke Ave. Robert's brother, Otis, owned the whole block down to Fred Street. It was all ghetto property, but it was low-cost, isolated, and private. The front building on Second Street had been completely refurbished; red brick with large windows, a long circular drive with lush landscaping. A small black sign was discreetly recessed into the brick with the name SHADOW, LLC in gold letters. Under the name in small cursive letters was *Detective Agency*. Not only was the office on Second Street frontage, it was a front for Otis' other businesses. At the end of Luke Ave was a large junk yard, great for writing off taxes, and next door was an old airplane hangar where Robert ran a mechanic shop, Uber and limousine service.

Robert eased the Suburban through the tall hangar doors and parked it next to an older white Rolls Royce. He told one of the workers the Suburban needed gas and walked out the door and up the block to talk to Otis.

Otis was on the phone when Robert walked into his office. Otis shooed him out with a wave of his hand. He needed to take this call in private. Robert didn't need to know all of Otis' business. When Zira was diagnosed with breast cancer, Otis bought her private detective agency and was doing a lot of business with city and county politicians including the mayor. He had established a reputation of trust and secrecy, no one ever knew all that Otis was involved in. He opened the door and motioned Robert into his office.

"Guess who I just picked up on Uber?" Robert said.

"LeBron James."

"Judge McKenzie O'Connor."

"Did you thank her for sending me to jail?"

"No. But I thought you might want to know she's moving to Key West and marrying your old boss."

"Mack Shannon?"

Robert nodded his head smiling.

"So?"

"Well, while I was unloading her suitcases, a man ran up and grabbed her, twirling her around and around, and kissing her. They went upstairs together;

he was carrying his luggage."

"Maybe it was her brother?"

Robert shook his head smiling as he walked toward the door. "No, no, not the way they were kissing."

"Did you find out who he was?"

"Nope. But they have camaras."

"Get me some pictures."

"Ya'sir, boss man." Robert said over his shoulder as he walked out of Otis' office."

Otis sat thinking. *This is touchy. Would I want someone to tell me my wife was screwing around on me? Better question yet is, if he found out that I knew and didn't tell him.*

Otis picked up his phone and tapped in Mack's number. He didn't answer. Otis left a message then called Robert and told him to take his camera with him and stay watching the judge till he got some defining pictures. His phone started ringing, "I got to go."

"Hello stranger, thanks for calling me back."

"I invited you down to go fishing. We wouldn't be strangers if you'd get your ass on down here." Mack said.

"I've been so busy, man, I'm lucky if I can find enough time to sleep."

"Come on down, take a break. The weather's great and the fish are jumping."

"I will, I promise. The first real cold spell up here and I'll come down."

"Okay, I'm going to hold you to it."

"I hear congratulations are in order, you finally getting hooked?"

"Yeah, I am. You remember McKenzie O'Connor, the red hair judge."

"I do. I thought you said you would never get married again?"

"The love bug got me, Otis. Bit me hard. I've never been this happy in all my life. She's top shelf."

"I'm glad for you, man. You deserve it."

"Thanks, Otis. Can I help you with anything?"

Otis wavered . . . "Ahh. No man, I'm fat."

"Oh, McKenzie is in Memphis now selling her condo. Maybe you two could . . ."

"Mack, I've got to take this call coming in. It's, my doctor, I've been waiting on his call all day. I'll call you back."

"Sure, call me back."

Shit! I can't tell him the woman he loves is shacking up with someone else. I need more proof than just Robert's word. He punched in the number of his top investigator. "Traci, get with Robert, I want 24/7 on Judge McKenzie O'Conner and lots of photos, ASAP."

Always suspicious, Mack questioned Otis's phone call. He called for a reason, what was it? How did he know that I was getting married? And that bullshit about 'the doctor's on the other line.' Mack had used that pretext many times to get off the phone with someone. Something's fishy.

The next day Robert and Traci were in Otis' office with photo's spread out on top of his desk. Some from the camera mounted on the front of McKenzie's high-rise condo showing the man swinging McKenzie around and around and then kissing her on the mouth. Although, true enough, she didn't resist nor did she participate. There were photos of them loading boxes and light furniture into a PODS container with playful banter. They took photos of them walking to Katharine and Mary's Italian Restaurant on South Main, eating dinner and later photos of them walking down Beale Street stopping outside at BB King's listening to the music. But the coup de grace photo was the two them walking into the elevator at one o'clock in the morning to her one-bedroom condo.

After Robert and Traci left Otis' office, he sat studying all the photos on his desk. Otis felt like there was not enough proof for a conviction, but it weighed enough suspicion of distrust to call Mack.

Mack looked at his phone ringing and saw Otis' number. "Okay, now you can tell me what this is all about."

"Believe me when I tell you it's not something I *want* to tell you. The rule I used was 'would you tell me if it was reversed' and I know *you* wouldn't hesitate."

"Get on with it, I'm a big boy. I'm sure whatever it is I've faced worse. 'What's it all about, Alfie.'"

"It's about Judge McKenzie O'Connor." There was total silence. Otis didn't know what to do. After almost a full minute Otis said, "Mack?"

"Go ahead." Mack said.

"My brother Robert picked her up at the airport on an Uber call. When he got to her condo a man ran out to greet her, whirling her around and kissing her. He had a suitcase and is staying with her in her condo."

Mack stood up, took a couple of deep breaths, trying to control the rage boiling up inside. "Are you sure he's not making this up out of revenge for sending you to jail?"

"I wouldn't put anything past my brother, and this sounded like something he might do. I sent my best investigator to back-check it and it's like he said. There's a camera in front of the condos, I saw the footage and we took photos just in case. I'm sorry, Mack. I thought you would want to know."

"Did you get his name?"

"We are checking on that. I wasn't sure how deep you wanted me to go. Robert said he thought he heard the name 'Niles,' does that ring a bell?"

Another long silence . . . "Can you pick me up at the airport downtown?"

"Sure Mack. What time?"

"I'll leave within an hour. It will take me about seven hours depending on the weather and one stop for fuel. I'll call you when I'm an hour out."

"Do you want me to keep the surveillance active?"

"Yes."

Otis was going to say something but heard a click. The phone was dead. He couldn't blame him.

There was no traffic as Mack turned on final for runway 35 at Dewitt Spain Airport. He lowered the flaps and adjusted the trim, the V-tail Bonanza floated to the threshold and practically landed itself.

Mack saw Otis standing on the tarmac outside his car as he taxied to the tie downs. A young man came racing out to the plane in a golf cart and tied the plane down. Mack told him to fill it up and took his bag and got in the car with Otis.

"Good to see you Mack, not under these circumstances of course, but you look good. You're welcome to stay with me or maybe The Peabody which is close to the judge's condo."

"Thanks for the offer but let's go to The Peabody."

In Mack's room at the hotel, Otis spread out the photos of McKenzie and Niles on the coffee table. He could see the hurt and pain on Mack's face as he studied each photo. He questioned himself again about exposing the judge's infidelity.

"Mack," Otis stood up. He felt uncomfortable, as if he was imposing. "I'm going to leave you now. If you need me at any time, just call me man and

I'll be there." He waited, dead silence, then turned and walked out the door.

Mack continued to stare at the photos. How could he have misjudged her that much? Photos don't lie. He felt sick as if he might throw up. He stood up, took a deep breath, and swallowed the bile in his throat and cursed himself for being so weak. He could feel his heart pounding now as it pumped blood to his brain with one overpowering answer to his pain . . . *VENGEANCE.*

Mack picked up his cell phone and called McKenzie.

"Hello, darling, I was just thinking of calling you." McKenzie said.

"Oh yeah?"

"Sure was. You okay, you sound a little tired."

"No, I'm good. You getting a lot done?"

"This is a mess. I hope this is the last time I ever move."

"Did you get some help?"

"Yes. Vickie, the real estate lady got me some boxes and I got a POD for moving. I miss you."

"For real?"

"What?"

"Someone's at the door, I'll call you back."

"I love you." She said. He didn't answer. She looked at her screen and the phone was dead. Something was wrong.

The doorbell rang and McKenzie opened the door. "I've got us a jumbo barbeque each with baked beans and fries." He walked over to the kitchen bar and sat the bags down. "Come on let's eat it now while it's hot. Can we sit out on the balcony and watch the river traffic?"

They had finished eating and were enjoying sitting in the sun watching boats and barges go up and down the river. Niles walked into the kitchen getting another beer when the doorbell rang.

"Niles, will you get the door, it's probably Vickie."

The last person in the world Niles expected to see was Mack Shannon. Niles stood frozen for a moment, not knowing what to say, then stuck out the hand holding the beer, "Come in, have a beer."

150-years ago, Mack probably would have been a gunslinger, and one of the fastest. His right hand was so quick; Niles never felt any pain or knew what had happened. Mack hit him so hard it broke his nose splitting it down the middle and smashed his top lip knocking out two teeth. McKenzie heard a loud crash and came running into the room and saw Niles spread-eagle, knocked out cold on the floor, his head in a pool of blood. She screamed when she saw Mack and ran over to him.

"What are you doing here?" She looked back at Niles. He wasn't moving. "Did you kill him, is he dead? Are you insane?" She shouted and swung her fists at him, both arms wind milling.

He blocked each punch then grabbed her by the throat, "Shut your mouth, you whore." She clawed away at his arm, as each of his fingers tightened down around her neck till she stopped moving and her legs gave way. He stood there in total silence. Her face was blood red as he dragged her by the neck like a ragdoll over to Niles and tossed her on top of him. He reached in his pocket and removed all the photos Otis had given him of McKenzie and Niles. "You want him, now you got him." He tossed the photos and watched them scatter on top of the two bodies.

Walking back to The Peabody, it was the first time Mack didn't feel good after a reprisal. Niles was no problem; he'd smash his face in again without an afterthought. Any dumbass jacking around with another man's woman is asking for an ass kicking. It was McKenzie his heart was aching over. Did he go too far? It really didn't matter it was all over. Any woman with that lustful wandering was poisonous, a toxic future.

He stood outside the hotel under the porte-cochere waiting for an Uber.

He watched a black SUV drive up slowly and stopped in front of him. A young girl with tight jeans jumped out and opened the back door. "You're Mr. Shannon?"

"Yes. Do you mind if I sat up front?"

She looked him up and down and shut the back door and stuck out her hand, "I'm TJ. No luggage?"

"I'm Mack." He shook her hand. "No luggage." He opened the front door and got in. He watched TJ hurry around and get in behind the wheel.

"You know how to get to the downtown airport?"

"Dewitt Spain?"

Mack nodded.

"Never been there," she pointed to her phone in the vent holder, "but I have it in my GPS."

"Just go to the end of North 2nd Street, you'll run right into it."

She already had the location punched in and hit the start icon. "You from Memphis?"

"Yeah. But I live in Key West now. Why do you ask?"

"You seem to know your way around Memphis. I've always wanted to go to Key West, lots of artists live there, right?" She turned north on 3rd Street.

"Yeah, a melting pot. Are you from Memphis?"

"Jackson."

"Tennessee?"

"No. Jackson, Mississippi." She turned left on North Parkway then right on 2nd Street.

"Is this your full-time job?"

"No. Just to make a little mad money. I'm an artist, a portrait painter."

"How long have you been painting portrait?"

"Most of my life."

"And how long is that?"

"You *mean* how old am I. How old do you think?"

"Well, you are a very pretty young lady, I would say in your early twenties."

"Thank you, kind sir, I'm 31." She stopped at the red light at Chelsea. Opened her door, hurried to the back of her SUV, and removed a brown leather like album. In the front seat she handed it to him. "This is a portfolio of my work."

Mack turned the pages of the portfolio and was amazed at what he saw. Her work was superior to anything he had ever seen.

She turned into the airport driveway and Mack pointed to the opened double gates.

"You want me to drive out where the planes are park?"

"Yes. Drive slowly. It's the last one at the end of the second row."

"I can't believe they let you drive out here with all these planes." She stopped in front of Mack's plane.

"What did you think of my paintings?"

"I'm very impressed." Mack walked around the plane going over a preflight checklist in his head. TJ walked right behind him. "I'm no expert, but for your age and to be as talented as you are . . . it's unheard of. Where did you go to school?"

"I always love to draw even as a child. I studied fine arts at UCLA for two years. Took some master classes in Nashville under Igor Babilov, a great teacher, and a few classes at the Steinhardt School in New York with Niki

Smith. Are you married?"

Mack hesitated. Climbed up on the wing and checked the gas tanks while thinking of McKenzie. *That's a dead issue.* "No, I'm not married."

"Do you have any children?"

"Yes, I have a daughter that lives in northern California."

"You are a super fine-looking man, Mack. You have that strong bone structure in your face that I'd love to paint. Have you ever thought of having your portrait painted for your daughter?"

"No."

"There are three things I like to do . . . four really, but I'll keep the fourths till I know you better. I love to paint portraits, barter, and travel. Would you be interested in a trade of a portrait of you for your daughter, for a place to stay in Key West while I paint you? It's going to get cold here real soon."

Mack was standing at the end of the wing ready to leave. "Let me think about it."

She reached out and shook his hand. With her other hand she removed a ballpoint pen and turned his hand over and wrote in his palm. 'Call TJ 901.324.5421.'

Mack stepped up on the wing and opened the door. He looked at the phone number again, smiled at TJ, and crawled inside the plane. He waited till she drove off before turning his starter on, taxied to the runway, and took off headed south over the great Mississippi River.

McKenzie rolled off Niles as he moaned over and over. She sat up with her back against the couch rubbing her neck and thinking over all that had happened. She saw a photo next to her and picked it up and then picked up a hand full more studying each one.

Niles moaned again and tried to sit up. McKenzie grabbed him by his bloody shirt and pulled him up across from her. They sat face-to-face on the floor looking at each other. "What happened?" Niles asked, feeling of his swollen nose covered in dried blood.

McKenzie handed him a hand full of the photos. "I told you what would happen if Mack found out you were staying here with me. We are both lucky we're alive."

Niles rubbed his hand across his mouth then stuck his finger inside and let out a scream like a little girl. "My teeth! My teeth are gone. Where are my teeth?" Niles struggled to stand up then staggered to the bathroom and McKenzie heard another loud shriek. She stood up and saw him standing in the doorway crying.

"Look at my face, he smashed my face in. I will never look the same. I'm going to sue his ass for everything he's got."

"No, you are not, sat down." She pointed to the kitchen table.

"All this is my fault. I gave in to your persistence knowing it was a gamble and I lost, big time. Hopefully it's not too late and I can convince him there was nothing going on between the two of us."

"But now, I've lost my job. Look at me, no one would hire me, and I have no money. I'm going to sue him."

"You're broke, you're jobless, and you're homeless, how are you going to hire a lawyer. There's not a lawyer in town that would take this case on a contingency. You're the guilty party, you were sleeping with an engaged women and you attacked him first."

"What? You know I didn't attack him, you're my witness."

"No, I was on the balcony. I didn't see a thing and you know I can't lie under oath. Imagine what the newspapers/TV stations would do with this case: 'Former Memphis federal judge McKenzie O'Connor, engaged to be married to Mack Shannon one-time Memphis real estate tycoon, caught in three-way sex brawl.' Your name would be all over the news too. You don't think Mack's lawyer would accuse you of throwing the first punch. Mack is the last person I would sue. He's an Irishman with a strong code sworn to an oath of vengeance."

"Then I'm going to kill the son of a bitch. I did nothing wrong. He's not getting by with this?"

"Don't be ridiculous, you would go to jail for life. Hopefully, he has gone back to Key West. If I were you, I would heed the saying 'let the sleeping dog lie.' I know the head of the legal department at IP; maybe you can call her and drop my name with a little white lie that you were in an accident. I'm sure they would delay your interview. Meanwhile you can go to my doctor and my dentist, those were caps on those two teeth anyway, weren't they?"

"You would pay for all that?"

"A loan. You can pay me back once you're back at work and you can stay here until then. I'll have to take my condo off the market, I'm sure the welcome mat for me at Key West is in the shit can."

CHAPTER 44

Mack had anchored his 18' Dolphin over a large coral head the size of an average 3-bedroom house. It was one of his favorite spots to bug hunt. He had stopped at Sandy's Café on White Street for a café con leche and Savanna begged him to take her out in his boat to catch some lobster. He was watching her now, 30 feet down on the bottom, tickle her last lobster of the day out from under a jutting stony coral. He leaned over into the water as she surfaced and took her net with 6 lobsters, the daily limit. With his six in the live well that would give her a dozen bugs. She was happy with that.

Almost a year had passed since the debacle in Memphis with McKenzie and not a day went by that he wasn't faced with a memory of her. She had called many times, but Mack refused to answer the phone. She had sent him a long text explaining in detail why Niles was staying with her. Mack didn't believe her. Irish and Jin tried to talk to him, but Mack was adamant, told them in no uncertain terms to backoff. He was there; he knew what happened. There were photos. He hadn't forgotten seeing them kissing in the laundry room at the New Year's party on Long Island. And he remembered when he was dragging McKenzie across the floor and tossed her on top of Niles that the condo was a one bedroom and there were no sheets, or a blanket, or a pillow on the couch.

It was one of those nights that writers write about, artists paint, and singers sing. The sky was full of bright stars, like sparkling diamonds floating on a dark velvety sea. A red supermoon looked as if it were sitting on the curb at the end of Whitehead Street as a warm salty breeze played soft music with the dancing palm fronds. Maybe it was the calm before the storm.

Mack had just left The Green Parrot Bar after a couple of hours of drinking and socializing. Everyone was talking about the hurricane changing course after tearing through Havana and now headed for the Florida Keys. No one seemed bothered by the news: music playing, people drinking, some dancing—typical conch. But he was headed home, riding his Conch Cruiser down Whitehead Street longing for McKenzie to be riding next to him to share this picture-perfect night. His phone buzzed; it was a text from Savanna, 'Your favorite band is rocking tonight at Sloppy Joe's . . . come dance with me.'

Why not. The wind had picked up a little but no sign of a storm.

When he turned off Whitehead onto Greene Street, he could hear the 'After Hours' band playing and singing Shake, Rattle and Roll. At the corner of Duval, he chained his cruiser to a bike rack and went into the bar looking for Savanna.

Sam, the bartender, saw Mack and held up a glass of ice and pointed to an empty bar stool on the far side of the bar close to the dance floor. The place was packed and rowdy. The music was booming, and the dance floor was overflowing with some dancing between the tables. Sam poured Mack a double shot of single malt and nodded toward the stage where Mack saw Savanna dancing in wild gyrations. The music stopped and immediately started playing Chuck Berry's 'Rock and Roll Music,'

Just let me hear some of that
Rock and roll music
Any old way you choose it . . .

Savanna came running up to Mack and grabbed his hand and started pulling him out onto the dance floor. "Okay lover-man, show me those old rock and roll dance moves of yours."

Mack thought, *'this is what you get when you're out with someone 20 years younger.'* He reached for his glass and drained it and let her pull him onto the dance floor. He knew better than leave his drink on the bar, you never know who or what someone would drop in your glass or just pick it up and keep walking, steal your drink. Mack was a good dancer years ago and from the buzz he got from the scotch and the loud rocking music, he grabbed her, swinging her around and around, twisting her body in perfect harmony with the music.

She was screaming with laughter as she held onto Mack. When he pulled her in close at the end of the song she shouted in his ear. "You never fail to amaze me. You're a great dancer."

Mack stood on the dance floor staring at two drunks, one tall and one short, that had been dancing together.

Savanna followed his eyes to the two men now standing on the dance floor holding hands. "What's wrong?" She asked.

He took her hand and led her back to the bar. Sam sat a cold beer on the bar for Savanna and a scotch on the rocks for Mack. Mack took a drink of his scotch and said, "Hold on. I'll be right back."

Savanna and Sam watched Mack walk across the dance floor and stopped in front of the table where the two men were now sitting. Sam shrugged at Savanna and said, "Beats me."

Mack stood staring at the two men, his hands on his hips. It was dark and smoky, but he was sure of who was in front of him.

"What are you staring at?" The short one said, standing up with his hands on his hips, staggering, trying to mock Mack.

Mack pulled a chair over and shoved it between the two men and sat down with his back to the short one. The man tapped Mack on the shoulder, "What do you think you are doing, this is *my* date."

"Not any longer, shorty." Mack grabbed him by the neck and pushed him down in the chair. "Now shut up or I'm going to throw you out of one of those doors into the street." Mack nodded toward the opened double doors all along the Greene Street side of the building.

Mack sat back down not taking his eyes off the tall guy, "You know who I am?"

"You think I would forget the son of a bitch who busted up my face." Niles said.

"Careful dumb ass. I could do it again."

"No, that won't happen again."

Mack shrugged, "What are you doing in Key West?"

"Vacation."

"Who's the midget?" Mack nodded behind him.

"We met online. He bought my plane ticket."

"We need to talk."

Niles' date stood up and pointed his finger almost in Mack's face. "Is this who you want to be with?"

"You don't want to piss him off." Niles said.

"Well, just . . . who is he?"

"I should have told you I was married. He's my husband." Niles slurred.

"Oh, my God! You're married? Just what I need to get involved with." He turned to leave, then stopped and shouted, "You slut," and hurried across the dance floor and out the front door onto Duval.

"Now what, you damn bully."

A waitress walked by, and Mack motioned for her. "What do you want to drink?" He asked Niles looking at his empty glass.

The waitress stood waiting with her hand on Mack's shoulder.

"Sex on the Beach, a double."

"The same for you Mack?" The waitress giggled.

Mack smiled at Niles as the waitress left to get their drinks. "Your husband, huh. That's funny."

"Yeah, it works all the time."

"Are you queer?"

"You mean am I gay, a homosexual? Why did you attack me?"

"You were sleeping with my fiancé, you idiot."

"You're the idiot. I'm gay. I couldn't *sleep* with McKenzie if I wanted to. She told you we were just friends."

The band started playing, "What about when I saw you two kissing on New Year's Eve?"

"Kissing is not screwing. It was the New Year, for God's sake. I might have kissed you if you were there."

He's telling the truth and so was McKenzie. What's wrong with me. Stupid, Irish pride.

"You want to dance, good looking?"

Mack looked up at a man with heavy eye makeup and a dangling earring in each ear. He dropped his head into his open palms on the table and moaned, "Piss off, fag."

"You don't have to be so nasty mouth about it. Do you want to dance sweetie?" He asked Niles.

Niles stood up, lost his balance, righted himself and took a big gulp of his Sex on the Beach. "Delighted," he said, taking the man's hand.

Mack finished his drink and walked back to the bar while looking over the crowded dance floor for Savanna.

What was he going to do? McKenzie was all he could think of. What a fool he was.

Sam came over to Mack and sat two shot glasses on the bar. "My liquor distributor gave me this bottle of single malt to try." Sam filled the two shot glasses. "It's silky-smooth man. Cheers." They clicked their glasses and downed their drink. Mack scanned over the floor again for Savanna.

"Oh, Mack, I forgot to tell you, Savanna said she would be over at Captain Tony's Saloon."

"Thanks for the drink, Sam. I think I'll head for home."

"Be careful, bro, a storm is coming."

Mack finally got the key in the lock on his bike then lost his balance, tripped on the curb, and fell into the street pulling the bike with him. He looked around, embarrassed, it was a crowded corner, but no one noticed him. Just another drunk crashed on his bike lying in the gutter. How many drinks had he had? He lost count but did remember most were doubles. A strong wind blew up Duvall from Mallory docks carrying large drops of rain. He picked up his bike and started walking and remembered what Sam said, "A storm is coming." Mack wasn't worried, most hurricanes turned up the Gulf or out to the Atlantic bypassing Key West.

At Whitehead he turned left and started to mount his bike when the text tone sounded off on his phone. His heart skipped a beat when he saw it was from McKenzie. He took a deep breath and sat on the curb to read the text.

'My darling Mack, where are you? I'm in Key West. I was going to surprise you and stopped by The Green Parrot but Jimmy said you had left over an hour ago. I've tried to call you but keep getting a busy signal. They say a bad storm is coming so if I don't hear from you, I'm going back to the house to wait.'

He tried to call her but got a busy signal. The wind and rain had intensified. He didn't care, she was here in Key West . . . "Unbelievable!" He shouted and started texting.

'I cannot believe you're in Key West. I love you so much and I'm so sorry for not believing you about Niles. I can't wait to hold you in my arms. Are you still at The Green Parrot? I'm on my bike headed your way on Whitehead.' He jumped on his bike and started pedaling as fast as he could.

He stopped his bike when he felt the vibration of his phone. He covered it with both hands protecting it and read the text from McKenzie.

I'm on Whitehead too, across from the Post Office. I'm walking my bike toward you and can hardly see with all the rain.

There was no warning. The sky opened and dark turbulent clouds rolled over the island as high winds overturned garbage cans, blowing leaves, sticks and loose debris in whirling gusts. Mack fought to protect his eyes and face from the pelting rain mixed with sand as he looked for McKenzie.

McKenzie had laid her bike down and was standing behind a power pole for protection waiting on Mack. She was on the corner of Caroline Street and Whitehead and saw Mack pedaling hard out of the dark roiling clouds. She screamed helplessly as she watched a large palm tree limb flying down Caroline Street explode into the side of his bike. The wind, now hurricane strength, propelled him, his bike, and the palm branch, like a huge tumbleweed down the street slamming him against the front concrete half wall of The Banyan Resort.

McKenzie raced across the street into the howling wind and struggled to lift the bike off Mack. He was semiconscious as she pulled him out from under the palm branch, blood and rain streaked his face. It was pitch dark, no streetlights. The city's power must be off. She shielded her eyes with her hand and scanned her surroundings. She moved quickly dragging Mack to the front steps of the resort with a dim solar light on each side. She sat thinking, trying to get her bearings. She jumped when a small boat and trailer crashed into the wall next to them and flying coconuts, like artillery shells, falling from the sky destroying whatever they hit.

She needed to find a safer place and quick. Mack moaned. She wiped the rain from his face and saw by the solar lights more blood this time than rain. *Damn, what's bleeding?* Searching his forehead, she found a deep three-inch cut right at his hairline. She took the heel of her hand and pressed as hard as she could against the cut while looking around. A black shadow loomed to her right; it was the ginormous Banyan tree, an icon in Key West.

She duck walked the 20 feet over to the tree, Mack helping her now crawling on his knees as she led him by the hand steadily dodging the overhead barrage of debris. At the tree, she pushed Mack inside one of the buttress roots. Each side of the root was about eight feet tall.

They moved deeper into the base of the tree and fell back onto a bench like root. They sat there leaning back against the smooth surface holding each other in their arms. They were totally secure now, the rhythmic howling of the wind forcing their exhausted bodies into a deep sleep.

McKenzie awoke with Mack's head in her lap. With the flashlight on her cell phone, she checked the cut on his head. His face was covered with dried blood, but the bleeding had stopped. She wiped the hair back from his cut to get a better look; he opened his eyes.

"I can't believe this, it's really you. I've missed you so much." Mack said.

She leaned over holding his face with both hands and kissed him on the lips. "It's me, my love, and you are never going to get away from me again . . . never." She kissed him again.

He could hear the wind roaring outside. He sat up and looked around, "Where are we?"

"We're inside the Banyan tree, you don't remember? There's a hurricane blowing outside. You got a deep cut on your head when you crashed into the concrete wall outside."

Mack felt around on his head for the cut.

McKenzie grabbed his hand. "Careful, I had a hard time stopping the bleeding. We'll need to get you some stitches when we get out of here."

"You saved my bacon, lady. I owe you big time."

"You owe me nothing. I'm so happy you're alive and we have another chance to be together."

Mack sat up, "I do owe you an apology though. It was all my fault, that confrontation in your condo. I ran into Niles at Sloppy Joe's tonight, and he was with his date, another man. We had a long talk and he chastised me for not believing you. Don't worry, I didn't hurt him, I even bought him a drink, Sex on the Beach. I had no idea he was gay. I'm so sorry and I truly beg your forgiveness. I love you so much. I have never stopped loving you and never will."

"Oh, Mack, I'm so happy. I'll never let *anything*, I don't care what it is, separate us again."

The hurricane wind roared through the top of the tree shaking the ground and roots under their feet. McKenzie hugged Mack. "Listen to that wind. Do you think we are safe in here?" She asked. "You think the hurricane will rip the tree out of the ground and carry us away?"

"No, I don't think so. This old man has been here a long, long time and been through many hurricanes. Remember, the banyan tree represents eternal life because of its ever-expanding branches that send down aerial roots making it virtually impervious to death."

McKenzie looked up at Mack, "Like us now, 'eternal life . . . impervious to death.'"

A foggy rain mist drifted down between the limbs and leaves as the steady sound of the hurricane screamed directly overhead like a jumbo jet.

Mack wrapped his arms around McKenzie and leaned back against the side of the tree, rocking her slowly back and forth in the dark, as they listened to the wind. Soon, they were both sound asleep.

Mack awoke to the sound of chainsaws and wood grinders. He worked himself out of the tree roots, across the yard, and sat on the steps of The Banyan Resort. There was no wind, no rain and no clouds, just a bright Key West sun. He looked up and down Whitehead Street and saw a car upside down, bicycles in trees, scattered boats and trailers, garbage cans, and trees down everywhere. Mack sat thinking how lucky they were. He got up and walked back to the tree. He stood over McKenzie studying every feature and thought about what she said,

"Like us now, eternal life, impervious to death."

She was right.

He now finally realized and knew he had made . . .

THE RIGHT CHOICE.

Other Books by Jim Carson

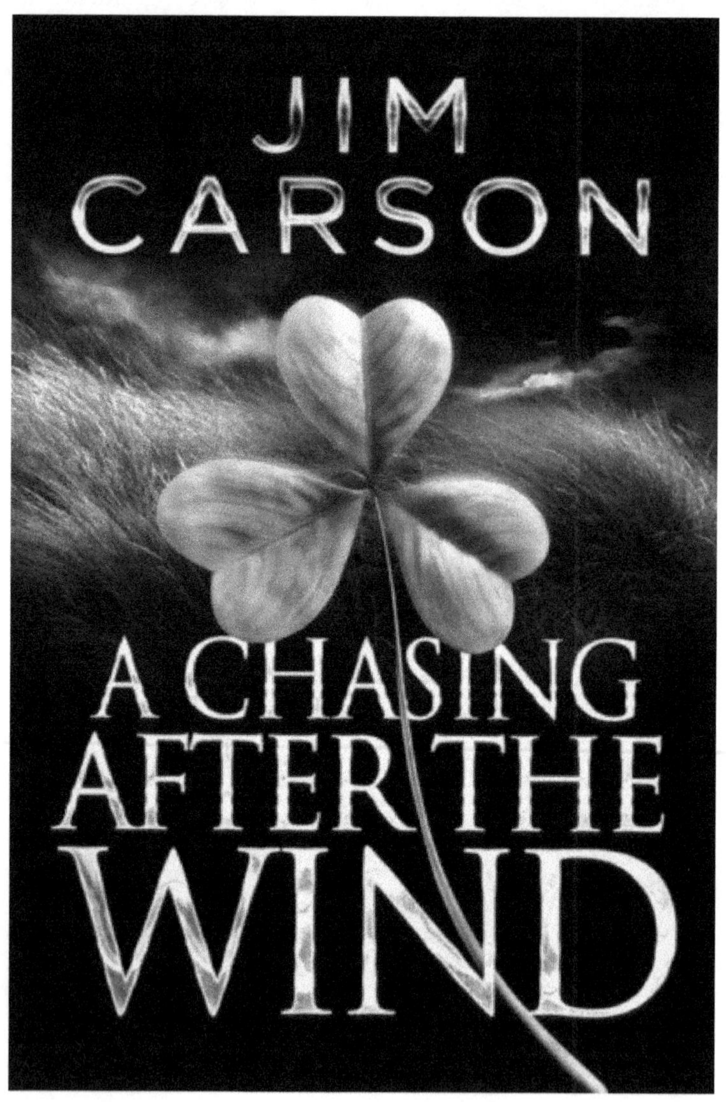

A sequel to *A CHASING AFTER THE WIND*

JIM
CARSON

A MAN'S
HUNGRY
HEART